E. C. Bateman is a novelist  Having made the questionab. she moved to Stamford and dreamt up the idea for this series whilst living in a converted Georgian flat overlooking St. Mary's Church in the heart of town. They've since decamped to the surrounding countryside with their baby daughter, but can still be spotted around the cobbled streets on a regular basis, usually being dragged along by their effervescent cocker spaniel, Audrey.

instagram.com/ecbatemanbooks

Also by E. C. Bateman

The Stamford Mysteries

Death at the Auction

MURDER MOST ANTIQUE

The Stamford Mysteries

E. C. BATEMAN

One More Chapter
a division of HarperCollins*Publishers* Ltd
1 London Bridge Street
London SE1 9GF
www.harpercollins.co.uk
HarperCollins*Publishers*
Macken House, 39/40 Mayor Street Upper,
Dublin 1, D01 C9W8, Ireland

This paperback edition 2023
1
First published in Great Britain in ebook format
by HarperCollins*Publishers* 2023
Copyright © E.C. Bateman 2023
E.C. Bateman asserts the moral right to be identified
as the author of this work

A catalogue record of this book is available from the British Library

ISBN: 978-0-00-856493-3

Printed and bound in the UK using 100% Renewable Electricity
by CPI Group (UK) Ltd

Prologue

I t was a midsummer's morning in middle England. Colin Creaton stopped on the wooden footbridge and gazed out at the town he loved so much. Stamford seemed to glow with promise at a time like this. Quite literally, in fact; the early sun had set the golden stone ablaze, making shimmering silver pools of the vast sash windows which adorned every Neoclassical façade. A sense of languid expectancy filled the air, the familiar hallmark of a rural province in which, even once awake, nothing was expected to ever really happen.

And indeed, nothing had. Until, of course, that innocuous day two months ago when a body had fallen out of a wardrobe in the middle of an antiques auction, sparking a devastating series of events which would have shaken any other small community for decades to come.

But not Stamford, Colin reflected, with a swell of pride. After all, this was a place which had sat placidly on the sidelines after its Georgian heyday had passed, slipping into the realms of long-forgotten backwater with barely a well-bred splutter of protest. Blissfully circumvented by all forms of modernisation and advancement, change had gradually become a concept which remained firmly on the other side of its expensively maintained, honey-coloured boundaries. And it wasn't about to break the habit of centuries over a handful of trifling murders.

Alas, though, it would seem that this attitude which Colin so prized about his beloved town was beginning to come with a price. Because that sense of suspended reality, the time capsule of lost Englishness which had once condemned Stamford to obscurity and irrelevance, had now become the very thing which was getting it noticed.

With a reluctant sigh, Colin turned, widening his viewpoint to accommodate the whole of The Meadows, where the evidence of that notice was making itself glaringly unwelcome. The much-photographed spot was ancient common ground, formed into a sort of island by the River Welland splitting at one end beneath the arched Town Bridge – which formed part of the main traffic route through the centre – and bracketing the wide green space between two meandering streams. With the river at its heart, Stamford boasted several bridges, all affectionately known and named. He was standing on the most unprepossessing of them all, the one which, perhaps, only true locals would know existed. To call it a bridge, even, was probably generous. It was more of a plank, placed across the narrowest part of the stream at the remotest end of The Meadows. From here, half hidden beneath the willows, he had a vantage point of the space where townsfolk and visitors alike flocked to stroll, picnic, and fight for their ice creams with the resplendently rotund – and very entitled – resident duck population. The ducks were as much a part of Stamford's identity as cobbled squares and head-to-toe tweed; loved and reviled in equal measure, they nonetheless enjoyed the sort of protected status afforded to peacocks and swans in other places ... a fact which they seemed gleefully aware of and ever ready to exploit to its limits.

They were stirring now; he could see them from here – his long vision was still excellent, despite his wife Margaret's insistence to the contrary – shaking out their feathers, hustling errant offspring into line, and, with no picnickers to harass yet at this early hour, turning their lively interest to the latest additions to their dominion. One was attempting to climb the peppermint striped helter-skelter, sliding back down each time with an audibly disgruntled quack. Another was poking its head beneath the Punch and Judy tent, whilst a third was, apparently unaware of the irony, swimming around in the hook-a-duck pool. Despite himself, Colin couldn't resist a small smile of gratification at the chaos they were causing; the organisers of the Georgian Fair were going to have a job on their hands when they got down here to set up later.

Bells were chiming from somewhere close by, breaking the morning hush. They could be coming from any of the five Medieval churches which clustered within the town's nucleus, but in any case, they made Colin's heart jolt in alarm. He fumbled for his watch, turning it on his bony wrist and squinting at the tiny gold batons (long vision aside, he had to admit that his short vision was getting worse by the month). She'd be sitting up in bed by now, plump fingers drumming impatiently on the quilted bedcovers, wondering why her morning cup of tea and local newspaper was late. In truth, the paper was a habit he'd instilled, an excuse to get out for his early stroll. A brief, glorious moment of peace and solitude, when the sky was pearled with blue, The Meadows glittered with moisture, and his only company was the odd half-asleep runner or the fluted song of the mistle thrush from high in the trees.

But with the sound of those bells, the enchantment was broken. They were a warning, a clanging reminder that he was running out of time. All too soon, the Town Bridge would bloom with the red of brake lights, wooden shutters peeling back from the surrounding windows to welcome in the morning sun … and he would have to return to the ire of a wife who had become more refractory and caustic than ever of late. Usually, he would make the natural assumption that it was down to something he'd done – that was generally a safe bet – but in this instance, for once, he didn't think that was the case.

It had all started, he thought, with a retrospective bristle, when that police sergeant had come to the house during the investigation in the spring. It had been a thorough mix-up, of course; Colin and Margaret had just happened to be at the auction, and they'd just *happened* to be standing next to the wardrobe – as Margaret had expounded since, how were they *supposed* to know that there was a body in there? Was one *expected* to be prepared for corpses in all manner of strange places these days? Is *that* what the world was coming to? – and it had been by pure chance that they'd needed to go back for Colin's forgotten scarf. But by this point, the police had got it into their heads that they'd been acting suspiciously, and…

Anyway, it had just been one of those ridiculous coincidences – the very *thought* of Colin and Margaret being involved! Such upstanding, long-time residents of Stamford – which had become apparent when they'd finally arrested the *right* person – also, come to think of it, an upstanding, long-time resident of Stamford, but that was besides the point – but not before the police had tried to get access to Margaret's

4

cleaning room. Colin shivered beneath his thin anorak at the mere memory. Her prized space. Even *he* didn't have a key. He'd tried to explain that to the officers, but they hadn't seemed very sympathetic. And then Margaret had come home, and she'd been so *furious* ... he'd never seen her like that before, not in all their married life. He would never admit it out loud, but it had almost frightened him a little.

That had all been bad enough on its own. But then that woman had come, later on, after the arrests ... Colin hadn't heard what was discussed between them, and he'd never dared to ask. Margaret hadn't mentioned it since, but he could tell that the whole episode had upset her deeply.

He'd since told himself – rather insightfully, he liked to think – that it was all bound to have shaken her up a bit. After all, a sensitive woman like his Margaret ... well, she just *felt* things so. No, by far the best thing he could do was keep his head down, spend as much time in his train shed at the bottom of the garden as humanly possible, and generally try not to aggravate her any more than was strictly necessary.

With that in mind now, he stepped a loafer-shod foot forwards, prepared to hurry on home. He began to cross The Meadows, although he hadn't got far before something crunched beneath his sole. He hesitated, looking down in perplexity. Glass twinkled like crushed ice on the lush grass. Shaking his head in faint disapproval, Colin stepped gingerly around it, wondering, not for the first time, what on earth young people thought they were about these days. Teenagers, no doubt, lurking around here at night as they were wont to do, away from parental eyes. Or Friday night revellers, staggering out of the pub with their bottles, perhaps celebrating the eve of the festival weekend. Not that Colin was *against* a bit of merrymaking, of course. He'd been to a disco or two in his own youth, but really, people ought to be more careful. Someone could have been seriously...

And then he was brought up short. For there, in the middle of his mental monologue, it happened. Again.

Colin had only ever had what he termed 'the feeling' once before in his life. It hadn't been all that long ago; two months, in fact, to be precise. On a chill April day, in a gloomy corner of the local auction room, standing in front of a dark wooden cupboard. Something had gripped him, just for a moment. Something he'd never told another soul about. Not Margaret, nor the police.

A choking sense of being watched. Of paralysing foreboding. He'd only had to think about it since to feel the goosebumps on the back of his neck all over again.

And now, out of nowhere, on a balmy morning in mid-June, he felt it once more.

His head whipped around, cold perspiration pricking along his scant hairline as he searched vainly for the source of it. But there was nothing there. No-one on the bridge. No-one on The Meadows. No-one on the water, save a couple of moorhens, which were picking their way delicately between the rocks and not paying him the slightest attention.

Colin mopped his brow with a handkerchief, wondering if Margaret might be right on those occasions when she crossly accused him of beginning to go senile. Tucking the paper – now damp and crumpled by his palms – under his elbow, he scuttled quickly on his way.

In truth, it was probably a very good thing that Colin didn't look down at that moment. Because if he had, he would have seen that there were indeed eyes watching him, albeit unseeing ones. Glassy eyes, staring at him from between the gaudily striped poles of the hook-a-duck pool, set into a white, bloated face. As Colin moved away, they continued to gaze on past him, into the cloudless expanse of blue sky which promised that, for once in an English summer, the unthinkable seemed absolutely guaranteed.

It was the perfect day for a fair.

Chapter One

"I can't believe you managed to talk me into this." Felicia Grant winced as the laces of her corset were yanked again, even more tightly this time. She gripped the back of the chair in front of her, turning her head to look accusingly at her best friend. "I must have been absolutely mad to agree." She paused, reconsidered for a moment. "Or perhaps drunk. They're the only two possible explanations."

If someone had told her two months ago that she'd be spending her Saturday morning in a damp, frigid cellar beneath the streets of Stamford willingly having her ribcage compressed to half its original size, she would have thought *they* were the mad one, she reflected wryly. But then, her home town had a way of changing the parameters of what could be considered normal in a way which few other places possessed.

"It wasn't me, it was Robyn," Cassandra Lane, Mayor of Stamford and, as of this moment, bearer of a towering grey powdered wig which trembled precariously each time she moved, began to protest, before an unceremonious wrench on her own laces cut her off with a grit of the teeth. She recovered, continuing in only a slightly more strained voice than before. "And as you well know, when it comes to my daughter, you don't agree; you capitulate."

On that point at least, Felicia couldn't argue. Her eighteen-year-old goddaughter was a veritable force of nature, a strawberry blonde Joan of Arc with an exhaustingly boundless sense of social responsibility. Where she got it from, no-one was quite sure, but Cassie tended to blame Robyn's father; an easy option since he'd exited their lives shortly after the positive pregnancy test, never to be sighted nor heard from again. Felicia was the only person who knew that her friend secretly toasted the fact every year, from a purpose-bought bottle of Aperol which she hid under an old dog blanket in the cupboard under the stairs. The unwashed state of the dog blanket was an ingeniously deliberate deterrent, although not one that anyone was likely to suspect, given Cassie's notoriously casual relationship with anything organisational.

"At least *you* get to change into your ceremonial robes later," Felicia said, a touch resentfully, as she tugged ineffectually at her stomacher in an attempt to get some air into her lungs. Her efforts were immediately reprimanded with a stinging rap to the knuckles from a tortoiseshell shoe horn.

"None of that!" barked Edith Babington, local tailor and the Georgian Fair's indomitable wardrobe mistress. The cellar they currently stood in – if that wasn't too prosaic a word for the sprawling kingdom of ancient, damp, windowless rooms which hulked beneath the town's theatre – had been designated as the fair's wardrobe department, and thus was, for the next couple of days at least, hers to command. "You'll dislodge your costume. I don't spend all year painstakingly making these things as historically accurate as possible just so that you can go slouching out there wearing them all anyhow. I thought you of all people would appreciate that. Some sort of antiques dealer, aren't you?"

"I'm an auctioneer," Felicia replied patiently. The two things really weren't all that similar, aside from sharing a general subject area and occasionally, the same air space, but it was a stubbornly persistent view that they were interchangeable. It hadn't helped that during the tumultuous events of the spring, some bothersome local journalist, delirious with the prospect of news which didn't revolve around livestock shows and permit parking charges, had zestfully dubbed her 'Lincolnshire's Lovejoy'. It was a moniker which, in common with all the most unflattering and inaccurate of its kind, had stuck fast, like chewing gum to the underside of a park bench.

"Hmph," Edith pushed her red-framed glasses – the only accession to flair in her otherwise rather sombre outfit – up onto the bridge of her nose, from which they promptly slid straight back off again. "Funny sort of job to want, I've always thought. All that banging of mallets and shouting. Yes, very odd." She narrowed her eyes, looking at Felicia assessingly over glinting lenses. "Say, weren't you the one who sold a dead body? I remember seeing it in the news."

"I didn't actually *sell* a body." Felicia looked beseechingly at Cassie for help, but her friend just grinned, clearly enjoying all of this immensely. "It happened to be in the wardrobe, that's all. It was a complete coincidence."

Edith didn't look entirely convinced, which Felicia couldn't say surprised her. After all, her return to the town she'd grown up in after a decade-long hiatus hadn't exactly been without incident. Within hours of her arrival there'd been a murder (in her own auction house, no less, as Edith had so tactfully reminded them all) and two more had followed swiftly in the coming days. Somehow, Felicia had found herself at the heart of the case – more by accident than design, as she was quick to point out to whoever might intimate otherwise – and despite the fact that she'd actually had a hand in *solving* Stamford's first murder investigation in living memory, some people still seemed wary of the Londoner, as they now saw her, who'd brought such upheaval to their quiet idyll in her wake. Whilst no-one had actively said anything of the kind to her face, Felicia had good cause to suspect that her decision to stay on permanently hadn't been universally welcomed.

"Yes, well, I don't go getting involved in things which aren't my business," Edith said, with a hint of reproach which implied that it must still have been Felicia's fault *somehow*, even if only by choosing to run such a strange and ghoulish enterprise. Presumably, such a thing would never dream of happening in her genteel, expensively seemly tailor's shop just down the street on St. Mary's Hill, with its polished mahogany fittings and lingering scent of beeswax wafting on the hushed air. "And my business is clothes." She looked Felicia up and down, tweaked her skirts, then said, not entirely enthusiastically, "well, I suppose you'll have to do. Tara!"

She snapped her fingers, and a pallid, dark-haired girl rose obediently from where she'd been putting some last stitches in the hem of Cassie's dress.

"Come along, duck. There's no time for that. We've got the soldiers to do next. Seventy of them!" Edith shook her head with a tsking sound, addressing the room in general now. "More to the point, I'll eat my trusty tape measure here" – she tapped the article in question, which was looped around her neck – "if most won't fit into the coats I've made them *and* then have the cheek to suggest it's my sewing. Thirty four waist indeed!" She scoffed. "Do they think I was born yesterday? A couple of dozen pork pies ago, maybe." She began to pack scissors and thread into a cracked leather case with what seemed unnecessary ferocity, the clatter of metal on metal ricocheting within. "But of course, it's always the same with men; never their fault. There's a good reason I gave up on them in my private life, and honestly, if my business didn't rely upon them..." She broke off abruptly, blinking rapidly behind her glasses, then seemed to shake herself, blurting out, "come along, now, Tara, chop chop! Stop drifting about. We've got work to do."

And without another word to Felicia or Cassie, she stomped out, leaving Tara to scuttle unsteadily after her, slight form buckled under armfuls of breeches. Cassie raised sandy-coloured eyebrows at Felicia, exhaling with a low whistling sound.

"That's what *you'll* sound like in years to come if you won't let me set you up with anyone."

"Cass, you know I've got far too much on my plate to be bothering with that sort of thing right now," Felicia retorted, exasperation getting the better of her. She began to tick items off on her fingers, just to elucidate her point. "Where do you want me to start? We've upended our whole life from London, we still haven't got anywhere to live, Algernon's started a brand new school, I'm having to re-learn the ropes of running the auction after ten years away while Dad's out of commission ... and, incidentally, getting more and more cantankerous about it every day..." dizzy with overwhelm just talking about it, she went to rub a hand across her forehead, then remembered at the last moment that her face was covered in white powder. "Plus, you know, it's not exactly easy to think about romance with my ex-husband still lurking about on the scene."

All right, so *lurking* was perhaps a bit harsh, Felicia amended, with a mild throb of guilt. Really, she ought to be pleased that Dexter was taking some responsibility for once. To call him a reformed character would be a stretch, perhaps, but she couldn't deny that he'd surprised her at almost every turn after what had almost happened to their son, Algernon, back in the spring. When he'd announced his intention to do the unthinkable and put his precious television series – and, by extension, his globetrotting existence – on ice for a while, she hadn't really believed him. Not because she doubted he meant it at the time; Dexter's one saving grace, sometimes infuriatingly so, was the genuine goodness of his intentions. But his pronouncements tended more towards the exuberantly, earnestly dramatic than the well thought through.

And the idea of Dexter living in a place like Stamford? Well, it was just … unthinkable. He was a glittering London personality to the core, far more so than she had ever been. The notion of him lasting more than a week in a provincial community where the biggest buzz of the year – when there wasn't an uncaught triple-murderer roaming around, naturally – was over the replacing of cobbles for tarmac in Red Lion Square, or a proposed new housing estate on the fringes of town, had been enough to make her laugh inwardly.

She wasn't laughing now, though, she reflected, with a slight sense of discomfort. Her scepticism had been forcibly eroded with each passing day as he'd moved out of her father's tiny cottage, into which they'd all been crammed whilst the investigation was going on, taking on the rent of a flat in the luxurious Riverside development just across the water. But as for what it had been replaced with … whilst she knew that Algernon was adoring having his father so close by, from her own perspective, things weren't quite as clear cut.

They'd been like satellites for so long, even when they were married, that it was a strange feeling having him so close, knowing that she could almost see into his flat through the warped old glass from her father's kitchen window. It was even stranger still seeing him around town; Stamford was a small place, after all, and not bumping into people was nigh on impossible.

"I don't know that I'm really the lurking kind," as if summoned like a well-bred poltergeist, an amused voice emerged from the doorway. "That would necessitate a certain ability to blend into the background, wouldn't it?"

An amused and very familiar voice. Felicia swallowed a sigh, counting to five before she turned.

Chapter Two

Certainly, no-one could call Dexter Grant nondescript, Felicia admitted privately, looking at the tall, broad-shouldered form whose shadow was filling the low cellar doorway now. One of her ex-husband's key attributes had always been his ability to make female (and quite a few male too, if his fan mail was anything to go by) hearts flutter like a standard on a windswept battlement. Felicia, on the other hand, felt only the faintest flicker of irritation in his presence; a sensation which rapidly intensified as he stepped into the light of fuller view.

"I thought your talk was supposed to be on Georgian art," she said, unable to keep the accusation out of her voice as she took in the sight of a costume she'd wanted to throw on a bonfire for almost as long as it had been in existence: safari shirt, desert boots and – worst of all – a battered old fedora, which currently swung from the tips of his fingers. It was an outfit designed to evoke a vision of Indiana Jones, of daring adventures across the wilder parts of the globe; and indeed it did … for anyone who hadn't been married to the wearer while those supposedly wild adventures – in actual fact rather cushier than they appeared on screen, Dexter not being one to rough it – had steadily corroded any illusion of a functional family unit.

In reality, it was nowhere near that simple of course; whatever was? And 364 days out of each year, Felicia was perfectly, contentedly aware of the other factors at play: of how young they'd been when they got together, of how frangible their conflicting ambitions had always made things between them. Of how the divorce had been entirely her idea, borne, perhaps (although she'd never dared look this notion directly in the eye) as much by the innate, fey-like restlessness she'd inherited from her mother as by strict necessity.

However, for some reason, and despite all of that, the mere sight of that outfit still seemed to bring her out in Pavlovian waves of irritation and resentment. Arbitrarily, she found that she held a particular animosity towards the hat. She tried not to scowl at it now.

"I am, but they wanted me in the whole Treasure Seeker get-up." Evidently she'd failed, because for once, Dexter looked faintly sheepish. "After all, most people know me from the television, so…"

There was a brief, awkward pause, which Cassie, ever strident, refused to let sit for more than ten seconds.

"Well, whilst on a personal level I'd be quite happy to never see that botulism-ridden hat ever again, in my official capacity I'm very grateful that you've agreed to it. You'll be a big draw for the fair."

A Georgian fair in Stamford wasn't exactly a big surprise; indeed, it was all but inevitable. As the best preserved

Georgian town in the country – often described as a microcosm of its grander, more famous metropolitan cousin of Bath – the only real surprise was that it hadn't got around to holding one sooner. As it was, this would merely be its fifth year, and it was understandable that Cassie, in her debut role as host, would want to make it the best one yet. Felicia sensed that her friend felt a strong need to draw a line under everything which had happened in the spring, before Stamford became known more for its body count than its honeyed Regency Squares and quaint, carriage-width streets.

"It's the least I can do for Algie's godmother." Dexter pecked her on a heavily be-rouged cheek. "And while we seem to be getting along for once, may I take this opportunity to tell you how smashing you look?"

Felicia rolled her eyes. Honestly, the man just couldn't help himself, could he? Even with Cassie, probably the only woman other than Felicia who was firmly impervious to his charms.

"I look like a brothel madam," Cassie said bluntly, hoiking up her gaudily brocaded bodice, from which her own copious charms were currently making a bid for escape. "Felicia got off much more lightly. They even let her use her own hair."

"Not that it feels like it," Felicia added, turning to look at herself in the full length mirror. They'd managed to pile her thick bronze hair atop her head in a way which looked airily romantic, but she knew that if she touched it, it would feel like a helmet. Her neck was already beginning to ache from the weight. "I think it's at least half hairspray." Which was better than the pig's grease they would actually have used at the time, admittedly. She was heartily glad that in that respect at least, authenticity had been jettisoned in favour of modern sensibilities.

Discomforts aside, though, she had to concede, as her gaze moved the length of her unfamiliar reflection, she couldn't deny that the whole effect was rather dazzling. Her dress was of the sack-back style popular in the latter half of the 1700s, with a tightly nipped waist and cape-like train of fabric flowing from the shoulders down the back, all rendered in exquisite ice-blue silk which shimmered with every play of light. The split skirt revealed a lustred white petticoat underneath, and the entire thing was studded with tiny pearls which matched the ones in her hair.

Never mind dazzling, she silently amended, as she turned to study the back, which was just as exquisitely worked. It was nothing short of breathtaking. Although, by this point, she perhaps shouldn't be so surprised.

When the notion of the Georgian Fair had first been floated in front of her, Felicia had – somewhat naïvely, she saw now – envisaged a jolly sort of country bash, thrown together by a few elderly ladies over a glass of elderflower wine and a piece of Battenberg in the Methodist Church Hall over the course of a few Tuesday evenings. Home-laminated posters advertising the event would be cable tied to the wrought-iron lampposts dotted around town, a few people would gamely hire ill-fitting, garishly synthetic costumes perhaps … maybe there would be a nod to some vaguely 18th century activity in the form of a performance or two, but otherwise it would be business as usual for an English midsummer fête: candyfloss, Morris dancers, a forced and vastly unenjoyable spin on the tea cups…

Clearly, though, she'd missed something vital in the years she'd been away. She'd noticed it the minute she'd set foot back in her home town. The shift was subtle rather than wholesale; the stalwarts of old, eccentric Englishness were still very much there, occupying their positions on the High Street. The country outfitters with their seemingly endless selection of tweed suits beside flamboyantly patterned socks and pocket handkerchiefs. The hardware shop where anything, no matter how obscure, could be found – although notably, not by the shopper themselves, no matter how long they desperately scoured the haphazardly stacked shelves. A simple enquiry, however, and the proprietor would dive beneath a random pile of sieves or bucket of plant pot feet with a knowing twinkle, producing the arbitrary item as though it should have been obvious all along. The tearoom – *not* café; heaven help anyone who uttered that word while in there – where the waitresses still wore white frilled aprons and served a selection of edibles which had last been popular in the Second World War.

But between them a new breed was appearing, like dandelions sprouting in the pavement. Glossy-looking boutiques with foiled writing above the door. Gleaming kitchen shops filled with entirely unnecessary but oddly seductive gadgets in ice cream shades of enamel and neon bright silicone. Bakery windows filled with sourdough baguettes and cardamom buns.

Stamford was still very much Stamford, Felicia had soon deduced, but with a new wick of tourist-luring polish. A place where day-trippers and weekenders alike could bask in history and tradition without missing out on modern luxuries such as a freshly ground flat white or plush accommodation with velvet armchairs in the bedroom and a freestanding bath.

As such, it seemed that the town's Georgian-ness, which had always been its major charm but in an understated sort of way, had now exploded into something to be taken deadly seriously: big business. And this weekend was the crowning jewel of that; far from the elderflower wine-fuelled amateur affair of her imaginings, it was instead a juggernaut, a meticulously organised whirlwind of satin and string music, with big-name speakers from around the country peppered amongst the local acts to add to the glamour and excitement.

It was also, as Felicia was already finding, utterly exhausting. And it hadn't even officially begun yet.

"Everyone ready in here?" Gavin March, Cassie's ultra-efficient secretary, materialised out of the gloom – the lighting down there was terrible; Felicia wondered how the theatre actors, who used the place as their dressing rooms for most of the year, could stand it – wearing a clipboard around his neck and an uncharacteristically flustered expression. His lacy cravat was askew, and there were two bright spots of colour on his cheeks. Whether that was down to makeup, or the multiple layers of silk he too was wearing (one thing Felicia could say for eighteenth-century fashion was that at least for once, men didn't have an easier time of it than women) was anyone's guess. "The opening ceremony is set to start in twenty minutes. You *have* got your speech to hand?" He asked Cassie, not sounding especially hopeful.

"Naturally," Cassie said blithely, with a regal wave of her hand, then hesitated, looking slightly less certain. "Somewhere."

With a long-suffering exhale, Gavin produced a crisply folded sheet of paper from his waistcoat pocket.

"If I give you the spare, can you promise not to lose it between now and the procession?"

"Yes, yes, of course, you don't need to fret," Cassie said dismissively, about to stuff it into her bosom until, at Gavin's horrified look, she sighed and fumbled for the reticule which dangled from her wrist instead. "Now, how's everything going out there? Chaos, I presume?"

"It is a little ... disorganised, yes," Gavin said, with a visible shudder, the very word clearly an anathema. "The Stamford Players are trying to get a final rehearsal in..." A resounding thump from the theatre above, followed by a strangulated aria, confirmed that fact. Gavin flinched. "And there was a bit of a ... erm, duck problem ... at the fête, but they got it sorted in the end."

"That doesn't sound too bad, considering." He looked so harassed that Felicia felt obligated to soothe him, despite an overwhelming impulse to enquire further into what, exactly, the 'duck problem' had consisted of. "These things are bound to have some teething troubles."

"Especially in Stamford," Dexter piped up cheerily. "Just be glad there hasn't been a body yet."

Everyone took a moment to glare at him. As usual, he didn't seem to notice. Just then, a reedy voice barked from the doorway, making them all jump.

"Have you found her yet?"

Felicia was sure she heard Cassie groan as Dennis Stanworthy, her deputy mayor and self-styled nemesis, swept into the room. At least, he attempted to sweep, hindered inelegantly by having to stoop beneath the low stone lintel to gain access. Even once inside, the top of his grey wig hovered perilously close to the ceiling, something which only exacerbated the impression of him as the most impossibly tall man Felicia had ever set eyes upon. Whilst she knew that in reality it was nothing more an optical illusion – standing near to Dexter as he was now, it was apparent that their heights almost matched – the effect was a discombobulating, persistent one. Everything about him was elongated, as though he were fresh spaghetti which had been rolled and then hung to dry, stretching glutinously in the process.

"Jesus." Cassie looked between the two council men in exasperation. "Don't tell me we've lost her already? Surely that can't be possible; she only arrived last night."

"I thought that Gavin here was supposed to be keeping an eye on her." Dennis turned his laser glare onto the back of the assistant's head, then swivelled the beam across to Cassie. "You promised me that there would be no trouble, Cassandra." He wagged a hectoring finger. "*Promised!* After last time..."

"I did try," Gavin protested, looking stricken to be found wanting. "But I couldn't watch her all of the time. Short of stalking her around town..."

Felicia, realising that this was going in no good direction, did her best to bring everyone back onto the matter at hand by asking calmly, "What's happened? Someone's gone missing?"

"Only the bloody headline speaker!" Dennis snapped, eyes bulging. The effect was eerily halibut-like, an image which Felicia tried not to dwell upon. "She was supposed to be giving a talk to accompany the statue unveiling of Fitzwilliam Trendlehart this morning." He gazed wistfully at a point somewhere over Cassie's shoulder, quoting words which, Felicia suspected, were already sitting on a draft tourist pamphlet in his office somewhere. "Groundbreaking new research into one of our most illustrious but, until now, elusive local figures." When no-one responded with suitable reverence, his face, which had briefly softened, soured again instantly. "But with..." He checked his pocket watch, flipping open the silver case to peer at the time. "Fifteen minutes to go, it's not looking very likely." His voice sharpened to a finely pointed blade. "We need a contingency plan, Cassandra. *Without* delay."

"I thought *I* was the headline speaker." Dexter, who'd been boredly fiddling with a pair of curling tongs, looked up in wounded indignation. "Cassie, you said…"

"Of course you are." Cassie patted his arm distractedly, already turning back to Dennis with a visible effort to be conciliatory. "Look, I'm sure she'll turn up any minute. She's probably just overslept, that's all. There was a…" She flushed a little under her makeup. "Well, a fair bit of wine flowing at the party last night, let's just say."

"You're telling me," Felicia muttered, touching her temple, with was starting to throb faintly, even her father's infamously tar-like tea having made only the slightest dent in it.

"I've already been to her rental cottage," Gavin ventured quietly, with a wary glance at Dennis. Felicia watched this silent exchange between the two of them, trying to detect anything beneath the surface. This was the first time she'd seen them both in the same room since Cassie had found her deputy's private phone number in Gavin's desk – a mystery which she knew had been eating away at her friend, who was paranoid that they were plotting against her. "And I'm certain she's not there. I knocked loudly enough to wake the dead."

"Well, that's just capital, isn't it?" Dennis spat. He was ruddy with barely repressed rage now, the tip of his beak-like nose quivering. "This is all we need. We've not even started and it's already a fiasco!"

"I'd have thought you'd be thrilled," Cassie snapped back, the strain finally making itself apparent. "After all, it's *my* fiasco, isn't it?"

There was a tense beat of silence. Gavin stared fixedly at his clipboard. Dexter whistled unhelpfully.

"It will also reflect upon *me*," Dennis said tightly, at last. He puffed out his bony chest. "As deputy mayor…"

"Yes, yes," Cassie cut him off hastily, clearly recognising the opening bars of an impending, unpleasantly familiar soliloquy. "But this is getting us nowhere. We need another plan." She went to scrub her hand through her hair, looking momentarily confused to find the usual unruly tangle of blonde curls absent. Instead, she settled for scratching her head through her wig. "I suppose I'll just have to do it myself. I'm making my own introduction speech anyway. I'll just ... whip the sheet thing off the statue quickly, ad lib something vague about what a great guy he was and what an honour it is for the town..."

"Whip the..." Dennis looked as though he might be about to faint from the irreverence of it all. "*Ad lib*? Cassandra, you cannot be serious! This is *Fitzwilliam Trendlehart* we're talking about. To treat him thus..."

"Well, what do you expect me to do?" Cassie retorted crossly. She was beginning to look flustered, her usually irrepressible buoyancy cracking under the strain. "Even if I knew what she was going to say – which I don't – I couldn't begin to present something like that. I'm no scholar."

"It's true," Felicia felt compelled to agree. "She flunked out of GCSE history because she thought that Henry VIII had sixteen wives rather than six."

"And that was with cheat notes written on the palm of my hand," Cassie added morosely. Then her face lit up, eyes shining in a way which had always made Felicia wary. It usually meant that someone...

"Of course; it's staring me right in the face!" She grabbed Dexter, linking her arm through his as though presenting him for a curtain call, then, to Felicia's horror, did the same to her on the other side, looking between them expectantly. "Tell me, how do you two feel about saving the day?"

Felicia eyed her friend's beatific smile and immediately felt wariness turn to a sense of impending doom. Her head began to shake reflexively.

"No, Cass." She said emphatically. "Whatever you're thinking, the answer is absolutely *not*. Never in a million years."

Chapter Three

"I can't *believe* she managed to talk me into *this*," Felicia muttered under her breath, as she and Dexter stood on the narrow, twisting thoroughfare of Austin Street, looking up at the front of a bijou dwelling whose engraved slate sign professed itself to be Honeysuckle Cottage. The honeysuckle itself wasn't in evidence, but Felicia decided to give it the benefit of the doubt and assume that there was some growing around the back. "I *must* be mad. It's the only explanation. I certainly don't have the excuse of being drunk this time."

"Is this some sort of warm-up routine, or are you going to get on with it?" Dexter was lounging against the wall beside her. "We haven't got all day, you know."

"You're the expert at breaking into places," she said tartly. "Why don't *you* do it?"

He moved his eyes heavenwards, as though requesting divine forbearance.

"You're never going to let that go, are you?"

"Curiously, no, I'm not." Considering he'd lied to everyone – including the police – and in doing so nearly let a murderer go free, she added; although she did so silently. After all, he'd said sorry more than enough times. There was no benefit to anyone in keeping on punishing him. She'd decided some time ago that if this was going to work – whatever *this* was, this new, unconventional family arrangement the two of them and Algernon seemed to be settling into – then she was going to have to learn to forgive ... even if she couldn't quite bring herself to forget.

Something which was easier said than done when Dexter was being especially vexing, as she was all too forcibly reminded by his next words.

"I really don't see what you're making such an almighty fuss about, anyway." He crossed one leg over the other, tapping the reinforced toe of his desert boot against the cobbles in an irregular rhythm. "It's not as if it's especially difficult for you. And you heard what Cassie said. It's not about us; it's for the good of the whole town." He paused, then added, rather worthily, "hence why I agreed to do my bit."

Felicia looked at him disbelievingly.

"For the town," she intoned, voice dripping with sarcasm.

He didn't so much as bat an eyelid, the swine.

"Indeed."

She folded her arms, knowing she shouldn't rise to this but unable to help herself.

"So it's nothing to do with the fact that she buttered you up like a plate of teacakes, then? All of that gushing about what a *famous* historian you are?"

"I *am* a famous historian," he shot back, looking slightly piqued. Then he muttered bitterly, "far more so than Iris Breadmore. Headline speaker, indeed. She has a certain *following* ... but nothing like..." He clicked his tongue irritably.

"I mean, the woman hasn't even got a TikTok account, for Christ's sake."

Felicia felt her eyebrows raise of their own accord.

"And you have?"

"Naturally." He inspected his fingernails. "My fans like to see what I'm up to."

Said without a single trace of irony. Felicia shook her head in stupefaction, deciding on the spot that there was no answer she could make to that which wouldn't take them into even more surreal territory than they were already in. Instead, she returned her attention to the door in front of her, trying to reassure herself that he hadn't been quite such an insufferable berk when she'd married him. At least, she sincerely *hoped* he hadn't. In any event, it was certainly saying something when a spot of breaking and entering seemed like the saner topic for contemplation.

"I'm still not sure I like this." She studied the door in front of her, chewing her lip as she tried to articulate the reasons for her reluctance. "For the good of the fair or not, it doesn't feel ethical, somehow." Then, suddenly hearing how prim and stuffy she sounded, she pulled a face, tugging a pin from her elaborate updo. "Oh, for God's sake, let's just get it *over* with. No-one's watching, are they?"

"Relax. They're all down on The Meadows, waiting for the start of the opening ceremony."

He was right. The lane was absolutely deserted, save for a curious silver and white tabby, who was watching them from a low, erigeron-frothed wall. In the near distance, Felicia could just about hear the first strains of music floating up from a couple of streets beneath them. Before she could think better of it, she dropped to her knees in a pool of stiffened silk, trying not to imagine the expression on Edith's face if she could see the way she was treating her costume. Widening the hairpin between her fingers, she pushed it into the lock.

"What d'you think dear old Sergeant Pettifer would say if he knew that you counted picking locks as part of your resumé?" Dexter asked, watching with palpable amusement.

"It's a very useful skill for an antiques valuer to have," she frowned, manoeuvring the pin within the lock. "All of those boxes and cabinets people bring you which they have no idea what's inside. You'd be amazed what … *aha*," she broke off as, with a decisive click, the heavy mechanism within released. She tilted her face up to look at Dexter, shielding her eyes against the aureole which blazed around the edges of his hat. "I believe we're in."

"Marvellous." He held out a hand and helped her up, then reached around her to turn the brass doorknob. The door swung open of its own accord, which wasn't surprising. Almost every other entranceway in town had the same quirk, the result of shifting old foundations built onto a slight slope. "And since we wouldn't want to compromise your delicate morals, if you'd rather stay out here and keep watch…"

He was trying not to smirk. She scowled at him and stalked past through the open doorway without a word.

"Ah, now this takes me back," he said fondly as he followed her down the slender hallway, Felicia's wide skirt scraping against the walls on either side. "You and me, prowling around someone's house together. Just like old times."

"Let's just hope it doesn't end the same way as on the last occasion," Felicia murmured, preferring not to think about what they'd found on that cold, starlit night. Having said that, it was hard to imagine anything of the kind on a glorious day like this. Sunshine streamed through the windows, illuminating the pale tan carpet with a geometric pattern, while dust motes sparkled on the air, rendered temporarily beautiful by light. Besides, this house was about as far away from the neglected, decaying mansion of her memories as it was possible to get. *That* place would have felt eerie even in broad daylight, whereas this cottage, whilst probably just as old, had been briskly buffed and updated until any lingering aura of dark history was all but undetectable. It had all the cosy, practical feel of a holiday let, the walls painted in cotton white, the furniture of serviceable pine – although there were a few more antique pieces placed here and there, presumably to give the place some individuality.

Felicia moved through the open door into the living room, drawn inexorably to the fireplace, where a Victorian bronze sculpture of a hare sat. She ran a hand over its cold, roughly-textured flank, peering for the all-important maker's mark and edition number.

"You just can't help yourself, can you?" Dexter's exasperated voice followed her into the room.

"Sorry," she smiled self-consciously, although her hand dropped with some reluctance. There'd been a fire in the grate, she noticed, the ashes cold but fresh-looking. It seemed an odd choice, considering the time of year, but it was an old house, she supposed. They could feel chill even in the warmest of weather. "Occupational hazard."

"Don't I know it," Dexter grumbled. "I was married to you for all of those years, remember? The phrase 'busman's holiday' doesn't do it justice."

He had a point, Felicia conceded, making to follow him back out into the hall. In fact, busmen probably got far better holidays. At least they could probably visit someone's house or get through an entire party without being pressed for their opinion on timetables, or have their approval sought as to the exact route someone's great-grandmother had taken to get to Bognor Regis in 1955. Auctioneers weren't so blessed. Sometimes, Felicia thought that the phrase, "While you're here, maybe you could just take a look at this..." might as well be her epitaph.

Although, those were the easy cases; at least then there was an actual *object* to study. More challenging were the new acquaintances she found herself seated next to at weddings or christenings or dinner parties or school carol concerts, whose eyes would light up at hearing what she did for a living. The next twenty minutes would then be taken up by a strikingly long-winded – yet amazingly parched of any detail which might prove pertinent or useful – description of an object which they'd inherited/won at a tombola/bought at a bank holiday car boot/been using as a cat basket for the past seventeen years, which they would then expectantly wait for her to pronounce priceless. When she would inevitably fail to be so unequivocal, the eyes would dim, lips pursing in disappointment, and she would immediately become rather less popular.

She'd often joked that it wasn't easy making friends as an auctioneer; most people only heard about the highs, but in reality, for every hope realised, you'd dashed at least five others behind the scenes. And not just individual hopes; in many cases, you were shattering myths which stretched back generations.

After all, which family didn't have 'the thing' which Great Granny had assured them was a priceless artifact destined to make the family fortune one day? 'The thing' which was then treated with a reverence usually reserved for holy relics and proudly paraded in front of guests for subsequent decades?

No-one would fancy being the one to reveal the humiliating truth, that it was nothing more than a 20th century reproduction, worth ten pounds on a good day. And yet, that was her job. Or at least, a large, and, at times, vaguely disheartening part of it.

But it wasn't all of it, she reminded herself, with a longing glance back over her shoulder at the bronze hare. Occasionally, something came along which made everything else worthwhile. Something which explained why people like her still willingly worked in a sector which was, at its heart, dusty, unglamorous, and woefully underpaid.

The beautiful, the rare, the fascinating. The sense of holding history in your hand, of turning someone's inspiration over between your fingers. Reflecting on what it had meant at the time it was made, and what it continued to mean now. It wasn't strictly linked to monetary value, either. Some things were spellbindingly curious but not worth a lot despite it, whilst others were highly prized by collectors whilst not being particularly thrilling, or even in some cases particularly old. Like many auctioneers, Felicia was caught in a constant tussle, her business head knowing that her energy should be focused on the latter, whilst her heart...

"Felicia!" Dexter's voice boomed through from the hall, making her jump guiltily, her hand half outstretched back towards the hare. "Can we maybe focus on what we're *actually* here for?" A pause, then, "If it's not all a bloody wild goose chase, that is. Are we sure it's even here to find?"

"Cassie seemed adamant she'd seen Iris's file of notes when she greeted her yesterday. They'll be here somewhere." A thought occurred to her as she hastily re-joined him. "We should probably check upstairs, you know. Just in case."

He gave her an arch look.

"In case of what? A body?"

"Of course not," she said, relieved that he'd already turned away so couldn't see how he'd flustered her. She followed him up the narrow, vertiginous stairs, striving to change the subject. "So, what do you think this big new discovery is going to be? Iris seemed to have got Dennis quite worked up about it."

"Dennis would get worked up over an extra cherry on top of his currant bun," Dexter said dryly. "I wouldn't read too much into that."

"I'm surprised you're not more interested." She frowned at the back of his head, trying to work out what was going on in there. "After all, it has been everywhere recently."

That was an understatement if ever there was one. Sometimes, it seemed you couldn't move around Stamford these days without hearing the name Fitzwilliam Trendlehart bandied about in association with something. Even the least historically-interested person in town probably knew more than they wished to about Stamford's newest – and, rather uniquely, deadest – celebrity by now. In a way, it was hard to imagine that there could be anything else left to say about the saintly nobleman with the passion for social reform. Establishing ground-breaking orphanages, assisting unmarried mothers, rescuing maidens from rivers ... for someone who'd fallen into reasonable obscurity until very recently, there seemed to suddenly be an awful lot of lore surrounding his exploits. So much, that it was becoming difficult to tell what was based on solid evidence and what was more excitable extrapolation bordering on the fictitious. Not that many people seemed unduly worried by whatever he had or hadn't done in his lifetime. He was fulfilling a whole new role now, as a welcome boost to both local pride and tourism. For most, that was more than enough for them to get behind.

"I wouldn't get your hopes up for anything too sensational," Dexter replied flatly. "Iris didn't exactly build her career on making history exciting."

"You don't seem to rate her much." One of the steps was bowed in the middle. As a veteran of old-house living, Felicia knew the signs of a creaking floorboard when she saw them. She repositioned her foot, stepping neatly over it. "Or are you just jealous?"

He faltered on the small square of landing, his shoulders tensing for a split second before he made a shrill scoffing sound, disappearing through the single doorway which branched off it. Felicia could see the blank space of wall where there ought to have been another; presumably, the owners had decided to turn the small second bedroom into an en-suite to the master instead. After all, there would have been no provision for an upstairs bathroom when the place was built – or indeed, a bathroom at all, their invention still languishing a good century away in the future. It was one of the factors which made these tiny dwellings so well-suited to holiday lets; rebranded as cosy boltholes for couples, the cramped confines were magically transformed from – well, cramped – to swooningly romantic in a single trill of a marketeer's fingers across a keyboard.

Once upon a time, she and Dexter used to whisk one another away to places just like this, she reflected wistfully. Now they just broke into them together instead. How time changed things.

"Well, she's definitely not here," he concluded, somewhat unnecessarily, as she joined him inside the bedroom. It was a cheerful, sunny space, belying its steeply sloping ceiling. A lot of that was down to the Velux windows, which currently showed cut-outs of brilliant blue sky. There was a suitcase on the floor, thrown open to reveal a hastily-packed array of clothes. But it was the bed which mostly caught Felicia's attention. It was snowy and crisp, the pillows plump and undented, the sheets pleated into hospital corners so precise they could have been measured by mathematical compass. It clearly hadn't been touched since the housekeeper had put new bedding on yesterday. A quick open of the wardrobe door also confirmed her rapidly growing suspicions.

"The clothes she was wearing last night aren't here either." Even as she said the words, they made her feel uneasy. She turned to Dexter, experiencing a jolt of surprise to see him already rummaging through the bedside drawer.

He looked at his watch and swore under his breath, switching his focus to the bookshelves.

"Five minutes. Let's just find this blasted speech and get out of here. Maybe if you look downstairs? It'll be faster."

She blinked. He didn't seem concerned in the slightest, and she felt a small quiver of doubt, wondering if she was being paranoid.

"I'll just check the en-suite first," she said, moving towards the door, which stood ajar.

Her first impression was that it was like a bomb had gone off in there. Makeup scattered across the marble-topped washstand, vying for space amongst pots of various lotions and potions. There was no sign of the woman herself, though. Felicia didn't know whether she felt relieved or not.

There was a blusher brush on the tiled floor, its bristles tinted bubblegum pink. Automatically, Felicia bent down to pick it up, then froze in mid crouch.

Something was tugging insistently at the corner of her eye,

making her head turn as though pulled by marionette strings. For a split second, she wasn't sure what it was which had caught her attention. Then she saw it.

Sheaves of paper, folded over. With her eye in direct line with the edge of the sink, she could see the edges. They curled slightly, as though they'd been thumbed over several times.

"I've found it!" She yelled, straightening up and dragging the papers out from beneath a mascara, two eyeshadow palettes and a tube of lid primer. Immediately, she could see why she hadn't spotted it from above. Against the white marble, and buried under half a chemist's worth of makeup, it had been expertly camouflaged.

Dexter popped his head around the door.

"In the bathroom? Really? I wouldn't even have thought to look in here."

"That's because you're not female. She was probably going over it while she got ready." Felicia was unfolding the papers, scanning the ornate handwriting. Although it was unlikely to be anything else, the cautious adult in her told her to check. Amusing as it would be to send Dexter onto the stage with some florid diary entry to read out, she didn't think Cassie would find it quite so amusing at this point. Or Iris herself, if she ever turned up.

Dexter sighed showily.

"I could take this moment to expound on the many strange behaviours of women, but alas, we haven't the time." When she didn't respond, he glanced up, his smile slipping uncertainly. "What's the matter?"

"Dexter," she whispered, still staring at the page in horror. "You can't read this speech."

"Is it not very good?" He asked hopefully, clearly trying not to look too gleeful at the prospect. He craned over her shoulder, trying to see. "Because I'm sure I can jazz it up a bit; you know, give it a bit more panache…"

She choked on a hysterical laugh.

"Oh, it's already got plenty of that." She shook herself back into focus, urgency returning to her voice as she grabbed his arm and steered him away. "We have to go. *Now!*"

Chapter Four

As a policeman in Stamford, Detective Sergeant Pettifer was used to a life which was decidedly less than high-octane. Generally, he liked it that way; he'd seen more than enough of the rougher side of law enforcement during his brief stint in Leeds as a young PC. No, these days, with three children and a mortgage under his belt – a belt which was, regrettably, expanding year on year thanks to the excellent cream teas served at The George, the town's famous coaching inn – he much preferred the quieter roster of work which Stamford's meandering, carriage-width streets occasionally offered up: lost handbags, lost spaniels, the odd half-hearted fracas which broke out on the steps of The Golden Goose on a Saturday night...

Or at least, he amended reluctantly, he perhaps ought to say that that *had* been the case. Before Felicia Grant had appeared on the scene in a flurry of spring blossom and briefly turned his genteel, uneventful patch into the sort of frenzied bloodbath worthy of a late-night horror flick. Only with a lot more tweed.

Of course, it had only been temporary. Thank God, he added hastily, shifting his weight from one size 15 foot to another. Things had had swiftly settled back to the bucolic, monotonous status quo like sand sinking to the bottom of a glass. Efficiently, inevitably. Within weeks, it was like the disturbance had never even taken place.

Which suited him perfectly; of *course* it did. Just...

He frowned, displeased to find his thoughts heading in this direction once more. He'd always prided himself on being a gratifyingly plain sort, enjoying an easy, satisfied relationship with whatever life chose to serve up in front of him. He certainly wasn't one to yearn for unnecessary drama, as so many out there seemed to these days. It was a modern plague, one which a policeman was often forced of observe – and, on many occasions, deal with the consequences of. Folk who indulged in pointless arguments, pointless affairs, pointless spurts of speeding or driving just over the limit on the way home from the pub. None of it for any good reason; none of it, he suspected, because they even really wanted it. They didn't really *want* the last drink or the fumble in a hotel room with someone they barely knew. They didn't really want to get home that badly – or anywhere else, for that matter. It was all just a bit of a thrill, that was all, a way to make life feel more exciting than it was.

Frankly, it made him want to knock their heads together half of the time.

And so this niggling sense that since returning to normality, the day-to-day hadn't seemed *quite* so comprehensively fulfilling ... it was more than unfamiliar, it was downright aggravating. Hell, he was actually beginning to disapprove of *himself.*

He looked across The Meadows, which were heaving with

people by now, the grass barely visible under the assortment of boots and silk slippers which clad their feet. The funfair was set up expectantly behind them, pinstriped tents billowing invitingly in the balmy breeze. Music was playing from somewhere; something jaunty and classical, although he couldn't begin to say what, his listening habits being contentedly limited to Test Match Special and, occasionally, when he struggled to sleep, the shipping forecast.

It all looked perfect. Everyone looked happy. Nothing was even remotely amiss.

At once, out of nowhere, like a monster rearing its head, he felt it again. A frisson of something; restlessness, irritation…

Boredom, a small, unhelpful voice supplied. *Admit it. You're bored, aren't you?*

The thought made him flinch. He shook his head ferociously to clear it, thoroughly disgusted with himself.

"All right, Sarge?" PC Jess Winters, the other officer who'd drawn the short straw of sacrificing their Saturday to watching over the fair, had sidled up to him. She grinned. "You don't think we ought to have dressed up, do you? In the interests of blending in?"

"Certainly not," he growled, but it was for show, really. He liked Jess; insubordinate ribbing aside, the lass was earnest and hardworking, probably the most promising recruit he'd ever come across. All of which was more of a feat considering the pale blonde hair and baby face which worked against her daily in the quest to be taken seriously. Plus, she was a fellow incomer, and while he shuddered to think what his parents would say if they knew he considered himself in kinship with someone from *The South* – that scourge of all places – he was satisfied that here was a strong case for extenuating circumstances. When it came to somewhere like Stamford, somewhere so steeped in its own history and identity, anyone else who shared that sense of being on the outside looking in, of not quite getting it, was a welcome ally. Even if they *did* think that putting gravy on your chips was an act of vandalism.

"It's going to be a long day, isn't it?" The amusement had slipped from Jess's voice. She sounded resignedly weary. Pettifer watched her rub her eyes and made a mental note to check the rota when he got back. How many shifts in a row had the lass worked recently? She seemed to be constantly on duty. If he found out that she was picking up the slack for older, decidedly more male officers at the station, he was *not* going to be pleased.

Nonetheless, he acknowledged privately, she wasn't wrong. The two of them had a lot of ground to cover today. Most of the action revolved around the town's eponymous Arts Centre, a jumble of Georgian recreational buildings including the original assembly rooms – now known as the ballroom – and theatre, which still functioned as such today. Over the intervening years, its remit had grown dizzyingly, the sprawling corridors and higgledy-piggledy rooms becoming home to an ever increasing roster of workshops, art exhibitions, and local clubs. There was a café, a bar, a dazzling white cube of a gallery space which morphed into a temporary polling station on election days. The front desk was also the town's Tourist Information Centre, a one-stop shop for visitors in search of maps and walking routes – none of which were much good, if the daily inability of anyone looking even vaguely local to get five feet without being stopped for directions was anything to go by.

In short, it was fast becoming a case of what the Arts Centre *didn't* do rather than what it did. In the early years of the Georgian Fair, it had managed to contain the entire event within its stately walls, Pettifer thought ruefully. Not so any more. Now, the thing had grown so monstrously that it seemed to have infected the whole town. There was the funfair down here on The Meadows, an open-air market on Broad Street ... and that was before you'd even considered the glut of smaller concerts and talks tucked away behind the stone walls of Medieval churches and timbered pubs, businesses having soon seen the savvy of getting in upon the act. It was going to be an impossible task to keep an eye upon it all.

"Surely they don't actually *need* security for this," Jess muttered disbelievingly under her breath. "It's got to be the most middle-class event I've ever seen. The biggest ruckus will probably be in the tea tent."

With any luck she'd be right, Pettifer thought. The assembled crowd was looking up in anticipation now, at where the temporary stage – ornately gilded, naturally – had been set up next to a ghostly form shrouded in a satin sheet. He could only hope that no-one had added any 'amusing' additions to the statue whilst it had been unattended; that was the sort of crime which did happen in a small town dominated by a large, prestigious public school. Perhaps he ought to have checked on it earlier, although it was certainly too late now.

"Our illustrious leader thought there should be a police presence," Pettifer said sourly, then furiously reprimanded himself for letting his feelings show. The fact that he didn't like or – much as it pained his loyalty to the badge to admit it – have much in the way of respect for their Chief Inspector, wasn't something he should be revealing to Jess. It was the height of bad example.

"Not enough to be here himself though, I note," Jess

observed quietly, promptly confirming Pettifer's fears. He hastened to rectify the situation.

"I believe he'll be along later," he said neutrally, not adding what they both well knew: that DCI Heavenly was very much of the school of ruling from a distance. Namely, from the middle of a golfing green somewhere. "He's giving a talk on Georgian policing methods."

He didn't add that the council had actually asked *him* to do the talk initially, a decision which had affronted their very dapper and – in his own mind, at least – exceptionally personable superior no end. Any amusement at observing Heavenly's humiliation at being passed over was soon superseded by the effects of his ire, however, and Pettifer, never one for public speaking anyway, had fallen on his sword with no need to feign relief. Tedious it might be, but he'd still rather be on security any day of the week. Especially when the weather was like this, he thought, looking up in slight wonderment at the arc of unsullied delphinium blue overhead. Usually, one only had to so much whisper the word 'fête' in the vicinity of this sceptred isle for the clouds to slam shut overhead like a pair of iron curtains, the wind to start howling in straight from the Arctic circle, and rain to pummel down in Biblical quantities. Apparently, someone up there was on the side of the Georgian Fair ... even if it had come to his attention lately that not everyone in town was.

Grateful for the timely reminder, he scanned the crowd again, checking for any potential disturbances. All looked well. He allowed his shoulders to relax infinitesimally.

"Looks like they're about to start," Jess nodded towards the stage, which a rather unstable-looking Mayor Cassandra Lane was attempting to ascend in her enormous dress. "Where do you want me? By the jetty?"

"Better be," he agreed, still eyeing Cassie as she wobbled precariously on the top step. "In case some idiot manages to trip over their petticoats and fall into the river."

To the mayor's credit, she'd found her way on to the podium without assistance – not that Dennis Stanworthy, who was standing nearby, had looked predisposed to give it in any event – and was tapping at what even Pettifer could confidently declare to be a particularly un-historically appropriate microphone.

Apparently, even Stamford had to make the odd concession to modernity here and there. He found that the thought amused him for some reason.

"Good morning, everyone." Cassie's voice, which was, frankly, quite loud enough without artificial amplification, rolled across the open space like a clap of thunder. Any of the few hundred or so heads which weren't already swivelled obediently in her direction promptly did so now, and Pettifer found himself scanning them for a familiar pair; one bronze, one dark, both standing shoulders above the rest of the crowd. But there was no sign of his usual suspects. He felt his brow begin to crease of its own accord.

"By the way, sir," Jess whispered, as she slipped lightly away. "You should probably know that I volunteered you to judge the best dressed urchin competition this afternoon."

"Wonderful," he muttered. As if this day couldn't get any worse.

Up on the podium, Cassie was beginning to look uncharacteristically flustered as she neared the end of her welcome speech, head swivelling from left to right as she desperately scanned the crowd. Pettifer frowned; clearly, there was already a problem. Not one which need trouble him, granted; it was probably just an organisational glitch, but still, he didn't like it. Problems, in his experience, tended to flock together like sheep; one moved, and others followed indiscriminately.

"So, then, if we're all ready, it's time for…" With one last, slightly hopeless glance around her, Cassie visibly gave up on whatever she'd been waiting for, pasting an overly bright smile across her face as she blurted, "the traditional gun salute by our fabulous militia!" Flinging an arm out maniacally, she indicated the cluster of red-coated soldiers waiting to one side.

There was a beat of silence, and for the briefest moment before they could rearrange their expressions, astonishment registered on the faces of everyone on stage. The soldiers' reaction was milder; they simply looked at one another in bemusement, then shrugged, moving into line and lifting their muskets to the sky.

Pettifer, interest piqued, felt amongst the old sweet wrappers and confiscated packets of gum and cigarette lighters in the sagging pocket of his suit. It wasn't even that old, this suit, although his wife complained that he seemed to have an almost miraculous knack for aging clothing into something which wouldn't look out of place on a tramp within a matter of weeks. Pettifer had long since resigned himself to the fact that he was simply one of those people who couldn't look smart; it just wasn't in his DNA. He only had to don an outfit for jumpers to unravel, moth holes to appear in perfectly stored shirts, and polished shoes to scuff into an unrecognisable state. If his hair was slicked down, it sprung straight back up – or at least it had done before he'd had it shaved into a brutally short stubbly landscape years ago – if his tie was straightened, within moments it was crooked again. Unfortunately, whilst he might have made peace with it personally, those around him still despaired, often rather volubly.

True to form, the piece of paper, when he located it, was unrecognisable from the crisp sheet presented to him by the inexhaustible Gavin just yesterday. Now, it more closely resembled a crumpled chip wrapper. Smoothing it out as best he could, Pettifer squinted at the typed words.

Ah, he'd thought so. The gun salute was supposed to be at the *end* of the ceremony, acting as a sort of starting klaxon for the opening of the fair. Before that, there was Cassie's brief welcome, after which she handed over to an Iris Breadmore for a speech about that historical bloke everyone had been going all unnecessary over recently – God knew why; surely one dead lord of the manor was much the same as any other, but then, that was Middle England for you – followed by the statue unveiling. He couldn't see anyone who looked like a potential historian on the stage, mind. Presumably that was the source of Cassie's unease.

Truth be told, he was starting to feel a little uneasy himself, he admitted reluctantly. It was ridiculous, of course, but he had a horrible suspicion that it was something to do with the absence of Felicia and Dexter Grant. Wherever those two were, trouble was usually in attendance, too. And if they weren't *here*...

An explosion of gunpowder rang out across the grass, startling him and disorientating him all at once. Blinking, he noticed with some chagrin that the ducks on the bank beside him hadn't so much as raised their emerald-coloured heads at the sound. Then he looked up, and saw something else. From behind the trees. A flash of colour. Ice blue and bronze.

Impossibly, instinctively, he already knew what it was. In a subconscious way, he'd been waiting for it.

Felicia Grant was running across The Meadows, skirts

billowing out around her. Hot on her heels was a long-gaited vision in beige.

"Cass!" It was just a gasp, really, but into the pulsing silence following the gunshots, it rang out like a thunderclap. Instinctively, Pettifer found himself rocking forwards onto the ball of his foot, poised to lunge forward. But he held back, experience warning him not to charge in until he knew more.

She'd reached the podium by now; with one hand, she gathered up her hem, crushing the silk into a ball as she darted up the steps. Typically, she managed it with much more grace than Cassie had done. "Listen, there's something you really need to..."

"And *here* he *is!*" Completely ignoring her friend, Cassie reached past Felicia and yanked Dexter across the stage by his elbow, muttering to him in a low voice, "Thank the bloody *lord* for that. What took you so long? I was about to run out of waffle."

Unfortunately, she'd obviously forgotten about the microphone, which was blasting out her commentary at full volume. Dexter eyed it warily, then put a hand over it, bending his dark head down to whisper something to her. Even from here, Pettifer could see the urgency in his body language, the sharply defined movement of his lips. That alone was enough to resurrect the feeling of unease, which had simmered down briefly.

Because Dexter Grant wasn't what he would call a serious man. He approached almost everything in life with a flippant ennui which women seemed to adore and men absolutely hated. Pettifer could already see that, at his mere presence on the stage, a number of women had nudged their way to the front of the crowd and were gazing up at him. Although whatever he was saying to Cassie, it was falling on deaf ears.

She was shaking her head, swatting away his objections irritably, already shoving the microphone into his hand.

"May I present...the Treasure Seeker himself, Professor Dexter Grant!"

Applause broke out, swelling into a crescendo before gradually falling away, leaving a rather awkward pause as Dexter stood on the stage, looking, unusually, as though he'd rather be anywhere else but the centre of attention. At last, he cleared his throat.

"Er, well, hello everyone," he ventured uncertainly. "It's very … um … I mean, I'm honoured to be…"

He trailed off into a beat of silence. It lasted for one second … two…

Then the air around them all imploded.

Chapter Five

P C Jess Winters had been blissfully dreaming about a Saturday morning in bed when the piercing scream made every sinew in her body snap to attention. Her legs were already moving before her mind realised what was happening, urged into a sprint by a combination of instinct and training.

Jess was well aware she didn't inspire much confidence on the outside. At five foot three inches and weighing in at just over seven stone, she was well used to being overlooked – in many cases, literally – and underestimated, both professionally and in her day-to-day life. But she also knew that she had two things in her favour: she didn't freeze in a crisis, and she was fast. She was very, *very* fast.

It was those two things, working in tandem, which had propelled her through police college. It was also what got her onto the scene now before anyone else, despite having been stationed at possibly the farthest distance away.

The scream had come from the funfair, however, for a confusing moment, Jess couldn't see anything amiss. Then, as she drew closer, she spotted a dark-haired girl standing next to the hook-a-duck pool, white and shaking convulsively as she stared down into the depths. Jess skidded to a stop next to her, moving her gently but firmly to one side and craning over the edge.

What she saw there made her recoil in sheer horror.

A chalky face, hideously distorted by the water, pale bulging eyes staring straight up at her. Jess steadied herself, taking a deep breath in a bid to settle her suddenly churning stomach. She'd graduated at the top of her intake – to everyone's surprise except her own – and as such, her theoretical knowledge of finding a body was excellent. However, starting your policing career in a place like Stamford didn't exactly afford one many opportunities for coming face-to-face with a real corpse, and, as she was suddenly discovering, it was quite different to looking at a photograph of one. She'd been on the scene, of course, for the last three murders – two of which had actually been quite bloody – but by then the forensics team had all set up, and she'd been required to keep out of their way; only the briefest glance had been sufficient before the information she'd needed to know had all been relayed to her anyway.

She felt a hand on her shoulder, and looked up to see that Felicia Grant was next to her. By rights, she probably ought to have felt a degree of professional annoyance at the way the woman was trampling onto the scene, but instead, Jess found she could only feel relieved to see her. There was something reassuringly otherly about Felicia; she was like the subject of a favourite portrait, lovely, captivating, and eternally unruffled. And, Jess reminded herself wryly, probably more experienced at this sort of thing than she was. After all, she'd found those bodies back in the spring. She knew what it was like.

"They've been shot!" Someone cried out hysterically from

the crowd, who were pressing around the scene in a perfect crescent, held back by an invisible line at a distance which managed to be just about respectable whilst still affording a good view.

"No-one's been shot," snapped Cassie, who was standing a little further forward. But she immediately looked at Jess, and her face was beseeching, pleading with her to confirm it. Immediately, Jess understood; her eyes slid to the militia, who were muddled in amongst everyone else now, garish splashes of scarlet amongst the shimmering pastels. Their muskets were still clutched to their shoulders; they were supposedly loaded with blanks, but they were still real guns from the era. If someone had managed to spike one with live bullets instead, there was no telling where this could go. The mere thought, improbable and overwrought as it was, was enough to send a judder down her spine. She closed her eyes briefly, reminding herself that she was the professional here. She needed to keep it together, not get carried away with half-baked speculations.

As it was, she didn't get a chance to enlighten Cassie either way, because Pettifer came puffing into view, last as usual, his square body heaving with exertion.

"What have we got, Winters?" He spluttered.

"She's definitely dead, sir." Jess risked a glance at the awful, distorted face and suppressed a shudder.

"How?" Pettifer, never one to pussyfoot around, asked bluntly. Beside him, Cassie looked panicked.

Jess steeled her nerve and applied herself to further study of the body. Everyone waited, the silence so absolute it was almost deafening.

"It looks like drowning," she concluded at last. Then she pointed at a reddish stain on the side of one of the poles which held up the roof. "I suspect we'll find a head wound somewhere, conducive with a fall. At a rough estimate, I'd say she's been in the water since last night."

The crowd, which had been fairly silent up until this point, began murmuring to each other, a droning buzz, like an annoying bee in the ear. Cassie, far from looking relieved, was aghast as the pronoun seemed to resonate with her. A hand flew to her mouth, green eyes blooming wide with shock.

"*She?* Oh God. Surely it can't be..."

"Iris Breadmore," Felicia said. She only spoke quietly, but she'd been so still that Jess had temporarily forgotten she was there, and the sound of her voice made her jump. "The historian," she elucidated, presumably for Pettifer and Jess's benefit. "She's been missing all morning. Now I suppose we know why."

Was it just Jess's imagination, or did she and Dexter Grant, who was standing silently next to Cassie, share an uneasy glance as she spoke? Jess looked over at Pettifer, wondering if he'd seen it too. He had. He was watching them both, mouth a thin wafer of disapproval.

"You'd better call it in, Winters," he said at last, with customary lack of inflection. "In the meantime, we'll have to do what we can to secure the scene."

"The *scene*?" Blurted a voice. A face appeared over Cassie's shoulder. Jess recognised him immediately: the mayor's assistant. Gavin, she thought his name was. He'd been bustling around the police station for the past week like an officious, clipboard-brandishing wasp, haranguing them about every minor detail. Then, he'd been a categorically crisp, well put-together individual, but he didn't look it now. His face was almost as ashen as that of the corpse which floated nearby, and he was stammering his words. "But I mean ... you can't think

... it was an *accident*, surely? She must have ... I mean, after the party, on her way home...!"

"Party?" Pettifer's gaze, which had been hooded to the point of boredom, suddenly turned hawkish. "What party was this?"

Jess was starting to get cramp in her calf. She rocked back onto her heel, and as she did so, something crunched beneath her shoe. Glass, broken into tiny shards, some of it ground almost to powder. No-one else had noticed; they were all too caught up in conversation. Except Felicia. She was staring straight down at it, a look of deep thought on her face. Immediately, Jess really wanted to know what she was thinking. She'd discovered that Felicia's powers of observation were matched only by her intuition.

"For the opening of the Georgian Fair," Cassie was explaining now, Gavin having apparently quailed under the sergeant's intense stare. "Just those of us who were involved in the organising. Maybe forty, fifty people or so." She gestured at the little group clustered around the pool. "We were all there."

For the first time, Pettifer's eyes fixed definitively on Felicia's face.

"Of course you were," he said darkly.

She narrowed her eyes – now a stormy grey, which was curious as Jess could have *sworn* they were silver just a moment ago – and was just opening her mouth to make a retort, when a stifled sob made all of their heads rotate. The dark-haired girl was trembling violently, chin tucked tightly into her chest, arms wrapped around herself like a vice. She looked as though, if she let go for so much as a moment, she might simply shatter into pieces like the glass beneath their feet.

"She's in shock," Jess said, stating the obvious somewhat,

but knowing that someone had to say it. "We need to get her away from here."

"We need to get them *all* out of here," Pettifer scowled, jerking a thumb over his shoulder at where the crowd was watching on avidly, ears straining to hear what was going on. "This isn't a bloody pantomime. It's a potential crime scene."

He was glaring expectantly at Cassie, who started.

"Of course," she said automatically, but the affirmative rang hollow. Instead she seemed dazed, at a loss for what to do. Felicia, who had her arm around the crying girl, looked up.

"Why don't we take them to the ballroom?" She suggested gently. "It's a big enough space for everyone."

"*Yes*." The word came out in a whoosh, the relief and gratitude palpable in Cassie's voice. "Good idea, Fliss. The ballroom it is."

Chapter Six

"Here you go, Tara," Felicia put a chipped mug of tea on the tablecloth in front of the still trembling girl. "Sorry it's not a better cup. They wanted to save those for later, in case..."

In case it all still goes ahead. The end of the sentence hung unfinished between them.

The situation was an awkward one, to say the least. Pettifer was still waiting on the final opinion of the crime scene team, but right now, it all seemed to be looking very much like an accident. Dennis had swiftly been on the phone to DCI Heavenly, who had apparently abdicated all responsibility for the decision, instead choosing to leave it in the hands of the town council. It had thus gone to a hasty vote, one which Felicia was in no doubt had threatened to split the cabinet down the middle. One look at Cassie's strained face when she'd emerged with the results had confirmed that suspicion, and Felicia promised in that moment that she would never ask which way her friend had voted. The choice was an impossible one, with seemingly no right answer, and she knew that Cassie would agonise over it endlessly whichever way she'd gone.

However tense the process might have been, however, the consensus was that it would be a shame for a tragic mishap to put a stop to everything the town had worked so hard towards for the past year. Especially as the couple of hundred people who'd been on The Meadows – and now crammed into the ballroom awaiting the verdict – were mostly locals; the official start time wasn't for another hour or so. By the time main visitors began to arrive, there would be no need for them to even know what had happened here this morning.

Felicia couldn't say she was surprised, even if she wasn't entirely sure how she felt about it. After all, that was life in the English countryside for you. Through World Wars and plagues, deaths of monarchs, changes of government, societal upheaval and – of course – the weather, the show always went stoically on. It was at once both extremely comforting and tremendously alarming.

"Thank you." Tara raised the mug to her lips. Felicia reached for her own tea, trying not to grimace as she noticed that the mug was emblazoned with the Treasure Seeker logo. She'd been obliged to run over to the auction house to supplement the Arts Centre's rather paltry supply of staffroom receptacles.

She looked at the girl out of the corner of her eye, trying not to be too obvious in her assessment. One of the soldiers had dropped his red jacket around her shoulders, and that, combined with the steam rising off the hot tea, made her look less frozen, at least. Some of the colour was even beginning to return to her cheeks, although she still looked impossibly frail and stunned. Felicia wondered how old she was; nineteen, twenty maybe? This may well be the first time she'd come into contact with death.

"I'm sorry," Tara said abruptly, seeming to shake herself. "I just … I can't take it in." She squeezed her eyes shut. "I keep seeing her face."

"It's all right, it happens like that." Realising she ought to expand, Felicia continued, "I've … er, been there myself. Once or twice. I know what it's like."

The eyes flew open, huge and shimmering.

"Does it get better?"

"Of course!" Felicia tried to sound suitably strident, not having the heart to tell her that while it faded dramatically in time, it never really left you. Finding a body was a gruesome, haunting sort of club, one which nobody had wanted to join but ended up with a lifetime membership to nonetheless. "It's just the initial shock, that's all. You'll feel better soon." She hesitated, tapping her teaspoon against the rim of her cup; then, driven on by an impulse she couldn't explain, added, "Did you … know her? I mean, I understand she was only in town for the weekend, but…"

"No, I never even spoke to her." Tara looked down into her drink. "But I'd seen her. She was at the drinks reception last night at The George. I was next to her at the bar at one point; not that I think she noticed me standing there." She gazed up at Felicia from beneath a heavy fringe. "Most people don't, as a rule." She smiled wanly, her gaze travelling over Felicia with something approaching wistfulness. "Although, I don't imagine you ever have that problem."

Before Felicia could work out how to respond to that, she was saved by a shadow falling over the table.

"Tara." The man's voice was courteous, full-bodied with sympathy. He had a patrician face, lined in an attractively lived-in sort of way, his salt and pepper hair swept back from a domed forehead. There was an aura of capability about him as well as a certain grace. The thought flickered across Felicia's mind that this is probably what Dexter would look like in twenty years' time. Feeling rather hot all of a sudden, she abruptly banished it.

"Oh," Tara faltered, not looking up at him. "Hello."

"Such a dreadful thing to happen." He'd placed a hand on the back of her chair. His fingers were strong, yet elegantly formed. There was no wedding ring, Felicia noticed, and no telltale pale line where one might have been until recently. Not that that was entirely conclusive on a man of his age, particularly out here in the country, where tradition tended to lead over modern sensibility. "The whole company is so concerned. We wanted to check that you're all right." He looked at Felicia then for the first time. "Although, I can see you're being well looked after by Ms. Grant here."

He'd got her name right, Felicia noticed. Or at least, her title. People here had a habit of automatically calling her Mrs. Grant, which needled the hell out of her. Not only because she and Dexter were very much divorced, but because Grant was actually *her* name, taken by Dexter when they'd married; a fact which only the smallest application of common sense would reveal to anybody, given that it was emblazoned above the door of the auction house begun by her father. Alas, not many seemed able to make that connection that set this man apart, made her immediately warm to him.

"Have we met?" She asked.

He held out a hand towards her.

"James Riverton. But I already know who you are. I should think everyone in town does by now."

She gave a wry smile. He wasn't wrong about that. She was still getting used to being a local celebrity, especially one at the slightly more infamous end of the scale.

"I was away on business at the time it all happened, but I read about it afterwards," he explained. *The Stamford Bugle* covered the whole thing quite extensively."

"They certainly did," Felicia said flatly. It had been a sensation for a while – how could it not be? – but soon enough, the other media outlets had grown tired and moved onto other, newer stories. Not so *The Bugle*. The area's slightly unedifying gossip rag was well-known for putting people's backs up; Cassie had had any number of run-ins with them over the years. Perhaps inevitably, they'd latched onto the story of the murders – they were the ones to blame for the 'Stamford's Lovejoy' moniker, incidentally – and refused to let go, releasing a gleeful barrage of dubiously researched, preposterously-headlined speculation which had barely seemed to abate in the intervening months. Every time she began to hope it was all settling down, she'd open the front door in the morning to find a brand new hypothesis screaming at her from the mat. "I only got a glance at the front page before we had to leave earlier, but I believe that today's suggestion is that Charles I is haunting my auction house."

His responding smile was droll, self-effacing.

"I'll admit that some of their shots go a little wild, but at least they're still asking the questions. I'm like you, Ms Grant; I can't stand loose ends. And there were so many in that case. There was clearly more to it all than the police were saying." He opened his palms in a gesture of mild, quizzical frustration. "Who broke into the house on Barn Hill, for one thing? There's never been a satisfactory answer to that, in my opinion." He raised his eyebrows at her, his eyes registering a newly keen interest. "Then again, I'll wager you have some theories."

Felicia suddenly found herself *very* keen to change the subject. She dropped her teaspoon with a clatter.

"So, you two ... work together?"

It took him a second to catch up. Then his face relaxed into a well-bred laugh. "Oh, no, not *that* kind of company. Although I can see where the confusion might arise from. No, we're both in the Stamford Players. We're putting on an adaptation of *The Beggar's Opera* early this evening."

"Or we were," Tara said quietly. "I don't suppose the play will happen now, will it? None of it will happen."

"Oh, I wouldn't be so sure," Riverton said confidently. As both women looked at him in surprise, he drew back, shaking his head as though annoyed with himself. "I apologise, that was crass of me. I oughtn't have said that. It's only ... well, with her reputation..." He glanced back and forth between them, apparently puzzled by their lack of comprehension. "Her little problem with ... imbibing? I thought everyone in town knew ... surely, after the incident..."

"I...wasn't part of the fair then," Tara stuttered, looking down at the table. "I wouldn't remember."

Riverton looked down at her for a long moment. Felicia thought he looked faintly disappointed, as though she'd failed some undefined test.

"No, I suppose you'd have been too young," he said blandly. Then, "Your suitor is looking somewhat perturbed, Tara. You'd probably better settle his feathers."

Felicia followed his gaze to the corner of the room, where a gangly, sandy-haired boy was glowering at Tara from beneath fair eyebrows, crumpling the brim of his tall hat between oversized pink hands. He was wearing the military uniform of white breeches and waistcoat, long black boots encasing his calves, but the most striking part of the outfit, the scarlet and gold coat, was nowhere in evidence. It wasn't a massive deductive leap to work out that it was currently draped around the slight shoulders of the girl sitting next to her.

At that moment, Riverton was hailed from across the room, and he inclined his head in a small bow, explaining, "Excuse me, but duty calls. I'd better do the rounds."

He took his leave, clapping his acquaintance on the back as they fell into genial conversation.

"Popular man," Felicia murmured.

"Oh yes, everyone looks up to James ... Mr. Riverton." Tara bit her lip, glancing nervously across the room, then stood hurriedly, catching the underside of the table and causing it to pitch back and forth. She snatched at the edge to stop it, stammering apologetically, "I really ought to speak to Ambrose, before he..." She swallowed. "It's just ... *he* just ... worries so much about things. Thank you for the tea, though. I'm feeling much better, really."

Felicia watched her scuttle away, then allowed her gaze to carry on around the perimeter of the room, taking in the sort of scene which only a place like Stamford could call normal. The ballroom in which they were sitting was the earliest surviving example in the country, and frankly, little had changed within it since its construction in 1727, bar a few modern conveniences such as electric lighting – a necessity as the room was perennially dark despite its large arched windows to either end. It was a reminder, along with the mirror-lined walls and deep rose paintwork, that this was a place designed for night, for the shimmer of candlelight on glass and silk, for whispered confidences behind fluttering fans and stolen kisses in shadowed corners. That said, it occurred to Felicia that if you discounted the weak daylight filtering in from above, this was probably the closest thing the room had got to its original usage in almost three hundred years. It was already set up for this evening's dance; long, cloth-clad tables lined the far end of the room, and plush velvet seats were in place for the string quartet hired to play for the evening. Combined with the clusters of historically-clad people milling around, it was easy to imagine, just for a moment, that it wasn't the 21st century at all. That none of today was happening.

That was, until she saw the grim-faced figure beckoning to her from the doorway. She sighed.

"Right," Pettifer growled as she approached, skirts swishing on the polished wooden floorboards. "I just need to know one thing."

"Why can't everywhere be more like Yorkshire?" She quipped. Then, at his stony expression, she relented. "Sorry, long morning. I thought we could both do with some levity."

He harrumphed, shoving slab-like hands into crumpled pockets.

"There'll be plenty of that in about an hour, when the body's been moved." At her raised eyebrows, he elucidated, "It's all been arranged, apparently – well over my head. Stitched up very cosily by Heavenly and Dennis Stanworthy. Turns out nothing stops a good old English fête."

Bitterness fairly radiated from his tone. Felicia realised she'd better tread cautiously.

"So ... it definitely was an accident, then?" She ventured.

"Nothing to indicate that it wasn't," he said shortly.

She'd been dealing with him long enough by now to know that what Pettifer didn't say was almost as important as what he did. You had to look for the negative space between his words.

"But anything to indicate that it actually *was*?" She pressed.

He pursed his lips. For a minute, she thought he wasn't going to answer her. But then he started to speak in a low voice.

"Jess was right about the head wound. It's on the side, towards the back of the skull. On top of that, one of her ankles is badly bruised, and there's a small patch of churned up grass which is consistent with the spike of a heel twisting and then coming out at an angle. The natural conclusion is that she got her shoe stuck and lost her balance, hitting her head. She'd have been unconscious when she landed in the water; never stood a chance. She'd obviously been drinking; the shattered glass still has traces of red wine in it."

Felicia hesitated, wondering whether to say more. But the woman was dead; nothing could hurt her now.

"Apparently she had been known to have a slight ... problem in that department," she admitted reluctantly. She had a feeling this wasn't going to go down well.

She was right.

"Oh, really?" He turned a laser-like gaze upon her. "And how, exactly, would you know that, Ms Grant?"

Oh dear, Felicia thought, with an internal gulp. When he used her full name like that, she knew she was really unpopular. Or at the very least, about to be.

"Just ... something someone said to me," she said cagily. "That's all."

"Hmm." His expression was thunderous. "People seem to have a habit of 'just saying' things to you, I've noticed."

"I must have an understanding face," she retorted. "You would too, if you'd spent years valuing dead people's things to their relatives." Being an auctioneer sometimes felt like moonlighting as an unofficial therapist, bereavement councillor, and mediator all at once. Some of the things she'd been told over a table of antiques put anything she'd heard during the course of her springtime murder investigation in the shade. But she wasn't about to try and explain all of that to Sergeant Pettifer. It would only make him even crosser.

"Hmmmm." Pettifer had an entire catalogue of 'hmms', Felicia had come to learn. This one denoted deep scepticism tempered with resignation. He knew he wasn't about to win this discussion, so, for the time being at least, he gave up. "You were at this party thing last night, I take it? Did she seem particularly…"

"In her cups?" Felicia only realised belatedly that she'd chosen an appropriately Georgian phrase. "I'm afraid I didn't notice."

He raised a bristly eyebrow.

"I thought it was an auctioneer's job to notice detail?"

Of *course* he would take any opportunity to throw that back at her. She resisted the urge to roll her eyes – too puerile – and instead put her hands on her hips.

"I was at a *party*, Sergeant. I was off duty!"

"Plus it was a free bar." Cassie's voice piped up from the doorway behind them. She squeezed her skirts through the opening with difficulty, her anxiety-creased face belying the teasing tone. "What's going on, both of you? You're looking all furtive out here. If you've found out what happened to that poor woman…"

"Of course, I promised you'd be the first to know." Pettifer said, then added neutrally, "all signs are pointing to an accident."

Cassie stared him down.

"I wasn't born yesterday, Sergeant. That's police speak for you're not convinced."

Felicia swore that she saw Pettifer's panoramic shoulders drop.

"Personally, I would be ... if it weren't for one thing." He looked at Felicia, so pointedly that she sighed. Of course, she should have known he wouldn't miss that. The man didn't miss *anything*. It could be rather vexing at times.

"Fine," she said, throwing up her hands. "But not here. Cass, you'd better come along too; you need to hear this."

Chapter Seven

The tiny, lopsided cottage on Water Street was a picture of bucolic innocence. Lemon-hued roses bloomed across its honeycombed frontage, and the blue slate roof sagged in a way which delighted the ambling tourist as equally as it alarmed any professional tradesperson who happened to set eyes upon it. In front of the house, the narrow lane was succeeded by the wide riverbank, which unfurled to the water in a flower-speckled carpet of green. Even the Welland sparkled appealingly on a day such as this, the recent prolonged dry spell having transformed it from its usual opaque olive hue into a glass-like substance which revealed a bed of rippling reeds, between which minute silver fish darted furtively. Above it, the ironwork bridge arched gracefully in a high-Victoriana confection of sage-painted lacework swirls. The effect was one of almost overbearingly lovely peacefulness, Felicia thought. It was hard to imagine that she and Algernon had almost been killed on this spot not so very long ago, or that the toybox cottage in front of her had become the headquarters for a very unorthodox – and decidedly unofficial – murder investigation.

This had seemed like the safest place to come, away from prying ears, but as she pushed open the diminutive front door – she no longer assumed it would be locked, something which was still alarmingly common to find in Stamford – she immediately realised her mistake on that score. The first thing which greeted her was a hubbub of voices coming from the kitchen, shortly followed by a small figure, which barrelled down the narrow hall, flinging itself at her with abandon.

"Mum! They're saying that you found a body." A pair of bright grey eyes gazed up at her expectantly. "Again."

"It wasn't actually *me* who found it this time." Feeling slightly defensive about the 'again', which she hadn't felt was quite needed, Felicia was moved to uncharacteristic pedantry. "I just … happened to be nearby, that's all."

"Your mother has something of a knack for that," Pettifer supplied dryly, from over her shoulder, and despite herself, Felicia started slightly. For such a large man, it was unnervingly easy to forget his presence. Alas, the same couldn't be said of Cassie, who'd somehow managed to get herself entangled in the hat stand and was thrashing about like a warring hippopotamus in an attempt to free herself. As usual, everyone politely ignored her.

At the sight of Pettifer, Algernon's eyes lit up with barely repressed excitement.

"If Sergeant Pettifer's here … does this mean it's another murder?"

Felicia bit back a groan. At twelve, Algie was still at the age where the full horrors of murder were yet to dawn. To him, it was all just very thrilling, especially seeing as being involved in it last time had made him a bit of a celebrity. Their moving back had compelled him to join his new school at an awkward time, just after the Easter holidays, and she'd worried about how he'd fit in and make friends during the narrow sliver which the final term of the year afforded. After all, it had taken him years to settle at his old school in London. Algernon wasn't a straightforward child; he was fascinating and strange, ever shifting from childish effervesce to levels of gravity and comprehension normally only found in those who'd lived a long and complex lifetime on Earth. He could be talkative and sunny one moment, silent and dreamy the next. He was unknowable even to those who knew him best. You had to take him as he was; something which even adults struggled with sometimes, never mind other children.

But her fears hadn't come to pass. Secretly, she had to admit that his local fame had probably helped to smooth the way somewhat with his new schoolmates, and he already seemed happier than she could have imagined when he'd first begged her to move them back here for good. That said, she did rather wish that the close shave he'd had in the spring might have dampened his enthusiasm for investigating just a *bit* more.

Pettifer was evidently of the same mind. He gave Algernon a warning look.

"Now then, lad, remember what we spoke about. A police investigation..."

"Yes, I remember." Algernon was far too well brought up to *actually* roll his eyes, but the sentiment was there in his voice. "It's all very boring really and nothing like it is in books. That's why policemen do it and not normal people."

"Er, I don't think that's *exactly* what I said..." Pettifer began, not seeming too keen on such a cursory dismissal of his career.

"But it *is* a murder, isn't it?" Algernon pressed. "Because you wouldn't be here if it wasn't. And you certainly wouldn't have that look on your face."

Pettifer did a visible double take.

"What look?"

"Your murder expression," Algernon replied loftily, with the self-satisfied air of one who knows all.

"I don't have a *murder* expression," Pettifer said tetchily, but Felicia saw him glance surreptitiously in the hall mirror nonetheless.

"Leave the Sergeant be, Algie," Felicia's father boomed, hobbling through the kitchen doorway on crutches. The cast was off his leg now, but he was still struggling to get around after the fracture he'd sustained in the spring. The confinement hadn't been good for his temper, which was irascible at the best of times. The only silver lining was that he hadn't been able to get to the auction house much, so Felicia had been able to resettle into her old role without his critical interference. In truth, she knew that it was only delaying the inevitable; as soon as he was back, the conflict between them would spark again, just as it had the last time they'd run the place together. "It was an accident, surely. Everyone knows how slippery The Meadows get underfoot, especially when the dew's on them. And in the dark like that..." He looked at Pettifer then, and his robust confidence faltered momentarily, his broad, burnished face registering an almost pleading expression. "It *was* just an accident, wasn't it? There's no need to make a song and dance about it."

Pettifer gave him an assessing look.

"I wouldn't have thought you'd be such a keen proponent of the Georgian Fair, sir."

Clearly, he was trying to imagine her gruff, earthy father all trussed up in pastel breeches taking part in a quadrille and struggling.

"Oh, I'm not," Peter said forcefully. "All of that poncing about the place ... load of old cobblers, if you want my opinion."

"Thanks, Peter," Cassie said dryly, pausing briefly in her efforts to disentangle a portion of her wig from the spokes of an umbrella. "Good to know we have your endorsement."

"It's Auntie Juliette he's worried about," Algernon piped up, in that singularly unhelpful way he had. "She was utterly furious when she found out what happened before. She said it was all Mum's fault..."

"She says *everything's* my fault," Felicia muttered.

"Well, you do have something of a tendency to attract drama," Cassie supplied, finally wrenching herself free with a ripping sound.

"Or *it* has a tendency to attract *me*," Felicia shot back. "Has no-one thought of that?"

"...and that if Mum couldn't be trusted to look after Grandad and me properly and was going to get us involved in *dangerous murders*..." Algernon continued, doing his best to ignore the interruption.

"The thing is, if this turns out to be another murder," Peter took up the mantle, turning to Pettifer almost apologetically. "My other lass, she's ... well, she'd be over here like a shot, you see. Probably never get rid of her."

There was a sombre silence whilst all contemplated that. Even Sergeant Pettifer, who'd yet to make the acquaintance of the redoubtable Juliette, looked vaguely wary at the prospect.

"Christ, it sounds like someone's died down here." A cacophony of creaking oak announced that feet were descending the stairs. Within seconds, Dexter came bounding into view. He paused in the doorway, appearing to consider what he'd said rather sheepishly. "Perhaps not my finest choice of phrase, given the circumstances."

"*Mr. Grant*." Pettifer looked as aghast as his boulder-like visage would permit. "What are you doing here? All witnesses were instructed to remain in the ballroom!" He paused, then added, somewhat bitterly, "It's not as if you're new to this process."

"Yes, well," Dexter didn't seem particularly contrite. "Sorry about that. But I figured that you'd know where to find me. Besides, it's all just a formality, isn't it? It's not like last time…" He trailed off, glancing between them all quickly. "What? Why are you all looking like that? Have I missed something?" His cobalt blue gaze settled on Felicia. "It was an accident, surely? It couldn't have been anything else."

"So everyone keeps assuring me," Pettifer said tautly. "Perhaps I should just pack up and go home. After all, Stamford clearly doesn't need a policeman; the whole town appears to be experts on crime."

Algernon stood up on tiptoes to whisper to Dexter, "I think you've upset Sergeant Pettifer, Dad."

"It's all right." Dexter patted his head, not bothering with a whisper, stage or otherwise. "We're always upsetting Sergeant Pettifer. He likes it really; it keeps his life interesting."

Pettifer, who, thanks to the proportions of the cottage, was standing only about a foot away, glared at him.

"So," Dexter continued, ignoring this completely. He raised his eyebrows. "A murder, hey? What makes you think that?"

"Your wife," Pettifer said stonily.

"*Ex*-wife!" Felicia ground out. "How many times?"

"Never mind all of that, duck," said Peter, with a

dismissiveness which belied the fact that he'd been more pleased than anyone when the decree absolute had come through. "What's this all about, then? You know something you're not telling us? Spit it out!"

Everyone's head swivelled to look at her expectantly, and Felicia felt the full absurdity of it all hit her. Surely other families didn't have conversations like this? She threw her hands up in exasperation.

"I'm going into the kitchen to make a nice cup of tea. Anyone who wants to come is welcome." She paused, then added darkly, "It's not as if I could stop you anyway."

Unsurprisingly, no-one needed telling twice, filing through the low-lintelled doorway like ducklings in her wake.

"*Hugo*." Felicia did a double take when she saw the poorly-attired figure sitting at the table. "What are you doing here?"

"How many more people can fit in this bloody house?" Pettifer grumbled, squeezing into the narrow space between the table and the Aga. Felicia was slightly surprised that he wasn't objecting more to such flagrant barging in on his investigation, but then again, perhaps he was simply resigned to its inevitability.

"Hello." The auction house's junior valuer, prone to flushing at the slightest provocation, found this scenario more than sufficient to produce a violent red bloom across his cheeks. "I ... ah ... well, Gavin ... he's rather ... tetchy at the moment, you see. I can't seem to do anything right. Thought it was best if I got out of his way for a bit."

He managed to look both abashed and wretched at the same time. It had been a long while since Felicia had last been in the early, heady days of a relationship, but she remembered well enough the first signs of the person you loved not being a permanent paragon of sweetness and light. The moment when you realised that after all, they were just human, and more to the point, they were beginning to realise the same of you. Suddenly, adoration didn't preclude irritation in the way it once had. It was a natural progression of course, but at the time, it was an unwelcome shock to the system.

"He's like that with everyone at the moment," Cassie said sympathetically. "We're all on the sharp end of his temper. I think it distresses his sense of perfect order that he can't control every aspect of a weekend-long festival."

"You stay as long as you like," Felicia laid a hand on Hugo's shoulder, then added, "provided you don't mind us talking about murder, that is."

"My only conversations for weeks have revolved around timetables and spreadsheets," Hugo replied. "To be honest, murder sounds like a positively refreshing topic."

"If we've *quite* finished," Pettifer clearly felt he had to try and take charge, although really, Felicia reflected, by now he ought to know that it was a losing battle. He pointed at Felicia, then at Dexter. "You two. You looked at each other earlier. You know when I mean, so don't try and deny it. What do you know that I don't?"

"Hang on," Cassie interrupted, holding up a lace-ruffled hand. "I'll just put the kettle on. I'm sure we all want tea, especially if this is going to be interesting."

Hearty concurrence followed, and Felicia and Pettifer watched on in joint disbelief as the next few minutes were spent in a whirlwind of team beverage-making. Eventually, with everyone settled in a reasonably comfortable spot – even Godfrey, Peter's bruiser of a cat, had come to see what all the fuss was about – and looking at her expectantly, as though this were a performance they'd had tickets to for months, Felicia glanced at Pettifer warily, then took a deep breath, letting her gaze fall on her best friend's powdered face.

"There's no easy way to tell you this, Cass. But your star speaker ... now your *dead* star speaker ... was going to sabotage the entire Georgian Fair."

Chapter Eight

"I should probably start at the beginning," Felicia said, after the pandemonium which greeted that statement had settled down.

"It is traditional," Pettifer grunted, mopping tea off his lapel from where Hugo had sloshed it all over him in the kerfuffle.

"When Professor Breadmore went missing this morning," Felicia continued, trying valiantly to ignore her father, who was brushing the contents of the upended sugar bowl off of his bandaged foot, "Cassie asked Dexter if he'd take over her talk."

"I did," Cassie agreed, around a mouthful of garibaldi. Godfrey had tactically stationed himself at her elbow, and was watching vigilantly for errant crumbs. "I was worried she mightn't turn up, and I thought Dexter was the best person to ad-lib."

Godfrey, apparently bored of waiting for a biscuit, stuck his head in her tea instead. Cassie didn't notice.

"To which I agreed. For the good of the fair, of course,"

Dexter said modestly.

Several people choked into their mugs.

"Gavin had already been over to her rental cottage and couldn't get any answer." Felicia added quickly, before Dexter noticed the merriment at his expense. "Obviously, we needed the notes for her speech – it was all original research, you see – so we went over to fetch them."

"Wait ... cottage?" Pettifer held up a stubby hand to halt the narrative. "I understood that all visiting speakers stay at The George?"

"They do," Cassie agreed, dunking the rest of the garibaldi into her tea whilst Godfrey looked on smugly. "Usually. But Professor Breadmore informed us early on that we needn't book a room for her. She would organise her own private accommodation."

"And you didn't think that was a bit unusual at the time? I mean, has anyone else ever done that?"

"Well ... no," Cassie admitted slowly. "But she was known to be a little ... erm, particular."

"Diva-ish, more like," Dexter muttered, from his position perched on the arm of a peeling leather armchair. There wasn't really room for it in the tiny kitchen, but Felicia's father had a tendency to take pity on the auction strays nobody wanted and give them a home with him. It was a small sign of the softer centre few people would guess lurked deep beneath his forbidding exterior.

Pettifer's piercing gaze immediately swung onto Dexter.

"You knew her?" The words were sharp, accusing. "Why didn't you say so earlier? If I find you're withholding information from a police investigation again, this time I swear, I'll have you—"

"Calm yourself, Sergeant." Dexter made the sort of

patronising downwards motion with his hands which was guaranteed to make anyone feel entirely the opposite. Indeed, if the vein in Pettifer's temple was anything to go by, it was taking all of his willpower not to strangle him on the spot. "Yes, I knew her. But only insofar as both being professionals in the same field. History's a very broad subject, Sergeant, and our specialisms don't exactly overlap. In fact, there's more than two hundred years between them. A scholar of Medieval symbolism and an expert in Georgian etiquette ... we didn't have much common ground." He shrugged. "It was more of a case that I knew *of* her. She was what you might call infamous."

"Liked a drink, I understand?" Pettifer's eyes flickered briefly to Felicia, then away again.

"More than one. And couldn't hold it, either." Dexter raised his eyebrows, looking impressed. "I say, you did well to find that out. It's one of the worst-kept secrets in academia, but as far as I'm aware, that's where it's stayed. The people around her have always worked very hard to contain the truth."

Felicia glanced across at Algernon, who had hopped up onto the counter, and was following avidly, legs swinging back and forth. She began to wonder if he really ought to be listening to all of this, then mentally shrugged. After all, he'd heard far worse in the past couple of months.

"People?" Pettifer flicked through his notes. "I have it here that she was unmarried, no children. Lived alone."

"I mean professional people, Sergeant. Her university, the publishers of her books. Everyone who had a vested interest in maintaining her sugar-coated image as the nation's Austenian grandmother, showing them how to select the right bonnet or sweep a curtsey just so." Dexter made a little mock bow to accompany his point. "But it says something about a person when even the paid professionals can't handle them, and she razed through agents and editors like no tomorrow; oh, there was always a very believable reason given, but it was starting to look obvious. I don't think she even had an assistant at the moment; word had got around in the industry. No-one would touch her with a bargepole, no matter how much money she offered."

Felicia thought there was something rather sad-sounding about that, although, judging by the expressions on everyone else's faces, the same sentiment hadn't occurred to them. They were simply watching on avidly.

"If you want to know more about that, Sergeant, you'd do well to ask my predecessor," Cassie offered now. "I understand there were a few … er … hiccups … last time she was here."

"*Wait!*" Pettifer's voice was like a crack of thunder. It made Hugo jump. "Professor Breadmore was here before? *In Stamford?*"

"Well, yes." Cassie looked nonplussed by his reaction. "Didn't you know? She was at the first ever Georgian Fair, five years ago." She hesitated, then added, "I get the impression that she left under a bit of a cloud, if the opposition to her returning this year is anything to go by. Several members of the council were quite up in arms about it, although no-one would say exactly why." She sounded a bit put-out by this, and Felicia didn't wonder. Her friend liked to know everything which went on. "I've tried to find out from other sources, but people are ridiculously close-lipped about it. You'd think it was a bloody state secret."

Felicia shared her exasperation, but it wasn't surprising. Stamford had many wonderful qualities, but a place which traded on its perfect image also had to be unexpectedly cut-throat in its protection of that perception. It had been closing ranks on the less bucolic elements of its existence for decades now; for a town which could sweep a few serial killings under the carpet within the space of two months, a minor, embarrassing indiscretion from five years ago was mere child's play.

A deep groove had appeared in the middle of Pettifer's forehead, almost cleaving his face in two.

"And you don't recall *anything* yourself from that time? You were living here then, weren't you?"

"In body, yes, but not in anything else." At his confused look, Cassie explained with a wry smile, "I had a small baby who'd decided to start crawling vindictively early. I wasn't in a position to notice much of anything which was going on. Besides, the idea of joining the council wouldn't even cross my mind for another couple of years. I'm afraid I was well out of it."

Pettifer moved his attention to Peter, who shrugged apologetically.

"You've heard my views on the subject. As far as I'm concerned, the thing's best avoided. I was probably working at the auction house all weekend, trying my damnedest to do just that."

"And I'd just been promoted to junior valuer around then," Hugo supplied. "So I was probably with you. I was working flat out learning the ropes all of that summer; I'm afraid I didn't go anywhere near the fair that year."

"We were all still living in London," Felicia added, gesturing towards Dexter and Algernon. "So we can't be of any help either, I'm afraid."

"And *I* was up in Yorkshire," Pettifer said, with a deflated sigh. His huge shoulders dropped. "I didn't transfer till the following year."

"Like I said, you'll have to ask James Riverton," Cassie said, blocking Godfrey with her arm as he made a play for the plate of biscuits. "He'll know all about it. He was the one in charge at the time."

"Hold on…" Felicia blurted out. "*He* was the mayor before you?"

"Yes, he's very popular locally." Cassie didn't seem perturbed by her astonishment. "He only did it for a couple of years, though. It's more work than people imagine," she added, with a certain level of feeling.

"Thank you, I'll speak to him," Pettifer said grimly, although Felicia thought he looked marginally more optimistic than he had a moment ago. By his standards, at least. He turned back to herself and Dexter, eyes narrowing. "So, you went to her cottage … *both* of you, I take it? Was that *really* necessary?"

"There's no need to sound so accusing, Sergeant," Felicia said primly. "I wasn't simply being nosy." When he looked flagrantly unconvinced, she continued hotly, "I *wasn't*! I was there to…" Abruptly, she stopped herself, realising that she'd almost said too much. "Anyway, never mind that now. We went inside…"

"*Wait.*" Alas, Pettifer wasn't about to be put off easily. "Details. How did you get inside? Was the door open by that point?"

For the briefest of moments, Felicia indulged herself with the notion of fudging the truth. Then she sighed.

"Well…*no.* Not if we're being technical about it."

"You picked the lock!" Algernon bounced up and down on the work surface. "She can do that, you know," he told Pettifer proudly. "I keep asking her to show me how, but she won't."

The tendons in Pettifer's neck suddenly looked dangerously close to snapping.

"Dashed useful, too," Peter rumbled approvingly from next to the fireplace, where he was sitting with his leg propped on a low stool. "An auction house can't afford to be without a lock picker. Young Hugo here had to learn after she'd gone flouncing off to London."

"I did not *flounce*, Dad," Felicia said testily. "I made a dignified exit from a partnership which simply wasn't working." Followed by a less-than-dignified re-entrance years later, although she wasn't about to voice that part.

Pettifer looked appalled. She could practically see him taking in the idea of an entire league of would-be criminals populating the nation's auction houses. Then he put a hand to his forehead, visibly recovering himself.

"All right, look, I can see that I'm going to have to take my policeman's hat off for a minute here. Go on. At least I know you didn't find the body this time, which is a welcome novelty."

"No, she wasn't there. For what are now ... obvious reasons," Felicia pulled a face. "To be honest, we just assumed she'd done a bunk. Her bed hadn't been slept in, and ... oh, thank you," she accepted, with some surprise, a hot buttered crumpet from a plate which was suddenly being proffered to her. "Hang on, when did we make crumpets?"

"Pikelets," Algernon said solemnly. "There's a difference."

Pettifer was visibly fighting for sanity by now. Felicia took pity on him, placing aside the dripping pikelet – promptly claimed by Godfrey – to reach into her reticule for the sheaves of paper, which she handed to Pettifer.

"These are her notes for the speech." She turned to Cassie.

"Brace, yourself, Cass. Like I said, they're not ... quite what we were expecting."

"I have three boys under the age of six," Cassie replied flatly. "I'm permanently braced."

"Fitzwilliam Trendlehart: A Very Georgian Villain." Pettifer read the title out slowly, then looked up, confusion reigning on his craggy features. "Wait, wasn't he the bloke everyone's been fawning over? The one the statue on The Meadows is of?"

Felicia nodded.

There was a brief, stunned silence whilst everyone absorbed this information, punctuated only by an unfortunately-timed slurp from Hugo.

"The things she's saying in here..." Cassie had taken the pages from Pettifer and was scanning them in mounting horror. "She makes him out to be an absolute monster. She's accusing him of poisoning his mistress, of sabotaging his best friend's horse before a hunt because he owed him money and didn't want to pay ... and that's just in the first paragraph." Her shoulders dropped disconsolately. "I don't understand why she would ... I mean, this would have *ruined* the fair."

"We can only assume that was her intention," Pettifer said, as diplomatically as he was able. "I know it's difficult to take in why she might..."

"No, it's not that." Cassie was shaking her head, making her vertiginous grey wig lurch back and forth alarmingly. "I mean, I *saw* her speech. She sent it to me weeks ago for approval. And this..." She waved the paper. "This isn't it."

"You're saying there was *another* speech?" Dexter leapt in with the question first, earning him a dirty look from Sergeant Pettifer. "A different one?"

"There certainly was." Cassie dropped the paper onto the table, where it narrowly avoided landing in a pool of melted butter. Pettifer tried not to look horrified to see his evidence treated thus.

"Just to be clear, Madam Mayor..." he stabbed a stubby finger against the tabletop. "You're suggesting that somebody *else* wrote this speech? *Not* Professor Breadmore?"

Cassie picked it up again with buttery fingers. Pettifer looked as though he might faint.

"No," she said, after a moment. "The handwriting's distinctive. It's definitely the same author. Although I'm afraid can't provide the original; she made me send it back." At the expression on his face, she explained, "She insisted on it. Even included an SAE." She held up a hand. "And before you ask me if I didn't think it odd, let me remind you that I'm the Mayor of Stamford. I deal with more eccentric people on a daily basis than most people do in a lifetime. As, I'm fairly sure, do you."

"It was known to be one of her foibles," Dexter supplied. "She communicated with everyone by letter. She preferred to pretend the Industrial Revolution had never happened."

Pettifer muttered something which sounded suspiciously like, "Bloody historians".

"So, if I've got this right." Peter had been uncharacteristically quiet throughout all of this – which might have had something to do with the plate of pikelets next to his elbow – but he leaned forward now, an unexpected light in his startlingly blue eyes. Felicia decided not to be worried by how her usually hard-to-engage father – unless it was on the subject of auctions, the right way to make tea, or Southern folk in impractical footwear – seemed so interested in this latest investigation. Or what her sister would say if she knew. "This lass ... sorry, this *professor*," he hastily amended, as both of the women in the room raised their eyebrows pointedly, "came to the festival five years ago, caused such an upset that no-one will talk about it, then came back again this year intent on mischief ... but she never got the chance because she conveniently fell in the hook-a-duck pool instead?" He selected another pikelet – Felicia thought it was his seventh, although she was trying not to count. "I'm no detective, but it sounds a bit dodgy, doesn't it?"

Only her father could deliver something so damning with such a sense of understatement. Immediately, everyone's head pivoted towards Pettifer expectantly. Algernon was practically vaulting out of his seat with anticipation. There was a long pause before Pettifer spoke. When he did, however, it was with a sense of resignation.

"As it happens, I agree. But there isn't a damn thing to be done about it." He put down his plate with a thunk. "Thank you for your time, everyone. And the pikelets."

And, leaving them all open-mouthed, he turned and shuffled out.

Everyone looked expectantly at Felicia.

"Don't look at me!" She protested. "How should I know what he's about? The man's just as much of a mystery to me as he is to the rest of you."

They all continued to stare at her. She sighed.

"Fine, I'll go."

She stalked out into the brilliant sunshine.

"Wait!" She called. The weeping willows on the riverbank were rustling in the breeze, creating a surprisingly loud backdrop which he had to shout over to be heard. "What are you doing? You can't just drop a bombshell like that then leave."

He turned. It took some time; she'd noticed that he seemed to find it difficult to simply twist his head, instead rotating his whole body as one like a solid boulder. She wondered if it had something to do with the rugby accident he'd alluded to previously, the one which had halted his burgeoning sports career and instead ricocheted him onto a different path. A path which, two months ago, had collided with hers. Now, they were enmeshed together by murder.

"Why not?" He didn't need to shout to be heard; his deep, sonorous voice carried easily. "You do it all the time."

"That's ... not the point," she said, feeling rather annoyed suddenly. It was one of his most vexing habits, to witness things like that, little foibles and caprices, then present them back to their owner on a platter. It was unnerving, uncomfortable; she was utterly certain he did it deliberately, to set people off-kilter. Like many of his odd tactics, it worked like a charm with witnesses and suspects, but as far as she knew, she wasn't speaking to him as either of those things. She put her hands on her hips. "*I'm* allowed to be dramatic. Policemen aren't. What was the purpose of that exercise, precisely?" She flung her arm back towards the cottage, where everyone had shamelessly crowded into the tiny window space and was watching them avidly. "To terrify us all at the thought of a murderer on the loose and then pronounce that you're not going to do anything about it? Haven't you ever heard of ignorance is bliss?"

He'd been waiting patiently throughout all of this, his expression unchanging. Now he spoke.

"I never said I wasn't going to do anything about it."

That threw her. She blinked, trying to find the next words as they skittered around her brain.

"So you *are* going to investigate, then?"

"I'll be keeping an eye out. Discreetly, of course." At her mutinous glare, he sighed. "Look, Heavenly has gone way over my head on this one. The last thing he wants is a murder at an event which attracts thousands of people each year." He looked at her levelly. "He's tied my hands. No unnecessary questions. The last time he did that..." He looked away, and something flickered across his crag-like face. "Well, you and Algernon almost died. I'm not in a hurry to repeat that scenario."

She opened her mouth, but he got there first, the words coming uncharacteristically quickly for him.

"I just want you to be on your guard ... all of you," he added, with a knowing look at the faces in the window. "But *only* on your guard. Trouble finds you quite easily enough as it is; I don't want you seeking it out this time. You understand?"

"Of course."

He stared her down.

"I mean it, Felicia. No capers, no unnecessary risks. This isn't St. Mary Mead." He broke off, stepping backwards from the river path as a man in tweed plus-fours and a deerstalker rode past on an ancient, rusty bicycle, a stuffed fox perched stiffly in the basket. Felicia looked at him, struggling to keep a straight face. Pettifer held up a warning finger.

"Don't, all right? Just..." He shook his head. "I have to go; they've already started arriving for the fair, and it'll be chocka in no time. I want to do a quick sweep before it gets impossible." He went to walk away, then hesitated, coughing awkwardly. "Listen, about what I said ... I mean, if you do *happen* to hear anything pertinent while you're going about your regular festival business ... *only* by accident, of course..."

"You'll be the first to know," Felicia said solemnly. Then she turned away to hide her smile.

Chapter Nine

Pettifer hadn't been exaggerating; within half an hour, the view through the diamond-paned windows of the cottage was filled with jewel-coloured skirts and powdered wigs, gold-buttoned coats and breeches capped by brilliant white stockings. Every few minutes a horse-drawn carriage clattered past, just one of the many which would be conveying fair-goers around town in true Georgian style.

Cassie had bustled off in her usual chaotic fashion, knocking over the fruit bowl, the cat, and a particularly spindly chair on her way out. Hugo had slunk off not long afterwards, muttering something about how he'd promised Gavin he'd help out on the doors at the Medicine in Georgian England demonstration. He'd had the look of someone going to the gallows about him; Felicia only hoped that Gavin would be in a better mood by now.

And that just left the four of them. Peter applied himself to the task of polishing off the last of the pikelets. Algernon gazed longingly out of the window, far too tactful to actually say anything, but radiating a desperation so apparent that Felicia eventually couldn't take it anymore. She stood abruptly, forgetting about her skirts and almost upending the very same chair she'd just righted. Godfrey snarled nervously at her, edging away.

"You know, I've got a couple of hours till I'm needed back at the Arts Centre," Felicia ventured, trying sound much brighter than she felt. "How about we all go down to the funfair for a bit? Show our support?"

Worryingly, Dexter looked almost as thrilled by the proposal as Algernon did.

"You know, you won't fix it by fretting, duck," a deep voice rumbled in her ear.

Felicia turned to look into her father's electric blue eyes; or at least, almost into them. They were too bright to stare at directly. She smiled ruefully.

"Am I being that obvious?"

"Not to everyone, maybe, but I know that look. You get it on your face whenever there's something you can't find the answer to. I remember when you were small, and you found a question no-one knew the answer to. Drove you mad, it did." His face turned serious. "It's how you looked before; you know … the last time." He looked edgy, and repeated, as though she might somehow have missed his meaning, "*You know.*"

"The last time there was a murder, you mean?" She said bluntly, not particularly bothering to lower her voice. A couple of heads turned.

"Steady, duck." Startled, Peter whisked her hurriedly to one side, behind the fortune-teller's tent, from which eerie music was emanating. "We don't want to alarm people, do we? Think of Cassie, if nothing else."

Immediately, Felicia felt a crest of guilt as his words sank in.

"You're right." She blinked, exhaling a long breath. "Of course you are. I'm just ... finding it hard to carry on like nothing's happened, that's all."

Her gaze drifted again towards the hook-a-duck stand, which had been discreetly closed off, a polite 'sorry, out-of-order' sign perched at a jaunty angle between the candy-striped poles. Something about the jollity of it made it seem even more sinister; surely a fête should be a safe, happy place, somewhere sunburnt, sticky-fingered memories were made. She wasn't sure she would ever be able to look a fairground ride in the same, innocent way again.

Not that anyone else seemed to be picking up any ominous energy from it. To them, everything was exactly as it ought to be. The air was thick with spun sugar and laughter, peppered with the odd tantrum as a toddler was denied another whirl on the teacups, or growls as a dog took exception to the obligatory giant teddy bears waiting to be won at every stall. How she wished she could be like these people: enjoying a perfect English summer's day in a perfect English town with nothing to darken their skies except the odd little scudding cloud straying across the edge of the blazing sun. How she wished she could be like her father, or Dexter, or Cassie, and put it out of her mind for a while, get on with the day at hand. Compartmentalise, that was what they called it.

But she couldn't. *Her* mind was like the sea, a boundaryless expanse of thoughts, green washing into blue crashing into silver grey until she didn't know where one part of her life ended and another began.

It was why she hadn't been able to forget last time. And why she couldn't now.

Peter Grant looked at his youngest daughter and sighed internally. The truth was, Felicia had always been a bit of a mystery to him. Juliette now, *she* was on his wavelength. A dyed-in-the-wool Grant, in the image of himself and his father before him. A practical, no-nonsense, just-get-on-with-it sort. She got things done, all right – sometimes whether you'd asked her to or not – and she didn't stop to look much beyond the end of her nose. A character type which, Peter cagily conceded, might have the *odd* deficiency here and there – although you'd never catch him saying so aloud – but at least it made for a simple existence, if nothing else.

Felicia, on the other hand … now, she took after her mother; restless, otherworldly, with a tendency to go into her head, to places Peter simply couldn't fathom. Half of the time, she felt so out of reach to him that it was hard to believe he'd had anything to do with making her. That he'd bounced her on his knee, taught her to tie her shoelaces, had once chased an overly-amorous teenage boy out of the house with an antique pikestaff on her behalf. And Algernon was built in exactly the same mould, he thought wearily, looking over at his grandson, who was attempting to outdo his father at the coconut shy. God knew, he loved them both, but sometimes he just longed for a bit of straightforward, plain-speaking folk for company. Someone you knew where you were with. That police sergeant, for example. He liked him. Always knew what he was about. A fellow Northerner, *and* he wore proper shoes.

"Now then," Peter made his best attempt to be soothing. It wasn't his natural metier. "That police fellow of yours has said he'll look into it, hasn't he? It's not like nothing's being done." He nudged her with his elbow. "Forget about it for a bit; try and enjoy yourself. It's not as if you don't deserve some light relief, the way you've been working lately."

Felicia raised her eyebrows.

"Careful, Dad. That skimmed dangerously close to sounding like a compliment."

He cleared his throat heftily, looking uncomfortable.

"Yes, well, you know me; I'm not given to this sort of ... I mean, I don't often..."

He tailed off incoherently. She peered at him, beginning to feel concerned.

"Are you all right, Dad?" His face was rather shiny and pink, now she noticed. "Is the sun getting to you? Do you want to—"

"Will you stop that, duck!" He barked, swatting her away crossly, and she felt herself relax in relief. That was more like it. "Let me say my piece! God knows, it's hard enough without your clever comments and your fussing and..." A family nearby was eyeing him warily. He took a steadying breath, placing a hand on the small of her back to turn them both in the opposite direction. "Look, if you hadn't stepped in like you did ... I don't know how the auction would have run with me out of action otherwise. You've..." He was looking excessively pained now with the effort of it, the words forced out between clamped lips. Anyone watching might have assumed that he was passing a kidney stone. "You've ... you've done me proud, duck. I'm grateful to you."

Felicia stared at her father, momentarily stunned into speechlessness. Peter Grant's epitaph could safely have been: *seldom satisfied*, never *pleased*. At least when it came to his beloved auction. It had been the main sticking point between them when they'd had a go at running it together all of those years ago. Her father's inability to loosen his grip on the business he'd started as a young man with barely two pounds in his pocket was something she could understand but not, ultimately, tolerate. It had created a gaping distance between them, both physically and emotionally, one which they were only just tentatively beginning to bridge.

Really, she ought to have been thrilled at what amounted to his idea of extending an olive branch, Felicia thought. But somehow, she wasn't. It was too soon, too discombobulating.

As though realising the same thing, Peter had turned a ruddy hue, sinking his chin into his chest.

"Of course, I'll have to fix it all once I'm back," he boomed. "God knows what you've been doing with the place. None of it good, I'll wager."

"Oh, you'll hate it all," she agreed quickly.

Their eyes met briefly, understanding and mutual relief flashing between them.

"Mum!" Algernon's excited shout formed a very welcome interruption. He was running towards them, a coconut clutched in both hands. "Look, I got one."

"Wonderful," Felicia replied, with a distinct lack of enthusiasm. In her experience, the things were a poisoned chalice for any parent. They sat in the fruit bowl, steadfastly repelling all attempts to break them open until eventually, they went off and had to be thrown out uneaten, leaving one on the receiving end of recriminatory comments and betrayed looks from one's own child for days afterwards. She would rather he'd won a goldfish. At least when *it* died she wouldn't be blamed.

"Grand job," Peter ruffled Algernon's hair with a callused hand. "I've got an axe in the shed at home that'll see to that nicely. You can even do the honours, if you'd like."

Algernon looked ecstatic. Felicia raised her eyes to the

cloudless heavens and bit her tongue. She'd learned by now that motherly protestations would get her nowhere when her father and her son had a scheme in mind. It was best to stay gracefully out of the way and just pray that no fingers were lost.

"Don't worry, I'll have some ice on standby," Dexter had appeared at her side, dropping his voice to murmur in her ear. "And if we misplace the digit, I'm sure I can find a suitable replacement in the freezer to take to the hospital with us. A chipolata, perhaps. Or a fish goujon."

She found herself smiling despite herself; she couldn't help it.

It was funny how things came full circle, she reflected now. As a free and single undergraduate all of those years ago, his irreverent charm had been impossible to resist. He'd courted her beneath Oxford's dreaming spires and over its ancient bridges until she hadn't wanted to be free and single any more. She'd been young, and all she'd needed in a partner was someone who made her heart flutter and her senses tingle and the laughter flow freely, her head thrown back.

It had been a wild few years; she'd been so confident then. It had never once occurred to her that she wouldn't feel that way forever.

They'd married, and it had been blissful. Then they'd had Algernon, and things began to shift beneath them; like tectonic plates, widening cracks which had always been there but which had been smoothed over by the glow of blossoming love. Dexter had, to be fair to him, been a doting and hands-on father in those early years; he'd been an undistinguished academic then, long before the bright lights of fame had beckoned and turned his head, and he'd happily toted Algie around between lectures, kept a crib in his tutor's office, and written papers between feeds whilst Felicia had gone back to her high-flying job at a prestigious contemporary art gallery.

As a husband, though, he'd been exhaustingly lacking in foresight, and she'd felt as though she was carrying the weight of their life on her own. Soon, she found that the laughs weren't coming so readily any more, the charm she'd once basked in now grating her raw until she didn't recognise the person she'd become. *He* was still Dexter, still devilish and capricious and wonderful, but she ... she'd become lost in marriage and motherhood, in a job she didn't like in a city she didn't love, trying to pretend she still felt the magic of youth but in reality feeling hollow and flat, like champagne the morning after a party which had long-since finished.

Now, however, things were different ... albeit in a deja-vu-like way. She was back in Stamford, running the auction again, and as Dexter's decidedly *ex*-wife – even though she still found him utterly exasperating – she was discovering a renewed appreciation for that devil-may-care attitude she'd once revelled in.

Coming back here had been good for them all, she concluded, turning her face to the sun with a contented sigh. Algernon had been right when he insisted on it. Now, if it weren't for the unpropitious string of murders which seemed intent on accompanying her every move, she might even be able to take her father's advice and relax just a...

Her eyes snapped open. Suddenly, she'd become aware of a prickling sensation across the back of her neck. A tingle of awareness she'd become uncomfortably well-acquainted with during the spring.

Someone was watching her.

Chapter Ten

Her heartrate skipped up a gear, pattering uncomfortably against her ribs. She strove to keep her expression steady, not to reveal outwardly what was racing through her mind. She put a hand to the back of her neck as though to gently stretch it – no-one would think much of that; everyone would have a headache from the weight of their hairstyles by the end of the day – using the motion as an excuse to angle her head one way then the other, discreetly scanning the crowd as she did so. But it was impossible to pick out anyone in particular; they were a whirl of busy, distracted colour, caught up in the delights of the fête, or chasing after a mixture of errant children, wandering old relatives, and over-exuberant dogs. No-one was looking in this direction.

She was beginning to feel slightly panicked now, a feeling she strove to quench. Logic told her that she was imagining things, that the shock of the morning was getting to her. But instinct screamed otherwise, a siren in her head, reminding her that she'd ignored her intuition once before, and it had almost ended in tragedy. That she'd been lucky. So, so lucky, in a way that she couldn't expect to be another time. Her gaze moved to Algernon, still animatedly discussing the best method of coconut-destruction with her father. He looked so radiantly alive, and her chest squeezed in terror at the thought of how different it could have been. No, she couldn't afford to make that mistake again. She *wouldn't*. She had to…

Then, at last, her eyes met another pair. Dark, steady. For a moment, her breath hitched, then relief flooded her muscles, unlocking them one by one.

"Oh." Dexter had followed her gaze. "*He's* here, is he?"

Surprised by the edge to his tone, Felicia turned to look up at him. His lips were pressed together in an unusually disapproving expression.

"Jack's a professional photographer," she said slowly, wondering why she suddenly felt she was having to defend his presence. "He's probably working." Surely, that much must be obvious to Dexter; why was he being so…

Then it dawned upon her. She stared at him incredulously.

"Wait, not you too. *Please* don't tell me that you've bought into all of that nonsense about him?"

"It's not nonsense," Dexter said crisply. "It's fact. The man's got a criminal record, hasn't he?"

"For a couple of teenage misdemeanours, yes." Felicia was beginning to feel more exasperated than perplexed by his attitude now. She went to put her hands on her hips, then realised the panniers beneath her skirt made it impossible. The discovery didn't exactly improve her mood. "It hardly makes him a supervillain."

"That wasn't what you were saying earlier this year," Dexter countered.

He had a point, not that she appreciated him making it.

"Yes," she ground out. "But I was *wrong*."

She didn't like to be reminded of how badly she'd misjudged Jack back then. It made her feel vaguely ashamed, even now.

"He might have won you over; personally I'm still not convinced," Dexter said stubbornly. He'd crossed his arms, and his face had taken on that closed, obstinate look which had always made her heart sink; there was something immovably childish about it, as though he'd been prevented from putting a frog on his grandmother's chair, or jumping in a muddy puddle with his Sunday shoes on. "And I'm not sure that you should be consorting with him. You've no idea what he's capable of."

She stared at him, flabbergasted. This whole conversation had taken on a surreal, disorientating edge, like in a dream where everything felt real and yet something was out of place. Dexter, usually so easy, so open, who took people as he found them all over the world ... falling prey to gossip peddled over cream teas and in the town's not-so-dark alleys, where the most nefarious trades were for jam recipes and the closest thing to a crime scene was an errant sprout fallen from a shopping basket? Perhaps living in Stamford wasn't so good for him after all.

"I will *consort* with whomever I choose," she said frostily, finding her voice at last and discovering that it was, in fact, really quite annoyed. "Because, despite what my current attire might suggest, it is *not*, in fact, 1754, and *you* are not my husband any more." She paused to take a breath, then added acerbically, "Even if you did keep my name."

And with that rejoinder, accompanied by a very satisfying skirt swish, she whirled and stalked away across the grass as fast as her uncomfortably pinching silk shoes would allow.

"That looked tense," Jack remarked mildly, watching on

with amusement as she approached in a zig-zagging, wobbling fashion, trying to avoid the most uneven bits of ground. "I take it he's not a signed-up member of my fan club yet?"

Felicia stopped, surprised to find herself breathing heavily. It wasn't easy lugging around the weight of so many layers on your body, especially not when your lungs were constricted by a corset. For about the fifteenth time that day, she thanked the stars to have been born on this side of the women's rights movement.

"That's an official thing now, is it?" She managed, with a raise of the eyebrow.

"So far it has two members," he replied, deadpan. "You and your dad."

"And Algernon," Felicia protested. "He'd be very upset to be left out."

"Two and a third, then. I'd better start getting the merchandise printed. Especially as it looks like I might be about to recruit the mayor, too." He held up his camera with a faint smile. "At the very least, she must be confident that I won't go around plundering and pillaging while I'm on the job. I'll take that as an endorsement of my character."

"You're here on business, then?"

"I am. Not sure that most of the council's too happy to have me as their official photographer, mind. God only knows how she swung it; she must have been very persuasive."

"You don't argue with Cassie when she's set on something," Felicia agreed.

Jack looked at her levelly.

"I suspect she still feels guilty that you all thought I was a murderer; this is her way of making it up to me."

He had a way of coming out with things like that, so calmly and matter-of-factly. Things most people would never say aloud, just tossed into the middle of a conversation like he was remarking on the weather. She was vaguely used to it by now, but it still threw her every time. She started now, flushed beneath her heavy makeup.

"We had our reasons," she said defensively. "Besides, you didn't exactly help yourself. All of that lurking about acting shiftily."

He put a hand to his chest, eyes widening.

"You wound me, madam, to be so dismissive of my arts. This level of shiftiness doesn't come about naturally, you know. It's the result of years of cultivation and dodgy deeds."

He spoke with his characteristic impassive humour, belying the sense of injustice which they both knew lay beneath the supposed facts. Because whilst Jack had certainly been no saint in the past, he wasn't responsible for every charge which had been laid at his door over the years; Felicia knew that now. She only wished that she could convince the rest of the town of the same. Unfortunately, the only person who could have corroborated the truth was now beyond the reach of anyone.

That said, looking at him today, it was impossible to believe how anyone could think badly of him. With the breeze ruffling his dark blond curls and the sunlight illuminating the dappled greens of his irises, he looked like a fallen angel, carefree and vital and young.

So young.

Felicia bit her lip, not wanting to acknowledge the all-too familiar sensations which were being stirred just by seeing him again. It was something she'd been able to forget about, during the past couple of months, buried in work at the auction, at settling Algernon in and reacquainting herself with her old hometown. She'd miraculously managed to avoid Jack the whole time – or perhaps not so miraculously, considering that there was an element of accidently-on-purpose about it on her end. On the days when he was due to come into the auction house to photograph the catalogue covers, she always found that there was a strangely pressing amount of work to do up in her office. Her walks through Burghley Park somehow never seemed to take her down to the corner where the two majestic bottle lodges stood. If she drove past them, she studiously averted her eyes, even as she longed to turn her head towards the windows of the right-hand lodge, to glimpse the kitchen she'd sat in only weeks ago, with a cooling cup of tea unnoticed in her hand as she listened to one of the most enthralling life stories she'd ever heard. All the more so because she knew that few others had ever been privy to it.

And now he was looking at her, and she could only hope that that entire thought process hadn't just played out across her face. She pretended to be diverted by a juggler moving amongst the crowd. Somewhere there were acrobats, although she didn't think they were performing until later.

"I saw you at the party last night," she said quickly, in an attempt to change the subject. "Was that official business too? You didn't seem to be taking many pictures."

She was trying to sound casual about it, but the truth was she hadn't just seen him; she'd been aware of his every move. She'd also been very aware that he hadn't come over to her. Despite the fact that *she'd* been the one avoiding *him*, that had stung. It still stung now, if she was being completely honest.

"I was, you just didn't notice me doing it. That's why I'm good at my job." He put the camera to his eye and snapped a picture of the juggler with a casualness which disguised the fact that it would probably be an award-worthy shot. He was one of those bothersome people who made everything look easy. "Besides, I think you'd sunk a bit of wine by the time I turned up."

Felicia threw up her hands, paste bracelets flashing in the sun.

"Why does everyone keep saying I was drunk? I was *not*—"

"—*As* had everyone else, I was about to say," he finished calmly. "That's what a free wine bar will do to a party."

"Oh." Feeling rather foolish, she put a hand up to her temple. "Sorry, long morning."

"I heard. You do like to find a body, don't you?"

She gave him an unimpressed look.

"I'm not going to dignify that with an answer."

His grin hovered for a moment, then slipped, his voice turning more serious.

"Look, joking aside, you're ... all right, I suppose?"

"Apart from the tail-end of a red wine headache," she said wryly. "We don't get along at the best of times, not since Algernon was born, at least. But Cassie had heard that Professor Breadmore was particularly partial to a certain vintage from the Pays d'Oc, so she got a whole case of it in." She winced. "Obviously, knowing what we do now about the professor's ... issues, a free bar was probably always going to be an absolute recipe for disaster. That it would lead to this, though..." She trailed off, feeling suddenly nauseous. Poor Cassie; what a thing to have to live with, even if it *had* been done in complete innocence.

Jack looked at her sharply.

"Wait ... they're saying she was drunk on red wine? The police?"

"Yes." Slightly taken aback by the urgency in his tone, she

stuttered slightly on the word. "She'd obviously carried it out with her; there was smashed glass all in the pool."

He was shaking his head vehemently.

"Then they're mistaken. That can't be what happened."

He reached for his camera, shielding the screen from the glare of the sun with one bronzed hand as he flicked swiftly through a kaleidoscope of photos.

"Everything from last night is still on here," he explained. He was frowning in concentration, a small, diamond-shaped dent between his eyebrows. "I've been so busy, I haven't had the chance to ... ah, here we are." He tilted the camera to show her. "See?"

Felicia squinted at the tiny rectangle of pixels, wondering if she was starting to need glasses. Wasn't forty supposed to be one of those rubicon ages, where parts of you which had always worked perfectly well before suddenly began to play up for no reason? Cassie swore that all manner of things had started dropping off and shrivelling up since she'd passed the milestone the previous October, although Felicia suspected it had more to do with the three children she'd popped out in five years than the inexorable passage of time.

"What am I looking at?" She said helplessly. It was a cluster of people in conversation, she could tell that much. It was taken in the hotel's walled garden, where the party had been held; a purplish midsummer's dusk swathed the scene, but she could make out the firefly-like orbs of fairy lights floating amongst the trees, the looming, ghostly mass of a white wisteria. Its perfume had hung cloyingly in the still night air, suspended in clouds which saturated your clothes as you walked through. Iris Breadmore was holding court off to the left, a figure impossible to miss with the cluster of sausage-like curls framing her small, lively face, the exaggerated, flouncing collar of her fondant pink dress billowing across her slight shoulders and fastened with a velvet ribbon at her throat. Privately, Felicia had always thought there was something vaguely unsettling about the way she dressed; almost like an antique doll, or a little girl from a sentimental painting. Not that anyone else seemed to mind; to many, she was a Miss Marple-like figure, bright-eyed and charming, delightfully quaint in her knowledge of long-forgotten etiquette and decorum. How to arrange flowers like a lady. How to differentiate between dining à la Russe and à la Française. How to send a love note across a crowded ballroom with the flick of a fan. Watching her shows or reading her books was like visiting a favourite grandmother; safe, serene, a sanctuary from an ever-hurtling world; that was what they all said, at least. That was the enduring appeal. Except, Felicia didn't think she was really as old as she made out; fifties, maybe? Certainly not more.

Felicia moved her gaze around the group, to the other people in the scene, but there was nothing of particular excitement. A couple of council members, what looked like Cassie's elbow about to knock over a carafe, Gavin watching on fretfully...

Then she saw something. A shift in the shadows in the background of the picture. A tall woman, almost out of frame. Half-blurred by the exposure, in the enveloping dusk, it was hard to tell where her eyes were looking, but she *seemed* to be staring straight at the professor, and with an intensity which...

Jack zoomed in on Iris Breadmore, cutting the woman out of the image completely.

"Look at the drink in her hand," he pressed.

Felicia shook herself mentally, trying to summon her concentration. She still felt scattered, out of sorts, and the suggestion that she was missing something which ought to have been obvious wasn't helping.

"Well, it's not red wine, I'll give you that. It looks like a G&T."

"She was drinking these all evening." He flicked through more photos. "Completely ruined the symmetry of my shots, I might add."

"So she went to the bar inside and bought herself something stronger," Felicia shrugged, not sure where he was going with this. "It doesn't mean she didn't pick up a glass of wine on the way out, though."

He hesitated. She gave him a searching look, the vague undercurrent of suspicion she'd felt throughout this conversation notching up into certainty. Because Jack Riding didn't hesitate. It was hard to know a lot about him, because he didn't allow it, but she knew that much.

"Unless, of course, there's something else?"

She folded her arms and waited. He looked pained.

"Felicia, you have to understand that I've spent the last seven years trying hard to keep my head down and as far away from any suspicious activity as possible. The police and I, as you're aware, don't exactly enjoy the most cordial of relations." He gave a humourless smile. "In fact, I don't think it's unfair to say that they'd relish any opportunity to toss me into the nearest cell."

He did have something of a point there, Felicia was forced to admit. The local police, like much of the town they defended, seemed stubbornly reluctant to embrace the notion that Jack might have changed. Even Sergeant Pettifer, who was usually such a level-headed, reasonable man … it had become a bit of a sticking point between them, actually, the elephant in the room of their admittedly offbeat, but otherwise strangely consonant relationship. These days, she avoided bringing Jack up altogether in his presence; it only made things awkward.

"Your name won't come into it," she promised.

He looked at her for a long moment, then sighed.

"Okay." He went back to the original photo on the camera, zooming in further than he had previously; this time, the small, pink-nailed hand holding the tall glass almost filled the screen. "This is just a hunch, understand? But I don't think that's a gin and tonic. See? It's got a wedge of lime in it."

"It's not unheard of."

"In London, maybe. Or some boutique hotel in the Cotswolds." He slanted her a glance. "Look, I know how this sounds, but back in the dim and distant past, when I was still considered vaguely employable, I worked at The George as a barman for a bit." Wryly ignoring what must have been a look of surprise on her face, he continued. "And what every bartender soon learns that there's fiercely polarised debate around exactly what garnish goes into a G&T. Lime is seen as avant garde, rather racy. Traditionalists insist upon lemon."

"The George is … fairly traditional," Felicia admitted, well aware that she was making the understatement of not just this century, but the thousand or so years the famous inn had stood in that spot.

Jack raised his eyebrows sardonically.

"Felicia, it's a place where you can still get sherry trifle on the pudding menu."

She opened her mouth, but he held up a hand.

"*All. Year. Round.*"

She closed her mouth.

"I think *that*," he tapped on the screen, "is a lime and soda."

She looked up quickly, and their eyes met.

"The drink people have when they want it to look like they're drinking," Felicia said softly.

"You'll need to check with the bar, obviously. But if I'm right…"

"Then she couldn't have been drunk when she fell in the pool." Another thought occurred to her. "And it couldn't have been her glass which smashed." Felicia put a hand to her forehead. "Someone was with her."

"Or someone was following her."

Her eyes widened.

"But then … that would mean…"

He nodded.

"It would seem that we all spent last night sharing smoked salmon blinis and melon balls with a murderer."

Chapter Eleven

Hugo Dappleton was in hiding.

Oh, not that he'd ever admit it. Not even, really, to himself. But as he sat in the low-raftered office at the top of Grant's auction house, listening to the sort of deafening non-silence which only an empty old building can create, he was hard pressed to come up with a better explanation for what he was doing right now. Sitting at his desk, at work, on a glorious Saturday evening, while through the deep mullioned windows the sounds of the Georgian Fair could be heard drifting on the balmy evening air.

Usually, the answer would come readily. Because Hugo, unlike much of the population of the British Isles, could truly say that he loved his job. He loved antiques.

Where this love had come from, no-one could really say. Certainly not from his parents, a volatile couple packed into a too-small house on a too-crammed estate on the edge of town who'd never really been suited but couldn't seem to make a decision on whether to be together or apart. Like an elastic band, they pinged to and from each other, his father storming out for weeks on end, his mother throwing crockery at the empty doorframe through which he'd departed and screaming at him never to come back. The one thing his mother actually *liked* about Hugo working at the auction was that he could bring home the unsold china lots, so they never ran out of plates. But that was about it.

Working at an auction was, his parents kept pointing out, unglamorous, unsociable, and – contrary to popular belief – decidedly underpaid. They just couldn't understand why he wouldn't go and sit behind a screen in a bank somewhere. But then, there were a lot of things they couldn't seem to understand about him. He was rapidly learning just how big the chasm was between them at the moment.

He sighed, tapping the screen of his phone, which was sitting face up on the desk next to his elbow. It lit up, revealing a picture of himself and Gavin. They looked happy, carefree, but in reality, that day had been a rare moment of unburdened breeziness in the midst of a turbulent and distressing couple of months. From his point of view, at least.

But no, that wasn't *really* fair. He knew how it hurt Gavin, having to watch him dealing with his parent's reaction to their relationship. He'd known they wouldn't be pleased; it had been at his insistence that it had been kept secret for so many months, something which Gavin had borne patiently. But it was different for him, Hugo told himself, feeling uneasily disloyal even as he thought it. It was true, though. Gavin had never grappled with his sexuality; he'd never had to worry about how his coming out would be received by the people closest to him, either. After all, it was only him and his dad now, and they had a preternaturally distant relationship. Something which, incidentally, Hugo was desperate to try and remedy. He couldn't bear the thought of them *both* being cut off from their parents.

He put his head in his hands, pushing back the skin on his forehead until it felt satisfyingly tight. This ought to have been the happiest week of his life. He ought to have been with Gavin now, radiant with the glow of all they'd achieved, of the future which still lay so dazzlingly full of promise before them. Instead, he was hiding – oh, yes, he was, no point in pretending otherwise – up here on his own, avoiding the celebrations down below whilst telling himself that he really *would* rather be chasing up unpaid invoices, which in reality was his least favourite task, one he avoided like the—

His ruminations ground to an abrupt and ungainly halt as he heard a telltale creak. His head snapped up, heart already beginning to thud. He tried to tell himself that he was being ridiculous. After all, old buildings like this creaked and groaned constantly, like a ship on the high seas. It was all part and parcel, along with sloping floors and window panes so ill-fitting that they rattled with the slightest draught.

Then he heard it again, and he knew he wasn't fooling anyone. There were creaks and there were *creaks*. Hugo was experienced enough to know the difference. One kind meant nothing; it was an empty sound, shifting timbers, settling beams, the odd ghostly footstep. The second kind was quite different.

It meant someone was here. Someone very real.

Two months ago, Hugo would probably have flown into a hopeless panic at this point. But, despite the local tourist board staunchly pretending otherwise, a mass murderer on the loose in a small country town hadn't been without its effect on the psyche of the local inhabitants. Any resident, even if they might not know it, had, at some point, prepared themselves for what they would do in a circumstance like this.

Hugo didn't hesitate. He reached for the nearest blunt object ... then, the antiques valuer in him getting the better, turned it upside down. On second thoughts, probably not worth wasting 18th century Dresden on the skull of an intruder. He put the porcelain candelabra back down and reached out behind him, his fingers scrabbling for purchase...

"Hugo? Are you up here?"

A familiar voice emerged from the blank charcoal rectangle of the doorway. Hugo felt his whole body sink with relief.

"Felicia?"

"Yes, it's me. Are you all right? Why are you sitting in the dark?"

She had a point. Despite the fact it was still light outside – it was June after all – the sun had dipped beneath the sightline of the small window by now, and the room was cast in a distinct gloaming. He pulled the chain on the green-shaded banker's lamp on the desk, and electric light banished the shadows to the remotest corners of the rafters.

"What are you doing here tonight, anyway?" She jerked a thumb towards the window. "Didn't anyone tell you there's a festival going on out there?"

He could see her better now, his eyes adjusting to the light. She was still wearing her 18th century style dress, but her hair was down in its usual style, creating an odd juxtaposition between past and present. He thought she looked incredibly tired.

"I could ask you the same thing," he pointed out.

"I suppose you could." She draped the garment bag she was holding over the back of the nearest chair, collapsing into the seat with a sigh. "You first, mind."

"Well..." He hesitated, but only for the briefest of moments. In truth, he was grateful for someone to talk to. He was well aware that most people wouldn't readily put their boss top of the list when it came to confidants, but then, Felicia had never been like most employers. She was a friend, and a very good listener to boot. He knew that whatever he told her would go no further than these sloping, timbered walls. "It's Gavin, you see."

She didn't seem surprised. But then, she never did. Instead, she just nodded, encouraging him onwards. He took a breath.

"It's just ... he's been in a funny mood for a couple of weeks now. I can't seem to do anything right. He's out almost all of the time; he pretends he's at the office, but I know he isn't. Sometimes, we'll argue, and he's gone for hours on end; I have no idea where he is." He scrubbed a hand across his face. "I know things aren't easy at the moment, with my family, and then there's the stress of organising all of this—" He indicated towards the window, the festival in full swing beyond the glass. "He takes it all so personally; if it doesn't go perfectly every step of the way ... I tried telling him that it's only one weekend, and it doesn't really matter..." His lips twisted in a rueful smile at the memory. "*That* went down well, I can tell you. Apparently I couldn't *possibly begin to understand the pressure he's under right now.* That's a direct quote, by the way." His shoulders sagged. "But how *can* I understand when he won't share it with me?"

Felicia looked at her valuer, marvelling at how the boy who'd once come shuffling into the office in an oversized shirt and his father's tie looking for a job had grown up so much since she'd been gone. He might still look under the legal firework-purchasing age, and his dress sense certainly hadn't improved any, but he was a young man now, mature beyond his years. At once, she felt a swell of pride in him.

"You're there for him, Hugo. That's the most important thing."

"Sometimes I wonder if that isn't making it worse. If *I* might actually be the problem."

Her heart plummeted. She ought to have seen this coming. Hugo was many wonderful things: kind, considerate, and a lot more capable than he gave himself credit for. But his confidence was fragile; ironically, being with Gavin had seemed to improve it, at least for a while.

"You are *not* the problem," she said firmly. "Don't start thinking that."

"But what if I am?" He said hopelessly. He'd begun to fidget with the book of antique silver marks which lay on his desk, his fingers ruffling the pages over and over, a canon of whispering paper. "What if I'm not ... if *it's* just not what he thought it would be, now we're together properly? Now that I'm there all the time, in his flat, not having to dash home before my parents start to wonder where I am?" He sighed. "I know I'm probably not the easiest..."

"No-one's easy, Hugo," she tried, and failed, not to let the exasperation show in her voice. She dropped to a gentler tone. "But if they are, you're as close as it gets."

"I'm not as tidy as he is," Hugo was saying, having clearly not heard a word she'd said. "And he can cook all these amazing things, whereas I can barely heat up a tin of beans. I know he finds *that* trying."

Felicia, who was about of the same culinary level herself, decided that she probably wasn't best placed to comment on that part. Dexter had always been the cook, and had never seemed to mind in the least. It was one of the nicer things about having him back in town; occasionally, he pitched up on the doorstep with leftovers, and the entire cottage rejoiced at the prospect of an edible meal. And as for not being as tidy as Gavin ... well, who was? She'd seen the man's desk at the Town Hall, and it was a veritable installation of meticulously arranged stationery. He even colour-coded his paper clips. In reality, she strongly suspected that *he* was the one who'd be challenging to live with, not Hugo. If his home was anything like his workspace, it would drive her loop-the-loop within days.

Obviously, though, she couldn't say that – mercifully, she'd managed to sidestep inheriting the infamous Grant Lack Of Tact – so she settled for simple, uncontentious facts.

"Look, Hugo, you're overthinking this." Wonderful, now she sounded just like her sister. It was happening with more and more regularity these days. She pressed on. "Gavin *loves* you. That's all that matters. Everything else, it's just..." She waved a hand expansively. "Teething problems. Everything's happened very quickly ... and I'm not saying he's not pleased about that," she added hastily, as Hugo looked anguished. "But it might just take a bit of getting used to, that's all."

"I suppose he *has* lived on his own for a long time." Hugo was looking marginally more hopeful. "I mean, he left home when he was sixteen. So, it must be strange, having someone else around."

"Exactly," Felicia said triumphantly.

A companiable pause fell between them. From around the room, carriage clocks began to chime the hour, all in slightly different time, a cascading, sweetly silvered song which instantly made her relax a little more in her chair. She looked around at the worn, slightly chaotic office, with its shabby leather chairs and wonky walls, antiques crammed upon every available surface, and felt her heart squeeze a little. This was home. Here, amongst the teetering piles of bidding forms, amongst the bulging boxes of fifty-piece dinner sets and trip-hazard stacks of gilt-framed paintings sprawling across the overlapping Persian rugs which covered the original wooden floor. Her father had slapped them down on the day he'd opened the auction thirty years ago, and occasionally, on quiet afternoons, they would indulge in fanciful discussions about changing them out for a proper fitted carpet, knowing all the while that no such thing would ever happen. Grant's didn't change; that was one of the best things about it. It had also, at times, been one of the worst, but generally she didn't dwell upon that.

Hugo groaned, putting his head in his hands.

"It's been doing my head in. You know, the other day, he came in reeking of perfume, and I actually found myself obsessing that he was having an affair."

"I highly doubt that," Felicia said dryly. "Unless it was distinctly masculine perfume."

"It wasn't. It was cloying, thick ... sort of flowery."

"Not only a woman, then, but an octogenarian. That narrows it down to ... ooh, about half of the Georgian Fair planning committee."

His mouth quirked faintly.

"It gets worse. I couldn't sleep that night, so I went and found his coat in the hall. That's when I realised ... it wasn't even perfume after all."

Felicia looked at him quizzically.

"It was pollen," Hugo finished, obviously trying hard to keep a straight face. "There I was, imagining him in the arms of a lusty pensioner ... and all the while he'd just brushed past a flower arrangement."

Felicia couldn't help it. She burst out laughing. Hugo joined in, then, abruptly, doubt clouded his face once more.

"D'you really think it's nothing, then?"

"Absolutely." She leaned forward, resting her forearms on her knees. "Listen, when Dexter and I were on honeymoon, we got into such a row that I threw all of his pants off the hotel balcony into the Grand Canal."

His eyes widened.

"What was it about?"

"Honestly, I can't even remember," she said vaguely. "I think it was something to do with jam. But the point is, it doesn't matter. We made up, bought some more pants – rather fetching ones with gondolas on; I think he might still have them – and it became nothing more than an amusing story." She reached across and touched his arm. "One day, you'll laugh about this together." She thought, then added, "Although maybe save it till after the fair."

"I'm not sure he'd see the funny side right now," Hugo agreed. Then his face softened, his voice dropping. "Thanks, Felicia. I needed that."

"Anytime."

"So," Hugo drew himself upright, visibly keen to move on. "Are you ready for tomorrow?"

"Are *we* ready for tomorrow, I think you mean," Felicia said archly, pointing at him. "You're responsible for managing it all while I'm up on the rostrum. And don't think it'll be any easier just because it's a charity do."

A Georgian auction. Felicia tried not to grimace as she thought about it, but she suspected that her feelings on the subject were written all over her face, just as they had been six weeks ago when Cassie had first floated the idea. Although, to suggest that Cassie would do anything so delicately was risible. In reality, her friend had burst into the valuations office in a tornado of blonde curls, oversized bags, and flapping hemlines.

"*Fliss*," she'd gasped, disgorging everything onto the seat of a nearby wingback chair and collapsing on top of it, apparently unconcerned by the ominous crunching sound this elicited. "I need a favour. It's urgent."

Felicia, who was well used to the locomotive effect caused by Cassie's entrances, waited patiently while catalogue pages ceased rippling, the sconce mirror on the wall stopped swinging, and the air had settled back into its usual, dustily torpid arrangement, before remarking calmly, "Cass, I'm in the middle of a valuation."

For the first time, Cassie seemed to notice the slack-jawed middle-aged couple sitting across a tableful of Beswick animal figurines. As usual, she rallied in a moment.

"Yes, well." She bestowed upon them her most radiant, mayoral smile. "I'm sure these fine people will forgive the intrusion in the name of vital town business. We Stamfordians stick together."

"We're from Skegness," the man supplied, blinking owlishly.

Cassie's smile dropped a few watts. She turned back to Felicia, clearly deciding the best policy was to simply ignore them.

"We've got a gap in the festival schedule. There was an … er, incident. Involving sausage rolls." She shook herself. "Anyway, the point is, I've had a fantastic idea for how to fill it."

"If you're about to suggest a Georgian auction, then don't," Felicia warned. "They've been on at Dad to do one for the past five years. He's always said no."

"But it's not him in charge this year, is it?" Cassie said, with a sly sweetness which reminded Felicia why her friend was so well suited to local politics. "It's you."

"And I'm … what? More gullible?"

"More community spirited," Cassie said diplomatically. "Look, it'll be great fun! And a Georgian auction would be so much simpler to run than it is nowadays. Everything on the day, no pesky catalogues to do in advance…"

"You know they *did* have catalogues in Georgian times?"

"Oh." Cassie's face fell temporarily. "Well, what else is different, then?"

"Nothing! Apart from the fact the room would have been full of men in suits." The clientele was, it had to be said, decidedly more diverse these days. "That's one of the things people like about auctions." They were one of the few things in life which had remained stubbornly the same throughout the centuries. "And what are we even going to sell?"

"You know," Cassie said vaguely. "Georgian-y things."

The look Felicia gave her must have been suitably withering, because she continued hastily, "Look, don't you worry about that. I'll scrape together some donations. We won't need much; it's more about the show, anyway. If all else fails, there's a load of stuff in the Town Hall I'm sure they won't miss for a bit. Ceremonial silver, and such the like."

"She's joking," Felicia said quickly to the couple, who were watching on, now looking scandalised.

"Come on, Fliss. It'll be a walk in the park for you." Cassie was putting on a good show, but some of the veneer of her confidence was wearing off, revealing a pleading underlayer beneath. "All you have to do is turn up, wave your hammer about…"

"It's called a gavel…"

"...Shout a few numbers, occasionally point at someone and say 'sold!' dramatically..."

Felicia was by now equal parts exasperated and amused.

"Is that *really* what you think my job amounts to? *Still?* After all of these years?"

"Please, Fliss," Cassie wheedled, flinging aside any semblance of mayoral dignity. She placed her hands together in a praying motion. "I'll never ask you for anything again, I swear."

That, Felicia knew, would turn out to be no more true than it had been the last forty-seven times her friend had said it. Just as she'd known that despite Cassie's blithe assurances, there would be nothing simple about this auction.

And she'd been right. It had already caused a massive headache in the amount of setup involved; now she was picturing the hordes of festival-goers due to descend on the building tomorrow with simultaneous dread and eagerness to get the thing over with.

And speaking of getting things over with ... she glanced at the grandmother clock in the corner behind her desk and sighed.

"I suppose we'd better think about getting ready for the ball tonight. Cassie will kill us if we're late." She rose, adding ruefully, "Let's hope I can come up with a good enough story for Edith as to why my hair needs redressing. Attacked by territorial ducks, maybe?"

"What's the real reason?" Hugo asked curiously.

"My head was killing me and I caved," Felicia said in a small voice.

Hugo nodded solemnly.

"I'd go with the angry ducks, if I were you."

Chapter Twelve

Stepping from the cool marble foyer of the auction house out into the heady, gilded luminosity of a midsummer's evening was like crossing into an entirely different world. The air was filled with bustle and the thick tang of warm stone. Felicia ran her hand along the front of the nearest building, relishing the heat trapped within its golden surface. It was one of the things she loved about Stamford at this time of year, how as evening fell and the air temperature dropped, the stone opened up like a night-blossoming flower, hot dust catching at the back of the throat.

Broad Street had been closed off to traffic all day, and people were making the most of it, strolling across the petal-strewn cobbles which held the evidence of today's Georgian market, their faces turned up to admire the town glowing in the dusk. Watching them, Felicia was aware of a small pang of envy.

Because she would never have that. This was her town, her home, and as such, the place would never have that purity, that untarnished wonder which can only come with a lack of connection. For her, these streets would always be bound up with the events of life. The bench she'd sat upon when she'd realised she had no choice but to leave the business she'd given her soul to. The café where her mother had announced, over a blueberry-studded scone and a pot of hibiscus tea, that she was leaving her father for a man she'd met through her work as a travel agent – with immediate effect, no less. Felicia still couldn't stomach the taste of the tea to this day; just a sip of it took her right back to that moment.

And now, of course, there were the houses. The lovely, tourist shot-worthy homes where she'd found the bodies of people she'd known, the life drained out of them. They were empty now, shuttered while the legal grindings which a death necessitated were carried out. From the outside as pretty as ever, only the most eagle-eyed of passers-by would observe the subtle, nascent signs of neglect. The paint beginning to peel on the miniature wooden gate leading through Betsy's cottage garden. The dead heads shrivelling on Evelina's beloved roses. Before long, the houses would be on the market, bought up by smart 50-something downsizers or middle-class families with young children. They would be renovated, no doubt, insofar as Stamford's punitive and pernickety planning laws would allow, and soon enough, they would become something new, their dark pasts painted over in tasteful Farrow and Ball shades. Gradually, people would forget what had happened within their walls. Except her. She would never be able to forget.

An overly enthusiastic dalmatian almost careening into her legs jolted her free of her thoughts. With a sympathetic smile at its mortified owner, she began the descent of Ironmonger's Street, this time keeping her eyes ahead, both metaphorically and literally. There was nothing to be gained by dwelling; she knew that, and God knew, her father had told her so enough times.

She emerged onto the pedestrianised High Street, but only ever so briefly, crossing its width in under ten strides and ducking down the narrow thoroughfare of Maiden Lane which sprouted off it like an awkwardly-set arm. Shortly, it brought her to the indistinct bend where St. Mary's Street melted into St. George's Square. Stamford was a warren to the uninitiated, every lane looping you back to somewhere else – quite often where you'd started – road signs clashing against each other as one street lurched into another with little to no logic or clear delineation. Felicia was quite surprised not to be stopped by any confused, map-wielding tourists en route, as she so often was. It was an unofficial job which seemed to come with living here, along with the PE9 postcode and eye-watering council tax bill.

The doors of the theatre were closed, indicating that the play was still running within. Felicia slipped through the empty foyer and down to the cellars below. They were eerily silent, most of the cast busy on stage for the final act. Distantly, she could hear the sounds of the performance; the thudding of feet on boards, the swell of projected voices, a dull bellow of applause every now and again. Felicia knew that it was emanating from above, but somehow, it was hard to pinpoint; it seemed to be everywhere, pressing around her, reverberating through the stones of the walls and floor. It was discombobulating, and as such, when a couple of soldiers rounded the corner in front of her, chatting amiably between themselves, she almost jumped out of her skin. They doffed their tricorn hats to her politely as they passed, and she shook her head at herself. She pressed on, trying not to notice how the constant hum, the reminder that light and colour and people were so near yet so far only made the chilly sense of isolation down here feel more acute.

Then she heard it. A furtive, scratching sort of sound. She faltered briefly in her step, biting her lip. She *really* hoped that wasn't a rat. Not that she was afraid of the things; you couldn't do her job and be timid about such matters. Some of the houses she had to visit for probate valuations had been empty for months. But nonetheless, she wasn't keen on encountering some colossal beast down here, trapped as she was in a narrow passageway with little room for manoeuvre. Not to mention the ridiculous skirts she was currently sporting, which were just asking to be run up by questing claws.

She heard it again, softly. She turned her head, just in time to see James Riverton emerge from the shadows. When he saw her, he did a double take.

"Ms. Grant. I ... didn't see you there."

He sounded strained, the cordial words not flowing quite as easily as they usually did. Felicia looked at him searchingly, something she'd never do so brazenly could he see her doing so, but this light made it possible. His face was lit from one side by the weak apricot light of an ineffective mid-century wall sconce, rendering it unreadable, but she could make out the tense set of his jaw. He wasn't happy to see her here, that much was apparent, although he was doing his best to pretend otherwise.

"I'm looking for Edith," she indicated her loose hair, wondering all the while why she felt compelled to explain her presence to him. "I need some help getting ready for the ball. Hence why I'm early." When he didn't reply, she added conversationally, "Anyway, it sounds like it's going well up there."

He stared at her uncomprehendingly.

"The play," she said slowly, pointing to the ceiling.

"Oh, yes. Of course." He wasn't just distracted, Felicia thought. He was actively rattled. Her suspicions were confirmed a moment later when he said, a shade too quickly, "You know, it's a bit desolate down here, isn't it? You don't notice when there are lots of people about, but they really ought to light it better. I'll mention it after the festival's concluded, see if something can't be done." He'd recovered himself while he was speaking; already he was back to his usual countenance, all concerned charm and graciousness. "Why don't I walk you to where you're going? Wardrobe you said, didn't you?"

"Er, yes..." Before she could qualify that, he'd taken her by the elbow and was steering her determinedly along the corridor. "I did. But you *really* don't need to ... I mean, you seemed to be in a bit of a hurry..."

"Curtain call," he said blandly. "Took me by surprise, that's all. But I've got a minute or two. Besides, I'm going this way. It's really no trouble."

There was something final about the way he said it. Something which brooked no argument, even wrapped in silky tones as it was. Felicia had been about to pull her arm free, but suddenly, she changed her mind.

"The accident doesn't seem to have dampened people's enjoyment of the fair, at least," she remarked, deliberately keeping her statement neutral, with no inflection either way. She didn't want to influence what he said next.

He was too sharp for her, however.

"Indeed," he agreed amiably, although was it her imagination, or did his hand tighten ever so *slightly* around her arm as he said it? "Although you must remember that not many people saw what happened this morning. Most of them

124

probably aren't even aware of it yet. There hasn't been anything in the press; nothing explicit, anyway. No names or specifics. It's all being kept well under wraps."

"You've been checking, then?" The words out of her mouth before she could stop them.

He halted so abruptly that he jolted her arm painfully. But he didn't let go.

"What exactly is this, Ms. Grant?"

She didn't like the way he said her name, with that inflection. But she stood her ground, falling back on the innocent look which she knew she did well.

"What's what? I thought we were just making conversation."

He shook his head slowly, a thin, humourless smile stretching his lips.

"You're questioning me. And I want to know why."

The light behind her was flickering, plunging his features in and out of view. Suddenly, she became uncomfortably aware of not just how oppressively small the space was, but by extension, what a big man Riverton himself was. He carried his size with such lightness that she'd never really noticed before, but now he was looming over her, and she found herself shrinking back, which appalled her. She prided herself on being a woman not easily intimidated; she'd faced down many an angry dealer, after all. But they tended to be all bark and no bite; they shouted and stormed and moaned operatically about their profit margins, but she never actually felt threatened. This was different; something about Riverton's silky, quiet sense of anger was more unnerving than any amount of bluster.

A burst of reprisal music thrummed through the ceiling, making the walls shiver.

"I think you're about to miss that curtain call," Felicia

managed calmly, forcing herself to meet his eye. Even as she spoke the words, though, she was regretting them. She'd just effectively reminded them both that they were very much alone down here; no-one would be passing now. Even those who hadn't been required for the final act would be up there, bowing and taking their applause.

Mercifully, he didn't seem to have been listening, because he carried on as though she hadn't spoken.

"You know, I've heard about you." He was eyeing her with distaste, no longer even feigning affability. "How you got yourself involved in that business back in the spring. Fancy ourselves as a bit of a detective, do we?"

"Not in the slightest," she snapped, indignation swiftly over-riding any sense of caution. "That *business*, as you call it, got itself involved with me, not the other way around. Believe me, it wasn't my choice. I'm an auctioneer, nothing more."

"An auctioneer with a police sergeant in her pocket?" He raised a silvered brow in disbelief. "Oh, don't deny it. I've seen the two of you together; very cosy." Suddenly, the grip on her arm intensified, fingers bruising the silk of her sleeve as his voice grew urgent. "Did he put you up to this?"

"I think you're being a little paranoid," Felicia said coolly, trying not to wince as pain shot through her arm. Mustering up her courage, she prized his hand away, stepping well out of his reach. "But I appreciate it's been a long day, and we're all slightly on edge. Now, if you'll excuse me, I think I'll walk the rest of the way on my own."

And then she strode off. It wasn't until she rounded the next corner that she finally allowed herself to take a breath.

Chapter Thirteen

S he was feeling more composed by the time she reached
Edith's door. In fact, she was actually beginning to
wonder if she might not have over-reacted slightly. After all,
the man was a pillar of the community; it was highly
improbable that he would assault her in a corridor. Chances
were, he just wasn't used to having questions asked of him.
Clearly, he was accustomed to being obeyed.

Even so, something had evidently shaken him up badly. He
hadn't been himself, and she highly doubted he would have let
his well-practised, charming mien slip otherwise. Whatever he
might be, if there was one thing James Riverton certainly
wasn't, it was careless.

Edith was collapsed in a plush velvet chair, feet propped on
a hatbox. She looked exhausted, and none too thrilled to have
someone disturbing her moment of peace.

"Oh, it's you." She put aside the magazine she'd been
reading and twisted in her seat, eyes widening in dismay
behind red frames as she looked Felicia up and down.
"Gracious, girl, what on earth happened to your *hair*?"

"Er..." Felicia scrabbled for a worthy response, but her mind was unhelpfully blank. "Angry ducks?"

Edith made a sound which was somewhere between a harrumph and a trombone being tuned.

"Honestly, I don't know, the lot of you." She swung her feet over the side of the chair, hoisting herself upright with a creak of springs. "If it's not Mrs. Waverley from the bridge committee loosening her corset in the loos so she could have another portion of charlotte, or that harebrained young Ambrose losing a piece of his uniform every five minutes, or half the men moaning at me that it's not manly to wear stockings ... why I bother with all of this is anyone's business. I suppose no-one else has the skills, though, nor the knowledge. The whole thing'd go to pot if it weren't for me." She sighed the most world-weary of sighs. So world-weary that Felicia could immediately tell that she was actually enjoying herself immensely. "Now, come along. Lord only knows what you've been doing with that dress, but it's a disgrace. Out of it, and I'll get the steamer on."

Felicia briefly considered running through what she'd been doing in the dress since this morning: breaking into a house, bending over a dead body, holding an unofficial debrief in her kitchen, wrestling with a local worthy in a dingy cellar...

On second thoughts, perhaps better to say nothing.

"We'll have to wait for Tara for the hair," Edith was tutting. "She's got nimbler fingers than me these days."

"I think they're just having the curtain call," Felicia offered, obediently slipping off her shoes and disappearing behind the screen to undress before she could get into any more trouble.

"Just as well. I'm going to need her down here sharpish. They'll start arriving for the ball soon, and most of them are going to need freshening up." Felicia heard, rather than saw,

Edith shake her head vigorously, large resin earrings clodhopping against themselves like wooden windchimes. "They insist that everyone has to look their best for tonight; it's a prime photo opportunity. Except how can they expect that after a day in heat like this?" Another sound, this time like the shaking out of satin. "And the poor old cast upstairs will have only just stepped off the boards! The turnarounds this year are really quite ridiculous."

"They have packed a lot in," Felicia allowed cagily, as she unfastened the overskirt, letting it pool to the ground. She wasn't prepared to get any more committal than that, for fear of setting Edith off again, although in reality, she did actually agree. Frenetic didn't begin to cover the celebrations, and it was only day one. Not even the *end* of day one.

Although, she reasoned hastily, suddenly feeling rather disloyal to Cassie for entertaining such thoughts, she could see why they'd be tempted to pack in as many events as possible. There tended to be a drive with these things to make each one bigger and better and brighter than the last ... sometimes, it had to be said, to its actual detriment. She continued out loud, "Although, I suppose it *is* only two days. And from what I can see, everyone seems to adore it."

Edith had come around the side of the screen by now, and was deftly unlacing Felicia's corset with practised movements. At this last sentence, though, her fingers stilled.

"D'you think so, duck?" Her voice was quizzical ... and something else Felicia couldn't identify. "I think you'd be surprised."

There was a clatter of quick footsteps outside in the corridor, a whoosh as the door opened.

"Sorry, Edith." Tara's voice, fluttery at the best of times, was like gossamer when she was out of breath. "I couldn't get away. *Three* curtain calls! Can you *believe* it!"

Felicia had never heard her sound so animated. She popped her head around the screen, and sure enough, the girl was glowing, all peony-pink cheeks and glittering eyes. For the first time, Felicia realised that she was actually very pretty.

"Congratulations," she offered warmly.

At the unexpected voice, Tara started like a baby rabbit, the radiance already beginning to drain from her face.

"Felicia," she stammered. "I ... I didn't realise you were ... I mean, that's very kind..."

"Stop wittering, girl, and make yourself useful," Edith said brusquely, stomping out from behind the screen, Felicia's dress draped over her arm like a great blue wave. "She needs her hair re-dressing."

Tara flushed miserably, dropping her chin into her chest as she scuttled towards the makeup chair. Felicia joined her, knotting her robe at the waist as she sat down.

"Sorry," she whispered. "I hope I haven't got you into trouble."

"Oh, no." Tara looked aghast. "You mustn't worry about that. Edith's great, really. She doesn't mean any of it."

She picked up a brush. Felicia sat as still as she could, trying desperately hard not to fidget. She'd never enjoyed being poked and prodded, even if the experience was designed to be relaxing. To distract herself, she struck up some benign conversation.

"How long have you worked for her?"

"Oh, I don't. This is just a hobby, really. I'm a receptionist at the GP's surgery in my real life."

She sounded almost apologetic about that, as though she were afraid she'd let Felicia down, somehow.

"It sounds like an interesting job." Felicia felt a maternal need to encourage her. "You must meet all sorts of people."

"Old ones, mainly," Tara said ruefully, gathering up a handful of pins. Then she seemed to catch herself. "But I mean, I shouldn't complain. It's a very good job, very secure." She nodded, more to herself than anything, Felicia felt. "I'm lucky to have it. I'm not academic you see. I wasn't very good at school. Most of my friends went straight on to uni, but ... well, it was never going to be for me. My parents told me that, and I can see now that they were right. They knew I'd fail, and they didn't want me to be upset when it happened." She jabbed a pin into Felicia's head with unprecedented force, then yelped, "Oh God, I'm so sorry! I didn't hurt you, did I?"

"Not at all," Felicia managed through gritted teeth, resisting the reflex to rub her throbbing scalp. "You were saying?"

"Was I? Oh Lord, but you don't want to hear about me." Tara gave an embarrassed laugh. "I've never done anything interesting. Not like you." She paused in what she was doing, her eyes meeting Felicia's in the mirror. There was almost reverence in her face. "You run your own business, and you've lived in London – I've only been twice, and once was a school trip – and now you solve *murders*." The last part was uttered with relish. Felicia opened her mouth to interject, but Tara didn't give her the chance as she gushed on. "Oh, and of course you were married to Professor Grant." She sighed dreamily. "That must have been *so* exciting. He's so handsome and dashing."

Felicia always wondered in these moments what Dexter's lovestruck fans would say if they knew that he snored like a tranquilised hippopotamus. However, tempting as it was, she always refrained from outing him. Even though they weren't together any more, they still kept one another's secrets.

"I wish you'd tell me your secret," Tara said wistfully, and Felicia started, wondering if she'd read her mind. "If I could hope for a life half as interesting as yours – scrap that, even a quarter – I'd be so happy." She gave Felicia's hair a final dousing of hairspray and stood back. "There. You're done."

"Listen, Tara, there is no—" Felicia was about to deliver an educational lecture. Then she looked at herself properly for the first time, and immediately the rest of the sentence flew out of her head, never to return. "Goodness, how on earth did you do that?"

Tara shrugged modestly.

"Well, I studied a few old fashion plates…"

"No, I mean, how did you *do* that?" Felicia craned forwards, turning her head this way and that. The style was similar to the one she'd sported earlier, piled up on top of her head, except this time, strands of hair had been overlaid across the front in an intricate looping pattern which resembled flowers and leaves. The centre of each bloom was studded with a diamond-headed pin, and a single curl had been allowed to sit loose against her collarbone. "You're a bloody *genius*. You should be doing this professionally."

"That's what I keep telling her," Edith said shortly, beetling back into the room with a garment bag held aloft. "Any theatre school in London would jump at the chance to have you, I say to her, if only you'll let them see what you can do. But *will* she? Will she heck." She glowered at Felicia over her glasses. "Maybe you'll have more luck talking some sense into her."

"She's right, you know," Felicia said gently. "You're very talented. And you *did* just say that you'd love to go to London."

"Well, yes, I did," Tara stuttered. Her face had lost all of its radiant prettiness now; it was pinched again, sullen. "But that was just talk. I couldn't really … I mean, my parents. *Ambrose*. I couldn't leave them. Besides, I'd be no good on my own." She turned away and began winding the cord around a hairdryer with shaking hands. "Please can we change the subject?"

And there was such pleading in her voice that Felicia, immediately feeling guilty, obliged.

"Is that my dress?" Feigning an enthusiasm for its reappearance which she certainly didn't feel – her preferred location for the garment now being at the bottom of the River Welland – she crossed the room and unzipped the bag. "That is … *not* my dress." She looked at Edith in confusion, only to receive an unrepentant stare back.

"It is now."

Felicia was beginning to feel wary.

"It is?"

"What's wrong?" Battleship grey eyes bored into her. "Don't you like it?"

"Of course I do," Felicia said hastily, then realised she hadn't even looked at it, and doing so might make her assurances more convincing. She pulled the skirt free of the bag, the weight of it pressing down on her hands. The ivory silk was pearlescent, reflecting every colour of the spectrum as it moved. It was embroidered all over with a scattered design of golden buttercups and pale green leaves, the latter colour reflected in the underskirt. This time, when Felicia spoke, she didn't need to feign her reaction. "It's a masterpiece."

"That's the idea. We spent months on it."

"But I don't understand. Won't someone else be needing it?" Then she looked at Edith's face. "Oh." She dropped the skirt as though it were radioactive. "*Oh*."

Tara let out a soft gasp.

"But Edith, she *can't* … I mean, that's…" her voice dropped to a whisper. "That's Iris Breadmore's dress."

"Not any more, it isn't," Edith said shortly. Then, looking between the other two with visible impatience, she put her hands on her hips. "Oh, don't be so squeamish, both of you! It's not as if she died in it or anything. She never even tried it on! I did it all off measurements." She eyed Felicia critically, pursing her lips. "Now let's see. You've got a bit more going on up top than she had, but there's some play with corsets. And we can let out the hem; that should make up for the height difference between you. It still won't be as precise as I'd like, of course, but I'm certain we can make it fit."

"Even so…" Felicia was struggling to articulate just how challenging she found the idea of wearing a dead woman's dress. She had never thought of herself as particularly superstitious before, but perhaps she was getting that way in her old age. Maybe Stamford, with its plethora of secrets and hidden histories, was starting to get to her. "It wasn't meant for me. It wouldn't feel right."

"And what would be?" Edith demanded. "All of this work, never seeing the light of day? Tara spent hours on that embroidery. Hours!" Tara looked mortified to have been cited, but Edith ignored her. "I won't let *that woman* … I mean, I won't let the fair be ruined because of an unfortunate accident. It was terrible, but people have worked hard for this one weekend. Some of us have put time and money and tears into this." She shoved the dress at Felicia. "Besides, once you're in it, you'll forget all about where it came from."

Felicia looked at Tara for help, but the girl just shrugged forlornly.

"I'll have to take your word for that," Felicia disappeared

behind the screen, only to poke her head back around as a hopeful thought struck her. "Won't some people think it odd, though? If I turn up in her dress?"

"No-one'll know it's her dress," Edith was already onto the next thing, fussing with a grey curled wig. "I keep the designs strictly under wraps. So don't worry; there won't be any Manderley Ball moments tonight. Not that one, Tara," she barked, as her assistant made to drape a chemise over the top of the screen for Felicia. Edith snatched it away, bundling it into a bag. "It's all wrong. Get one of those over there."

"But I thought that was the one which goes with…"

"Honestly, girl, is there nothing but air between your ears? It's a good thing you say you've no interest in going to London, because you'd have to screw your head on better to cope there." She threw up her hands. "You know what, never mind. I'll get it myself."

Tara looked away, letting her overlong fringe fall across her face, but not before Felicia saw the ripple of shock and hurt which passed across her features. Before she could say anything, though, a commotion sounded in the passage outside, and a gaggle of cast members burst in, all talking loudly over one another.

"Do I *really* have to wear this for the ball, Edith? It's so hot."

"I've got ten minutes to re-do my makeup. Can someone help me? *Tara!*"

"Wait, Tara, I need you first. This wig is itching me to high heaven. Can't you do something about it?"

Silently, Felicia drew back into the shadows behind the screen and began to dress.

Chapter Fourteen

"So, which one of them d'you think did it?" Dexter murmured, as he pressed a flute of champagne into her hand. "Come on, out with it."

She gave him an incredulous look.

"How on earth should *I* know?"

"Well, you worked it out last time, didn't you?" He took a draught of champagne, draining half the glass in a single gulp.

"So everyone seems to think." She raised a gilt-edged rim to her lips, muttering, "I remember it quite differently."

It had been a matter of chance, a fleeting moment of recognition in a grainy photograph. And it had almost come too late. If Algernon hadn't had the presence of mind to pretend to be unconscious ... she closed her eyes, suppressing a shudder. It was still too difficult to think about, even now. It had been enough at the time to make her swear to Pettifer that she'd never get involved in an investigation again, and she'd fully meant it.

She let her eyes rove around the ballroom. People were still arriving, gliding in through the vast double doors which were only rarely thrown open these days, bringing in the scent of honeysuckle in their satin-clad wake. Behind them, St. George's Square was bathed in lamplight, the still, balmy night air punctuated by the sound of carriage wheels clattering across cobblestones. Within the room itself, candlelight reigned, glittering off mirror-lined walls and gilded cornices. Laughter tinkled festively above the strains of a string quartet. Everything was sepia-tinted, dream-like ... perfect, many would say. But she couldn't relax into the spirit of it. To her, it was like watching a play, all fake. Each of her fellow ball-goers was just an actor, and she was on edge, trying to get a glimpse behind the disguises.

How had it come to this again? Looking at the people around her and seeing suspects rather than neighbours? Her business was antiques, not bodies. If she had any sense, she'd be sticking by her vow and staying as far away from all of this as possible. She could be just another civilian, innocently enjoying the weekend's festivities.

It wasn't as though she didn't already have enough to keep her occupied, she reminded herself. She wasn't a bored little old lady with too much time on her hands. She was a mother, a business owner, responsible for an errant ex-husband, a cantankerous father, and said father's even more cantankerous cat. She'd be well within her rights to leave it to the people who were actually *paid* to spend their time looking into these things. And yet ... somehow, she already knew she wouldn't be able to do that, even if she wasn't quite sure why. It was like an invisible thread, pulling her towards the unanswered, the unfinished.

"Well, everyone who was present last night is here now," Dexter was saying briskly, apparently suffering no such qualms. "It can't be that hard to narrow them down."

She almost choked on her champagne, bubbles razing the back of her throat.

"Do you really remember *nothing* from last time?" She spluttered.

He blithely ignored her, something he'd always been adept at.

"Our local grandee seems to be holding court," he observed, nudging her with his elbow. An elbow which, for tonight at least, was mercifully *not* clad in a beige desert shirt. In the interests of blending in, he'd been given a Georgian costume for the evening. Loathe as she was to admit it, Felicia couldn't deny that it looked sublime on him. But then, what didn't?

Distractedly, she followed his gaze, to where James Riverton was surrounded by a circlet of pastel-clad women, all plying him with fluttering glances and plates of iced fancies.

"Anyone would think it was *his* festival," Dexter muttered sulkily, glaring across the room with ill-suppressed envy.

"That's because it is." A rustle of skirts accompanied the low, smoky voice in Felicia's ear. She turned, surprised to find herself eye-to-eye with another woman. This was a rare occurrence; at five feet nine inches (and a third), she occupied an awkward hinterland, taller than most of her own sex but shorter than the majority of men. As a result, she spent almost all of her time either looking up or down at other people. It was odd to see someone else's face on a level. Odd and mesmerising. Felicia blinked, trying not to stare.

"Oh yes?" She said faintly.

Red lips smiled against a powdered face. There was a beauty spot pencilled to the right of the cupid's bow. Felicia found she couldn't take her eyes off it.

"So *surprised*! How sweet. Haven't you ever wondered

about how all of this gets paid for? The sheer scale of it, the speakers they attract ... the costumes alone must cost more than the entire fair makes in revenue." Pencilled eyebrows raised sardonically. "No? Well, you're not alone; most people don't. They prefer not to; it's all far too convenient for them the way it is. They'd rather just..." She waved her glass languidly, but her fingers gripped the stem like a vice. "Enjoy the fizz and the frolics."

There was something hard about the way she uttered those alliterative 'f's. Felicia immediately found herself feeling wary. This woman wanted something from her, that much was clear. She had the sensation that she was walking on cracked ice, keeping a steady eye on where she placed her foot next.

"That's very philanthropic of him," she said, carefully. "I had no idea."

The woman gave a tight little laugh. The flute tinkled festively against her bracelets.

"Oh, yes, James is nothing if not generous." She paused, then added smoothly, "That's the party line, anyway."

Felicia was beginning to tire of this particular game. She looked the other woman straight in the eye.

"By the way, I don't think we've met."

"Caroline Boughton, editor in chief of The Stamford Bugle." She thrust out a scarlet-tipped hand. "No need to introduce yourself to *me*, Ms. Grant. I already know all about you. Not least that you're quite adept at dodging phone calls."

Felicia felt her heart sink all the way to her beribboned shoes. This was all she needed.

She reached behind her and grabbed Dexter, who was being strangely quiet.

"Can I introduce you to—"

"Oh, your ex-husband and I are already acquainted."

Caroline craned her neck around Felicia's shoulder. "Evening, Mr. Grant. Ready to take me up on that evening at the theatre yet? The offer still stands, you know. And I reckon a night out in London might do you good. Surely our little town is getting a shade dull for you by now?"

"Not at all." Dexter straightened up, betraying no embarrassment at being caught attempting to hide in his ex-wife's shadow, and bestowed upon her his most charming, and simultaneously most oblique, smile. "I keep myself busy. There's my son, for one thing. I've been away more than I'd like for the past few years, so I've got a lot of time to make up for."

"So it's pleasure then, not business?" Her mouth made a little moue of regret, but the heavily made-up eyes were sharp, predatory. Felicia could see why they called her the Rutland Rottweiler. She'd assumed the name was only used behind her back, but now, Felicia could see that the woman might actually relish such a moniker. She might even have invented it herself; it certainly had a Bugle-ish ring to it. "Our readers will be disappointed to hear that. There was a hope that the Treasure Seeker might be onto something new right here in Stamford. After the discovery of the Charles I cupboard…"

"A nice idea, but alas, no." Dexter's voice was pleasant, jovial even, but the edges of the words were faintly clipped. There was a tautness around his eyes, too, which Felicia recognised well. He wanted to move on from this conversation. "As you'll recall, that cupboard was empty. What we call a historical dead-end, I'm afraid. Disappointing, but they happen. Sometimes, the past just doesn't want to give up its secrets, and one has to respect that." He shrugged. "No, right now, I am just what I claim to be. A family man and an academic just waiting for the muse to strike."

That line was a bit too polished for even Dexter to have come up with on the spot. Felicia gave him a sideways glance, wondering why he'd felt the need to practise his alibi, as it were.

"And one half of Stamford's newest detective duo?" Caroline suggested, looking at Felicia pointedly.

There was a handsomeness to her, Felicia thought, in the strong aquiline nose, the long line of her neck. Her hair was very dark, and unpowdered for the occasion, gathered atop her head in a pillow of tight curls which didn't quite match her roots for colour. Felicia suspected that her actual hair was cut quite short, and the rest was a hairpiece. She was wearing a dress of vivid scarlet. It glistened like blood beneath the candlelight. Felicia drew herself up at that last thought; perhaps she really did have murder on the mind. It couldn't be healthy.

"Nothing so thrilling, unfortunately." Felicia smiled coolly. "As Dexter says, there really is no story to tell."

The rouged lips flickered down at the corners, green eyes hardening. For a brief, disorientating moment, Felicia felt a flash of recognition from somewhere. But just as quickly as it had appeared, it was gone again, dissipating like smoke into a sea of half-remembered faces. Somewhere as compact as Stamford was like that, and running a local business only made it worse. She'd probably seen or come into contact with just about everyone in town by now, sometimes without even realising it.

There was a heavy pause. For half a second, Felicia thought that Caroline was about to persist further. Then her gaze caught something across the room, and she appeared to change her mind.

"Well, if anything ... comes to you." She produced a

business card from somewhere on her person – where, exactly, Felicia dreaded to think, as these dresses didn't possess anything approaching a pocket – and tucked it into the front of Dexter's waistcoat, patting it with polished fingertips. "You know where to find me."

And then she was gone, a flash of red crossing the ballroom and disappearing into the crowd. Dexter looked at Felicia, eyebrows raised quizzically.

"Something we said, perhaps?"

Felicia scanned the room, but all she could see was Robyn, stalking towards them with tulip-pink skirts gathered in her hands. There was a grimly purposeful look on her heart-shaped face as she drew up beside them.

"What did *she* want?"

"Gossip, I expect," Felicia said, slightly taken aback by the ferocity of her goddaughter's tone. Robyn was usually so mild, so unruffled. She'd never known her to take against anyone. "Isn't that what all journalists are after?"

"Yes, well, most of them manage to stick to reporting the gossip, not making it." Robyn put her hands on her hips. "Mum's going to be furious when she sees her sharking around, and she's cross and bothered enough as it is already." Seeing that an explanation was in order, she added, "Dennis insisted that they wear their ceremonial robes tonight instead of their Georgian costumes. God knows why; it looks really odd."

Felicia didn't think there was much of a mystery there. After all, Dennis was odd. And he relished any chance to flaunt his position. He probably even wore his chain of office to bed.

"Mum's convinced he's done it to spite her, of course," Robyn concluded wearily.

Felicia shared her exasperation. Ever since Cassie had been elected, she'd had a strange persecution complex over her second-in-command, insisting that he was out to show her up and undermine her at every possible turn. No-one seemed able to convince her otherwise. Privately, Felicia wondered if it was actually guilt which fuelled the fire of her friend's paranoia. After all, it had been Dennis's lifelong dream to become the mayor of Stamford; a dream he might finally have attained if council newbie Cassie hadn't swept in and stolen everyone's hearts – along with their votes – in a last-minute landslide. Felicia was one of the few people in Stamford who knew that behind the bravado and the jolly hockey sticks demeanour, their mayor sometimes felt like a bit of a fraud. That she was all too aware of the fact that she'd fallen into the role – or rather, she'd been pushed into it by Robyn – as an outlet from full-time motherhood, and as such, she felt like she wasn't a 'real' politician. That although she moaned about her role, she actually took it very seriously, and the thought that she wasn't doing it well enough kept her up at night sometimes.

Felicia looked across the room at her oldest and dearest friend – who did indeed look rather cross and hot – and felt a wave of affection for her.

"At least he's saved her from the corset," she said, trying not to tug at her own. She could practically feel Edith's gaze boring into her from here. "I'd swap with her right now. Give me a sweltering fur-lined cloak any day of the week."

Robyn looked her up and down.

"I don't know … that's a pretty amazing dress. What happened to your blue one, though? I thought everyone only got one costume for the entire weekend."

Much to Felicia's relief, she never had to formulate a reply to that question. At that moment, the string quartet struck up a haze of shimmering notes. Robyn's head whipped around.

"That's the cue; the dancing's about to begin." She eyed Felicia with concern. "You're sure you know all the steps, Aunt Fliss? Because it's going to be a disaster if no-one—"

Felicia held up a hand to halt her in her tracks.

"Relax. It'll be fine."

It had been her god-daughter's idea to send out a video link with each ticket so that guests could learn the moves to the eighteen-century dances beforehand. And judging by the way everyone was confidently moving into position, forming two lines facing one another, it looked as though people had got into the spirit of it and done their homework. Well, perhaps not everyone; there were still a good few wallflowers hanging around the edges of the room, clearly content to be observers, but there were more than enough enthusiastic participants on the floor to make up the dance.

Robyn was biting her lip, not looking convinced.

"Aren't you with Hugo for this one?" Felicia spotted her valuer moving towards them, and swiftly offloaded Robyn onto his Wedgwood blue velvet sleeve. "Go. And Robyn? *Enjoy* yourself."

She turned to see Dexter proffering his own arm.

"Come along then, former wife. Let's show them how it's done, shall we?"

Chapter Fifteen

"Mum, what have you done now?"

Felicia looked down into a pair of serious grey eyes. There was an accusation within them which was mirrored in her son's tone. Immediately, she found herself feeling guilty without even knowing why. How did children have that ability?

"I don't know." She ladled flaming punch into a small-handled glass, trying to seem nonchalant. In truth, she'd probably done any number of things wrong in the past half an hour alone; that was the dispiriting reality of life as the mother of a pre-teen. "You tell me."

"That man over there." Algernon was too polite to point, instead managing to indicate James Riverton with a tilt of his bronze head. "He's been staring at you all night. And he doesn't look very happy." His eyes went round. "You didn't accuse him of murder, did you?"

Felicia almost choked on her drink, and not just because of the indecent amount of rum it appeared to contain.

"Of course not! Why would you say that?"

"Because people only get annoyed with you for two reasons," Algernon said simply. "One's when you accuse them of murder; the other's when you tell them that their antiques aren't worth as much as they thought they were. And since he's wearing a gold Rolex Submariner, I don't think he needs to worry about money."

As so often happened these days, Felicia looked down at her son and felt a strange mixture of emotions. Concern over the fact that a twelve-year-old boy had to think about protecting his mother from potential murderers ought perhaps to have been at the forefront, but it was mingled with a glow of maternal wonder which, she was slightly ashamed to admit, was winning out in this moment.

She couldn't deny that Algernon had inherited the antiques gene. He saw things few other people did. She could see the watch in question now, half hidden beneath the lace trim of Riverton's cuff, a small incongruity in their otherwise period-perfect surroundings.

Cassie billowed up to them.

"God, I *hate* these things." She tugged at her robe tetchily. "I feel like a trussed up Christmas turkey. One which is slowly roasting." She swiped the drink from Algernon's hand and took a long gulp before pulling a disenchanted face. "What is this revolting, sickly stuff? Why doesn't alcohol taste like alcohol anymore?"

"It's lemonade, Aunt Cass," Algernon said. "I'm twelve."

She stared at him for a long moment.

"So you are." She patted him on the head affectionately before putting her hand to use as a makeshift fan, flapping in front of her gleaming face. "You see, I can't even think straight in these ghastly things; I'm so hot, it's broiling my brain." She scowled across the room. "Bloody Dennis. When this is all over, I *swear*, I'm going to stick this medallion right where the sun…"

"Punch, Cass," Felicia thrust a glass of clementine-coloured liquid at her hastily, aware that her friend's voice was carrying as usual, cutting above the genteel stains of the orchestra. "Take the edge off a bit."

"I'm going to change," Cassie muttered, between slurps. "Even the damned corset's preferable to this. And I'm supposed to be re-opening the dancing with James Riverton after the supper break. There's no way I'm spinning around that dancefloor like a giant crimson bat."

"At least it might distract from your dancing," Felicia said innocently.

Cassie gave her a flat look.

"Charming friend you are. I suppose I won't bother telling you that Jack's here, then."

As a matter of fact, Felicia was well aware of that. Powers of observation did, after all, come with the job title. She'd lost count of the number of times she'd visited someone's house for a valuation to be proudly confronted with the 'best bits' laid out on the dining room table. Often, they turned out to be nothing of the sort; coronation memorabilia (the whole *point* was it had been manufactured in industrial quantities), Granny's old tea set (no good if the pot was missing, unfortunately, and that was often the bit which got broken first), paintings which turned out on closer inspection to be prints … but then, in a dingy corner, she would see *it*. Usually called into ignominious service as a plant stand or a cat food bowl or a door stop. And her heart would start to patter, her pulse spark. She would draw closer, almost holding her breath with anticipation, all whilst sternly telling herself that it would probably be nothing. The dashed hopes of a printed maker's mark or the bitter taste left by an incorrect colourway were all too familiar to the seasoned antiques valuer, and you quickly learned not to get too excited, for the sake of your blood pressure if nothing else.

And nine times out of ten, it would be just that: a quick check of the base, or the gallery label pasted on the back of the frame, or just the benefit of nearer viewing, would reveal it to be not as hoped. But that tantalising ten percent of the time ... that was enough to keep her hooked, enough to keep her coming back for more, even when she was working on a weekend again or the money in the business account shaved rather too close to the overdraft with several days still left in the month. It was the reason she loved her job, what she'd missed so much when she'd left it to work for a contemporary art gallery in London for those intervening years. It had been glamorous, and secure, and *so* much better paid that it still hurt a bit to think about it ... but there had been no mystery, no thrill, no heartstopping moments when the air seemed to have been sucked out of the room, and the blood danced in your ears, and you experienced the realisation that you were holding something in your hand which was rare and beautiful. Something which had lain dormant and unnoticed for so long. It was a little bit like archaeology, she'd often thought, except instead of walking over things hidden beneath the ground, her treasures were in plain sight, walked *past* instead, in a box of bric-a-brac at a car boot sale, or amongst a cluster of ornaments on a relative's mantlepiece, so familiar and unchanging that they had almost seemed to become part of the fabric of the house itself.

It was also, she had to admit – albeit privately – to herself, the reason why she understood Dexter so well. Why she'd always managed to forgive him, in one way or another, whenever he'd done something idiotic, or selfish, or, on occasion, downright dangerous. They shared that same thirst for discovery, the one which Algernon was starting to display worrying signs of too. It was where the three of them, usually distant corners of a triangle, met in the middle. It was their family tie.

It was also why she was certain that her ex-husband had been protesting too much earlier. He wasn't simply rusticating as he claimed to be. He was onto something, she *knew* it. He would never just give up searching. He wouldn't be able to forget, just as she couldn't forget that Iris Breadmore might have been murdered.

And suddenly, she knew exactly why she couldn't let it go. Antiques and murder weren't often comparable to one another, but Felicia knew that not to ask questions about a suspicious death would be as impossible as walking away from a potential lost masterpiece without checking it over. It was about something important going unknown, something left hanging in the ether.

And speaking of hanging in the ether ... inexorably, her eyes were drawn across the undulating, bejewelled sea of dancers to where she already knew Jack would be, despite never once looking directly at him until now. She'd known where he was all night, just as she had been at The George the previous evening. His presence was like static, prickling at her, distracting and impossible to ignore.

Unable to avoid it any more, she looked up ... straight into the glint of a lens. Surprise must have registered on her face, because he lowered the camera, giving her a half smile.

Cassie was following her gaze, looking insufferably smug.

"But clearly there's no need. Looks like you've found one another anyway."

Her friend's tone dripped with suggestion. Felicia angled her a warning look over the top of Algernon's tousled head, wishing she hadn't given away her glass of punch. Cassie was famously indiscreet when she was tipsy. Algernon was looking out across the floor in the opposite direction, to all appearances watching the dancers, but Felicia knew that her son never missed a thing. They said that you'd done your job as a parent when your children surpassed you, and Algernon had certainly done that.

Her musings were interrupted yet again by someone barrelling into the middle of their group. This time it was Dexter, looking unusually harassed.

"For all that's holy, save me from that *infernal* woman!"

"Which one?" Cassie was looking decidedly jollier in the face of Dexter's obvious distress. She fished a slice of orange out of her punch. "A fair few of us here proudly answer to that description."

Dexter ignored her, instead looking pleadingly at Felicia. She couldn't help but notice that his cravat was askew.

"If you ever once loved me, Fliss, you'll hide me from her." He threw a haunted glance back over his shoulder. "*Please.*"

A voice rolled over the heads of the crowd like a sonic boom.

"Mr. Grant! *There* you are."

Dexter went pale.

"Christ," he muttered. "It's too late. She's found me."

Chapter Sixteen

Felicia adjusted her eyeline down a few inches, just in time to see the Countess of Kesteven emerge into view, her diminutive form encased in midnight blue velvet embroidered with countless silver stars. Hers was a seemingly ageless beauty, lustrous brown hair – sufficient enough, like Felicia's, to warrant foregoing a wig – combining with dazzling bone structure and large, doe-like eyes to give her the appearance of a fairy queen tonight. In reality, as Felicia had discovered firsthand, any suggestion of fragility was wholly deceptive; the woman was in fact dangerously steely, her tenacity sheathed in finely-honed graceful manners in a pairing which was almost impossible to say no to. While Felicia harboured a healthy wariness for the countess, she also couldn't deny a certain admiration. After all, she carried the entire burden of responsibility for an ancient, crumbling estate upon her slender shoulders every day, fighting to preserve a home which wasn't hers and a legacy which would never belong to her. It was a job Felicia wasn't sure she would have been able to dedicate her life to with such resolute good cheer.

"We were just in the midst of the most *fascinating* conversation," the countess declared, to no-one in particular, as she reached Dexter's side, clamping a proprietorial hand onto his arm. "Dear Mr. Grant has had a simply *wonderful* idea…" Bewitching green eyes, only faintly feathered by tell-tale fine lines, fixed upon him, gimlet-like. "*Haven't* you, Mr. Grant?"

Dexter looked utterly steamrollered. Felicia found that she, too, was beginning to rather enjoy this encounter.

"Well," he stammered. "I'm not sure I'd quite put it…"

"*An evening with our local celebrity*," the countess blazoned over him, gazing up rapturously towards the gilded ceiling as though reading from a billboard. "Star of the small screen, swashbuckling adventurer … the Treasure Digger himself."

"Treasure *Seeker*," Dexter protested weakly, but she swatted him away as though he were an irritating wasp, or an overly solicitous footman.

"I can see it now. We'll serve champagne, naturally. And canapés … although no fish, of course. Not after the incident with the bloater paste." A small shudder passed through her narrow shoulders at the memory. "That's the last time I buy off a man with a dip and strip tank in the back of his van, good deal or not."

Felicia clamped her lips together and tried very hard not to look at Cassie. Not that the countess would have noticed anyway; she'd rallied, and was proceeding to set out her vision with aplomb.

"…A jolly little talk about your exploits, maybe." Then she frowned, a single furrow appearing in the lovely alabaster expanse of her forehead. "Although, blast, I've just thought. Aren't you giving something similar here this weekend?"

"Tomorrow afternoon," Cassie supplied, chasing a punch-soaked strawberry around the bottom of her glass. "*Wildly* popular. Sold out months ago."

Dexter glared at her. She smiled sweetly back and stuffed the strawberry into her mouth.

"Even so," the countess was shaking her head, her star-studded hair flashing in the candlelight. "We'll need something fresh, different. Something people will pay ... I mean, something people will travel for," she amended swiftly. Then she clapped her hands together gleefully. "I *have* it! A preview of your newest project. Let us all have a sneak peek into what you're working on in our *dear* little town. Something suitably thrilling, I hope." As Dexter began to demur, she cut him off stridently. "Oh, now *don't* be coy. We all know you're not staying around here just to take in the Lincolnshire air."

Behind them, the quartet struck up a familiar melody. Dexter grasped the opportunity like a drowning man at a raft.

"A waltz," he blurted out. "How wonderful! Felicia, would you—"

"I thought you'd never ask,' the countess interrupted, with a coy smile. Still with a vice-like grip on his forearm, she forcibly dragged him away onto the heaving dancefloor.

Cassie and Felicia decorously waited until they were out of sight before giving in to laughter.

"Well, that's cheered me *right* up," Cassie dabbed at her eyes. "Now enough stalling. Get over there; the suspense is killing me."

Felicia pointedly didn't follow her gaze. She knew exactly who her friend was looking at.

"He's working, Cass."

"Yes, and as the person who's paying him, I think it's time

he took a break." Cassie wiggled her fair eyebrows. "Wouldn't want to contravene any employment laws." When Felicia didn't respond, she leaned in, muttering exasperatedly, "Oh, come on Fliss. It's a party, isn't it? Why not?"

"Yes, Mum," Algernon piped up. As usual, he'd clearly heard everything – although given Cassie's decidedly broad notion of a whisper, that wasn't so surprising – and he looked up at her enquiringly now. "Why not? Has something happened between you and Jack?"

If only. Felicia felt herself flush, then immediately cursed herself as the worst mother in the world.

"Of course not, darling," she managed, in a strained voice. She shoved her glass into Cassie's hands, rather more forcefully than was perhaps necessary. "I'll go and ask him now."

She squeezed around the perimeter of the ballroom, her image reflected back at her in mirror after mirror, a paper doll multiplying endlessly into a vanishing point of flame and glass. The amber glow of the candlelight seemed to be growing richer as the evening wore on, rendering the gilt ceiling molten and the plum pink walls a deep ox blood hue. The atmosphere was one of light within dark, hot and oppressive. She sucked in a breath, but felt nothing pass her lips.

He was lining up a shot of the dancers as she approached from behind. She put a hand on his shoulder, without really thinking, then realised her mistake as the muscles tensed reflexively beneath her fingers. She opened her mouth, about to apologise, but then he turned, and his face was so characteristically impassive that she almost began to wonder if she'd imagined it.

"You look very ... floral," he said, by way of greeting, looking her dress up and down.

"You look very…" She looked him up and down, taking in the faded black t-shirt and jeans. "Well, like you always do, to be honest." Presumably, dressing up was beneath him – much like her father, who'd remained at home in curmudgeonly fashion with Godfrey, not even bothering to give his broken leg as an excuse, although it would have sufficed. "I suppose it would be offensive to your artistic sensibilities to blend in?"

"Something like that." He waited a beat before adding lightly, "Plus of course, it's very convenient if I get the urge to rob a house on the way home."

"Will you stop that?" She chided him. "We both know that half the people here are probably just as criminal as you, when you boil it down."

"And we also both know that it's entirely different."

After all, removing a few items from a late relative's house before the probate valuation, or totting up the odd wine-soaked pub lunch on expenses … well, they were just things one *did*. They might not be legal, but they were acceptable crimes. There was almost something faintly patriotic about getting a minor victory over on the taxman; frankly, it would be almost un-English not to. Whereas anything which disturbed the beauty and tranquillity of the countryside … loud music, graffiti chalked onto a bus shelter, cars racing each other through the empty streets at night … they might be lesser crimes in the eyes of the law, but not to most people.

In somewhere like Stamford, such things were enough to provoke a rash of letters to the newspaper suggesting the reinstatement of stocks and pillories in Red Lion Square, together with a long-standing resentment and suspicion which became a stubborn stain, reluctant to ever fade. Eventually, the memory became almost collective, absorbed into the fabric of the town itself, until even people who weren't around when a thing happened 'remembered' it nonetheless.

Jack could probably reach the ripe old age of ninety and people would still be watching him warily … as indeed they were now, Felicia couldn't help but notice. Not overtly, of course, but eyes were definitely turned in their direction from behind fluttering fans and glasses of punch. There was a small halo of floorspace around Jack, too – ill-afforded in the jam-packed room – as if people were reluctant to get too close. Felicia felt a hot flash of irritation. In case he … *what*? Ripped the paste jewels from their ears? Grabbed a hostage and demanded everyone stand and deliver? The whole thing was so patently ridiculous that it spurred her to be bold. She stepped closer, until she could see the copper flecks which encircled his irises.

"Shall we dance?"

He didn't move.

"I'm not exactly dressed for it."

"You're hardly likely to ruin the photos, are you?" She looped the camera strap over his shoulder and foisted it off onto a surprised-looking Dennis, who was standing nearby.

Jack still didn't move.

"It's a waltz. Some of us didn't go to finishing school, you know."

"It's basically a box step. You can't get it wrong." She pulled him onto the floor, having to use rather more force than was flattering. They found a space, slotting into the whirling ouroboros of couples. Felicia went to place his hand, when it suddenly found exactly the correct point on her back, and before she knew it, she was being spun around the floor in perfect time with everyone else.

"You know exactly what you're doing," she accused, as he steered them in a flawless turn.

He ignored her, instead remarking flatly, "People are looking. I did warn you."

The warmth of his hand was bleeding through the silk which covered her back. The washed cotton of his t-shirt rasped against the bare underside of her wrist where it rested upon his shoulder. At once, she was extremely, almost painfully aware of the pulse in her throat, like a butterfly trapped in a jar, hammering clumsily at the sides. She wondered if this hadn't all been rather reckless, although not for the reasons he was talking about.

"And I thought I'd made it clear that I don't care," she managed, hoping that he'd attribute her breathlessness to simple exertion.

"Are you sure? Your husband doesn't look too pleased."

That did it. Her head snapped up, and she gave him a cold look.

"He is *not* my husband."

There was a surge of silence between them as their gazes met.

"No," he said at last. "I know that."

At that moment, the dance came to a close; perhaps fortuitously for him. Felicia bobbed a brief curtsey along with everyone else and whirled away before she could say something she might regret later.

Cassie and Algernon were gone from the refreshments table upon her return, but now that she was here, she realised just how parched her throat was, dry with overuse and suppressed anger. She filled a glass of lemonade and tossed it back, trying not to shudder at the burning sweetness as it hit the roof of her mouth. Cassie was right; it was vile stuff.

Belatedly, she became aware of another presence at the table with her. A squat man, looking ill-at-ease in his costume, browsing the sweetmeats with an unenthusiastic eye. He didn't look much in the mood for conversation, and Felicia couldn't say she was feeling too gregarious herself at the present moment, but politeness dictated, so she offered up a breezy, "Lovely night for it, isn't it?"

Later, when Felicia would revisit this moment, it would occur to her that if he had replied in the accepted fashion, that probably would have been it. A simple smile, or murmured affirmative, and they could both have contently gone on with their respective business, duty done. But he didn't. Instead, he grunted, not looking at her as he snatched a couple of petit fours off the nearest plate, scattering several more onto the table in the process. They'd been lovingly arranged in a chrysanthemum shape, and something about this small act of vandalism irritated Felicia and captured her interest simultaneously. For the first time, she looked at her companion properly. Her initial, fleeting impression had been correct; his costume looked to be sitting all wrongly on him, despite Edith's unmistakably precise tailoring. Closer inspection revealed why: he'd clearly been tugging at it all evening, his cravat askew, the cameo brooch which had held it in place at his throat almost hidden by the disarrayed folds of unravelling fabric. His wig had gone a similar way, listing on a crudely cropped head which, from the slither of it she could see, was inflamed and mottled, presumably from incessant scratching.

"It looks set to hold for tomorrow, too." She pretended to peruse the plate he'd just defiled, taking a perverse pleasure in forcing conversation upon him. She was in a perverse sort of mood; Jack had seen to that. "Wouldn't that be lucky?"

He finally glanced at her, clearly mystified as to why she

was still talking to him. For the first time, she got a proper view of his face. Unfortunately, *pugnacious* was the word which immediately sprung to mind, the features all crammed too close to the centre, leaving an awkward moat of flesh all around which seemed to serve no purpose.

He looked her up and down, so slowly that she began to feel hot with discomfort, although she tried not to let it show. Then at last, a pair of small, deep-set eyes met her own.

"Nice dress," he said softly. "Where'd you get it?"

There was something unpleasantly insinuating about the way he said it. Almost menacing. Felicia could feel her skin crawling. However, she was rescued from having to reply by a commotion springing up at the back of the room. The huge double doors were heaving open.

And there, in the curious blend of silver and gold as moonlight and lamplight blended, stood an angry mob.

Chapter Seventeen

Of course, Felicia noted wryly, this was an angry mob, Stamford-style. So ... a politely put out mob would probably be a more appropriate phrase. They looked like they'd dropped in for a cup of tea rather than a threatening showdown. A more complete selection of sensible shoes would be hard to find this side of the Greenwich Meridian.

"Oh, Lord." Cassie had materialised at her side, and was groaning. "I should have known he'd pull a stunt like this. The man gets more bonkers with every passing day."

"I assume you mean their ringleader?" Felicia said, trying not to look too amused. "The little chap at the front with the bow tie?"

"Aloysius Drummond," Cassie clarified, through gritted teeth. "He's the local librarian. And a thorn in my *bloody* side." She strode forward, folding her arms sternly. "What's going on here?"

"I might ask you the same question." His voice was thin, querulous. "I thought we'd discussed this, Cassandra."

"No, *you* discussed it, ad nauseum. I listened politely, but that's all. And frankly, I wasn't obliged to do that much." She exhaled, clearly trying to maintain her patience. "I know the Georgian Fair isn't your thing, but look," she spread her arms wide. "At lot of other people enjoy it."

"Because they're *brainwashed*!" Drummond snapped. He had particularly large head in proportion to the rest of him, Felicia observed. It was one of those peculiarities which, once noticed, proved fascinating to the point of distraction. "Seduced by a commercialised past which never existed..."

"Oh, come now," Cassie said wearily, clearly having had enough. "It's just a bit of harmless fun."

Drummond's mouth went slack with shock.

"*Fun?*" He squawked.

"Yes," Caroline Boughton said languidly. She was inspecting her cherry red nails, making a show of boredom, although Felicia could tell she was enjoying all of this immensely. "I know you're not the most up-to-date of individuals, Aloysius, but even you must have come across it at some point. It's not an especially new import."

"*You!*" He whirled on Caroline, apparently noticing her for the first time. His nostrils, already an unfortunately prominent feature, only became more so when he was angered. They flared in and out, quivering like a moth next to a flame. "You've got some nerve." He jabbed a bony finger at her. "A lot of this is *your* doing."

"Mine?" But she looked more entertained by the accusation than indignant. Felicia could only imagine the headlines in tomorrow's Bugle.

"That filth you print," Drummond spluttered. "This used to be a respectable town. Now it's some sort of circus! Just look at that business in the spring!" This was greeted by a rumble of agreement from the small cluster of people behind him. Evidently buoyed by this, he continued with relish. "*Murders! Here! We hadn't had a murder in Stamford since the war. It's all these ghastly new developments, bringing in outsiders...*"

The pugnacious man visibly bristled, looming forwards with clenched fists.

"Now, listen here, you..."

"Tony," James Riverton's voice broke in, quiet but commanding. "That's enough."

The object of his censure clamped his lips into a sullen, resentful line, but obediently stood down.

"We want Stamford returned to the way it was," Drummond said staunchly, as though nothing had happened. Felicia had to admit, the little man had pluck. "A quiet, out-of-the-way place. And that reclamation begins with the Georgian Fair."

There were jeers of approval from his entourage. For the first time, Felicia noticed that one of them was wearing a cap, which seemed a bit odd indoors. And at night to boot. It occurred to her that perhaps some people wouldn't want to be identified publicly as anti-fair. Who knew a harmless festival could prove so polarising?

"I agree," Riverton spoke up again. "We should discuss it, Aloysius. Let's not spoil anyone's evening with our dull conversation, though. We'll go outside." He held out an arm, funnelling the librarian and his motley crew towards the doors through which they'd arrived, addressing the assembled room as he went. "My apologies, everyone. It's been a challenging day for us all. Emotions are running high. Please, continue to enjoy the party."

After they left, the room exploded in a buzz of excited conversation. Cassie visibly exhaled in relief, her bravado slipping for a moment.

"That could have been a lot worse. Thank God for James."

"Yes." Felicia had to admit that, despite her opinion of the man, it was an impressive feat, the way he'd mastered the situation. Clearly, he had a way with people ... when he wanted to use it. She leaned in closer to Cassie, indicating the pugnacious petit-four pilferer with a subtle tilt of her head. "Out of interest ... who's that man over there?"

"Oh, him." Felicia thought she saw a flicker of distaste cross her friend's usually amiable face. "That's Tony Chandler. He's a local builder. Done the last few big developments in town."

"Ah." That made sense of a couple of things. The anger he'd shown when Drummond had mentioned building expansion. The defensive, tightly-wound nature. After all, few people in a small, picturesque town were less popular than a developer.

"He doesn't seem like the type who'd be friends with James Riverton," Felicia observed. "They're like chalk and cheese."

"Friends? I wouldn't say that." Cassie raised blonde eyebrows. "Actually, it's a bit awkward between them. Tony was supposed to be developing some of James' land – he owns a bit around the edges of town – but at the last minute it was discovered to be the site of one of Fitzwilliam Trendlehart's great moments of derring do. Rescuing some orphans, or such the like. He seemed to do a lot of that. Anyway, that put paid to the whole thing. They're hoping to make a special site of it now. There's even talk of running the Georgian Fair from there going forwards." She shrugged. "Obviously, for James it's just another feather in his cap, but for Tony ... he'd put a lot of time and backing into that project. He had big plans for it. It was quite embarrassing for him, I think." She frowned. "To be honest, I'm not really sure what he's doing here tonight."

Felicia looked thoughtfully at the man, who was currently skulking at the edge of the room, scanning it with barely disguised contempt.

"A very good question," Felicia said, under her breath. "A very good question indeed."

"Come on," Cassie slapped her on the back. "More dancing for you. We need to get this party re-started."

And before Felicia could protest, she was dragged vigorously back onto the floor.

———————

Thank *God* for pudding, Felicia thought, an hour or so later, as she sagged discreetly against a plasterwork frieze, trying valiantly not to look as done in as she felt. Nothing could be better relied upon to distract the British from their woes. To be fair, the glittering table of sugarwork, candied fruit and flowers had provided quite the show, and soon enough, it seemed that the scene from earlier was all but forgotten. If anything, Felicia thought, people appeared more enthusiastic that ever, more determined to have a good time.

Unfortunately, she found she couldn't get into the swing of things quite so easily. Something about that confrontation kept going around in her head. But then, it had been an interminable day, and maybe all she really needed was sleep. She was eyeing the clock hands ticking steadily towards midnight for about the tenth time in as many minutes when Cassie snagged her, looking unusually worried.

"You haven't seen James Riverton, have you?" She'd

changed back into her Georgian dress at some point, and the shot silk oscillated under the lights, making Felicia's tired eyes begin to cross. She shook her head, partly in answer to the question, but also to banish the hallucination.

"Sorry, can't say that I have."

Cassie exhaled through tightly pinched lips, making a faint whistle of annoyance.

"Well, this is just grand. He's supposed to be dancing the minuet with me. Everyone's waiting for us to start." She went to check her watch, then obviously realised she'd taken it off for the night. "It's unlike him to forget. If he doesn't show up soon I'll have to dance with..." she closed her eyes briefly. "*Dennis.*"

She uttered his name as one might Mephistopheles, or Beelzebub. Despite her exhaustion, Felicia laughed, making her friend's eyes fly open accusingly.

"It's not *funny*, Fliss! The man seems to think he's some sort of Hanoverian Fred Astaire."

"So I see." Felicia looked over to the dance floor, to where Dennis was employing a technique which could safely be described as enthusiastic. "Who knew he could get his leg that high?"

"Nice as it is to see you getting so much enjoyment out of my predicament, do you think you might actually try and be helpful?" Cassie said. "Like going and finding my dance partner for me while I stall things here."

That wiped the smile of Felicia's face.

"Er ... I'm really not sure I'm the person..."

"Why?" Cassie shot back, her face immediately morphing into a plaque or horror. "What have you done, Fliss? You haven't upset him, have you? Because he's a *very* important..."

"Nothing!" Felicia said hastily. "Nothing at all. Look, he can't have gone far. I'll ask around, find out who saw him last."

Unfortunately, it wasn't quite as straightforward as she'd hoped. Robyn thought she'd spotted him heading towards the foyer, but that was a while back, and she wasn't sure he'd still be there. Gavin was convinced that he'd seen him not five minutes ago, just on the other side of the ballroom, although he hadn't been able to see who he was chatting to in the crush. Eventually, Edith suggested that it might be worth checking the men's dressing room, so, failing any better suggestion (and with an increasingly frantic-looking Cassie meeting her eye) Felicia set her course in that direction.

She didn't relish the prospect of returning to the cellars on her own again, especially not after what had happened last time. But her fears turned out to be unfounded; as she navigated the crepuscular corridors, it soon became clear that she wasn't the only one who'd strayed from the party. As she passed the door to Edith's wardrobe department, the murmur of voices floated out towards her.

"Honestly, Ambrose, you'd lose your own head if it wasn't screwed on." A feminine tone, young and breathy. Tara, sounding weary and a little strained, despite the affectionate choice of phrase.

Another voice responded, gruff and petulant.

"I told you, it's not there."

"Let's have another look, shall we?" Tara suggested, overly brightly. There was a screech of hangers along a rail, a metallic clicking sound as something was removed. "Here we go; it's right here, amongst the others."

"It wasn't there before."

"It must have been."

"It *wasn't*."

He sounded angry. Felicia hesitated, wondering if she ought to announce herself. On the one hand, this seemed like a private matter. And yet...

"All right, well it doesn't matter," Tara soothed. "We've found it now, and..."

"It *does* matter," Ambrose said, in a strangled voice. Felicia could imagine his face flushing a dull red, those over-large hands curling into fists. In an instant, she had a flash of those hands – of their strength, the barely-repressed emotions of the man who governed them. Of just how easy it would be for them to shove a woman to her death. Like swatting a fly. The thought was unsettling to say the least. "You don't believe me. You think I'm ... I'm..."

"Oh, Ambrose, don't." Tara's voice was pleading, almost desperate. "Not here. We can talk about it later, all right?" A rustle of fabric. "Come on, let's get back to the ball. Before we're missed."

Felicia moved on quickly, not wanting to get caught eavesdropping. All the same, it was hard not to marvel at the behind-the-scenes dynamics of other people's relationships. Who would have ever guessed that the towering, burly Ambrose would be the needy one in the pairing, rather than his tiny sprite of a girlfriend?

A scuffing sound to her right made her head whip around, but the low-lit corridor was empty. Felicia frowned, reminding herself to get a grip. It wasn't as if she weren't used to creaking old buildings with a mind of their own. Admittedly, she wasn't too keen on the whole underground part of it; perhaps it was claustrophobia which was making her edgy tonight.

Then she heard it. The sound of shoe leather scraping against flagstones. It was a sound she knew well from childhood, familiar as her face in the mirror. Her father, dragging furniture across the saleroom floor at Grant's, while she sat swinging her legs on the rostrum, covertly sucking a humbug she'd purloined from the secret stash in his desk. A hazy memory of youthful boredom, now precious and gilt-edged, preserved in a special photograph frame within her mind. Usually, that sound comforted her; now, it made her go still with fear.

Someone had drawn back into the shadows. She could feel their eyes on her now, watching her.

A cold sensation broke out across the back of her exposed neck, the fine hairs at the nape rising. She fought for calm, not to descend into panic.

"All right, that enough." Her voice was loud, surprising her with its stridency. "Who's there? Show yourself."

Silence greeted her demand. Felicia felt something else kindling within her, something perhaps not wise, given the circumstances, but very welcome nonetheless. Its heat melted the chill within, emboldening her. She raised her voice even further, letting it ring off the stone walls.

"Mr. Riverton, if this is your idea of trying to intimidate me, you're going the wrong way about it."

Just a few months ago, that would have been an outrageous lie, she realised. But not now. Living in London for all of those years, she'd naturally presumed herself streetwise. What a laugh that seemed now. A week back in the countryside had thoroughly disabused her of that notion. But she wasn't sheltered anymore.

"You're far from the first to have a go at it," she continued, although declined to add how close the last person had come to finishing her off in the process. She didn't fancy putting ideas into his head. "And if you listen to those around me, they very much doubt you'll be the last. So if you *don't* mind, I have places to be."

Then she marched off. Her heart was hammering with adrenaline, energy rushing to her head and making her feel vaguely spaced out. It was only after a minute or so that she realised she had absolutely no idea where she was going. Not that she was lost; she could see the door to the men's dressing room at the end of the passage, a seam of light marking its edges. But she'd come down here to find Riverton, and if that was him behind her...

A hand emerged from the darkness, clamping down on her shoulder.

For a second, all rational thought flew out of her head. She swallowed back a gasp, too frozen to turn around and face her assailant. But then her senses began to return. The hand on her was enormous, the palm spanning almost the entire width of her collarbone. For many, that would have only been more terrifying, but to Felicia, it was a balm to her soul.

"*Pettifer*," she breathed. "What are you doing here?" She finally turned, relief making way for another, less benign emotion. "And why are you following me?"

"Following you?" His wide, flat face corrugated with confusion. "No, I was just doing my rounds, is all."

"Your..." Her eyes travelled up and down his regular attire of crumpled suit, frayed tie and shoes which would look more at home on a building site than the pristine pavements of a conservation town. "Wait, are you still *working*?"

He looked uncomfortable, shifting from mammoth foot to mammoth foot.

"Not officially, no. As far as Heavenly is concerned, I'm off the clock and tucked up in bed with Mrs. Pettifer."

What a thought. Now she found herself wondering what he wore to bed. Probably that suit; she'd never once seen him out of it. Perhaps he was like a Medieval peasant and sewed himself into it.

"And unofficially?"

He hesitated.

"I just … wanted to keep an eye on things, is all."

She felt any residual annoyance at being crept up on dissipate.

"Have you been around all evening?" She asked softly.

"Here and there. Trying to stay out of sight." He gave a rueful smile. "I'm perhaps not built for undercover work, mind."

Felicia tried to keep a straight face.

"Some of these passageways are pretty useful for getting around." He slapped the wall next to his head. "Once you work out where they go, that is. I've gone round in circles a few times. It's like a bloody maze." He looked at her then, suspiciously, as though a thought had just occurred to him. "What are *you* doing down here, anyway? Aren't you supposed to be at the knees-up?"

"Ball, Sergeant. It's a ball." She wondered how the Georgian Fair organisers would feel about having their meticulously researched and lavishly appointed event described in terms more suited to a spontaneous carousing session in the sticky recesses of a dodgy pub. Probably best they never found out.

Pettifer made a dismissive trumpeting sound through his squashed nose.

"Never mind what it is. Why aren't you at it?"

He sounded put out, as though she were an inconvenient child who just *had* to ruin things for everyone else by refusing to behave.

"I was sent to find someone," she said, defensively. "I was on my way to the dressing rooms."

He didn't miss a beat.

"Fine. I'll come with you."

She looked at him, unsure whether to be more puzzled or irritated.

"It's literally just there," she said slowly, pointing to the glowing doorway. "I think I'll be fine."

His granite-like jaw set even harder, if such a thing were possible.

"Even so."

She opened her mouth to argue, then decided against it. Instead, with an exaggerated sigh – just so he knew how ridiculous she found all of this – carried on towards the door. But something was bothering at her, and as she raised her hand to knock – just in case there were any half-naked men in there – she found her hand stilling, fingers curling into a fist in mid-air. Her head whirled, and she looked at him through narrowed eyes.

"Why are you being so strange? What do you know that I don't?"

"Nothing! I…" He faltered, flushing so thoroughly that she could see it even in the semi-darkness, before saying in a low voice, "I mean, it's more of a … feeling."

She couldn't help herself. She grinned, knocking jauntily on the door, which swung open of its own accord with an unhealthy-sounding rasp.

"I see," she said, with mock seriousness. "And here I

thought a dyed-in-the-wool Northerner like yourself didn't believe in such frivolous things as intuition."

He didn't smile back.

"I don't. That's what worries me."

As one, they turned towards the open doorway. And Felicia felt the mirth sliding from her face towards the flagstones below.

Chapter Eighteen

It was the legs she noticed first.

For a moment which was brief but equally not nearly long enough, she thought she was hallucinating. Then her mind caught up with her eyes, puzzle pieces slotting into place as she made sense of what she was seeing. The legs weren't hovering above the floor at all. They were dangling, feet hanging limply en pointe. One shoe had fallen off, the stockinged toes looking horribly bare and vulnerable. She couldn't bring herself to look at the face, but not to look at all felt cowardly somehow, almost disrespectful, so she fixed her attention on a point somewhere below the knee instead, which felt just about manageable.

"Christ," Pettifer swore softly from behind her. It was only then that she noticed he hadn't moved forwards; neither of them had. Clearly, it was apparent to both of them that there was no point. Even so, she was taken aback when he calmly pulled out his phone, already turning away.

"I need to call it in," he said shortly, as he put the handset to his cauliflower ear.

She knew he was right, but something about the abrupt invasion of procedure into such a moment felt positively inhuman. It spurred her to action. She moved further into the room, reaching out her fingertips to touch the underside of the pale, lifeless wrist, before immediately yanking them away again in horror.

"He's still warm," she whispered.

"He will be." Glancing up, he must have seen the look of horror on her face, because he sighed, placing the phone against his shoulder. "I'm sorry. I know I must seem..." His face convulsed briefly. "Look, the best thing I can do for him right now is my job. You understand?"

She nodded, swallowing.

"Good, because I need you to keep your head. You may well have been one of the last people to see him before he..." He trailed off, looking at the body properly for the first time, at the stool tipped over beneath the suspended feet, and she saw the expression of appalled pity cross his features before he could hide it. "Bloody hell, he must've..." He took an unsteady breath. "What even *is* that thing around his neck?"

"It's his cravat," Felicia said scratchily. "Part of his costume." At his uncomprehending look, she elucidated, "Basically a Georgian tie. It goes around the..."

She faltered, realising the awful irony of what she'd been about to say. Because it *was* around his throat, only not in the way it was meant to be.

"Well, it was the closest thing to hand, I suppose." Pettifer scratched his bristly head, looking bleak. "Still, I don't like to think how desperate he must have been. I mean, there are easier ways."

"Wait ... what are you saying?" She spun to face him, eyes round. "You can't possibly think that he did this to *himself*?"

He'd been in the process of returning the phone to his ear, but he paused, looking at her in disbelief.

"The man's hanging from the ceiling, Felicia," he said slowly. "How else d'you think he got there?"

"I can't ... I mean, I know it's the most likely explanation, but ... I just can't imagine him doing a thing like this. What possible reason would he have? He was wealthy, admired..."

"There'll be a reason somewhere. Doubt we'll have to look far. Everyone has their demons after all. Especially the rich and successful." His mouth turned down at the corners, an expression she couldn't decipher. "Didn't you say he was some local big shot? There's a lot of pressure right there: an image to maintain, a constant fear of letting people down ... it wouldn't be the first time it's got too much for someone in his position."

"Yes, but he wasn't like that. If you'd met him..." Felicia bit her lip, frustrated by how difficult she was finding it to convey the essence of the man. The vitality, the leonine pride. Of course, she understood that people could be hiding things, that everyone was masquerading, to a more or lesser degree.

Pettifer looked at her for a long moment. When he spoke, his voice was gentle, soothing.

"Look, Felicia, I understand that after last time ... after Betsy..."

She felt herself go very still, a coldness seeping through her muscles.

"What exactly is *that* supposed to—"

"Hello?" A voice sounded behind them. Gavin was walking down the corridor towards them, his pale green coat glowing in the dim light. "Oh, it's you two. What's going on? Why are you both just standing there like..."

His gaze, which had been following a natural path across

Felicia's face, now fixed upon the open doorway beyond her shoulder.

Felicia was, by now, no stranger to the finding of bodies, and she'd also seen more than one person in the aftermath of stumbling over a corpse of their own. But it occurred to her, as she watched Gavin's jaw go slack, his eyes oscillate in disbelief and dread, that she had never actually witnessed anyone in the moment of the most unthinkable of discoveries. It seemed to happen impossibly slowly, and was by turns unbearably awful and utterly compelling. She found that she couldn't look away, no matter how much she wanted to.

"As you can see, sir, this in now the scene of an incident," Pettifer said, although Felicia could tell that he was making a concerted effort not to sound too brusque. "So if you could please just…"

Gavin didn't even appear to hear him. He was still staring at the body, transfixed.

"No," he whispered, through bloodless lips. He'd begun to sway. "Oh my God, *no*."

Instinctively, Felicia reached for him, but she was a fraction of a second too late. Her fingers found only air as Gavin's eyes rolled back in his head, his body plummeting towards the floor.

Chapter Nineteen

"I t *might* have been nice if you'd chosen to tell me that James Riverton was Gavin March's father," Pettifer growled, as he stalked into the cupboard which masqueraded as the Art Centre's staff kitchen, the door thudding shut behind him. "I would obviously have handled the situation differently."

Directing his anger at Felicia probably wasn't going to make him feel any better, Pettifer conceded guiltily. But it was a damned sight easier than admitting the rather more self-directed truth.

He'd made a hash of things, he knew it. Another death, and this time right under his nose. Never mind that it appeared to be a suicide, and not another murder; that wasn't the *point*. He ought to have prevented it nonetheless. Hadn't he known something was going to happen tonight? That's why he'd been here all evening, skulking in the shadows like a fifteen stone, Yorkshire-bred Phantom of the Opera. Feeling like a prize ass for most of it, and wondering why on earth he wasn't back at home with his wife as he was supposed to be, feet propped up on the settee, puzzles section of the paper in hand, cold beer at his elbow ... he hadn't even told the missus what he was really up to tonight, nor Jess, whom he would usually trust with his life, lest they think he'd gone crazy.

But he hadn't been crazy, he reflected now, desolately. Someone had died tonight, just as he'd feared they would. He'd been right. Not, perhaps, in the way he'd envisaged, but right nonetheless. The knowledge gave him absolutely no satisfaction whatsoever.

"I had no idea, honestly." Felicia's eyes were orb-like, pearlescent with innocence. She still looked as fresh as she had at the beginning of the night, he noted. Anyone would have thought that she'd nipped away and retouched her makeup, smoothed over her hair, but even if he hadn't been with her the entire time, he'd have known that she hadn't. Felicia had a natural ability to appear outwardly untouched by events, which was ironic, really, as he knew that beneath it all, she felt things more deeply than anyone could have imagined. Far more so than most people did. And yet, it didn't show at all on the mirror-like surface. It wasn't a trait which always worked in her favour. Pettifer knew from experience that most people didn't trust calmness in the face of a crisis. It made them wary.

"Cassie never told me," Felicia insisted, catching sight of his unimpressed expression. She turned accusingly to the other occupant of the room.

"I assumed you knew!" Cassie protested, snatching up the kettle as it rattled to a boil, steam immediately engulfing the tiny kitchen.

"How was I *supposed* to know? They didn't even have the same last name!"

"Well … no, granted, they didn't," Cassie admitted sheepishly, dunking a teabag into a mug and swilling it around briefly before squashing it violently against the side with the back of a spoon. Pettifer tried not to wince openly at this sacrilege, making a mental note never to accept a cup of tea from the mayor if it could be helped. "Gavin took his mother's maiden name years ago. Before he came to work for me."

"Not to mention that he never once gave any indication that they were related," Felicia persisted. "In fact, I don't think I've seen them exchange as many as two words together."

"I did tell you that they were estranged." Cassie flipped the compressed tea bag in the direction of the bin without looking. It missed entirely, landing on the floor with a doughy squelch. "On Gavin's side, at least. James always hoped that there would be a reconciliation one day, but I think he knew better than to try and force it. Gavin can be incredibly stubborn."

"And what exactly was it that they fell out about?" Pettifer didn't pussyfoot around the question. He could tell that she knew.

Cassie's face tightened, cracks appearing in the thick white makeup which still caked her face. She heaped two teaspoons of sugar into the mug, then, after a brief consideration, another half, stirring the resulting concoction with a furibund motion. When she finally spoke, he got the sense that she was choosing her words with care.

"I'm not sure it's my place to tell you that. You'd need to ask Gavin himself … provided he's up to it, of course." This last part was added with meaning. She handed the mug to Felicia, the liquid inside sloshing dangerously close to the lip. "You take this to him, Fliss. And make sure that *he* treads gently." She indicated Pettifer, who gritted his teeth, sorely tempted to point out that he *had* done this sort of thing before, just the once or twice. Then he decided that now probably wasn't the moment for sarcasm. Instead, he silently followed Felicia back through to the now-empty ballroom – empty save for a small cluster of people gathered around a figure on a chair. The candles had all been extinguished, replaced by electric lighting which chased away the enchanted illusion of the evening. Now, it just looked like any room after a party had ended, drooping and a little forlorn.

They'd managed to get everyone out all right; the ball had been drawing to a close anyway, the clock hands creeping closer to midnight, and Cassie had explained away the arrival of the ambulance with some veiled story about a small accident. She'd been the consummate professional in that moment, and he'd been glad to have her. Managing the public had never been his forte.

He watched Felicia hand Gavin the cup of tea, murmuring something sympathetic as she bent over him. Hugo, who was sitting next to him, arm around his shoulder, looked up and smiled gratefully. Jess was hovering at a discreet distance, pity written all over her young face, despite her obvious attempts to remain professional. He hoped she never changed, never lost that soft core of empathy; it was one of the things which made her a fantastic officer. If only she could see that and stop trying so hard to suppress it.

Gavin was staring into the cup in his hands with a faraway, helpless look, as though he'd never seen anything like it before and hadn't the first idea what to do with it. Freckles stood out starkly against the sallow skin on his face like constellations. Pettifer recognised the symptoms; this went beyond shock and into something deeper, more unfathomable. Nonetheless, he forced himself to step forwards, trying not to loom too imposingly over the hunched figure on the chair. There was no point delaying the inevitable. Questions still had to be asked, even if, in moments like these, he briefly found himself wishing it wasn't he who had to ask them.

"Are you up to answering a few questions now?" He endeavoured to keep his voice low, aware that its deep rumble could be alarming. Like a landslide beginning in the distance, Felicia had once described it, with her customary zest for a simile. "I know it's late, but the sooner we do this…"

"I understand." Gavin's head snapped up suddenly, eyes focusing sharply on Pettifer's face. Pettifer was struck by their blue, pale and piercing, the colour of a clear sky on an October day. It was the first real resemblance he'd seen between the boy and his father, but even so, now he cursed himself for not noticing it before. Another slip-up which would be playing on his mind later.

Gavin shifted in his seat, divesting himself abruptly of the blanket which had been placed around his shoulders as he sat bolt upright. There was none of the dazedness left about him now. "Ask me whatever you need to."

Hugo eyed him uneasily.

"Are you sure? I mean, don't you think you need—"

Irritation convulsed across Gavin's face.

"I'm fine. Stop fussing over me; you know I hate it." As Hugo's face fell, he relented slightly, saying in a softer voice, "The sergeant wouldn't be asking now if it wasn't important. He's well aware, as am I, that the time window we have for keeping this quiet is running out fast. By morning, the whole town'll know what's happened." He turned his attention back to Pettifer, tilted his chin. "What is it you want to know?"

"What were you doing down in the cellars in the first place?" Pettifer knew the question sounded brusque, but it couldn't be helped.

Gavin blinked.

"Well, looking for my father, of course. After that message…" his hand flew to his mouth. "Gosh, I'm sorry. I've just realised that you don't know."

"Know what?" Pettifer shot back. Out of the corner of his eye, he saw Jess tense, her face taking on a keen expression.

"It's easier if I show you. You'll need to see it anyway." Gavin was fumbling inside his jacket, producing a phone. "He sent me a text."

He handed the phone over without another word. Pettifer looked at the tiny glowing screen, dwarfed within his palm. Five words jumped out from it. Just five.

I'm so sorry. For everything.

As suicide notes went, it was short. But then, they often were. And it was unequivocally to the point; at least, he hoped that for the person for whom it was intended it was. Judging by Gavin's reaction, it had meant something very meaningful indeed.

With the lack of embarrassment police work instilled in a person, Pettifer shamelessly scrolled back through their previous correspondence. Not that there was much to it, and what there was was so one-sided that to call it such was misleading in the extreme. Cassie had been right; Riverton had clearly longed for a relationship with his son, although judging by Gavin's complete lack of reply to any outreach, it hadn't looked like it was coming soon. And now it never would. The thought was oddly affecting. Pettifer cleared his throat.

"And this is why you went looking for him? You were alarmed?"

"My father never said sorry," Gavin said dully. "Never."

He'd tiptoed around long enough, Pettifer decided now. Time to get to the big question, the only one which really mattered in a case such as this one.

"Can you think of any reason why he might have wished to end his own life?"

Gavin stared at him, as though he couldn't quite comprehend the question.

"Did he seem in any way odd recently?" Felicia helped him out, her voice soft and encouraging. "Distracted? Disturbed?"

Pettifer gave her a grateful look as Gavin nodded, clarity returning to his expression.

"As you've no doubt gathered, Sergeant, we didn't exactly enjoy the best of relationships. In fact, to say that I actively went out of my way to avoid him would be an understatement. Frankly, you'd be better off asking one of his business associates that question than me."

Jess had been making feverish notes, head bent over her notebook. She looked up at that, however, surprise flickering across her face at his matter-of-fact tone. Pettifer, with the benefit of experience, was finding it easier not to judge. After all, shock and grief manifested themselves in myriad ways. He tried a different tack.

"What was he apologising for?"

Gavin shrugged.

"As he said, I suppose. Everything."

Not good enough. Pettifer dug in.

"Everything *being*?"

Gavin looked at him steadily. There was a moment's pause.

"What you're really asking me is why my father and I didn't get along. Well, the answer is at once both rather complicated and incredibly simple: we just never have. I wasn't the son he hoped for, you see. I was never interested in following in his footsteps, and that irked him greatly. He thought I should be overwhelmed with gratitude to be a Riverton, with everything that came with it. The money, the status..." he threw out an arm theatrically. "Elysian Fields, my boy! The world's your playground. So long as you follow the path I've paved for you, that is." He dropped his arm, the sarcasm in his voice fading. "It became a bit of a game, really, trying to thwart him, to get as far away from his expectations of me as possible." He exhaled. "Although, I suppose he's got his way in the end, as usual. Everything'll come to me now ... whether I want it or not."

An awkward silence settled on the room following that statement. Jess caught Pettifer's eye, and he saw the message there clear as day. She was thinking that it was a good thing that there was no suggestion of anything suspicious in Riverton's death, because Gavin was going the right way towards giving himself a strong motive. Pettifer didn't think he was unaware of the fact; he was an astute young man. Presumably, he just didn't care.

"I know I must sound heartless to you all," Gavin spoke again, his voice chiming through the stillness. "But none of you knew my father like I did. He got where he did because, at his core, he was ruthless. He'd learned to always get what he wanted, even if it came at a price to those around him. And everything he did was for himself. Nothing was ever without a catch. Probably no-one would believe me if I told them this, but it's true. I'm the only one left who knows what he was really like, underneath it all."

"Your mother..." Felicia began, leaving the question hanging in the air.

"Dead. A long time ago now. Alcoholism, before you ask.

And my brother died of leukaemia." His voice was growing tauter with each word. "As you can perhaps gauge by now, Sergeant, we weren't a happy family. Perhaps it's for the best that we're dwindling." He stood, shaking Hugo off him roughly. "I need some fresh air."

He left, banging the heavy double doors shut as he disappeared into the lamplit night. Jess moved to follow him, but Pettifer shook his head. The lad wasn't going anywhere. Best let him be for the time being.

It was then that he noticed Felicia watching him. The expression in her grey eyes was indecipherable, and he immediately felt annoyance stirring within him. He knew that in truth, it pricked his professional pride; after so many years in the force, he could read most people pretty easily, but not her. He never knew quite what she was thinking. It made him defensive, uneasy. He ended up second-guessing himself, jumping to conclusions as he tried vainly to fill the gaps. Even now, he was wondering if she wasn't silently judging him for questioning Gavin too harshly. The thought was entirely baseless, but it tugged at him nonetheless.

"He doesn't mean it, you know."

This was blurted out by Hugo, who was looking frail and exhausted and, in all honesty, more in need of the blanket and the cup of tea than Gavin had been. "He's more upset than he's letting on. He just ... doesn't show his emotions like other people, that's all. I don't want you to think..." His expression became stricken. "He's not some sort of monster..."

"We don't think that," Jess said quickly. "Do we, sir?"

"Of course not, lad," Pettifer rumbled. "Look, perhaps it's best if we call it a night for now. It's been a challenging..."

But Hugo didn't appear to have heard him. He was staring, apparently at a plasterwork festoon of harebells above the mirror, although Pettifer suspected that he wasn't seeing it at all. It was the blank look of someone suddenly overwhelmed by their thoughts.

"I don't understand how this can have happened. Just when Gavin and I … James was so *pleased* for us…"

"Wait. I thought there was no contact between Gavin and his father?"

"There … wasn't," Hugo admitted cagily.

Pettifer stared him down. Hugo's face crumpled.

"I did it for Gavin, all right? I didn't *want* to go behind his back, but…"

"But you did anyway?"

"I tried not to! But every time I brought it up he'd just get angry. Say I didn't understand. But I couldn't bear the thought of it being like this for the rest of our lives." He put his head in his hands, dislodging his grey wig. He pulled it off, revealing a line across his forehead where the white makeup ended. "Our relationship has already caused enough problems with my family; the idea of us being estranged from everyone in our lives … that's not how it's supposed to be, is it, when you fall in love? It's meant to bring people together." He looked beseechingly at Felicia, who moved towards him, put a hand on his shoulder.

"So you met him?" Pettifer pressed. "When was this?"

"Oh God, no. Not in person. I couldn't, not around here. It'd get back to Gavin in a minute. You know what this town's like. We just used to talk on the phone sometimes, that's all. I'd tell him about Gavin. I sent him a couple of photos, as he didn't have any from recent years. He seemed genuinely grateful; it was rather sweet, actually." He fiddled with a tassel on the seat cushion, then said, "It wasn't strictly true, you know, what Gavin said just now. They didn't *always* get on so badly. But after his little brother died ... well, Oliver was the apple of their father's eye. The perfect child, quite a few years younger. Gavin has a photo in his wallet of them catching butterflies together. When I asked, he said he used to take him off for long walks out into the fields, get him out of the house while their parents argued." Hugo grimaced. "Then, the week after Oliver died, James sent Gavin off to boarding school."

Jess's fair eyebrows had almost disappeared into her hairline by now. He could tell that it was taking all of her self-control not to react.

"I didn't know that," Cassie had entered the room at some point, almost uniquely silently. She looked aghast. "He never told me. God, how *awful*."

"In James's defence, I think it was a mistake made with good intentions," Hugo said quickly. "He thought he was protecting Gavin by sending him away."

Or at least, that's what he told himself, Pettifer thought privately. It was incredible the ways people could find to justify their actions, especially after the fact.

"Well, it's heartening to know that you've got such a good grip on it all," an acidic voice said from the doorway.

"*Gavin.*" Hugo started, turning puce with horror. "I didn't..."

"Know I was here? Evidently. But don't let me stop you. Do carry on. What else having I been wrong about for all of these years? You seem to know better than I do, after all."

"Don't be too hard on him, Gavin," Felicia said softly. "He's only trying to defend you."

"Well, there's no need." He stalked over to the piano, gripped the edge of it with whitened fingers. "You all want to know why my father died? Because *I* killed him, that's why!"

He looked around at them all savagely. "There. Are you all satisfied now?"

There was a stunned silence. Eventually, after a brief clearing of the throat, Pettifer was the first to speak.

"I think, sir, that perhaps you'd better explain further."

Chapter Twenty

Oone thing Felicia couldn't fault about Sergeant Pettifer was his prescient timing. The kettle was just beginning to whistle on the range when his familiar bailiff-style knock shuddered through the diminutive cottage.

"I'll get it," she said hastily, as Peter reached for his crutches, wobbling precariously on his bandaged foot. "You stay here and keep an eye on the toast."

She saw his mouth flatten mulishly as she turned away, and made an exasperated mental note to ask the doctor if there was anything which could be done to speed along the recovery period on a broken leg. Her father wasn't exactly the most patient of patients, and...

There was a crash from the kitchen behind her. She winced, fumbling with the awkward locks on the cottage's original 18th century front door. Never mind the doctor, she thought, with increasing desperation; if Western medicine couldn't do the trick, she'd go to the herbalist, the witch doctor, the *runes* ... anything if it could save their collective sanity.

It took several tugs at the door – it always swelled in hot

weather – before she found herself face-to-face with Sergeant Pettifer. Or rather, face-to-crown-of-head; he was a good couple of inches shorter than she was. Behind him, almost blocked by his poorly-suited shoulders – Sunday's version of Sergeant Pettifer, apparently, looked exactly like every other day's version – she glimpsed what was rapidly blooming into another ambrosial June day, rustling lime green canopies vivid against a cloud-dolloped sky. But a glimpse was all she was destined to get, as Pettifer stomped into the cramped hall, shutting the sunlight out behind him – both metaphorically and literally. The sombre look on his face dispelled any potential lightness of heart in an instant, reminding her why he was here. After all, this wasn't a social call. He wasn't here as her friend, but as a policeman. And policemen, on the whole, were harbingers of doom.

It must be nice for them, she thought, as she watched Pettifer exhaustedly rubbing a hand across his unshaven face, on those occasions when they were a welcome presence, bringing something good in their wake. A lost cat, or a stolen purse. They must savour those moments, brief as they were. Until they were called on to the next thing; another fight, another accident, another death.

"Breakfast, Sergeant?" Peter plunked a plate of hot buttered toast in the middle of the kitchen table, balancing on one crutch. "Tea's just mashing, if you want a cup."

"Not for me, thanks." Pettifer hefted himself into a chair with an exhale like a tyre deflating. "I've already had enough tea to sink a battleship this morning. I don't think I can stomach any more."

Peter and Felicia stared at him, agape. Even Godfrey blinked owlishly from his position on top of the Welsh dresser.

"Well, I never thought I'd hear a Yorkshireman say that,"

Peter said incredulously, pouring liquid the approximate colour and consistency of treacle into two chipped mugs. Felicia felt her insides contract in anticipation of the tannins coming their way. Technically, both father and daughter were Lincolnshire bred, but the county was enormous, and each hailed from its furthest, polarised corners. Peter's taste in tea, having been forged dangerously close to the Yorkshire border, was rather too Northern for Felicia's softer Midlands palette, but she knew better by now than to request a shorter brewing time, or, heaven forbid, an Earl Grey instead. She'd only made that mistake once since returning home, and the reception it had met with had been enough to cast a hard frost over the Serengeti.

"Yes, well, clearly no Yorkshireman ever came up against the women of Stamford before." Pettifer was eyeing up the toast, clearly trying to resist. "I couldn't get six feet through town this morning without someone dragging me into their front parlour to tell me what a *wonderful* man James Riverton was, what a loss it'll be to the community, etc." He leaned back in his chair, which squealed in protest. "Of course, what they really wanted was for me to let slip why he did it."

Felicia had been lavishly spreading marmalade onto a triangle of toast, but suddenly she found her appetite had vanished.

"How is Gavin this morning?" She asked, in a low voice.

"Still asleep when Jess checked in with Hugo earlier. The paramedics gave him something pretty strong last night."

Seeing the normally constrained, perfectly buttoned-up Gavin going to pieces hadn't been easy to watch. He'd told them everything, the words running over one another in their haste to be out in the open. How he'd found out about Hugo's contact with his father. How he'd confronted Riverton, furiously telling him exactly what he thought.

"I was ... brutal." Gavin had closed his eyes against the memory, face ashen. "I can't even repeat what I said. It's too ... I mean, I never imagined he would actually..." He'd looked at Hugo beseechingly. "I as good as strung him up myself, didn't I?" He'd begun to tremble then, the trauma finally setting in. He hadn't been in a state to say anything more after that. And now, it sounded like he wouldn't be for a while.

"Poor lad," Peter shook his head, the effect only slightly impeded by his crunching loudly on a piece of toast at the same time. Nothing dampened her father's appetite, Felicia thought dryly. Ten minutes after her mother had packed up and left him, she'd found him in the kitchen making a sandwich. She worried about many things happening to him, but wasting away certainly wasn't one of them. "What a burden to have to bear."

"It wasn't his fault, Dad," Felicia interjected.

"People are responsible for their own actions," Pettifer agreed. "Unfortunately, the human heart often doesn't see it that way. People blame themselves for these things, when in reality, it's much more complicated than that. People don't just kill themselves over one cross word." He sighed, fingers inching longingly towards the plate of toast. "Hopefully young Hugo can help him to see that. The lad seems to have his head screwed on right."

Felicia sipped her tea, trying not to wince at its stewed taste. She certainly hoped so, for Hugo's sake. She wasn't sure that their relationship could take much more strain at the moment. And if anyone deserved to be happy...

"Felicia?" Pettifer's voice broke into her thoughts. She started, the sunlit kitchen coming back into focus. Dust motes sparkled in the shafted light through the mottled panes of the window. No matter what happened, this room looked the same: cluttered, cosy, its surfaces permanently scattered with biscuit crumbs and spent tea bags no matter how many times she wiped them down. The familiar sight comforted her, grounding her back in the present.

"Sorry." She put her cup down on the table. "Were you saying something?"

"Only asking what time your auction is later." Pettifer peered at her, concern on his face. "You sure you'll be up to it? You look a little…"

"Of course." She cut him off, making a loud performance of clearing up the breakfast things to cover up the sudden defensiveness she felt. "Why wouldn't I be?"

"Er … because you found a body last night, perhaps?"

"So?" She said crisply, clacking the cups together between her fingers as she scooped them off the table. "As everyone keeps pointing out to me, it's hardly my first."

"No, but…"

"I think what the sergeant's trying to say, duck, is that no-one's exactly feeling in a festival-like mood today," Peter said sagely, taking a rare stab at reading the subtext and proving exactly why he was better suited to inanimate objects as he missed by a county mile.

"Gavin was emphatic that the fair should carry on," Felicia said neutrally. "And if that's what he wants, then we all have to do our best to put on a good show."

He'd actually seemed almost stricken at the suggestion that they do anything else. And no-one had wanted to argue with him at that point, so…

"Crackers, if you ask me." Peter supplied bluntly. "Whole thing's clearly turned the lad's brain. But I suppose it's up to him in the end; after all, it was his father." He swivelled his crutch around, leaving a rather obviously manufactured pause. Felicia could practically see him counting to five in his head before saying, "you know, if you're really not feeling the thing, I could take the auction later. Help you out. Might need a bit of help getting up onto the rostrum, of course, but after that..."

Felicia scrubbed at a stubborn tea stain on one of the mugs, trying not to hear the hope in his voice. Trying not to feel guilty at being the one about to stamp on it.

"I'll be fine. It's only a short auction; I could do it in my sleep."

Unfortunately, he wasn't so perceptive. He didn't hear the warning in her tone.

"Even so, duck, it's really no trouble. If you aren't up to it..."

"Will you both *stop* bloody saying that?" She snapped, finally pushed beyond endurance. She crashed the cup into the sink as she spoke, sending soap suds sloshing over the draining board as she gripped the cold metal edge. "I am absolutely *fine*. Perfectly capable of functioning. I'm not about to go down with a fit of the vapours like some nineteenth-century debutante. So just *leave* it, all right?"

And then she waited. For a good few moments, a stunned silence reigned behind her, and she took a certain satisfaction in the effect her little outburst of temper had had. Then Pettifer spoke.

"Felicia ... can we have a word?"

Chapter Twenty-One

His voice was gentle, but there was an ominous undertone to it which made her tense. Trying not to show it, she threw down the washcloth with a put-upon sigh.

"If you insist."

She wasn't surprised when he moved towards the front door; her father's cottage was so poky that it was impossible to conduct a private conversation anywhere within its walls, solid stone though they might be.

She'd been expecting him to steer left, heading for the relative cover of the weeping willows which lined the riverbank, but instead he carried straight on ahead, ascending the steps onto the Victorian ironwork bridge which arched gracefully across the water. He stopped in the centre, leaning his elbows on the sage green-painted railings, waiting for her to join him. It was a familiar spot for them, but also a challengingly evocative one. She was in no doubt that he'd chosen it on purpose.

"Why are you here?" She got straight to the point. "It's not to update me at all, is it? You're checking up on me."

He didn't reply straight away, instead making a show of studying the reeds beneath the crystalline surface below. When he spoke, his words were measured.

"It's pretty standard to want to check on someone who's found a body, wouldn't you say?"

"Bollocks," she declared loudly, before remembering there were children playing on the riverbank nearby. She dropped her voice. "You'll have to do better than that."

"What do you think those fish are?" He asked idly, as if she hadn't spoken. "Every time I come here, I always mean to look it up, but I never do."

"I've really no idea." Her patience was beginning to fray. "Look, why don't you just say whatever it is you came here to say? I'm sure it'll be a relief to both of us."

"It's not what I'm going to say to you. It's what you're going to say to me."

"I don't—"

"All right, you know what, let me save us both some time." He was starting to sound as impatient as her now. "At some point during this conversation, you're going to tell me that you don't think James Riverton killed himself. Correct?"

Unable to think of a convincing rebuttal, she set her jaw, looking out across the river.

"Because I know you, Felicia." He answered her next question without her even needing to ask it. "Because I know how your brain works. And because..." his voice melted into something which sounded worryingly like pity. "I was afraid of something like this. You're projecting."

That did it. She spun around, looking at him incredulously.

"I'm *what*?" She spluttered. "Have you been on some new police course or something?"

He ignored her, continuing doggedly.

"What happened before…"

"Oh, I see." The sunlight was so bright, so harsh. It was too much. She squeezed her eyes shut briefly, and at once became aware of everything else. The rustling of the willow leaves, the flapping of ducks on the water's surface, the yelping of the children as they chased one another around. The breeze on her face, so close to skin temperature that she almost couldn't feel it at all, the sensation a disconcerting one. The rapid beating of her heart. She reopened her eyes, focusing on the lopsided form of her father's cottage across the river. The chimney was leaning at such a precarious angle it was a wonder it didn't topple off the roof altogether. "You think that I'm hysterical. That what happened to Betsy has deluded my mind, turned me into some sort of fanatical suicide-denier…"

He held up two hands like clay tablets.

"No, what I *think* is that a very devious killer set up your friend's death to look like a suicide. What I *think* is you accepted that version of events despite your doubts, and that you've blamed yourself for it ever since." He paused. "And, by extension, for what happened afterwards."

She shot him a warning look, and he continued swiftly onwards.

"But Felicia, this isn't the same. We have a note…"

"We had one of those last time."

"…And a solid reason why he might have done it. Regret is a powerful motivator. For all of his outward success and popularity, he was clearly a lonely man."

"We had one of *those* last time, too. And before you say it, anyone could have put that stool there afterwards; it doesn't prove anything."

He made an exasperated sound.

"Fine, let's look at it another way. Why would anyone want

to kill him? If you listen to everyone around here, they seem to have viewed him as a candidate for beatification."

"Except Gavin."

"Yes, but Gavin's not exactly the most impartial of sources, is he? I think we need to take his opinion with a grain of salt."

Felicia shook her head.

"I don't know about that, but there was definitely something going on with Riverton. He got really defensive when I asked him about Iris Breadmore..." The memory came back to her, and she shuddered slightly. "Almost threatening. It was strange."

"You asked him—" Pettifer broke off, aghast. "Jesus *Christ*, Felicia; I said keep an eye out, that's all. Not barge around questioning people!"

"I didn't *barge* anywhere," Felicia sniffed, slightly affronted at the suggestion. "I was very subtle, as it happens."

"Evidently, seeing as he rumbled you straight away." He whistled out a breath. "How many times do I have to tell you not to put yourself in the firing line?" When she didn't answer, he threw up his hands in despair. "When was this, anyway?"

"Finally, you're asking the right question! It was last night, just before the ball. About quarter to eight."

A frown split his heavy brow.

"That's after Gavin claims they had their argument."

"Exactly. And he was hardly acting like a broken man with nothing to live for. Like I said, he was angry, defensive..." As he opened his mouth to interject, she held up a finger. "And, if that's not enough, might I remind you that he then went to the ball and spent the next three and a half hours dancing and socialising, apparently without a care in the world?"

"So he was putting on a final show. People do."

"You can't seriously believe that?" She stared at him, not

recognising the man in front of her at all. Could he even hear himself? "Don't you think it's just a bit coincidental? A supposed accident ... which, incidentally, you were the first one to call murder ... and now a suicide on the same day? And you're just ... ignoring it?"

For a moment, she saw a flicker of emotion, a wavering. Then his face closed in on itself.

"I'm not ignoring anything. But it's an urban myth that policemen are allergic to coincidences. In reality, they happen every day. And for the record, I never said that Iris Breadmore's death was murder ... I only said that I intended to carry on looking into it. But you didn't hear that; you just..." he exhaled heavily, rubbing a hand along his jaw. "This is all my fault. I should never have brought you into any of this. It was hugely irresponsible of me."

She crossed her arms over her chest.

"You weren't saying that last time, when I solved your case for you."

She was resorting to playground tactics now, but he didn't rise to the bait. Instead, he just looked back at her stonily.

"Last time's the problem. It's clouded my judgement, made me forget ... I mean, you're an *auctioneer*, for Christ's sake."

"So you're saying I'm ... what? Not reliable?"

"I'm saying you're bloody civilian!" He finally snapped, banging his fist on the iron railing. It startled a pair of moorhens below, who started making a commotion on the surface of the water. "More than that, you went through a harrowing experience only weeks ago, one which you're clearly still not over..."

She felt her own temper flare.

"Don't psychoanalyse me. I think I can be the judge of my own mind."

"Can you?" He looked at her intently. "Tell me, do you still have nightmares about that day?"

She froze, momentarily incapable of speech. He nodded.

"So do I. But the difference is that I'm trained for it. I've been here before; you haven't. You have no idea just how not all right you are just now. You probably won't until it's long behind you."

"You're not going to listen to anything I've just said, are you?" She said wearily.

"I have listened, and I'll treat it with the same consideration I've given to any other statement I've heard this morning."

He was brushing her off. The realisation burned through her, a mingling of hurt and humiliation. She swallowed, but found there was a lump in her throat she couldn't speak around, so she nodded jerkily instead.

"All right, well, I'd best be off." He touched her arm briefly. It was probably about the most contact they'd ever had. "Good luck later, all right? Maybe I'll be able to step in and watch a bit of it, if work takes me in that direction."

She found it too hard to watch him walk away. Instead, she focused on the familiar row of cottages across the river, willing herself to keep her emotions in check. She looked at that chimney, her mind ticking over ... and then, to her horror, she heard her own voice blurting out, calling after him.

"You probably won't be interested in this." Her words dripped with hurt sarcasm, and she winced inwardly. "But Iris had a fire burning in her grate the day before she died." She folded her arms, glaring at his retreating back. "I suppose that's just nothing too though. Just my *fevered* imagination, reading too much into everything again."

He hesitated briefly, but didn't break stride. And he didn't turn either. Just a single, curt dip of the head to indicate that he'd heard.

She waited until she was sure he was gone before she allowed herself to sag against the bridge, fingers biting into the flesh of her palms as she fought sudden, ridiculous tears.

So, he thought she was a liability, did he?

It wasn't exactly a new sensation for her, she reminded herself. After all, she was a woman in the very male-dominated world of antiques. She was more than used to being underestimated. Over the years, she'd come to see it as part of the challenge, almost an entertaining game, to make a show of confounding those prejudices.

She'd never thought she'd hear them coming from Pettifer, though.

Was it as he'd said, and that the last investigation had muddied the waters of what should have been a distant, purely professional relationship? Or perhaps that in itself was the problem; there should never have been a relationship at all. But being thrown together like they had been ... it had changed things. Made them friends of sorts. Made them a team. Or so she'd thought. But clearly, that had just been her delusion. The mortification which accompanied that realisation was white hot, but all the same, she sensed that it wasn't the sole reason for the way her breath was suddenly not coming so easily. It was something else Pettifer had said.

Do you still get nightmares about that day?

She felt her eyes unfocus, the starbursts of sunlight on the surface of the river blurring together into translucent orbs of memory. Blood gushing from Dexter's shoulder, soaking his geranium pink jacket. Algernon, lying still and pale on the sofa; so still her heart had almost stopped in her chest. The glint of a blade as it arced towards her...

Enough. She forced her eyes to readjust, taking in the view upriver, the busy Town Bridge and The Meadows beyond ... and tucked away to one side of them, the house where it had all happened. She couldn't quite see it from here, but she felt its presence nonetheless. For the first time, she allowed herself to wonder if it really had been the best thing, moving back here, living in the shadow of it all.

Not that it seemed to be bothering anyone but her. Algernon had his new school, his dream of getting to spend more time both with his grandfather and at the auction house, and while she knew that he thought about Betsy often – probably far more so than he admitted to – he was only twelve, and the forwards pull of life was always going to win at that age. And as for Dexter ... well, his shoulder had healed smoothly, and apart from bemoaning his tennis swing, which apparently would never be the same again, he seemed as untouched by the ordeal as he was by anything else which had happened more than fifteen minutes ago.

No, she was the only one who still had nightmares, that was for sure.

"But that's not a failing," she told herself, pushing away from the side of the bridge. "And it doesn't mean you're wrong about this."

She walked determinedly back towards the cottage, feeling suddenly resolute.

"Algernon?" She called up the stairs. "Are you dressed yet?"

A small face appeared above, encircled by a halo of unruly bronze hair.

"Yes. Why?"

"Excellent. Get your shoes on, then. We're popping out for

a minute." She paused. "There's a little something I need your help with."

Sergeant Pettifer walked heavily along the riverbank, lost in his own thoughts. He crossed Water Street, disappearing down a narrow lane between two houses. Barely a car's width wide, it was more of an alley than a true roadway, and although the odd vehicle did brave it, the cobbles below were generally quiet save for the pounding of footsteps.

Pettifer passed by a long row of cottages, each with a small garden to the front, summer flowers spilling over their neat fences. He passed a number of school buildings, with their polished burgundy and white plaques, their names bound in institutional traditions only an insider would understand. He passed the rear of St. Martin's church, with its leafy churchyard and lichen-covered headstones.

There was a shabby-looking car parked up on the side of the road, pressed against a weather-beaten stone wall. He got into it, sank into the driver's seat, and let out a weary sigh.

"Have you done it?" A voice to his left asked.

"Yes." He ran a hand over his rough, misshapen face, feeling his broken nose, the raised areas where scars had healed over. Once, he'd hated any reminder of how he looked. He'd avoided mirrors for years. But now, it didn't bother him so much. In fact, at times he almost found himself feeling proud of it. It reminded him of the somewhat unorthodox path he'd taken in life.

"And? How did she take it?"

His lips twisted.

"About as well as you'd imagine."

"You've done the right thing, Sarge." Jess's blue eyes met his own, soft and understanding. "You had no choice. There's a murderer out there."

One whose agenda was still murky, he added silently. Who could easily be planning more deaths even as they sat here talking. It didn't bear thinking about.

"I know," he admitted at last. "It doesn't make me feel any better about it though."

An image of Felicia's face filled his mind, and he winced inwardly. He'd hurt her, and he knew it. She was good at hiding her feelings, but not that good. Not to someone who knew her. The knowledge made his stomach churn with guilt, and he cursed himself for caring so much. It was his job to protect her, but he could only do that properly with a sense of distance and perspective. Clearly, he'd lost both of those somewhere along the way.

This was why the precious line between professionalism and friendship should never be crossed, he reminded himself fiercely. It could only ever cause problems.

"All right," Jess was briskly flipping over the pages of her notebook in search of a crisp new canvas, her mind evidently already onto the next thing. "So what's our next move?"

She almost sounded quite excited. He wished he could summon up some of her youthful exuberance. Instead, he harrumphed, then immediately felt older than ever.

"We need to find out who might have wanted to kill Stamford's most popular man." As Jess looked dubious, he continued, "Even saints have enemies, Winters. Start with a general background check. History, financials..." He hesitated, suddenly realising where he was going with all of this. "Unless, of course ... look, I shouldn't just assume..." By continuing to investigate, they would be going directly against

Heavenly's orders. He had no right to expect her help; in the sparest terms, he was putting her career at risk just by broaching the subject with her. "If you're not comfortable with this..."

She cut him off emphatically.

"Sir, you don't even need to ask."

He was well aware of that, just as he knew exactly what she'd say. She was fiercely loyal; it was a trait which was admirable, but not always in her best interests. He wanted to make sure she was thinking this through, so he persisted, "You have to look out for yourself, lass. Think about your future. I'm an old hand; it doesn't matter so much to me if I get caught. The worst they can do is retire me early." Or put him on traffic cone duty, but it wasn't exactly as if he was in line for promotion anyway. His career had stalled a long while ago; his idiosyncratic investigative style had seen to that. But Jess ... she had so much potential. She could go anywhere. Provided he didn't screw it all up for her, that was.

"I've made my choice," Jess insisted, obviously guessing the line of his thoughts. "So there's no point trying to convince me otherwise. We'll just waste time. Besides, Heavenly's not going to find out. He's never even around." She tapped her notebook pointedly, signalling a return to the matter at hand. "Anyone else you want me to look at, while I'm snooping?"

She knew him well, knew he was already turning over potential suspects in his mind. Many officers would have waited for the hard data, but he worked on instinct.

"Yes," he said immediately. "Tony Chandler."

She stared at him in astonishment.

"*He* was at the ball last night? I'm finding it hard to picture that."

"Exactly. I want to know why he was there. Because it certainly wasn't for dancing."

"Okay." Jess was scribbling in her notebook with a minute stub of pencil. Why the woman wouldn't just get a pen was beyond him. "Who else?"

Pettifer thought for a moment.

"That gangly boy was down in the cellars last night with his girlfriend. It was just before we found Riverton's body. It might have just been a case of wrong place, wrong time, but…"

"They were on the scene, so we can't rule them out," Jess agreed. "You think they might have been in it together?"

"Too early for that sort of speculation, Winters," he said, with gentle sternness, and she flushed sheepishly. "But let's cross the t's and check them out."

"What about the group who stormed the ball last night?" She asked, recovering herself. "The anti-fair lot. Surely they're worth a look … if we can find out who any of them are, that is."

"Unfortunately I wasn't there, or I might have been able to identify a few of them," Pettifer said ruefully. "Just find out what you can without arousing too much suspicion. See if there's anyone who raises flags."

"Apart from that creepy librarian, you mean?" Jess pulled a face. "He's their ringleader, isn't he?"

Pettifer was internally debating the ethics of referring to a suspect as 'creepy', and wondering if, as her mentor, he really ought to reprimand her for it – even though, as it happened, he fully agreed with her – but before he could respond either way, Jess's phone pinged. She glanced at it, and her face fell.

"It's Heavenly. He wants to know where I am. Apparently he wants to talk to Drummond." Her eyes widened in horror.

"How did he…" She dropped her voice to a hiss. "D'you think he's bugged the car? That he's listening in?"

Pettifer tried not to look too amused by her flights of imagination.

"Calm yourself, Winters. It's a coincidence. He'll just be box-ticking, that's all. Remember that Drummond was the last person who we know saw Riverton alive." He drummed his fingers against the steering wheel, thinking. "Go with him, but don't say much. And certainly don't question Drummond. We don't want Heavenly getting wind of what we're doing." He started the engine after a couple of tries. The car, like everything else in his life, was on the tired side. "I'll drop you back at the station. You can tell him we've been patrolling."

She leaned back in her seat, regarding him quizzically.

"And where will you be, while I'm engaging in this subterfuge?"

"Iris Breadmore's rental cottage." Pettifer's hands tightened around the wheel. "Felicia said…"

He trailed off.

"You still really trust her, don't you?" Jess said softly.

"Yes," he said simply, as the car finally responded, lurching forwards with a crunch of gears. "For my sins, I do."

Chapter Twenty-Two

"Are you sure we should we doing this, Mum?" Algernon gazed at the stone columns which towered above them, a dubious expression on his face. "It looks closed."

"Of course it's closed. It's Sunday." Felicia reached over the top of his head and knocked on the door again, more forcefully this time. "But you heard what the neighbours said. This is where he'll be."

Most places, Felicia thought wryly, housed their libraries in singularly unprepossessing buildings: a brutalist concrete block, or a portacabin. Stamford's, on the other hand, was a miniature pastiche of a Roman temple. Wide stone steps floated towards its classical façade, across which Doric columns marched imperiously. Anywhere else, and it probably would have looked ridiculous. Here, however, one had the sense that anything *else* would have looked strange.

"If he is, I don't think he can hear us," Algernon said. He tugged at her arm. "Come on, Mum. I promised Grandad we'd be there to set up for the auction in plenty of time."

It was telling that her father had more faith in a twelve-year-old's capacity to manage his precious auction than he did in hers, Felicia thought flatly. Nonetheless, Algernon did have a point. She checked the dainty Art Deco watch on her wrist – a wedding present from Dexter, and thus technically a symbol of their marriage, but she hadn't been able to bring herself to slough it off along with the rings and the marital title – and bit her lip nervously. Behind them, the High Street was quickly beginning to fill up with festival-goers.

"All right," she said reluctantly. "Maybe we'll have to…"

As she said it, a rattling sound emitted from beyond the closed door, and it scraped open an inch. A slither of suspicious face peered out at them.

"What do you want? Can't you see we're closed?"

As welcomes went, it wasn't the most encouraging. But Felicia pressed on.

"Actually, it was you we were hoping to see, Mr. Drummond." Felicia put her hands on Algernon's shoulders and gave her most charming smile. "We wondered if you could spare us a minute?"

"Me?" What began as a harrumph of derision swiftly morphed into a hacking cough. Felicia kept her smile fixed and fought the natural impulse to step back. "What on earth d'you want to see *me* for? No-one ever wants to see me."

If this was the way he greeted everyone, it wasn't much to wonder at. Felicia took a breath, forced her smile wider.

"Maybe if we just could come inside?"

He scowled at her for a minute, then obviously realised she wasn't about to go away. He sighed dustily.

"Fine. If you must." He opened the door just wide enough to let them pass through, whisking it shut quickly after them as though afraid that someone else might take advantage of the opportunity and sneak in on their tail. "But

I can't stop. I'm working on a very important project just now."

"Of course." Felicia gave Algernon a nudge, then, when he seemed reluctant to move forward, another, more forceful one. "We understand that you're a busy man. Don't we, Algie?"

Algernon gave her a disbelieving look. She raised an eyebrow at him in return, warning him to play along.

The interior of the library was disappointing, given the dazzling promise of grandeur it exhibited from the outside. To a local, it wasn't such a mystery; after all, the façade was just that. A portico, or gateway, originally leading to the meat market. It had only been filled in much later, sides and a roof added to make it into a useable building.

The result was that from within, the library looked much the same as any other, with fluorescent strip lights suspended from a low ceiling over rows of white shelves, the books within bathed in a washed-out bluish glow. Laminated tables were dotted about here and there, where on any given weekday the elderly residents of the town could be found perusing the newspapers and furtively sucking on a boiled sweet under the watchful eyes of the librarians. Their favoured table, Felicia had noticed, was right next to the rack of Mills and Boons, and she'd often wondered if that was a telling choice on their part, or a show of impish humour from some long-departed library employee.

Through the swing doors, she could see the children's section, a welcoming space complete with colourful bean bags and a giant paper caterpillar sprawling across one wall.

Drummond saw her looking and made a sound between a grumble and a cat coughing up a hairball.

"Absurd, isn't it? A library should be a place of learning."

Felicia decided it was better not to venture an opinion.

Instead, she and Algernon followed obediently, until Drummond bellowed, without breaking stride, *"French!"*

Algernon jumped, looking this way and that as though anticipating a battalion of blue-coated soldiers to emerge from behind a bookcase. Or perhaps a giant croissant; her son had a vivid imagination.

"Your name," Drummond barked, turning to face him. He had a peculiar habit of tilting his chin and looking at one as though over a pair of spectacles, even though he wasn't wearing any. "It's French, you know. People always think it's Victorian – damned Oscar Wilde – but…"

"I know," Algernon nodded. "I'm always telling people that."

Drummond's eyes gleamed with sudden interest. Felicia had the sense that Algernon had passed some sort of test.

"Indeed? A smart young man, I see. You like history, then? Perhaps you'd be interested in some of my works. Come with me."

The followed him to a dark, dingy corner, as far away from the main hub as it was possible to get. Drummond motioned down at the bottom shelf proudly, where a curling array of bound pamphlets were propped. Felicia could just make out some of the titles: *Sewage Solutions in Victorian Stamford. Granite Setts: A Study. A Comparison of Pork Ratios 1839-42 (Itemised by Piemaker).*

"This all looks … fascinating," she managed weakly, wondering how on earth she was going to get out of this one. "It's just … well, Algernon was *really* hoping to learn more about Fitzwilliam Trendlehart, weren't you, darling?"

Algernon, still staring in horror at the pamphlets, needed no prompting this time. He nodded so fervently that she heard his neck crick.

"Oh." Drummond looked so crestfallen that Felicia was almost inclined to feel sorry for him. "I see."

"I was told that you're the expert on all things local history," she said, aiming for a reverent tone.

Flattery clearly worked as anticipated, because he seemed to perk up a bit.

"Well, yes, I suppose I am, rather." He puffed out his pigeon chest, stroking a hand over the front of his claret-coloured waistcoat. "It's easy to be seduced by more glamorous subjects, of course. The bright lights, and all of that. But some of us have to do the real work." He gave a rasping sniff. "Unfortunately, Stamford seems to be attracting the wrong sort at the moment. I hear that Treasure Seeker bounder is still in town. The man's a disgrace to the profession, if you ask me."

Felicia put a hand over Algernon's mouth as he opened it to speak. Luckily, Drummond seemed oblivious. He was lovingly rearranging his pamphlets.

"So, you want to know about Trendlehart, do you? Well, I warn you, you won't get the scripted version from me. I'm not interested in inventing a new town hero."

"I thought he was supposed to be a great philanthropist."

"Of course." Drummond was disparaging. "That's what they *want* you to think. The whole thing's been cooked up by a lot of self-interested parties."

Felicia thought back to Iris's speech, the accusations she'd read in there.

"So it's true then? That a maid threw herself in the lake following an ill-fated affair with her master? And that her sweetheart, the groom, hanged himself shortly afterwards? And then…"

"Whoa, there!" Drummond flung up sinewy hands.

"Where the blazes did you hear all that? What a load of old claptrap!"

"So it's not true?"

"Of course it's not! Does it sound true to you?"

"Well … no." To be honest, she'd always had her suspicions on that front. After all, it was a ridiculous list; surely no man could have been involved in that much intrigue. You'd need more than one lifetime just to fit it in.

"The truth, I'm afraid, is probably the least palatable option to most," Drummond fiddled with the watch chain suspended from his waistcoat pocket. He was in constant nervy, jerky motion, like a skittish woodland animal. "And that's that Fitzwilliam Trendlehart was neither a great man, nor a particularly wicked one. He was just a rather dull aristocrat. Yes, he made a few charitable donations here and there, but nothing more than was expected for a man in his position. Certainly no great heroic leaps of philanthropy. Equally, he no doubt had his fair share of dalliances and minor scandals, but again, that was what they did in those days." He scowled. "I bet you read it in The Bugle, didn't you? It sounds like their brand of scuttlebutt. Well, I'll be having strong words with them. That woman's gone too far this time."

"Caroline Boughton?" He hadn't seemed too enamoured with her last night, come to think of it. "I'd have thought you'd be encouraging her. After all, she's doing her bit to disrupt the fair. Isn't that what you want?"

"I want the truth, not sensationalism." He gave her that over-the-invisible-glasses look again, which was quite a feat considering she practically towered over him. "Now listen, I know that to you young people this probably all sounds harsh, but the Georgian Fair is no good for this town. It cheapens its noble history, and it leaves a trail of devastation in its wake. It's almost as though the town itself is rejecting it, telling us it doesn't want it."

Felicia looked at him, starting to feel wary. Stamford, like any small country town, had its fair share of unconventional types, but she was beginning to question the wisdom of locking themselves in here alone with him.

Drummond was frowning to himself. "I tried to tell Riverton this last night, of course. I tried to warn him. But he won't have paid the slightest heed; his sort never do."

Felicia reminded herself that Drummond wouldn't know about Riverton's death yet. She had to be careful how she trod from here.

"You ... had words, then?" She dropped her voice slightly; Algernon had grown bored and wandered off to look at some books, but she couldn't see him, and he might be just behind the nearest shelf. "After you left together?"

"We had a friendly discussion. Like I said, I tried to warn him. I don't know what he's playing at, but it'll come to no good."

"What do you mean?"

Drummond looked at her thoughtfully for a moment, then sighed.

"I suppose it's not my job to keep his secrets. He was the one who pushed to have Iris Breadmore invited back to the fair this year." At her obvious surprise, he gave a reedy, humourless smile. "How else do you think it got through the council? She caused quite the ruckus last time she was here."

"Yes, what happened back then?" It was a bold move, asking so openly, but Felicia deemed it worth the risk. Drummond didn't seem the discreet type, and he certainly had no loyalties. She hoped he might be the one to tell her. "It seems to be something of a town secret."

He looked at her, and she immediately got the impression that he was much shrewder than he appeared. He knew she wasn't really here for the reasons she'd claimed. For an awkward moment, she thought he was going to say as much, but instead he obviously decided to humour her for a little longer.

"There were several instances, I recall. Abusive behaviour towards the staff at the hotel, almost missing her talk entirely then turning up intoxicated ... it was all very embarrassing for the organisers." He paused. "And of course, there was Edith. Now there's someone who certainly won't have been pleased to see Iris Breadmore back in town. Not after what that woman did to her."

He broke off, waiting for her to ask. Apparently, he was enjoying himself in some strange way. But if he told her what she wanted to know, Felicia was willing to indulge his whims.

"What happened?"

"Why, she ruined her life. Edith's husband was an alcoholic, you see. Sober for ten years ... until Iris came to town. She persuaded him to keep her company at the hotel bar ... the next thing, he was off the wagon. Never got back on it again." He pursed his lips. "Edith got rid of him eventually, but by then, he'd frittered away everything, including most of the business savings. She's been fighting to stay out of the bankruptcy courts ever since." He stared at Felicia reproachfully. "So you see, whatever it is you might be insinuating, there are plenty of people other than me who have a grievance against the fair. To trifle with the past ... it can be a dangerous thing."

"I ... see." She wasn't sure she did, exactly, but it seemed like what he wanted to hear.

"Do you?" The next thing she knew, he'd stepped forwards,

until his face was very close to her own. "This town ... it has a unique history. One which needs to be protected."

He was looking at her with an intensity in his colourless eyes, as though trying to see straight into her mind. She swallowed, feeling faintly uncomfortable. Then, suddenly, he shook his head, moving away, and the atmosphere dissipated.

"No," he said quietly, and there was something like regret in his voice. "I had thought you might understand. But I was mistaken. I can see you don't."

She had the sense that she'd failed him in some way, but she wasn't quite sure how. All she knew was that a wall had come down. She wouldn't get any more out of him, she could tell.

"I need to continue with my work now," he said abruptly, proving her suspicions right. "I've wasted quite enough time as it is." He began to hustle them both out, flapping like an agitated pigeon. "If you want information, you should come on the days the library is open. The times are clearly displayed outside."

The door closed behind them, with rather more alacrity than was perhaps necessary. Felicia could hear the bolts being drawn across hurriedly, scraping into their sockets.

"Well," she managed brightly. "What an ... *interesting* man."

Algernon eyed her disbelievingly.

"He was weird, Mum."

Algernon's choice of adjective was undoubtedly more correct, but Felicia didn't think it would be a very good example to admit as much.

"I'd say more eccentric," she said. "And there's nothing wrong with that. It's a thoroughly English trait, eccentricity. No-one else does it quite like we do."

Algernon didn't look convinced.

"You know he's written an entire pamphlet on Stamford's old public toilets?"

The man did seem to have an obsession with sewerage, Felicia marvelled.

"Well, I suppose someone has to take an interest in these things," she said weakly. "As he said, it's history too."

She placed a hand between Algernon's slight shoulder blades, turning him away from the door.

"Did you get what you wanted, anyway?" At her look, he sighed in that world-weary way he had, the one which was more suited to someone of seventy than twelve. "Obviously we weren't there for my education." When she didn't answer, he pressed again. "I *know* there's been another murder. There's no point pretending. Do you think he's a suspect?"

Felicia froze mid-step. Did she? Trust Algernon to cut right to the heart of the matter.

As usual, she'd been acting on a sort of instinct, the gauzy, enchanted skein of feeling which had always materialised at life's most vital moments, drawing her where she needed to go. Now, though, she forced herself to ask the questions, to follow her own logic. Why were they *really* here?

The answer rose up easily, like bubbles through water.

Because Drummond was the obvious loose thread in the tapestry. The one which invited plucking at. He was the most vocal opponent of the Georgian Fair. Clearly, he wanted it stopped. Iris Breadmore had been on the cusp of making that happen, or at the very least, seriously upsetting the apple cart.

Could they have been in it together? They seemed unlikely bedfellows, but it was surprising what a common goal could do to unite people. And talking to Drummond had at least given her a clearer idea of what the motivation behind that goal might have been, at least from Iris's side. She'd been struggling to imagine why a nationally successful historian would bother herself with causing such a fuss over what amounted to a fairly small-fry local personage. Not to mention why she'd choose to do so in such a public, embarrassing way, one which could have potentially backfired on her badly. After all, the resulting scandal would have rocked her sweet, grandmotherly image no end. Of course, there was always the 'no publicity is bad publicity' line of reasoning, and perhaps she'd calculated the potential boost to her ratings as worth the risk, but...

But now, here was another, more tantalising solution. A desire for revenge on the town which had tossed her out so unceremoniously years before. Humiliation for humiliation. An eye for an eye. Her mind flipped back to the last photograph she could recall of the woman, gracing the cover of a newspaper supplement. She'd been perched like a frothy, pastel-coloured poodle amongst teetering stacks of lusterware teacups. Just looking at it had been enough to make the teeth ache. And yet ... there'd been something steely in the doe-like blue eyes, the set of the rose-pink lips. Felicia had had the impression of a woman who was a lot sharper on the inside than her sugary shell would imply.

Could she see Iris killing someone? Probably. But Iris was the one who was dead; in which case, it would have to be Drummond who killed her. A falling-out among thieves, perhaps? After all, they had no way of knowing what she actually would have said, had she the chance to get up on that stage; what if she'd got cold feet at the last moment, told Drummond she was pulling out? Would that have been enough to drive him to murder? Felicia summoned up an image of the man they'd just left behind, puttering around in the darkened shell of the library. Clearly, he had a passionate temper, beneath all of that tweed, but was he cold and calculating enough to be a murderer? To be honest, it was difficult to imagine, but then she'd had to learn the hard way that anyone could become a killer if suitably provoked.

And then there was Riverton. Where would *he* fit into all of this? He was more than capable of doing the necessary provoking; she knew that firsthand. If he'd found out what Drummond had done ... could that explain the fear she'd sensed in him last night, the edginess which had underscored – and perhaps even provoked – his threatening behaviour towards her when he realised she was asking questions about Iris's death? Because he knew for a fact that she'd been murdered, and by whom?

By now, Felicia's head was spinning, and she was beginning to feel no small measure of despair. Every question just seemed to sprout about a dozen more, with nothing firm or concrete to grab hold of anywhere. Everything she'd just thought was pure conjecture, wild stabs in the dark which didn't seem to be narrowing down the field a single jot. The truth was still the same as it had been yesterday; anyone could have done it, and, as it stood, for a myriad of potential reasons. It was a disheartening realisation, not improved by the rumble of an engine behind her as a sleek black car swept ostentatiously in front of the library steps.

Chapter Twenty-Three

I f Felicia could have groaned out loud, she would have done, but the passenger door was already opening. Jess hopped out, bright blue eyes widening as she spotted Felicia and Algernon standing there. She opened her mouth, but as she did so, there was an imperious rapping from the interior of the car. Clamping her lips shut, she scuttled around to the driver's side, hastily opening the door and standing aside to allow a glossy black brogue to alight on the cobbles. A pinstriped silver leg followed, then a pinstriped silver body, then a familiarly pointed, fox-like face ... one which was, to Felicia's dismay, already looking straight in her direction.

"Ms. Grant." Detective Chief Inspector Heavenly stepped forwards, leaving Jess to close the car door behind him like a chauffeur. Felicia half expected her to doff her cap. "Fancy seeing you here."

The words were light, cordial even, but Felicia knew to look past the impeccable, urbane exterior if she wanted to see the truth. She risked a glance into his eyes and saw the anger lurking there.

Only one thing to be done, she decided swiftly. Brazen it out.

"DCI Heavenly," she said breezily. "What a charming coincidence."

He bared pearly teeth, and Felicia tried not to blink. Despite his antagonism, it was impossible not to be dazzled; he really was an astonishingly beautiful man, from his mercury-coloured hair to the eerie smoothness of his skin. Like a fallen angel.

"A strange day to be at the library," he remarked. "You must have forgotten it's Sunday."

Over his shoulder, Jess was looking increasingly uncomfortable. She'd begun to twist the little silver moon in her earlobe, around and around.

"We did." Felicia put an arm around Algernon's shoulders, squeezed in a way which would have looked reassuring to an observer but was in actual fact a warning. He'd understand. He was supremely quick when it came to the unspoken; in fact, he could pick up a tacit cue much faster than an articulated one. "Don't know what we were thinking. We got our days all mixed up, didn't we, Algie?" She looked between the two police officers. "I didn't take you two for library buddies. Let me guess..." She tapped her chin thoughtfully. "Bodice rippers?"

Jess gave her a look which was half warning, half abject pleading.

"We're here to see Mr. Drummond," Heavenly said shortly. There was a vein beginning to pulse in his right temple; a small imperfection in an otherwise flawless canvas, the tiniest sign of a temper which was just a bit too controlled to be entirely safe. "His neighbours told us he would likely be here. They seemed rather surprised to be asked, in fact. If I were of a more suspicious nature, I might even wonder if they hadn't already answered that question once this morning." His eyes bored into her, and despite herself, she felt an uneasy chill run down her spine.

"A good thing you're not, then," Felicia said lightly. She looked past him, at Jess, directing her next question to the PC even though she knew it would irritate Heavenly no end. "Why do you want to talk to Drummond? I thought it was an open-and-shut..."at the last moment, she remembered Algernon beside her. "Er ... passing."

"You *can* say suicide, Mum." Algernon rolled his eyes. "And death too. I'm not a child."

"Nonetheless, we must be seen to be doing our best," Heavenly said silkily. "Such a *fine* man, a true *pillar* of the community." He gave a sorrowful, and entirely staged-looking, shake of the head. "Took his responsibilities to the town seriously right to the end, even dancing through the night of the ball. Truly remarkable."

If he'd cared that much about the Georgian Fair, Felicia thought privately, he'd hardly have hanged himself right in the middle of it. But there was no point saying such. She knew Heavenly too well by now to waste the breath. If he'd decided he didn't want the deaths to be suspicious, then that was that. She supposed that a murderer at large during an event which drew thousands of people wouldn't exactly look good on his resume. And to Stamford's new DCI, image was everything.

Algernon looked dismayed.

"So, you're not going to investigate, then?"

"Dear boy, there's nothing to investigate," Heavenly spluttered, finally beginning to lose his composure. "It was a tragedy, yes, but we mustn't lose perspective. I understand that you had a ... traumatic experience," this conceded reluctantly, as though it was of the highest inconvenience. "But not every death is suspicious."

"But my mum doesn't think Mr. Riverton killed himself." Algernon persisted. His face had taken on that sweetly stubborn look which made her maternal heart both glow and sink simultaneously. She suspected he hadn't taken kindly to being patronised. "And she's usually right about these things." He paused, then said pointedly. "She was last time."

"Oh, she *is*, is she?" Heavenly sounded strained, although he was clearly trying hard to maintain his composure in a public space. "Well, how ... *reassuring* that is to know."

If he'd been furious before, he was practically livid now. Felicia decided it was probably time to make a move before she and Algernon both ended up arrested. She had visions of having to ask Peter to bail them out. Or, God forbid, Dexter. She'd never live that down.

"Well, come along, Algie," she said brightly. "Best leave the police to their work. We'll have to come back to the library another day." She gave a rather strained smile. "How foolish of me to get so mixed up. If I'm not careful, I'll forget my head one of these days."

It was only as they were walking away that she heard his reply, soft and menacingly lustrous.

"Yes, one really *must* be careful, Ms. Grant. You never know what might happen ... otherwise."

She almost faltered, but she didn't. Instead, she carried on walking, head high. But the arm around Algernon squeezed just that little bit tighter nonetheless.

Chapter Twenty-Four

The auction room thrummed with activity. Margaret Creaton browsed slowly between the long tables laden with lots, waiting for something to catch her eye. She'd done this many times before, and she knew to take her time; it had to be something just right. Something special.

Having said that, this was unlike any viewing she'd been to previously. The room was filled with costume-clad men and women. Margaret was an island of beige in a sorbet-hued sea, disapproving and incredulous at the circus going on around her. She didn't believe in dressing up. If people had nothing better to do of a weekend than truss themselves up in ridiculous costumes like something out of a pantomime ... well, she didn't know what the world was coming to, she really didn't.

She was tutting out loud, she realised. Colin glanced at her cautiously as he trailed beside her. She could tell he was wondering why they were here, even if he didn't dare to actually ask. Usually, it was he who wanted to come to the auctions, to look at his precious trains. But there was no toy section here today. Margaret ignored him, as she often did. She found it the best thing; looking at him only made her feel the bitter taste of disappointment and disillusionment all the more keenly.

Colin Creaton hadn't been her first choice of husband, nor her second. Margaret doubted he'd have been her 75th, if it had been up to her. But he was what she'd got, and in time, she'd learned to live with it. Away went dreams of art and travel, replaced by jam, Jerusalem, and a house full of toy trains. The trains she'd managed to relegate to the shed – along with Colin, for as much of the day as she could manage – but the space they'd left hadn't been filled by anything more satisfying.

These days, Margaret didn't have dreams. She had vices.

The penny toffees she kept in an old tea caddy marked 'knitting needles—mismatched', safe from Colin's bumbling attempts at tidying. Tuesday mornings, when she was supposedly at a Citizens of Stamford meeting but in reality she went into town and bought herself a lottery ticket and a large mocha with all the trimmings. She'd sit and savour it, taking her time, spooning whipped cream into her mouth and thinking about what she'd do with the money if she won.

And of course, there were the things she stole. Those were her biggest vice of all. Her treasures.

Not that any of them were that valuable. They couldn't be; their absence would have been noted if they were. They weren't even particularly interesting or unique. She chose her items for the thrill of the taking over anything else. They'd been small at first, naturally, when she was still learning the ropes. But over time, the game had become stale. It had almost been *too* easy. And so, she'd started making it more of a challenge.

Colin gave that irritating little wavering cough he had, the one which made her silently scream inside. That cough had been the soundtrack to her life for almost forty years, and like all minor quirks, it had become a totem of bigger resentments, deeper unhappiness.

She could see him out of the corner of her eye, bobbing in and out of her vision as he scuttled to keep up. He was wearing his anorak, as he always did regardless of the weather, the toggles pulled taut beneath his weak chin. It gave her a certain vindictive thrill to know that *he* was the one who looked suspicious, while in reality he was innocent as a lamb. No, it was she they needed to watch out for. She, the bored wife who trailed her husband around the auction viewing days, complaining loudly about how *long* it was all taking, and when *would* they be going home, *surely* he didn't need another blasted train ... and all the while, she would be slipping her chosen treasure into her pocket, or under her arm. Right beneath the noses of everyone. It had given her such a buzz, the audacity of it. Such a sense of power, of *superiority*, to know how easily she could manipulate people's attention, play on their expectations.

That's why she'd wanted to come today. She'd hoped it might calm her nerves, give her a boost. But something was wrong; it wasn't working like it usually did. She waited in vain for her fingers to itch, the familiar tingle. But nothing was speaking to her.

The magic was gone, and she knew exactly who'd taken it.

Two months ago, she'd come home to find that woman standing in her room of treasures. And with a few words, her world had been blown apart.

Someone knew her secret.

After she'd left, Margaret hadn't been able to stop shaking

for almost half an hour. Suddenly, it hadn't been thrilling any more. When Margaret looked at her treasures now, she no longer felt pride. She just felt nauseous. Frankly, she wanted the things out of the house, as far away from her as possible, but it was too risky to get rid of them.

She'd been waiting on tenterhooks ever since. Waiting to find out the price of silence.

But so far, no instructions had come.

Margaret spotted a distinctive bronze head up on the rostrum, and her lips turned down at the corners. She was almost inclined to feel sorry for Felicia Grant. Because whatever she was going to be made to do, the auctioneer was almost certainly going to be the target of it. It didn't take a great leap of deduction to work that much out.

At once, being here felt wrong, sordid. Margaret almost felt ashamed of her presence, as though she were a voyeur of sorts, watching an impending car crash.

"Colin," she snapped. "Come on. We're leaving."

He looked woefully puzzled.

"But I thought … you said you wanted…"

"*Do* stop stuttering, Colin. Do I have to repeat everything several times?" She clamped her bag under her arm. It was almost empty, ready to be filled with treasures. But there were no treasures here anymore. She looked around the room distastefully. "There's nothing here I want."

And she stalked out, Colin trailing pitifully in her wake.

Chapter Twenty-Five

"Here are the selling sheets for you." Amelia handed Felicia a hefty wad of papers. "Are you almost ready to go up?"

Felicia looked at the rostrum, which hulked over them like a behemoth. A cross between a pulpit and a stage, it dominated the saleroom in which they stood. For many, it might have seemed intimidating, to have to stand up there, but to her, it was a safe space, as comfortable and familiar as an old, favourite armchair. It was one of the few places on Earth where she felt truly in command, where she knew exactly what she was doing. Up there, unpredictability didn't faze her; it was all just part of the complicated dance that was a live auction. A dance she knew and loved by heart.

She tested the weight of the gavel in her hand. Her favourite, worn smooth to the shape of her palm. No-one else had used it in the years she'd been gone. An auctioneer's gavel was precious, personal thing; an extension of your arm for hours at a time, you got to know each other, understand each other. This gavel would never feel right to anyone else who picked it up; it only fitted her.

"I'm ready if you are." Felicia looked searchingly at her young assistant. "Are you sure you're going to be okay to manage on your own? It'll be a challenge."

Amelia was a rare gem, a local girl who'd been working as a saleroom assistant at the auction since she was in her mid teens. Now she was away at university for much of the time, but she still came back to work in the holidays, and her knowledge of the business made her invaluable. If it weren't for her, they would have had to cancel today's sale altogether; with Hugo missing, she was the only experienced staff member they had. Of course, it would have been different if Betsy were still...

Felicia stopped herself before she could finish that thought, forcing herself to look around the room instead. It was something she always did before an auction; it was important to observe, to get the lay of the land, see who was here. That would usually give an indication as to what the mood would be, how the bidding would flow, who would bounce off one another as old rivalries resurfaced. The world of antiques was a small one, and it positively crackled with dynamics. Everyone automatically – and quite naturally – assumed that the success of an auction was about the lots on offer, but in reality, it had just as much to do with the people present. That, and an artful auctioneer who knew how to play the notes of the room. Who understood that their job was a game of psychology as much as anything else.

An auction audience tended to be divided between business and pleasure; couples and families out for a coffee and a morning's entertainment rubbing up against brooding dealers whose livelihood depended upon getting the right item at the right price. It was an odd mix, the lively, sociable atmosphere underscored by intensity and even desperation. Although, of course, today wasn't an ordinary auction. It was a charity do, an event; everyone was here for the spectacle. Those who bid would do so purely in the spirit of altruistic fun; as a result, prices would be artificially high, and of no interest to professional dealers whose profit margins were often calculated to the nearest pence.

Having said that, she could see one of them here. David 'Dodger' Wells – a dealer of the most old-school breed, and her father's bête-noir. Technically, he was banned from attending auctions at Grant's, after several dozen transgressions, but that didn't seem to stop him. He sprawled in the front row now, flat cap pulled down over his eyes, the grubby overcoat he always seemed to wear no matter the weather and a newspaper occupying the seat next to him. He was regarding the pastel-clad festival-goers around him with a mixture of suspicion and derision. Felicia made a note to keep an eye on him, as she always did, but she doubted he'd cause her much trouble today. He wouldn't be able to afford anything, for one thing.

"I'll be fine," Amelia said reassuringly. "You might need to go a bit more slowly than usual so I can keep up, but we'll manage it."

"You won't have to," a voice behind them said.

"*Hugo*," Felicia admonished. "You shouldn't be here."

He looked shocking, she noted, with a jolt. She wondered if he'd slept at all. He'd obligingly donned his Georgian Fair costume, although it somehow already seemed to be hanging off his frame, despite the fact it had been tailored to fit. It was as though he'd shrunk overnight.

"You need me," Hugo insisted. "So I'm here. End of story."

Felicia looked at Amelia, who shrugged helplessly.

"All the same," she said gently. "Don't you think you should be at home today? With Gavin?"

"Gavin's gone out," Hugo said shortly. "So there's no point in me being there."

"Out?" Felicia stared at him. Where could he possibly have gone today?

Ostensibly Hugo heard the silent question, because he answered.

"To the Georgian Fair." His face was shuttered. "Where else? He's adamant that he needs to oversee the rest of it. Apparently no-one else can do it. I tried to stop him, but..." he sighed. "I get that he needs something to fixate on, to distract him, but this just seems..." He trailed off, then shook himself. "You know what, he's a grown man. He can look after himself." As Felicia opened her mouth, he held up a hand. "Nope. For the next hour, I don't want to talk about anything but auctions, all right?" He thought. "And maybe tea. But nothing else."

Felicia and Amelia nodded warily.

"Where's your dad, anyway?" Hugo was already busying himself at the side of the rostrum. "I wouldn't have thought he'd miss this."

"He's ... gone to see a woman about a costume." Felicia shuffled the selling sheets in her hands, although they hardly needed tidying. But it meant she didn't have to look either of them in the eye.

Technically, it was the truth, but even as she said it she knew it was a mistake. She could feel their disbelief boring into the crown of her bent head.

"A costume?" Amelia said slowly. "You mean, to dress up in? *Your* dad?"

"Oh look, is that the time?" Felicia made an overly acted

show of checking her watch. "We need to start, or we'll over-run our slot." She squeezed her skirts up onto the rostrum, switching automatically to her auctioneer's voice to address the assembled crowd.

"Good afternoon, everyone, and welcome to our special Georgian auction here at Grant's. I'll start by saying that while we've had to take a few liberties here and there with history ... myself for one thing," she indicated her dress with a wry smile. "The auction process you're about to take part in is very similar to how it would have been 250 years ago, and it's really quite simple. If you want to bid, just raise your hand. All lots are sold as seen and to take away at the end of the auction. Any questions? All right, let's begin."

For the first twenty minutes or so, it was one of the nicest auctions she'd ever run. The bids were flowing generously, as she'd expected, and there was a lot of good-natured banter as people competed against one another. But as time wore on, something began to bother her. The saleroom was filling steadily, people slipping in through the doors at the back until there was no space even to stand. In itself, this wouldn't have unsettled her; after all, this was supposed to be a show of sorts, and people were more than welcome to watch.

The problem was that they weren't watching the auction.

They were watching *her*. Staring, whispering to one another behind their hands. Hugo and Amelia had noticed it too; she could see them darting glances between themselves, then up at her, concern on their faces.

Felicia tried to ignore it, but it became increasingly impossible. Heat broke out across the base of her neck. She lost her concentration a couple of times, missing a bid, almost writing the wrong information on her sheets before Amelia murmured the correction in her ear. Eventually, she'd had enough. Without warning, she put her gavel down abruptly, almost cutting off the last bid of the lot they were on.

"I think we'll take a five minute break there."

Surprise rippled across the room. Hugo leaned in.

"Er, Felicia, you know that there's no break scheduled for..."

"Can someone tell me what the *hell* is going on?" She hissed. "Why are all of these people..."

Then she saw it. The corner of a newspaper, peeking out from the crook of a jacketed arm. On its own, it was nothing, but as her gaze travelled around the room, she saw another one. And another. Not everyone had one; in fact, there were probably only about half a dozen or so in evidence, but it was enough. Without stopping to think, she stepped down from the rostrum and snatched the nearest copy to hand ... which just so happened to be on Dodger Wells' seat. He immediately sprung forward, frothing with indignation.

"Hang about! I haven't read that yet!"

Hugo speared him with a glance.

"Unless you'd like to discuss your storage charges for that dresser you never collected, I suggest you sit down, sir."

The dealer meekly retreated to his seat. Felicia flipped open the paper, and her heart plummeted. The Bugle. Of course. Emblazoned across the front page was the headline, "A Dark Day for Stamford" on a thick black banner. It seemed that the news of Riverton's death had broken.

The article itself was, Felicia had to admit, tastefully done. A glowing hagiography of his achievements, with the death itself only alluded to in the barest of terms. No details, no mention of suicide ... and, she was relieved to note, no mention of her, either. So why...

She turned the page, and immediately got her answer. Amelia, who was reading over her shoulder, let out a gasp.

Across the double page spread, a ghoulish font blazed:

Going, Going … Gone! Is Local Auctioneer Stamford's Very Own Angel Of Death? Reporter Nick Naseby Investigates the Terrifying Rumours.

Underneath was a deeply unflattering – and surprisingly grainy, given that it was the twenty-first century—photograph of her walking down the High Street. Worryingly, she couldn't say when it had been taken, although it clearly wasn't this morning, as she was wearing a different outfit. How long had they been following her for?

Unable to look at it any more, let alone read on, she wordlessly handed the paper to Hugo, who immediately began to speed through the text.

"It says that you were there last night. That you found James." He looked up at her, aghast. "We were the only ones there. How can they possibly *know* this?"

"There's more online." Amelia had been scrolling on her phone. She tapped the screen with sparkly blue nails, turning it to show the other two.

An update from your dedicated reporter, it gushed. *Since we went to print this morning, Felicia Grant has been spotted having a very heated discussion with the Welland Police's Detective Sergeant Pettifer. Regular perusers of The Bugle will recall that these two have a hair-raising history of crime-busting together. This reporter can only speculate, but it seems there may be more to come on the sad case of James Riverton. Stay tuned to find out.*

It was accompanied by a photo of her and Pettifer on the bridge this morning. The image was, ironically, far better in quality than the one in the paper, presumably because it had been snapped on a phone rather than with whatever antiquated piece of camera equipment The Bugle doled out to its journalists. Felicia felt her stomach contract at the sight of it. The knowledge that someone had been there, watching them, photographing … it felt violating.

"How many people do you think will have seen this?" She managed, shakily.

Anyone else might have lied, but not Hugo. She knew he would tell her the truth.

"The online article?" He shrugged. "Hard to say. Probably not many people. They're mostly here at the fair. But the print…" He looked regretful. "They have newsstands up and down the High Street, Felicia. You know that. Almost everyone picks up a copy when they're passing."

He was right; she did know that. But she'd needed it said out loud. She closed her eyes, exhaling heavily.

"I'm sure it's not as bad as all that," Amelia glared at Hugo, clearly not equally grateful for his honesty. "No-one'll have time to read it today anyway, and even if they do…" She waved the paper, forcing a bright note into her voice. "Who really cares about this sort of thing? No-one, I'll bet."

As one, they all turned to look at the sea of people still staring at them.

"All right, so maybe a couple of people," Amelia blushed prettily as Hugo raised an eyebrow at her.

Just then, Felicia felt a hand upon her arm. The touch was feather-light, and she might have missed it altogether if it hadn't been accompanied by her name, breathily spoken in her ear. She turned to see Tara hovering apologetically behind her.

"I'm sorry to disturb you," she stammered. "But I just wondered…"

"Are you all right?" Felicia asked, resisting the urge to grab the girl as she swayed slightly on her feet. She was so pale today she almost appeared translucent, as if she scarcely existed at all. "Do you need to sit down?"

"No, I'm fine. Just tired." Her eyes were pink beneath her heavy fringe, and she was scratching her palms distractedly. When she caught Felicia looking, she explained, "nervous reaction, I think. Things have been ... getting to me lately." She dipped her chin, until it all but disappeared into her chest. "I know you're busy, but I was hoping we could talk. You seem like..."

"What happened to James Riverton?"

The shout rang around the high-ceilinged room like a gunshot. Tara started, shrank away as though she'd been lashed. The crowd was looking wildly amongst itself, trying to identify who'd spoken out, buzzing loudly in excitement. Felicia could sense the tension in the space ramping up, sucking out the air. She'd experienced this once before, when several bidders had come to blows in the middle of the saleroom floor, and she knew the signs. She needed to do something, and fast. Before things got really out of hand.

She turned back to Tara, only to find that the girl had disappeared. Felicia shook her head, putting it to one side. She'd deal with that later. For now, she had bigger problems requiring her attention. Squaring her shoulders, she marched up the steps to the rostrum.

"I'm sorry to interrupt our event, ladies and gentlemen," she said, raising her voice so it reached to the back of the room. "But it appears there are some things I'm going to have to address before we can go any further. Some of you may have read ... certain stories about me. But let me be clear: I do not know any more about the tragic deaths of James Riverton or Iris Breadmore than anyone else does. As far as I'm aware, the official line is that neither is considered suspicious in any way, and therefore that is the line I myself will be taking. If you have any more questions on the matter they should be addressed to the police, not me. *Now*," she banged the gavel on the rostrum, taking a certain pleasure in making several people jump guiltily. "If those of you who've come here solely looking for salacious gossip could kindly leave my saleroom, the rest of us can continue with the auction we're supposed to be here for."

There was an echoing silence. After a moment or two, a few people began to sidle out, but most stayed put, evidently too ashamed to admit to it publicly.

"Not as many as I suspect is really the case, but all right," Felicia said crisply, after she'd waited for the last to close the door behind them. "You've had your chance. Now, where were we?" She indicated to Amelia, who reached for the next item, holding it aloft. "Ah, yes. Lot 36. Who'll bid me fifty pounds?"

Chapter Twenty-Six

S unlight streamed through the gothic arched windows of the Welland Police's single-roomed station. The atmosphere was quiet, even slightly soporific, but that wasn't unusual. With only a handful of officers at its disposal, it wasn't uncommon for Jess to find herself alone here.

Alas, that wasn't the case today. The station had another unexpected, unwelcome occupant.

Jess carefully placed a steaming cup of lapsang souchong next to DCI Heavenly's divinely tailored elbow, trying not to let any spill over the bone china rim onto the saucer below. One of the station's rather motley collection of mugs simply wouldn't do; pottery impaired the flavour, supposedly. In fact, he'd brought everything of his own, distastefully moving the standard-issue teabags and crystallised lump of sugar in its bowl to one side to make way for his special tin of tea – from a shop in Piccadilly – and the glass teapot it had to be made in ... not that he ever had to go through the process of making it, of course. *That* particular task fell to Jess.

She set down a plate of biscuits on the desk, somewhat tentatively. She hadn't been sure what he'd like, so she'd chosen a few options from the selection box, allowing herself to a small moment of mischief by adding a pink and yellow party ring right on the top of the pile. One thing she was certain of was that he wasn't a party rings man. She tried to imagine him at a child's birthday, balancing a paper plate of jelly in one well-manicured hand whilst sticky fingers pawed at his immaculately pressed trousers. Unfortunately, the bubble of mirth that thought inspired caused her hand to shake as she set the plate down, biscuits spilling onto his paperwork. He brushed the crumbs away irritably without a word, although she was sure she heard a distinctive tut as she turned and scurried away.

Sergeant Pettifer was always telling her that she shouldn't feel obliged to make tea for everyone, Jess acknowledged guiltily, as she slunk back behind her own desk. But then, that was easy to say when you weren't languishing on the bottom rung and, more pertinently, the only female officer in a station of middle-aged men.

Besides, Jess thought, risking a glance around her computer monitor as she brought it back to life. She had an ulterior motive today. She didn't want to give Heavenly any reason to go to the kitchen; that would take him past her desk, and for all his faults, he could be annoyingly observant when he wanted to be. He would see instantly that she wasn't typing up reports. The last thing she wanted was for him to see what she was really doing.

The screen lit up, revealing the financial checks the sarge had asked her to do on James Riverton. She skimmed through them once again – keeping half an eye on the DCI as she did so

– even though she'd already ascertained that there was nothing of note there. Plenty of money flowing in and out, but it all looked above board. In fact, the most noteworthy thing about the man seemed to be just how much he gave away to good causes, particularly around the town. It was going to be difficult to find someone who might actually benefit from murdering him; if anything, his death was going to detriment a lot of people.

Jess bit her lip, drumming her fingers on the desk then abruptly ceasing when it drew a glower from Heavenly. There was one more thing she needed to do … but factoring in the DCI's presence made it significantly more dicey. If Pettifer knew, he wouldn't want her to take the risk … and a part of her was sorely tempted to follow that imaginary advice. She *really* couldn't afford to be caught. In fact, she couldn't afford to annoy Heavenly in any way; it was a large part of why she pandered to his caprices without complaint. It was in his power to have her reassigned to another station, and she couldn't chance it. She needed to be here, in Stamford. Needed it for reasons she couldn't tell anyone, not even Pettifer.

Ironically, though, he was also the very reason she *had* to go ahead with this. Because he was a stellar police officer, even if he'd be horrified to hear anyone say as much. His instincts were second-to-none; she trusted him implicitly, and if he thought that there was something off about these deaths…

She hesitated, torn between duty and self-preservation. Then, before she could talk herself out of it any further, she rose from her seat, moving across the station in a way which she hoped was both surreptitious and confident.

She nearly made it. Her hand was on the handle of the evidence cupboard when Heavenly's silken tones stopped her in her tracks.

"What are you doing, Constable?"

Jess gulped, discovering at this helpfully late moment that her mind had gone blank. Why hadn't she thought of a good cover beforehand? That's what Pettifer would have done.

"Just..." her eyes roved the room, eventually alighting on the ever-present stone cold mug of tea perched precariously on the edge of her desk. "Spilled my drink, that's all. I'm just getting something out of the cleaning cupboard to wipe it up." For the first time, she found herself feeling profoundly grateful that the station's bijou proportions meant the cupboard was forced to adopt a dual purpose. Or triple, if you counted the coats. She paused, then added casually, "of course, I could just use the sleeve of my uniform, but..."

"*No!*" Heavenly looked appalled. "Good gad, Constable. I understand you only have experience of a provincial force, but..." he let out a harrumphing sigh, evidently concluding that he was wasting his breath trying to educate such a peasant. "Get what you need. Just be quick about it."

"Absolutely, sir." Hoarse with relief, Jess ducked swiftly into the cupboard, clicking on the dim bulb overhead and beginning to scan the rickety shelves rapidly. She didn't have much time; knowing Heavenly, he was probably counting the seconds she was in there. Luckily, though, there wasn't exactly a lot of evidence to sift through. She passed over a silver letter opener, an empty spray can, and a cauliflower – she made a note to look into *that* particular incident later – and then saw what she was looking for. She held the clear bag up, the weak light glistening off the black phone screen within. At once, she felt the tingle she always did when faced with a potential lead.

"Let's see what you can tell us, shall we?" She said softly.

"Forty-three seconds, Constable," Heavenly called sourly. "Do they not teach observation in police college these days?"

Jess rolled her eyes, stuffing the phone into her pocket. Then she headed for the door, just in time remembering to grab a bottle of spray cleaner on her way out.

Chapter Twenty-Seven

On The Meadows, the funfair was still in full swing. Gaudily-striped tents flapped on a breeze laden with tinny fairground music and squeals of delighted laughter. It sounded appealingly innocent and carefree, but Felicia wasn't headed towards it this time. Instead, she made a beeline for the quieter end of things, where the river forked beneath the arches of the town bridge. The spot was marked by a willow tree and, beneath it, a wooden jetty. It was a place usually frequented by sweethearts or fishermen with more hope than expectation, but today, the grass in front of it had transformed into a picture-perfect Georgian picnic. A large sheet of gingham seersucker had been laid out across the ground, and people were lounging around the edges, gloves discarded by their sides, faces turned to the sun. Some were sipping lemonade and picking at the cornucopia of food spilling out of artfully arranged wicker baskets. Such a vision of peacefulness was more than welcome to Felicia's jaded eyes, and she flopped down gratefully, already reaching for her satin slippers.

"It is *so* good to get off my feet." She flipped the shoes off, wiggling her toes in the plush grass. "These things are lethal. I may never walk properly again."

"Ours aren't much better, you know." Dexter leaned back on his elbows. "I'm not surprised it's the only time in history men were foolish enough to dabble with heels. The relief they must have felt when the fashion changed to boots. I saved you a plate, by the way." He leaned closer, voice dropping to an indignant whisper. "You wouldn't *believe* what absolute gannets these people are. I've watched that man take three slices of pigeon pie in the last quarter of an hour." He took a huge bite of his own portion, muttering around a mouthful of pastry, "disgraceful behaviour. The English really can't be trusted with food."

Felicia picked up her plate, eyeing it dubiously.

"Is it really pigeon, do you think?"

"Well, no." Dexter dusted crumbs off his lapel. "I suspect it's probably a pork pie. But it's very good either way."

Felicia shielded her eyes with a hand, looking around them.

"Where's Algernon? You haven't let him wander off again, have you? Because you know what he's like…"

"A friend invited him over for computer games and pizza, and I said he could go." Dexter crossed one long leg over the other. "Apparently even the kids are all Georgian Fair-ed out by now."

"Oh … I see," Felicia fiddled with the edge of the picnic blanket, knowing he'd pick up on her stammer. He looked at her knowingly.

"He seemed like a nice boy, Fliss. I had no qualms about letting Algie go off with him."

"I'm sure he was." Felicia plucked at a buttercup, spinning it between her fingers.

"He's twelve years old," Dexter said, with sudden gentleness. "We can't let what happened..." his gaze met hers. "I worry too, you know."

Dexter wasn't often earnest, but when he was, he could fairly take your breath away. Felicia looked into his cobalt blue eyes and saw half a lifetime of shared experience unravelling backwards. She felt something lift inside her, somewhere in the region of her chest. She patted his hand, smiled.

"I suppose we couldn't expect to stay cool forever," she sighed theatrically.

"No, I'm afraid we're doomed to become the biggest losers on the planet. At least he still hangs out with us occasionally at the moment. Give it a year, and he won't want to be seen dead in our company."

The thought was bittersweet, a sugary arrow to her heart. No-one ever warned you just how much it hurt to watch your children grow up. But then, no-one warned you just how incredible it was either, watching this person who was part you, and at the same time completely *not* you, take the first tentative steps towards becoming someone. Every day that Algernon grew away from her was compensated for by him becoming more wonderful, and weird, and contradictory, and wise. More fascinating and yet more unknowable. However hard it might be to stand aside, she knew that she wouldn't freeze time even if she could. Well, not for long, anyway. She wouldn't mind keeping him at twelve for just a while longer, the teenage hormones still just at bay, him still just about her child.

She took an experimental bite of the mystery pie, conceding that it *was* good, vermin or not. Then her eyes landed on the newspaper under his glass of lemonade, and it turned to dust in her mouth. She put her plate down, appetite completely gone.

"You've seen it, then?"

"I have." His eyes were closed by now, hands cradled behind his head as he reclined on the grass. "Another fine piece of journalism from our local rag."

"I'm surprised you're so chipper about it," she said flatly. "Considering it describes you as a 'fame-hungry tv pundit'."

"True. It also calls me dashing, though, so I'll forgive them."

"Dear God," Felicia muttered. "Give me strength."

"They weren't entirely uncomplimentary about you, either," Dexter opened one eye. "Apparently you have 'fabulous' hair."

"Yes ... well ... *my* ego isn't so easily massaged," she stuttered primly, resisting the automatic urge to touch her head.

"Clearly not. I heard you gave an entire auction room a rollicking dressing down on the lasciviousness of gutter-press gossip earlier today."

Felicia put her head in her hands.

"Oh no," she groaned. Truth be told, she was already beginning to question the wisdom of that.

"It sounded like stirring stuff to me," Dexter said cheerily. "Why, it reminds me of the time you stood up at the Oxford Union in just your bra..."

"*Dexter!*" She hissed, as several curious heads began to swivel in their direction. She cringed behind a picnic basket, trying to stay out of sight. The last thing she wanted was to draw attention to herself. God only knew how many of their fellow picknickers had seen the story already, and if Dexter had heard about the incident at the auction, then it must already be spreading around town like wildfire. "Control yourself." She reached for the paper, partly to brandish at him, and partly to hide behind. "You do realise that Caroline Boughton is a direct source for this article? She taken your conversation from last night and twisted ... well, *everything*." She flipped to the page – trying not to look at the awful photograph of herself – and read, "*Professor Grant remains tight-lipped about the exact nature of his latest project, but revealed with a coy twinkle in his eye that Stamford has many more secrets to share. Is that the rumble of tv trucks on the horizon? You heard it here first.*" Felicia snapped the paper shut. "You never said any of that!"

"No, I didn't," he agreed mildly. "Although I might have been guilty of the coy twinkle."

She stared at him in exasperation.

"Are you going to take *any* of this seriously?"

"Nope." He reached for a strawberry. "Why should I? People will make things up when you're in the public eye. Unless..." he looked at her warily. "It's not entirely made up in this case?" When she didn't reply immediately, the wariness turned to suspicion. "What's going on? Don't tell me you *really* think Riverton was murdered?"

"Of course I bloody do!" She snapped, too indignant to be abashed. "Frankly, I'm astonished that I'm the only one."

"Doesn't that tell you something?" He sat up. "What does Pettifer think?"

"He says he believes it's suicide," she admitted, in a small voice.

"Well, there you go then. The man's not an idiot, Fliss – even if he does dress like one. Why would you be right and he be wrong?"

"Because..." she hesitated. Dexter was probably the only

person she could confide in without fear of judgement. "He doesn't exactly ... *know* everything I do." She placed the buttercup on her plate. "You remember I said someone was there with me, down in the cellars? The person I thought was Riverton but obviously wasn't?"

"Yes." A frown scored his brow. "But it was Pettifer, wasn't it? You said he appeared just after that."

"He did. But the thing is, it couldn't have been him. You've seen his shoes? The ones he always wears?"

"Of course I do. They offend me every time I have to look at them." Dexter shuddered. "Huge, clod-hopping things. More like work boots than shoes."

"Exactly. And yet what I heard..." she could recall it so easily. The feathery scrape of a soft sole, drawing across the flagstones. "There was no way it could have been made by those shoes. I know it."

He looked startled.

"But that means..."

"That someone else was there? Yes." She wrapped her arms around herself, feeling suddenly chilly, despite the warmth of the day. "Someone's watching me, Dexter. They have been since the start of this."

"Christ," he muttered. "And you haven't told Pettifer any of this?"

"I was going to," she said defensively. "But then he..." she dropped her voice in shame. "Well, to be honest, he annoyed me."

All right, so it didn't sound terribly mature, said like that. But he hadn't just annoyed her, Felicia reminded herself. He'd hurt her too, although that was something she'd never admit to aloud. Not even to Dexter.

"So you retaliated by keeping back vital information? Brilliant, Fliss. Way to potentially get yourself killed." Dexter sounded genuinely angry; she looked at him in surprise, but he was already pulling out his phone. "I'm going to call him. He needs to know about—"

"Hello, both." A shadow fell over them, and suddenly Robyn was there, a smile on her face, as ever. "This looks very cosy. Not interrupting anything, am I?"

She looked as innocent as a new lamb, but Felicia looked closely and saw that the smile was, in fact, more of a smirk. Felicia glared at her, but there wasn't any real heat in it. She held far too much affection for her goddaughter for that. And besides, she enjoyed the reminder that Robyn wasn't quite the po-faced, saintly miss her mother seemed to think she was.

"Absolutely not," she said, at the same time as Dexter snapped, "no."

"Okay, if you say so." Robyn raised strawberry blonde eyebrows, reaching between them for a slice of cake. "Don't mind if I pinch this, do you? And if you could just pass me that last piece of pie over there..."

"Hungry, Robyn?" Felicia said dryly, pouncing on it just before the man Dexter had indicated, who'd clearly been eyeing up his fourth helping. He gave her a wounded look, which she ignored, handing it over to Robyn.

"Oh, it's not for me." Robyn arranged a selection of sandwich triangles together, points aiming towards the sky. "I'm on a last-minute mission. Mum's sent me down here to put some things together for Caroline Boughton. She's modelling for the Georgian makeup talk soon, but her lunch hasn't turned up. Gavin's furious, of course; it was all I could do to stop him marching over to the caterer's himself." She sighed. "To be honest, it would probably be easier for everyone if he'd stayed at home today. He's making everyone..."

But Felicia had stopped listening. Suddenly, she had the shivery sensation of being watched. She wrapped her arms around herself, inexplicably cold despite the warmth of the sun.

For a moment, she entertained the idea that she was genuinely being paranoid, that it was all in her head. Maybe Pettifer was right, and she was seeing things which weren't there, imagining danger where there was none. But all the same, she had to be sure. She leapt to her feet, neck twisting back and forth as her eyes roved The Meadows all around her. She probably looked mad, a suspicion which was confirmed as Robyn stared at her in concern.

"Aunt Fliss? What on earth are you..."

"*I see them!*" Felicia cried, a rush of exhilaration as suddenly, she spotted a figure beneath the trees. She pointed wildly. "Over there! I *see* them!"

Heads turned, people stopped moving. For a stomach-churning moment, Felicia felt like she was falling into space. She'd shouted without thinking; what if she was wrong, and that was just someone waiting for a friend, or...

Then the figure began to move, backing away stiltedly.

And Felicia knew she hadn't been wrong.

"They're going to make a run for it," she breathed. She spun towards Dexter, who was on his feet by now, peering towards the trees. "How much do you remember from your rugby days?"

"If you're suggesting I tackle someone in public, then you must be mad," Dexter sniffed. "Most unseemly. Besides, I'm more of a cricket man; you know that."

"I bet I can catch them," Robyn was bright-eyed, the thrill of it clearly over-riding her usual cautious instincts. "I ran cross country for the school. I gave it up to focus on my grades, but..."

"Absolutely not," Felicia said firmly. "Your mother would never forgive me if..." She stopped as the distant figure began to break into a run. Any more prevarication and they'd lose them entirely. "Oh, bugger it. I'll get them myself."

And she took off. Vaguely, she heard Dexter shouting something after her – she thought it might have been an expletive, which was perfectly believable – but the blood was already roaring in her ears. The figure was running diagonally across The Meadows, forcing their way through the crowd. Felicia pushed forwards, just managing to keep them in sight, a task which was fortunately made easier by their dark attire. They stood out like a beacon amongst the ice-cream shades of the costume-clad fairgoers. It was just as well, because she wasn't as fast as she'd like; her dress tangled around her legs, dragging her backwards, and the uneven ground beneath her feet threatened to tumble her more than once. But she forced herself on, ignoring the screaming protest of her joints as the world around her fragmented into blurred washes of colour and snatches of sound. Green, blue, yellow, red ... the tinkle of an ice cream van, a dog yapping excitedly, the indignant quacking of a duck as it flapped out of her path...

And then another awareness. Dexter, pulling up by her side, long strides catching her easily.

"You go left; I'll go right," he bellowed above the wind. "We'll head them off by the bridge."

Up ahead, the figure turned to look back, stumbling over the tussocky ground. For a second, Felicia thought they were going down, but they managed to right themselves, staggering on. Except now they weren't heading towards the bridge anymore. They were changing course, swerving in an arc ... into the heart of the funfair.

Felicia didn't think, and she didn't hesitate. She plunged straight in after them.

Chapter Twenty-Eight

The first thing she was hit with was a wall of sound. Pinging, jangling. Lights blared in the corner of her vision. Rides whirled to her left and right, disorientating her sense of what was moving and what wasn't. She ducked between the stilted legs of a juggling acrobat, trying to catch sight of her quarry. Dexter skidded to a halt beside her, panting.

"Where'd they go?"

"I don't know," she said hopelessly. "It's going to take a miracle to find them in this."

Dexter frowned thoughtfully. Then, before she could blink, he'd leapt onto the carousel, hoisting himself up onto one of the horses.

"Oi!" Bellowed the ride attendant. "You're not supposed to be on here! Under twelves only."

"I'm just very developed for my age," Dexter replied distractedly, craning his neck as the horse rose higher. Then he pointed. "Over there. By the helter skelter." He wobbled, almost losing his balance as the horse juddered down again. "Grief, these things are more violent than I remember."

"And more expensive, I'll wager," the ride operator grinned toothily at him.

Dexter sighed and got out a tenner. But Felicia didn't wait; she darted in the direction of the helter-skelter. The crowd parted slightly in front of her, and she saw the figure again. They'd stopped, and were taking a breather, bent over with their hands on their knees.

Then they looked up. For a moment, hunter and prey just stared at one another. But only for a moment.

"Bloody hell," she muttered, as they broke into a sprint again. "You can't be serious." She raised her voice, pointing after them. "Somebody *stop* that person!"

It didn't have the effect she'd hoped. Everyone seemed to have frozen, uncertain whether to take her seriously or not. Felicia could see her target getting further and further into the distance, beyond all hope of catching.

And then something very strange happened.

One minute they were running, the next, they were flying through the air. They sprawled forwards, splaying face-first onto the ground with a heavy thud. Felicia skidded to a halt, momentarily confused. Then she saw the stilt, still sticking out across the path.

"Thank you," she panted, as the figure curled into a ball on the grass, groaning in pain. "Thank you very much."

"No worries," the acrobat carried on juggling casually, as though nothing had happened. "Always happy to help a lady in distress. He nick your purse or something?"

"Something like that," she agreed, as Dexter arrived on the scene, looking as unfairly fresh as ever. He didn't even appear to be out of breath.

"Aye, well, I'm not surprised," the acrobat said sagely. "He looks like a shifty sort."

The man – because now up close, she could see that it was indeed a man – stopped writhing abruptly to look indignant.

"How very *dare* you! I'll have you know I'm a professional."

"Wait..." As Dexter hauled him to his feet, Felicia looked him full in the face for the first time and gasped. "I *know* you! You were part of the anti-Georgian Fair demonstration." He was the one in the hat; she could see it now. "Were you following me then, too?" Another, even worse thought struck her. "Or were you there to commit murder?"

"*What?*" The man sat up sharply, spluttering. She could see now that what she'd fantastically imagined as classic 'murderer' attire of black parka and gloves was in fact just a rather adolescent outfit: an old band t-shirt beneath an open combat shirt, once black but obviously washed many times since then, and ill-fitting dark trousers which seemed to be held together with an elastic band where the button had once been. The man himself, however, was decidedly *not* a teenager. In fact, she suspected the last time he'd slammed a door or eaten his own body-weight in cereal without repercussions was around the time the clothes had rolled out of the factory. "No! *God*, you can't think ... I was *working*. Undercover."

"As what? 2005?" Dexter said derisively.

"I'm a *journalist*," snapped the man, glaring at him. "And if this buffoon will put me down, I can prove it to you."

"He's telling the truth, Aunt Fliss." Robyn appeared at her side. "That's Nosy Nick. He works for The Bugle."

"Nick, as in ... Nick Naseby?" Felicia turned on him accusingly. "The one who wrote that slanderous article about me in this morning's paper?"

"Now, see here," Nick whined, still hanging by his collar. "The public has a right to the truth."

Felicia folded her arms.

"I was going to give you a chance to put your side of the story, obviously," Nick sulked. Then his eyes lit up. "All right, you've twisted my arm. Double page, all-exclusive." He splayed his hands, as though performing a conjuring trick. "*Auctioneer of Death tells all*." He paused, looked expectant. "You see? It's kind of like *angel of death*. It's a play on words."

"Not really," Robyn said, almost apologetically. "I mean, it's not *actually* that close…"

"All right, we're not The Sun!" Nick muttered, looking hurt. "Christ, everyone's a critic."

Felicia couldn't help but feel they were getting off-topic. She looked at Nick's shoes – soft-soled canvas trainers – and then into his face.

"Have you been following me all weekend?" When he looked furtive, she persisted. "This is important, Nick. I need to know if you were in the cellars under the Arts Centre last night. While the ball was going on. You were, weren't you?"

"I … might have been there," he admitted slowly.

Dexter gave him a shake.

"All right, so I was there!" He squeaked. "But I was only doing my job. A reporter has a duty…"

"Yes, yes," Felicia cut him off, trying not to sound as impatient as she was beginning to feel. "But did you see anyone else down there? Besides me, I mean?"

"I don't know." When Dexter looked ready to shake him again, he protested, "No, really! I … I think someone might have passed me at one point, but I can't be sure. Just this flash of red, disappearing around the corner. But I'd been stuck in that tunnel for so long, I was probably oxygen deprived. I'm not good with small spaces, you see—"

"Wait." Dexter's voice, sharp and urgent, made them all look up in surprise. He was staring at Nick, intensity etched into his face. "Did you just say ... *tunnel*?"

"Yeah, I thought it'd be a good shortcut," Nick said ruefully. "But then I totally lost my bearings. It's an absolute warren down there, once you get off the main corridor. A person could get lost for years. I'm surprised I didn't find any skeletons." He looked faintly disappointed that this was the case, until Dexter set him down with a thump. Then he just looked put out. "Steady!" He straightened his shirt, rather pointlessly, and scowled. "I take it I can go now?"

"Not just yet, Nick." Dexter clapped him on the back. "First, we're going to take a little trip."

Chapter Twenty-Nine

"I was *really* rather hoping that I wouldn't have to come down here again," Nick complained, as they traipsed through the darkened passageways sometime later. "This place gives me the creeps." He tugged at his collar. "And did I tell you that I'm not keen on small spaces?"

"You *might* have mentioned it once or twice," Dexter said dryly. In actual fact, their journalistic companion had done nothing but moan since they'd got down here. "Just show me where this tunnel was, and you can leave."

Felicia slanted him a glance. In all the years she'd known him, she'd rarely seen him so focused. It still took her by surprise, how different work made him from the rolling stone he was in his private life. Because this *was* work, there was no doubt about that. It was the only thing which could draw out this intensity in him, this thrumming with barely-supressed energy. He was practically crackling with it. When he was like this, it was impossible not to get sucked in, to get swept along by the adventure; even Felicia, who felt she ought to be impervious to it by now, couldn't help the thrill of anticipation which shivered through her.

Because the other annoying thing was, Dexter was often right. Despite what insouciant appearances might suggest, he was in fact first-rate at what he did, and he had the instincts to match. They'd been on many goose chases in their time together, Felicia reflected, not without a hint of fondness, and they hadn't all led where Dexter had hoped, but they'd never been random or baseless. If he thought there was a lead down here, he was probably onto something very real. She only hoped it wouldn't get them in as much trouble as it had last time. Dexter might have an incredible mind, but he had absolutely no sense of self-preservation.

"Well..." Nick looked around him edgily. "I mean, it's not that easy to say. It all looks the same."

"*Try*," Dexter ground out, visibly fighting for patience. Nick eyed him warily.

"Well, let me see. I followed you..." He indicated Felicia "...down here from the ballroom." He began to move forwards. "Yes, we passed this. And that. Then you looked behind you, and I thought you might see me, so I was trying to find somewhere to hide..." He began to run a hand along the right-hand wall, peering at the stonework. "Ah. Here we are."

It took a minute for Felicia to see what he was talking about. It was only when she squinted that the form of a door began to emerge from the grey stone around it. It was ancient-looking, heavily studded, with blackened timbers buckling around rusted hinges. There was a grate in the top, presumably at what was intended to be face height, although Felicia couldn't imagine that anyone could have been that short, even when it was made. It was, without question, one of the smallest doors she'd ever seen; blending into the gloom as it did, it was no wonder she'd missed it.

"Are you sure?" She said, uncertainly, as Dexter began poring over it. "I mean, it doesn't look like it's been opened in centuries." Chances were, it was probably bricked-up behind there. It wasn't uncommon for old cellar doors like that to be left in situ even when there was nothing behind them anymore.

"Well, it was open last night," Nick said. "I'd never have noticed it otherwise."

"The mechanism's seized," Dexter tugged on the handle. "But I think with a little elbow grease…"

With a groaning worthy of a ship's hull in stormy seas, the door began to open, swollen timbers scraping against the flagstones below.

"Lead the way," Dexter stood aside for Nick, who immediately quailed.

"What? You can't be serious! You want me to go in … there?"

"Why not? You've already been in once."

"I only stood inside the door!" Nick shuddered. "That was quite arachnid-infested enough, thank you very much. I've no desire to see what other monsters might be lurking further within."

Dexter looked incredulous as to how anyone could possibly be so lacking in curiosity.

"Not very intrepid for a journalist, are you?" he said, stepping one foot through the doorway. "I'd have thought you'd be all over this. Before someone else steals your glory."

Nick looked blankly after him for a moment, then blurted, "Wait, what are you talking about?"

There was a sigh from within the tunnel, and Dexter reappeared.

"Let's look at the facts, shall we?" He spoke slowly, as though talking to someone very dim – which no doubt he felt he was. "A secret passageway undiscovered for hundreds of years, potentially now connected to a mysterious death. And *you* discovered it." He raised his eyebrows. "That, my friend, is what I believe you in the trade call a scoop."

"I suppose it is." Nick's face took on an awestruck cast as the idea sunk in. He yanked out a Dictaphone and began murmuring into it breathlessly. "As I scoured the *darkened, desolate* passageways, scarcely knowing if I would ever glimpse daylight again, little did I realise how closely I trod in the *footsteps of death…*"

"Are you sure this is a good idea?" Felicia asked Dexter, as they inched into the narrow tunnel, Nick trailing after them, still externalising – punctuated by the occasional squeal as presumably he came into contact with a cobweb.

"Why, are you worried he'll do us in?" Dexter sounded amused by the notion. "I don't think he's much of a threat. The oaf's barely able to dress himself."

"Oi! I heard that." A petulant voice said behind them. "And these clothes are vintage…" A pause, then a sheepish, "or at least, they will be soon."

Dexter gave her a 'see what I mean?' look.

"Well, all right, no. I'll give you that," she admitted, then dropped her voice. "But all the same, do you really think it was wise to bring a muckraking journalist along with us?"

"I heard that too." Nick's voice was fainter now, although no less peevish. "Sound carries in here, you know. And d'you think there's any chance you could you slow down a bit?"

Dexter ignored him, forging on. Felicia – who, incidentally, was struggling to keep up with him herself – watched him out of the corner of her eye, wondering what he was up to. Her suspicions were confirmed a minute or so later when he stopped abruptly, squinting back over his shoulder into the opaque darkness.

"Have we lost him yet?"

His voice was completely different now. It was hushed, serious. Felicia put her hands on her hips.

"All right, that's it. What's going on?"

He held up a hand distractedly, still looking behind him.

"Just … is he gone?"

Felicia strained to listen.

"I think so. For now." She frowned warningly. "Dexter, we can't leave him down here."

"Keep your knickers on, woman." She heard, rather than saw, him roll his eyes. "We'll find him in a minute. Believe me, I don't want a desiccated reporter on my conscience any more than you do."

She huffed, tapping her foot impatiently on the floor.

"I still can't see why you insisted on bringing him in the first place."

"You want Heavenly to get off his sculpted behind and start treating these deaths seriously, don't you?" He was crouching down now, scrutinising the stone walls.

"Well, yes, but…"

"Exactly. Muckraking journalists, under which umbrella you so charmingly termed our dear Nicholas, can be very useful." He ran a palm slowly across the roughly hewn surface, moving along it in sections. "So long as you only let them see what you want them to. And this next part isn't for public consumption. Not yet, at any rate."

He moved to the opposite wall, starting the laborious, odd

process all over again. She watched him for a few minutes, finally blurting out, "What on *earth* are you looking for?"

"Carvings, symbols." His voice was vague, preoccupied. "Anything which tells me this is the place I'm after."

Felicia looked around her dubiously.

"It's just an old service tunnel, surely?" It hardly seemed very promising. Then, dimly, something began to connect in her mind. It was a word; something she'd said ... something *Nick* had said...

"Oh God," she groaned, slapping a hand to her forehead. "Someone's told you that old fable about the tunnels, haven't they?"

The idea of secret tunnels running underneath Stamford was a myth well-known by locals. Most people remembered being enthralled by the stories as children, but later, as adulthood set in, they became half-forgotten, fairy-tales and legends as charming and familiar as the ones in their childhood bookshelf. Once so real, now gathering dust, the magic stripped from them.

To be fair, the idea wasn't *entirely* inconceivable; Stamford's centre being untouched for hundreds of years meant that almost every house was underpinned by a cellar. Many were unused now, some boarded up, but they still existed. Often they constituted of several rooms, and would have been large enough to make a living space of their own if it weren't for the fact that they were buried completely underground. The result was an entire layer of Stamford's architecture that no-one ever saw, a subterranean town all of its own, living out its ghostly existence beneath the streets. So the concept of them being linked by their own web of 'roads', or interconnecting passages, was certainly possible ... if decidedly on the fantastical side.

Dexter staunchly declined to reply, which told her everything she needed to know. She sighed.

"They were probably having you on. Seeing if you fell for it." Out-of-towners often did. It was a consequence of a place so otherworldly; people suspended common sense, believed anything. "Everyone knows it's a load of old codswallop. No-one's ever actually found them."

"No-one's ever *admitted* to finding them," Dexter corrected, in that obstinate tone which made Felicia's heart sink from well-worn experience. When he was in, he was in with both feet, entirely immovable in his conviction. There would be no stopping him now, no reasoning with him. "Not publicly, at least. But there are accounts, when you start to look. People have been in them." He took her shoulders between his palms, eyes alight. "They *exist*, Fliss. Believe me."

He was pulling her in, just as he'd always been able to do, and for a split second, she *so* wanted to let herself fall. But then reality came rushing back. She went rigid, throwing out her next question like an accusation.

"So ... you *are* working on something? You have been all of this time?"

He had the grace to look faintly guilty.

"Look, before you think ... I wasn't lying when I said I'm here for Algernon. I am. Mostly. But..." he exhaled. "All right, yes. I am ... following a thread. Or *unravelling* would probably be more apt. It's a complicated business, slow going. And it's very early days." His mouth quirked wryly. "You know long this stuff really takes. It's not like it looks on TV."

She certainly did know, all too well. She'd lived through it for long enough.

The breathless dash across continents shown on Treasure Seeker were nothing like the truth. In reality, those trails had taken years to map. Every tantalising clue solved seemingly on the spot was in fact the result of countless hours of pointless, at times soul-destroying poring over old documents and inscriptions. But no-one wanted to see that side of things. They wanted instant gratification. As a result, what everyone thought were Dexter's 'new' projects were almost exclusively anything but.

"This is to do with the Charles I treasure?" She managed, trying to keep her voice even.

"If I'm right, bigger than that." His eyes were alight, and she felt her stomach flip.

She knew she should ask more, but the truth was, in that moment, she actually didn't care. Her emotions were broiling in a confusing mix of hurt and betrayal.

He hadn't told her.

She knew, in a way, that it wasn't strictly rational to feel like this. After all, they weren't married anymore. Technically, he didn't have to tell her anything. But she'd always believed they shared an openness and understanding, a bond of trust which soared higher than the day-to-day realities of their relationship, unaffected by earthly preoccupations such as divorce and distance and disagreements.

He'd only broken that trust once, just two months ago. Of course, once ought to have been enough. But somehow, her illusion had held, like a crazed windscreen, damaged but still in place. He'd been so contrite, and she'd managed to convince herself that it had simply been a one-off. A blip. Except, clearly it hadn't been anything of the kind.

Fool me once...

"You promised me no more lies," she said, hating the tremor which had crept into her voice, despite her best efforts.

He let his hands fall slowly from her shoulders, looking at her warily.

"I didn't *lie*, Fliss. I just … didn't tell you. It's not the same thing."

Of course he would choose to believe that. How very convenient for him.

"That's a matter of opinion," she snapped, tugging her skirts free of some unseen snag and stalking away into the darkness. Suddenly, she just wanted to get out of here.

"Fliss, wait." Dexter called. "You don't know where you're going."

"Neither do you," she retorted, over her shoulder.

Then, without warning, she was lurching forwards. She flung a hand towards the wall, fingers digging into the crumbling mortar between the stones, but in reality – as she would reflect later, somewhat grudgingly – it was probably the corset that saved her, its rigid pressure preventing her from folding in half. She snapped upright like a sprung doll, belatedly becoming aware of a burning pain in her left big toe.

Biting back an expletive, she shone the beam of her torch down across a pitted stone step, then, slowly, back up again. Step after step melted out of the blackness, leading upwards in an apparently endless flight.

Wordlessly, they looked at one another across the beam of torchlight. Then Dexter moved forwards, beginning to climb. Felicia hesitated briefly, then followed in his wake.

The door at the top was unremarkable, and decidedly more modern than the one they'd entered the tunnel through. Dexter paused on the threshold. Once upon a time, Felicia thought, he would have turned back to her at this moment, shared the final seconds before revelation. But those days were gone. Now, he simply reached out and turned the handle.

A thin thread of gold appeared around the edges of the door. Then gradually, it widened, spilling light into the darkened passageway. Felicia discovered she was holding her breath.

And then the mystery vanished, banished by the clarity of daylight. Despite herself, Felicia couldn't help a small, self-deprecating smile as she recognised their surroundings.

"Where are we?" Dexter looked around them, clearly perplexed to find himself in a rather bland, magnolia-painted corridor. "This panelling seems familiar."

"We're still in the Arts Centre." Incredibly enough; it felt like they'd been walking for miles down there. "The ballroom's just around that corner."

"So it *is* just a service passage after all." Dexter did every emotion to its full extent; nothing was by halves, and that included disappointment. He kicked at a loose pebble in the doorway with barely repressed savagery. "What a bloody *waste* of time."

"I wouldn't say that, exactly." Felicia was looking thoughtfully at the uppermost bolt on the door. She reached up, drawing it back and forth, then touched a finger to it. "Someone's oiled this."

"So?" Dexter was disinterested, sulky. She persisted anyway, trying to make him see.

"*So*, it means that someone could have slipped away to kill Riverton, then back again, without necessarily being missed. More than that, I might know who." She looked at him sideways, head tilted inquiringly. "Fancy a makeover?"

Chapter Thirty

C assandra Lane was having a terrible day. In fact, she was having a terrible weekend full stop. She was beginning to fervently wish she'd never heard the words Georgian Fair. Frankly, she'd like nothing better right now than to slip away home, scrub the sticky makeup off her face, change into something which wasn't designed by a rampant misogynist with the aim of keeping women in their place, and curl up on the sofa with the curtains drawn and a tin of chocolate biscuits in her lap until it was all safely over.

But alas, that wasn't an option. Cassie dragged herself reluctantly back from her lovely daydream, forcing her most mayoral smile onto her face as she nodded to those who were filing into the theatre. From the outside, no-one would ever guess that behind the curved, closed lips were teeth gritted together in discomfort and exhaustion. It was a particular skill of hers, one well-suited to local politics but in fact honed many years earlier, when she'd returned to her high-powered job in finance just six weeks after having Robyn, her body still burning with mastitis and the sensation of having been pulled apart and put back together wrongly. She still remembered getting through meetings with her usual aplomb, only to burst into tears of agony and imploded identity in private, squashed into the knee-hole space beneath her desk so no-one would see.

"Mum?" Robyn appeared at her side, hair shimmering beneath the lights. "Everything all right? You seem miles away."

Of course Robyn saw through it. Robyn saw everything. Sometimes Cassie wondered if she ought to have tried harder to shield her daughter from having to read her mother's emotions. Maybe it had forced her to grow up too quickly. But it had only ever been the two of them, Robyn's father having swanned off on one of his eco-crusades at the first hint of blue on the pregnancy test, leaving behind not so much as a hemp shirt or an indigestible nut bar, let alone any kind of financial support system. The only thing he'd ever given Robyn was the red tint of his hair – although Cassie had always been careful never to vilify him in front of her daughter. As yet, Robyn had never met the man who made her. But one day she might, and Cassie wanted her to be able to make up her own mind.

"I'm fine, darling." She patted Robyn's hand, then decided she could do better than that, and linked their arms together. "Did you take the food down to Caroline?"

"Yes, and a pot of coffee, as suggested."

"And is it too much to hope that she appreciated it, after all of that?"

Robyn gave her a sardonic look, as if to say, 'What do you think?'

Cassie fought the urge to roll her eyes in sympathy. Caroline Boughton had a way of rubbing everyone up the wrong way; complaints about her were forever crossing Cassie's desk – complaints which she could rarely do much about. The truth was, Britain did operate a free press, and while privately, Cassie wasn't much keen on the woman either, as mayor, she had to keep the peace.

"Well, thank you anyway. At least we can say we've done our duty." Cassie rubbed her temples, trying to massage away the pressure headache which had been lingering around all day. "Go and have a rest, darling. I've got things covered here."

"You look like you need the rest more than me." Robyn was looking at her with concern in her bluebell-coloured eyes. "Are you *sure* you're all right, Mum?"

"Of course," Cassie said briskly. "Constitution of an ox, me. Just as long as nothing else goes wrong, I'll be fine."

"Ah." Robyn tucked a strand of hair behind her ear, looking nervous. "Well, perhaps now's not the time to mention this, then…"

Cassie immediately felt an ominous sinking feeling.

"Mention what?"

"It's nothing, really." Robyn was clearly trying to backtrack. It reminded Cassie of when she was a little girl, trying to minimise some mishap she'd created before she got into trouble. "Just a small hiccup."

"Mention *what*, Robyn?" Cassie ground out, in her most maternal warning tone.

"*Well*, the expert who did the apothecary talk this morning's been back in, a little worried. They're missing a vial of arsenic from their medicine case."

"Arsenic?" Cassie bellowed, momentarily forgetting herself. A few people looked startled. She dropped her voice to a hiss, turning them both into the corner to give their conversation more privacy. "Please tell me this is a prank." But of course she knew it wasn't; Robyn was far too earnest and responsible for that. "Bloody *hell*, this is all we need, on top of everything else. Some deadly poison rolling about the place, just waiting to be scooped up by a curious dog or child—" her voice was rising to a faintly hysterical squeak— "I mean, I suppose it's fitting. Whyever not? Wouldn't that just top off the most *disastrous* Georgian Fair in history? Wouldn't that *just* be—"

"Don't be dramatic, Mum," Robyn, who was never dramatic, said sternly. "It's a sealed bottle, so none can accidentally spill. You'd have to smash it to get the contents out. Besides, they're pretty sure they must have dropped it in here somewhere; we'll find it, and no-one'll be any the wiser." She squeezed Cassie's arm. "Chin up, Mum. It's almost over. Just think, only a few more hours and then the next one's a whole year away."

The next one ... Cassie felt a thrill of horror at the very notion. She wasn't sure her nerves could take another Georgian Fair.

She returned to the doorway, switching the megawatt greeting smile back on, murmuring welcoming words. But she was doing it all on autopilot; behind the façade, her mind was racing.

There was only one thing to be done, she resolved. She'd simply have to resign before next year. It would be a shame, but unless she could come up with a decent excuse not to run it...

Alternatively, of course, she could always give it to Dennis to organise instead.

The sly little thought popped up out of nowhere, halting her in her tracks. She paused for a moment, enjoying the sweet thrill of schadenfreude that idea engendered.

Yes, she decided, maybe she would do *just* that.

Feeling decidedly more perky, Cassie slipped into her seat, taking her place on the end of the row just as the crimson curtains in front of the stage began to rise.

The afternoon sun was inching around the gothic spire of All Saints' Church as Hugo Dappleton waited in Red Lion Square, resisting the urge to check his watch for the umpteenth time. All around him, Stamford was in full festive spirit, the sky above fluttering with bunting, the pavements thrumming with people. Usually, this part of Stamford was a busy thoroughfare, the cobbled square with its many offshoots and lack of modern street markings a jumble of filtering traffic, unloading delivery vans, and pedestrians. The latter tended to be in varying states of confusion, depending upon how local they were – and therefore how well they understood the town's idiosyncratic road system. The natural consequence of a street plan unchanged since wheels were only to be found on carts, and cars were mere science fiction, it tended to fluctuate between being charming or infuriating several times a day, depending largely on how much of a hurry you were in.

Normally, Hugo would have loved to see his town like this. Stamford shone at its brightest when it was full of visitors; not everyone was of the same opinion, he knew, but to his mind they made the place a little less museum-like, reinvigorated it with their awe. Today, however, it was taking all of his effort to try and get into the spirit of it.

He looked around him yet again, still searching for a familiar figure coming towards him even as his hope rapidly began to fade. In the end, it was time to give up. Shaking his head, he turned to walk away, when a hand snatched at his arm, yanking him back around.

"*Hugo.*" Gavin was out of breath. "I'm sorry. I got held up."

His cravat was askew; Hugo knew how much he'd hate that if he realised. The temptation to reach out and straighten it made his fingers itch, but he resisted, knowing how Gavin felt about public displays of affection. Instead, he tucked them away, folding his arms across his chest.

"It's all right. You're here now."

"What is it, then?" Impatience radiated from Gavin's tone. "Why did we have to meet here? Your message was cryptic. I'm not exactly in the mood for guessing games right now."

Hugo drew back a little at the shortness in his tone, then reminded himself not to take it too personally. What came across as brutal to other people was, to Gavin, simply efficiency. He probably hadn't meant that like it had sounded.

"That's because I wanted it to be a surprise." Hugo said brightly. He motioned around them, where open-topped carriages formed a higgledy-piggledy queue around the square, harnessed to patiently waiting horses. "I thought it might be nice get away for twenty minutes. Just us."

It had been Amelia's idea. Initially, Hugo had been sceptical, but she'd won him round.

"You two need some time together," she'd insisted. "Relaxing time. Away from everything that's happened." She'd raised her eyebrows meaningfully. "Besides, it'll get him away from work for a while, won't it?"

And it had indeed got him away from work – although he looked about as far from relaxed as was humanly possible right now, Hugo noted with some dismay. Every line of his body was tense, and he was darting glances around him as though he'd rather be anywhere else.

"It's not really my thing, Hugo. You know I don't like animals."

It was a flimsy excuse, and they both knew it. Hugo was starting to feel a flare of annoyance. He knew that Gavin was going through a lot, that he needed to make allowances, but he could feel his sympathy, stretched beyond its limits, now beginning to fray, buckling under months of resentment and unspoken hurt.

"Well, what about me?" He retorted. "What about what *I* might want to do for once?"

"Listen, Hugo," Gavin was already looking back over his shoulder, disconnecting from the conversation. "It was a nice idea, but I just don't have time for this right now, all right? I need to get back to work."

"And *there* it is!" Hugo threw up his hands in sarcastic triumph. "Your reason for everything. You know what? Forget it. Forget I even *tried*."

"Don't be difficult, Hugo," Gavin said wearily. He was looking around, clearly embarrassed by the attention they were attracting. "Please."

Hugo choked on air.

"Yes, because of course *I'm* the difficult one in this relationship," he spluttered. His blood was boiling, rushing to his head until he'd felt dizzy with it. His temper was usually as even as a mill pond, so impossible to stoke that he come to the conclusion that it was simply non-existent. He hadn't even known he could feel this angry. It was half invigorating, half terrifying. "It's *me* who's making us unhappy..."

That got Gavin's attention. He swung back around, shock rippling across his face.

"You're ... unhappy?"

"Of *course* I'm unhappy, Gavin!" Finally saying the words

out loud felt like the most fantastic relief, even as he saw the pain it caused. "You're making it impossible to be anything else."

"Look, I know I've been … on the stressed side lately." Gavin said quickly. "Maybe I've taken it out on you more than I ought to have done, but I've told you, when the Georgian Fair's over…"

"Bugger the Georgian Fair!" Hugo bellowed, making one of the horses start. By now, half the square had stopped to watch. Normally, he would have been mortified, but right now, he couldn't care less. "What about *us*?"

"You just don't understand, do you?" The contrition had vanished from Gavin's face. His voice was low, controlled. "You have no idea how hard I've worked, what I've done—"

"I know that I'm sick of you telling me that I don't understand when you won't share anything with me," Hugo replied tightly, turning away. "You want to insist on doing everything on your own? Fine. Knock yourself out. I won't get in your way anymore."

Then he pushed away through the crowd, before he could wonder what on earth he'd just done.

Chapter Thirty-One

"That is indeed a very red dress," Dexter murmured, as he and Felicia sidled into the plush oxblood interior of the theatre. They'd arrived just in the nick of time; the performance was about to begin, and the lights were down, the doors closed, creating that unique environment which only a theatre could produce. Like being inside a womb, or a toothless mouth: dark and muffled, the atmosphere close and intense, everyone's attention focused on the glowing rectangle of stage. "Although that adjective seems rather pedestrian. What would you call that? Crimson? Scarlet? Vermillion?"

"I'd call it a clue." Felicia stood up on tiptoes, skimming over the rows of powdered heads. "And as we've been a bit lacking in those of late, I'll take it." Spotting a couple of spare seats towards the front, she began to move forwards, motioning for Dexter to follow. "It looks like we'll have to sit through the show first though before we get a chance to talk to her."

"But why would Caroline want to kill Riverton?" Dexter mused, as they inched past the knees of a group of disgruntled-looking middle-aged ladies. "Unless she's decided to take the concept of creating the news to a whole new level."

"Well, she's been stirring up antipathy towards the fair since day one," Felicia said, as they reached their seats. "Perhaps he confronted her about it and they came to blows."

"I thought you said he was the one who brought Iris back here."

"I did."

"Well then." Dexter settled himself in his seat like a pedigree cat, fussing about for several moments before selecting a comfortable position. Once he was suitably ensconced, he continued, "Why would you assume that he actually *wanted* the fair to run smoothly? That little speech she was planning to make ... what if he knew all about it?"

Felicia sat back heavily as the thought sunk in. When he put it like that, of course it seemed obvious. But all the same, she knew why it hadn't occurred to her.

"Because ... well, he *is* the fair. *Was* the fair," she added, with a small grimace. "Why would he put his weight behind something only to watch it fail?" She shook her head. "I just can't see it. It wouldn't make any sense."

"Don't look at me," Dexter shrugged, patting a yawn and reclining back in his seat. Felicia really hoped he wasn't planning on having a nap; he had the singular ability to do that in the most implausible of places – including, on one particularly memorable occasion, the top of a rollercoaster. "I just ask the questions. But it seems to me that he's one you should be looking at."

He was right, Felicia conceded, albeit with reluctance. It did seem as though Riverton was the hinge upon which everything rested. But the problem was, and always had been, that she didn't really know who that man was.

The real James Riverton was still a shadowy figure, a mass of contrasting accounts and opinions, none of which could all be true at the same time. Was he a really great philanthropist, or just another ruthless businessman always calculating in his own interest? A heartless egotist, or simply a misguided man desperate to make amends with his only son? The truth was, she was no closer to having any idea. And until she knew, she was going to have a hard time figuring out who might have wanted to kill him.

"Besides, could a woman even do that?" Dexter was indicating Caroline up on the stage. "Strangle him in cold blood, I mean? He was a big man."

"Not with her bare hands, no." Felicia's answer came quickly. "But from behind, and with a chair to pull against ... he was in the dressing room, remember? What if he was sitting in front of the mirror, and..."

She trailed off, feeling rather sheepish.

"Been looking into it, have we?" Dexter seemed mightily amused by her discomfort. "Your internet search history must be raising flags in some interesting places at the moment."

Mercifully, a booming voice from the stage saved her from having to answer.

"*Welcome*, everyone, to our Georgian makeup demonstration," the woman in the left-hand chair was smiling in welcome. Felicia didn't recognise her, and she couldn't help but wonder why Tara wasn't doing this. She thought of the girl she'd seen earlier, pale and nervy, and wondered if she'd been taken unwell.

The presenter was indicating the other chair on the stage, and its occupant.

"*Please* welcome our model for the afternoon, Caroline. Many of you will, of course, recognise her as editor-in-chief of the *fabulous* Stamford Bugle newspaper. A real local institution, I understand."

There was a scoffing sound from Dexter. Felicia made a show of whacking him on the back. Caroline's thin smile froze in place.

"Now, as many of you are displaying *so well*, the first, and most important part of any 18th century lady – or gentleman's – makeup routine was a flawless white face." The presenter picked up a small glass pot and began to dab a brush into it, still talking as she worked. "Some of the ingredients in a face paint such as this would have been rice powder, vinegar, gum Arabic..." She paused for effect, brushing a smear of white paste across Caroline's forehead before continuing, "and a few other little things like lead, arsenic..." A smattering of laughter greeted this, and she smiled. Caroline continued to look stony as ever.

"It's easy for us to assume they were ignorant," the presenter carried on chirpily. "But in reality, people knew what they were putting on their faces ... although perhaps not *quite* how *deadly* they could be. Beauty then, as ever, had its price." She paused again, dropping her voice to a dramatic timbre. "And some were about to pay the highest price of all."

Hugo stalked across Red Lion Square, blinking back tears of anger and despair.

"Hugo, wait!" Gavin's voice rang out behind him. Hugo ignored it, ploughing on through the crowd, muttering apologies to those he jostled.

"Hugo, *please!*" The voice was louder now, closer, tinged with desperation. "Just ... stop. Let's talk about this."

Hugo wasn't, on the whole, given to moments of impetuousness. In fact, he tended to err in the opposite direction. But something about the demand in Gavin's tone – the automatic assumption of being obeyed – pricked at his temper, made him bold. Without breaking stride, he vaulted up into a waiting carriage, landing in the seat opposite a surprised-looking Tony.

"Mind if we share?" Hugo asked distractedly. He could see Gavin pushing towards them, fighting against the swell of people.

Tony's eyes flickered to Gavin, then back to Hugo. An expression passed across his face, half-assessing, half-leering. For a moment, Hugo found himself regretting his moment of petulance; after all, being stuck in a moving vehicle making small talk with one of Stamford's least winning denizens wasn't tempting. But it was preferable to the alternative, and when Tony nodded curtly, Hugo spun around gratefully towards the driver.

"Can we go, please?"

"Of course, sir. Anywhere in particular?"

As Hugo watched, Gavin broke free of the crowd. He looked around wildly, clearly having lost track of where Hugo had gone. Then his eyes fell on the carriage.

"No," Hugo said quickly. "Just drive."

They pulled away, leaving Gavin standing there in the middle of Red Lion Square, getting smaller and smaller with every turn of the wheels over the cobbles.

———————————

"Pettifer's here." Dexter's voice was low in her ear.

"Mmm." Felicia stared straight ahead. She felt, rather than saw, Dexter's quizzical glance.

"Trouble in paradise?"

She glared at him, and he grinned, sinking back into his seat.

"All right, all right. I've no desire to get in the middle of you two. Just ... keep it civil, okay?" He placed a hand on his heart. "Think of the children."

"Do you *mind*?" The woman next to them hissed crossly. "Some of us are trying to listen."

"My sincerest apologies." Dexter immediately turned his most bewitching smile upon her. "Beastly behaviour, I agree. I shall remove myself forthwith."

Felicia watched in disbelief as the woman's eyelashes began to flutter.

"Oh," she twittered. "No, I mean ... please, don't."

"Most obliging." Dexter patted her gloved hand, abruptly swivelling back to Felicia. "Now, where were we?"

"I wish you wouldn't *do* that." Felicia tried to ignore the woman's crestfallen expression. "It's a detestable habit."

"Feeling left out, dear heart?" He raised an eyebrow. "I can flirt with you too, if you like."

She rolled her eyes.

"Tempting, but no."

"And now for the rouge," the presenter up on the stage was gushing. "A red spot of colour on each cheek was the *height* of fashion, but that coquettish hint of blush came with its own risks. The vibrant hue was achieved using vermillion, which is made from cinnabar..." another dramatic – and, Felicia was beginning to find, slightly tedious – pause followed, then "... also known as mercury sulphide."

She droned on, but Felicia wasn't listening. She leaned closer to Dexter.

"Is it just me, or is Caroline looking a little … peaky?"

"The white paint might not be helping."

"Very droll." She bit her lip, trying to articulate the sudden sense of concern that was creeping over her. "But I'm serious, Dexter. She really doesn't look right."

Her gaze travelled across the rows of seats to where Pettifer was lurking by a column, clearly trying to be inconspicuous and failing miserably. He was watching the stage with the same granite-like expression he always wore, but she could tell he was intently focused on proceedings. She couldn't help but wonder what he was doing here. She doubted he was after cosmetics tips.

She looked back at Caroline, and immediately knew something was very wrong. Her lips were bracketed by deep grooves, beads of sweat glistening on her newly painted forehead. Out of the corner of her eye, she could see Pettifer obviously sensing the same thing; he was rocking forward on one huge foot, ready to move if need be.

And the need suddenly became very apparent.

A cry tore the air. Up on the stage, Caroline Boughton was grasping her stomach, bent over double.

Chapter Thirty-Two

G avin stared after the rapidly retreating carriage, numb with shock.

He'd gone. He couldn't believe it.

He felt a discombobulating sense of things he'd taken for granted turning on their head. When he made a plan, it happened. He never left room for it to do otherwise. And yet, in one fell swoop, Hugo had changed everything.

The carriage rounded the side of All Saints' Church, disappearing from view. And for the first time in his life, Gavin didn't over-think. He didn't try to plan.

He just began to give chase.

Inside the theatre, things were teetering dangerously on the verge of chaos. People were rising from their seats, chattering in panic. Caroline had slid off her chair by now, hitting the floor with a thud.

Pettifer didn't waste a moment. He surged forwards,

charging down the aisle, gesticulating ferociously at those foolish enough to get in his path.

"Bring down the curtain!" He bellowed, his voice hoarse. "*Now!*"

But he was too late. Up on the stage, the prone figure began to convulse.

———

Gavin's blood sang in his ears as he ran up the curve of All Saint's Place. The church was perched in the middle of the square like an island of grey stone, blocking the view of anything beyond it. As he rounded one hulking side, the carriage suddenly came back into view.

And what he saw made Gavin's heart stop in his chest.

It was tilting, veering perilously.

Then, slowly, it began to tip over.

The splintering crash of wood and metal seemed to go on for ever. Gavin skidded to a halt, momentarily frozen. It was as though his limbs had forgotten how to function.

He tried to call Hugo's name, but nothing happened. The sound just wouldn't come.

Chapter Thirty-Three

P ettifer looked down at the body lying in a pool of scarlet. The material of her dress glistened under the spotlights. It looked uncannily like blood. Or perhaps that was just his brain playing tricks on him.

He sat down heavily on the edge of the stage, feeling suddenly dazed. Guiltily, he was aware this was all a crime scene now, and he shouldn't be touching anything. Forensics would be swarming all over this soon enough; he was only waiting with the body until then.

It was the strangest feeling, being alone with a dead person. The silence was deeper, greater than anything merely auditory. Pettifer wasn't inclined towards contemplation, but in these moments, when it felt like he, too, was suspended in the unreality between worlds, it was difficult to do anything else. Unfortunately, the thoughts going around his mind at the moment were ones he'd rather not face.

Dimly, he became aware that he was no longer alone.

"You shouldn't be here, Felicia."

He spoke without turning his head, voice echoing around the empty theatre space.

"I know." But she didn't move to go, and he didn't tell her to. Instead, they just occupied the space together for a moment, shared the burden of silence. Then she spoke again, hesitantly, stepping out of the wings into the light.

"Are you … all right?"

"Me?" The unexpected nature of her question rendered his reply sharp.

"You were the closest when she…" She looked at the body, then quickly away again. He saw her swallow, the long line of her throat moving up and down. "I mean, I can't imagine many people have actually died in your arms."

She was right; they hadn't. Only Felicia would have thought of that.

Everyone else assumed that death was just a part of the job, that it happened every week, that he would be inured to it by now. But the truth was, it still shocked him, terrified him, broke a piece of him within each time it happened. It didn't get better with years or experience, either. He felt the same today as he had at his first fatality. No-one warned you of that.

Once, he'd gone into the evidence cupboard and overheard Jess having a secret cry behind the shelves. He'd retreated silently, closed the door, pretended it never happened. He wished he hadn't now. He wished he'd spoken to her about it. Told her that an inability to be unmoved wasn't a failing, but a very human strength. That it made them better at what they did.

But he was a hypocrite for even thinking it. After all, he couldn't even look Felicia in the eye now. He couldn't admit that she was right. The old habits were too hard to break.

"She didn't," he said shortly. "She was already dead by the time I got to her."

But he'd held her anyway, cradled her head beneath his palm as he felt for the pulse in her neck. It had felt right, somehow, that she shouldn't be alone. That was what most people feared most: to be alone at the end.

"You couldn't have saved her," Felicia said gently. "It all happened too quickly."

He felt a spike of anger as he saw what she was trying to do. Well-intentioned it might be, but he didn't want her pity right now. And he certainly didn't want to be told how he should feel.

"And that's your *professional* opinion, is it?" He said caustically.

She opened her mouth, then closed it again.

"Sarge?" Jess appeared in the wings behind Felicia. She didn't look surprised to see the other woman standing there, which spoke volumes about matters, Pettifer thought darkly. Maybe Heavenly was right when he ranted on about lax standards and parochial approaches to crime-solving. "I've put everyone in the ballroom like you asked. All the witnesses."

"Thank you, Constable," Pettifer inclined his head queryingly. "Although you seem to have missed one."

"Oh, him." Jess looked dismissively at Nosy Nick, whose arm she was gripping authoritatively. "I was just about to toss him out. I found him skulking around backstage, stealing sandwiches."

"They were curling in the heat; no-one else was going to eat them!" Nick protested. "But actually, I was doing my job. This is a big story, don't you know." He looked pointedly at his captured arm. "And I'm sure the public will be *very* interested to know about police brutality on display by our local force."

"Oh, don't be so dramatic." Jess looked disgusted. "I'm hardly touching you."

"Semantics," Nick crowed. "Sweet semantics, dear Constable. I *think* you'll find—"

Then he noticed the body for the first time. His jaw went slack, eyes bulging.

"Christ, is that..." He swayed on his feet, and for an unwelcome moment, Pettifer thought he was going to have to catch him as he swooned. But then he was scrabbling around in his satchel, muttering frenziedly, "Why, this is incredible! Nick Naseby, on the spot ... oh, blast." He belatedly realised that he was talking into a box of cheese straws and tossed them back within, rummaging around once more. "Where's my Dictaphone? I'd better not have left it in that rancid tunnel."

Jess, alarmed, leapt into action.

"Come on, out with you. You'll get your story later, along with everyone else."

"Everyone *else*?" Nick stared, full of righteous consternation. "But I have an exclusive here!" As Jess tugged on his arm, he stabbed a finger accusingly at Felicia. "What about *her*? *She's* here!"

"She's a key witness," Pettifer said calmly, wondering if he should be concerned by how easily the half-truth slipped off his tongue. Before the spring, he wouldn't have dreamed of bending the rules in this way. But Felicia had a way of making her own rules, he thought ruefully, and everyone else ended up getting pulled in as her accomplices, like it or not.

"But..." Nick wailed. He was practically clinging to the wall now, Jess doing her best to drag him away. Pettifer tried to keep his face professionally stony, deliberately not looking at Felicia as the journalist was inelegantly manhandled down the aisle and through the double doors at the back of the theatre, protestations and calumnies echoing in his wake. It seemed to take a remarkably long time. Eventually, the doors slammed shut, and Pettifer took a moment to relish the blissful quiet before turning back to his companion.

"He's right, you know," he said sternly. "You should go. I don't know how I'll explain your presence to my reinforcements when they arrive."

Felicia was looking at the body, seemingly far away. But she nodded, indicating she'd heard him.

"All right." She shook herself. "Sorry. I just keep replaying it. It was so … brutal, so violent." Ridiculously, her mind kept going back to the one incongruous fact she knew about the woman: that she'd been the owner of fourteen guinea pigs. In this moment, it seemed to make her more human than ever, her death more real. What would happen to those guinea pigs now, she wondered? "I know I shouldn't ask, but … I mean, it *had* to be poison of some kind, surely?"

"Yes." His words were still clipped, but softening. In truth, he was already regretting having his earlier snap at her. After all, she'd only been trying to help. It wasn't her fault that he'd failed. Failed at his duty, but most importantly, failed the woman lying in front of him, cold and irreversibly still. "Something pretty powerful, I think. Fast-acting. Something like…"

"Poison?"

A voice rang out, making them both turn. Cassie was standing in the space Jess had just vacated.

"Madam Mayor, this is a *crime scene*!" Pettifer barked, although with more exasperation than genuine anger. This was what happened when reinforcements were a good ten miles away; it was impossible to create any kind of security. "You can't just walk in here like…"

"Did you say *poison*?" She persisted, apparently not having paid heed to a word he'd uttered.

He gave up.

"I did," he confirmed wearily.

"Oh, *God*." A hand flew to her crimson lips. She looked utterly stricken. "You don't mean ... it couldn't be something like ... arsenic, could it?"

Pettifer was beginning to get a very ominous feeling.

"Why?" He asked, in a low, controlled voice.

"Because..." Cassie gulped. "We might be missing a small vial of it."

Pettifer closed his eyes and started to count to ten. It was one of the things he'd learned to maintain his equilibrium when things were spinning out of control.

Meanwhile, Cassie was babbling on, clearly feeling the need to explain.

"There was a talk earlier. The Georgian Apothecary. It's part of it, you see; they have this doctor's case with all the jars in it. For demonstration purposes. They hand them around..." She was talking so fast that she ran out of breath. She paused, inhaled, then added more slowly, "They're all sealed, obviously. For safety reasons."

Pettifer had only counted as far as six, but his eyes snapped open at that. He wasn't feeling any more relaxed. If anything, his temper was rising at a steep gradient.

"And you didn't think it *might* have been a good idea to tell me this earlier?"

"I only knew myself just before the show started! And we ... I mean, I..." Her voice dropped in shame. "I thought we'd find it."

"Bloody hell, Cassie!" Pettifer exploded, so livid that he

forgot to address her formally for once. "I know you're a bit of a loose cannon sometimes, but this…"

Cassie blinked, looking shocked at his outburst.

"I … I didn't think."

"Wait you two." Felicia was holding up her hands. Pettifer assumed she was about to jump in and defend her friend, but he soon saw that she was preoccupied with something else entirely. "Let's think about this for a minute. Arsenic; that's one of the things she mentioned this afternoon." She looked between them, eyes wide. "Remember? They used to put it in the makeup."

As one, they all looked at the pot of white face paste, still sitting open on the table.

"It would have been easy to tamper with, I suppose," Cassie ventured. "The props were all set out in here a good twenty minutes in advance of the start. And those doors weren't locked."

"And arsenic powder is white," Pettifer said. "Once mixed in, no-one would be any the wiser."

There was a lull as they all privately considered the implications of what they were suggesting.

A muffled vibration came from within Pettifer's detritus-filled pocket. He located his phone, peeling a chewing gum wrapper off its screen before putting it to his ear with a curt, "What? What could *possibly* be so important right now that?" He broke off, listening to the breathless voice on the other end, and when he spoke again, his tone had changed. "All right. I'm on my way."

He cut the call, turning grimly to Felicia.

"You'd better come with me. There's been an accident." He hesitated, then added, "It's Hugo."

The ambulance was parked up behind the church, back doors flung open. Two figures sat on the steps. Even from here, Felicia could see that they were holding hands.

"Hugo!" She rushed over. "My God, are you all right?"

"He's lucky, is what he is." A paramedic was applying a plaster to Hugo's brow with a brisk, expert motion. "He was thrown completely clear. It could have been a very different story otherwise."

Gavin shuddered, squeezing Hugo's fingers tighter.

"Don't, please. I can't even think about it. To know how close I came to losing you..." He broke off, looking momentarily torn. Then resolve swept in, settling over his features. "I had this whole thing so carefully planned ... I wanted to wait for the perfect time. But now ... I can see what an idiot I've been."

Hugo looked at Felicia, raising a hand to his temple.

"Maybe I did knock my head after all. Or is he not making any sense to you either?"

"I'm trying to ask you to marry me," Gavin said, slightly shakily. "I know I'm not doing very well at it. I haven't handled any of this well, to be honest. But..." He stopped, peering at Hugo – who was staring straight ahead – concernedly. "Hugo? Can you even hear me?" He glanced entreatingly at the paramedic. "Are you absolutely sure he hasn't got a concussion?"

"You're right," Hugo said, speaking up abruptly. "You are an idiot."

But there was a glow of affection in his eyes. Gavin

obviously saw it, because he immediately looked hopeful.

"Is that a very backhanded way of saying yes?" He took a quavering breath. "Because if so, I'll take it."

"Of *course* it's a yes!" Hugo flung his arms around Gavin. "What else would it be?"

"Well, he seems to be all right," the paramedic observed to the air at large, looking amused. "But you'll need to keep an eye on him. He has to rest. No strenuous activity."

"What?" Hugo made a pretence of being aghast, which he promptly ruined by grinning. "Didn't you hear? I'm a newly-engaged man!"

"Hugo!" Gavin was blushing furiously, looking like he wanted to sink into the floor.

The paramedic laughed warmly.

"Congratulations, both of you."

"Seconded." Felicia pulled Hugo into a hug. Then she turned to Gavin, and, while Hugo was chattering excitedly to the indulgent paramedic, said quietly, "Well, you're a dark horse. I didn't see that coming. But I'm happy for you."

"Thank you." His glow faded slightly; he pulled her aside. "Listen, there's something I need to tell you. Hugo wasn't alone in the carriage. Tony was there too." He faltered. "He ... didn't make it, unfortunately."

"Oh." Felicia leaned against the side of the ambulance, trying to assimilate that information. She hadn't taken to the man, but this...

"Hugo doesn't know yet, and I don't want him to," Gavin was saying. "You know what he's like; he'll torment himself with guilt about it, and I don't want to ruin this moment for him. He's been through more than enough today."

Felicia nodded jerkily, still feeling thrown.

"There's something else." Pettifer appeared beside them,

presumably having overheard the latter part of their conversation. He had remarkably good hearing for someone whose ears had been boxed numerous times in the scrum. "I've been and had a look over the carriage, and I'm afraid it's not good news. One of the wheels has been loosened."

Gavin's head swivelled.

"Deliberately?"

"Almost certainly." Pettifer gestured to the incline rising up behind them. "It would have been a foregone conclusion. On these cobbles..." He looked at Gavin, and there was almost apology in his face. "I'm sorry, but I'm going to have to ask if you can think of anyone who might have held a grudge against Mr. Dappleton?"

"Hugo?" Gavin looked startled. "No, you don't ... I mean, he wasn't even supposed to have *been* in that carriage. It was a spur-of-the-moment thing." He looked discomfited. "We'd ... had a bit of an argument, you see."

Pettifer nodded, saving him from having to divulge more.

"All right, well, that makes more sense. Thank you for your time; you can go back to your fiancé now." As Gavin walked away, Pettifer murmured to Felicia, "I have to say, I couldn't really see Hugo and Tony Chandler as simpatico. He must have been meeting someone else, then."

"Who said he was meeting anyone?"

"I've spoken to the driver. Luckily, he's unhurt. Apparently the carriage was booked in advance – by Tony himself, so that doesn't help us." Pettifer raised a bristly eyebrow. "However, I highly doubt he was out for a solo ride."

For what it was worth, Felicia agreed. Tony hadn't exactly seemed enamoured with the whole Georgian Fair experience; she was finding it tough to envisage him luxuriating in a fanciful clip-clop around town in his spare time.

"If he *was* meeting someone," she said, following the logical train of thought. "Then there would only have been the two of them who knew which carriage they would be using. Where it would be, and at what time."

"It would explain why his companion didn't turn up," Pettifer said dryly. "No-one would risk being involved in a crash like that."

Felicia gave an involuntary shiver, her gaze wandering towards the wreckage.

"What a way to do it. They must have been confident it would work."

Pettifer nodded sombrely.

"Someone's got nerve, all right."

Felicia looked away, towards the periwinkle-coloured sky. It was hard to imagine how anyone's thoughts could turn to malevolence on a day as beautiful as this. She sighed.

"Do you think Tony was involved in some way? With everything that's been going on?"

"I think we have to assume that, yes. Even if he didn't actually commit the murders himself, he must have known something about them. Otherwise why get him out of the way?"

She folded her arms, stared him down.

"Oh, so they're finally *murders* now, are they?"

"They were always murders, Felicia," he said levelly. Then, ignoring her attempts to interject, "and now we have four. There must be a link somewhere."

Felicia wondered briefly whether she ought to pursue the point, but decided to let it drop. At least she finally had him on her side.

"Well, I'm pretty sure that Tony was linked to Riverton." She recalled that moment at the ball, when Riverton had made the other man stand down. "They hid it, but there was a relationship there. I'm still not sure what it was, though."

"Okay."

"And Riverton was linked to Iris," Felicia was on a roll now, pieces fitting together in her mind, one by one. "*He* was the one who wanted her back in Stamford this year. And Caroline ... well, who knows how she fits in, but she was a dodgy journalist. She could easily have been involved with any one of them..." As she spoke, something slotted into place. A memory, a flicker of recognition she hadn't been able to place. Jack's photograph ... the blurry image of a woman in the background, staring at Iris ... that had been Caroline. She hadn't seen it before, but now ... the realisation made her spin towards Pettifer.

"You were at the makeup demonstration." She put her hands on her hips, glared at him interrogatively. Co-operation went two ways. If he was holding something back from her, after all of this... "Why were you there? Was it to talk with her?"

"No." A quiet voice said behind them. "It was to talk to *me*."

Chapter Thirty-Four

"My parents are out at the fair." Tara let herself into the house, beckoning for them to follow her. "They won't be back until this evening."

The row of cottages on St. George's Street were miniature doll's house versions of the grand mansions in the square beyond. Felicia had been in one of them years ago for an insurance valuation, and she remembered the layout well. This one seemed to mirror it; only two rooms deep, but with a glorious view over St George's Churchyard – in spring a foam of sugary blossom, now a watercolour blur of midsummer's green.

Tara sat next to the window, in a lumpy-looking armchair. Felicia tried to curb her antiques valuer's tendency to scan the room, although she couldn't help noting that Tara's parents didn't seem all that hot on redecorating; everything in here looked dated, and not in a good way.

Pettifer perched precariously on the edge of the loveseat – the room being too small for a full-sized sofa – clearly trying to appear serious, despite apparently being about to slide off the edge onto the floor.

"I'm here to ask you about—"

"I know why you're here." Tara's profile was silhouetted in the window, so her expression was invisible. "You want to know about James and I."

Felicia, who'd been temporarily distracted by the view beyond her, started. Had she missed something? Before she could stop herself, she blurted out:

"You mean, you were…"

"In a relationship? Yes, we were." Tara clasped her hands in her lap, drawing herself up, and in that moment, she looked more woman than girl. "In fact, we were more than that. We were getting married."

Felicia's mind flashed back to yesterday in the ballroom, when she'd seen the two of them interact. Tara had been nervous around him, jumpy. But then she'd accidentally called him by his first name. She'd corrected herself quickly; so quickly that Felicia had missed the incongruity at the time.

She glanced at Pettifer, who didn't seem to find any of this that surprising. Instead he just carried on calmly with his questions.

"How did the two of you meet?"

"At rehearsals for the play. I wasn't even supposed to be in it, just helping with the costumes. But then the girl playing Polly had to drop out and I…" She faltered self-consciously. "I've always loved drama, but the thought of getting up on stage terrified me. James, though, he helped. Showed me how to overcome my fears. He saw something in me no-one else ever had." Her eyes, which had become misty as she spoke, sharpened as she refocused on them both. "I know what you're thinking: older man, younger woman … but it wasn't like that.

If anything, I was the one who pursued him. I liked the person I was when I was with him; he made me believe I could be more than just..." She broke off. "No-one else has ever looked at me like that. But James ... I never expected it to go anywhere, of course. Me and him. How could it? But when I found I was pregnant..."

Felicia let out a stifled gasp. Pettifer sent her a 'control yourself' glower. She shrank back in her seat, wishing he'd thought to give her a bit of a heads-up first. To say that this was all absolute news to her was an understatement.

"I thought he'd be upset." Tara didn't appear to have noticed any of this. She was somewhere else entirely, gazing into the past as she spoke. "But he wasn't. He was thrilled. He doesn't have much contact with Gavin, so another child..." For the first time, her eyes glittered. "He was so excited. Said it would be a fresh start for the family. He hoped it would bring him and Gavin back together at last." She shook her head, a tear splashing onto her cheek. She wiped it away. "So you see, he couldn't have killed himself like they're saying. He just ... wouldn't. He had so much to live for."

"And your boyfriend." Pettifer leaned forwards, resting his elbows on his knees. "Does he know that you're pregnant?"

"No." She sniffed. "Nobody knows. I know I should have told Ambrose the truth sooner, broken it off between us, but it's difficult. We've been together for so long, you see. He relies upon me. If he knew..." Her face twisted. "I'm not sure how he'd cope."

"He has a temper?"

"He doesn't always know how to control his emotions. He says they're too big for him sometimes." She looked up, and her eyes were huge, beseeching. "But he's not violent. I don't want you to think ... he's a gentle giant. A good person." She fiddled with a tassel on the cushion beside her. "I'm very fond of him, but he sees me the way he wants to. The way my parents do. Whereas James..." She looked away, out of the window, but Felicia knew she wasn't taking in the view. "I don't know what I'm going to do now."

In the silence that followed – during which Pettifer looked supremely ill-at-ease – Felicia became aware of a muffled commotion going on outside. Pettifer obviously heard it too, because he was on his feet, craning towards the window.

"Was that a siren?"

"There's an ambulance," Tara said vaguely. She still seemed disconnected from the present. "I can't see any more from here."

Pettifer made for the door. It was at a pace which no onlooker would ever describe as speedy, yet Felicia knew that was him making haste. He was worried, and she didn't blame him. After the events of this afternoon, they were all on edge.

There was indeed an ambulance in the square, incongruous and fluorescent against the mellow old stone. The ballroom doors were thrown open, a stretcher carefully being manoeuvred out between them. Felicia felt cold dread lodge itself in the pit of her stomach, racing forwards. Surely no-one else could die today?

As she neared, however, loud laments put her mind to rest on that score.

"*Struck down in the pursuit of truth.*" The figure on the stretcher strained to sit up. "Wait. That's good. Where's my Dictaphone?"

"Nick!" Felicia skidded to a halt at his side. "What happened?"

"I've been poisoned. I got too close, and now they're trying to kill me too." He flung an arm over his face, moaning, "Oh nurse, it's terrible. The *pain*! I think I'm dying."

"He's not dying." The paramedic – the same who'd treated Hugo, although decidedly less willingly in this case, Felicia sensed – said wearily. She leaned closer and murmured, "Although I can't promise I won't kill him on the way to the hospital. Especially if he calls me nurse again." She eyed the writhing figure dubiously. "Is he always like this, or should I be worrying about hallucinations?"

"No, this is pretty standard," Felicia said. She was dimly aware that Tara had followed her out, and was standing over her shoulder, watching silently. "Is he right? Has he been poisoned?"

"Yep. Something nasty, although not enough to do any lasting damage. At the moment, it's anyone's guess what it is or how it got into his system. He claims the only thing he's had this afternoon is a slug of coffee and a leftover ham sandwich. But this is certainly no food poisoning."

"No," Felicia said faintly, as Nick was wheeled away.

"What's going on?" Tara had wrapped her arms around herself, looking shellshocked. "I don't understand. Why is all of this happening?"

Pettifer came puffing over.

"Are you absolutely *sure* that your boyfriend didn't know about your relationship? Or the child?" Before she could answer, he urged, "Think. This could be vitally important."

"I don't ... *think* so," Tara stuttered, looking like a rabbit in the headlights under his intensity. "But I suppose I couldn't swear to it. Ambrose ... he keeps things bottled up. Why do you ask?"

"Because he's just been arrested," Pettifer said grimly. "Under suspicion of murdering James Riverton."

At the police station, Jess was arranging biscuits on a plate for the second time that afternoon. On this occasion, however, she bypassed all of the boring ones; it was chocolate fingers, jammie dodgers and party rings all the way. *Several* party rings, in fact. One in each colour. She felt the circumstances warranted it.

Heavenly was preening at his desk, but as she passed, he looked up, glaring at the plate.

"Biscuits, Constable? This isn't a boutique hotel!"

"I didn't think it would do any harm," Jess protested gently.

Besides, she added silently, as she looked at the gangly form slumped behind her desk, head cradled in his impossibly large pink hands, it looked as though their suspect could do with some sugar. "Do you want me to call the sarge in for the interview?"

"Pettifer?" Heavenly looked indignant. "Of course not. I shall be conducting the interview personally." He drew himself up, clearly unable to resist adding, "After all, it is *my* arrest."

Jess gritted her teeth behind her obsequious smile.

"Indeed, sir. So it is."

She glanced over at Ambrose again, hunched and miserable-looking, and began to wonder if she hadn't made a mistake in telling Heavenly what she'd found on Riverton's phone. At the time, she'd thought she had no choice, that she was doing the right thing, but now...

The sense of foreboding only increased as Heavenly pulled up a chair opposite Ambrose, crossing one Saville Row tailored leg carefully over the other. It was a slow move, deliberate, and to Jess, it spelled danger. Because for all his smooth, urbane exterior, their new DCI had an unprecedentedly aggressive way with suspects. Everyone had already learned the hard way that the more controlled and cordial he seemed, the more unpredictable he could become.

And he was looking *very* controlled right now.

"So." Heavenly steepled his hands beneath his chin, eyeing the prostrate form before him with silvered calculation. "Shall we begin?"

Ambrose raised his head at last, blinking. His face was blotched and blank with shock.

"I don't understand what I'm doing here."

"You're here because your fingerprints were found on James Riverton's mobile telephone," Heavenly said languidly. "The same phone which was used to type his final message. What we believed to be his suicide note. Can you explain how they came to be there?"

"He was already dead," Ambrose blurted out. "I *swear*. I never hurt him."

Heavenly leaned in closer, still keeping his voice low.

"Isn't it true that he was having an affair with your girlfriend? And that you knew about it?"

"I ... found out, yes," Ambrose admitted hesitantly. His hands wrung clumsily on the desk in front of him. Heavenly's eyes gleamed.

"That must have made you very angry."

"Of course it did." When he frowned, his whole face got involved, screwing up tightly. "An older man like that, taking advantage. Tara, she's ... innocent, you see. Not worldly. She needs protecting from things she doesn't understand."

"That's what you were doing then, was it, when you were arrested for beating up another man in The Golden Goose three years ago? *Protecting* her?" Heavenly's voice had sharpened. He no longer sounded so friendly. "Oh yes, I know all about that. These things stay on file, you see. They haunt one. How do you think we matched your prints?"

Ambrose flushed dully.

"He was taking liberties."

"According to witnesses, all he did was look at her." Heavenly returned. "Hardly a crime, is it? But then, perhaps you have your own idea of what constitutes justice?"

Ambrose's eyes, beneath coarse, unkempt brows, widened as comprehension set in.

"I never hurt him," he repeated stubbornly, but there was an edge of fright to his voice now.

Heavenly looked unmoved. Instead, he pushed harder, accusation colouring his voice.

"You have a history of violent temper. You confronted him..."

"I just wanted to talk to him, is all! Tell him to leave her alone." Ambrose sagged against the back of his chair, looking beaten. "Tara had been skittish all night, casting glances towards the door. I knew something was going on. They were going to meet. So when I saw him sneak out ... well, I followed him." He sighed. "Before you ask, I don't know what I was planning to do if I caught them. Chances are, I wouldn't have done anything. But by the time I got down to the cellars, I couldn't see them anyway. I was about to give up when I..." He gulped, his Adam's apple quivering. "He was just ... hanging there. I've never seen anything like it. I can't stop seeing it, even now."

Heavenly's lips pursed. Clearly, he'd thought he was closing in on a confession, and thus didn't appreciate Ambrose coming up with a plausible alternative.

"Then how do you explain your fingerprints on the phone?" He demanded.

"The screen was glowing, so I picked it up." Ambrose shrugged. "I don't know why; I was in a daze. Then I saw the message on it, and I knew what it meant." He looked at Heavenly levelly. "I'm not quite as slow as everyone thinks."

"Why didn't you call for help?" Jess asked softly, gaining her a vindictive scowl from Heavenly. But she didn't care; she wanted to give Ambrose a chance, although she had to admit it didn't look good for him, no matter what he said.

"I was scared! I just … ran out of there." He was starting to droop with exhaustion; Jess wondered if he'd ever uttered this many words in one go before. "I'm not proud of it now. But then I saw Tara, and I just … couldn't tell her the truth. So I said I was looking for my coat instead. That wasn't a lie, by the way. I really *had* lost it. But I know how I come across. If no-one even believes me about a small thing like that…"

"And where is this coat now?" Heavenly asked. His eyes were piercing. "I notice you're not wearing it."

"I…" Ambrose stuttered. "I can't find it again."

Heavenly just raised his eyebrows. Ambrose cast a desperate, entreating look at Jess.

"Look, please. I may be a coward, but I'm no killer."

There was a small, loaded silence. Then Heavenly got to his feet.

"You're right," he said silkily. "I don't believe you. About any of it."

And then he swept away, pausing only to snatch the plate of biscuits off the desk as he passed.

Chapter Thirty-Five

"Well, that settles it; someone's definitely playing a game with us." Pettifer collapsed onto the bench, pocketing his phone. "That was the pathologist. Apparently it's categorically impossible for the arsenic to have got into Caroline's system through her skin. To act that quickly, she had to have ingested it."

"So it wasn't in the makeup after all," Felicia frowned pensively.

"No. Just designed to look like it." Pettifer shook his remarkably cuboid head, looking perplexed. "Someone went to a lot of trouble. Although right now, I'm struggling to see why. I mean, what was the point?"

Felicia looked out over the river. A pair of swans was gliding downstream, like melting snow on the surface of the water. Their dazzlingly, almost unnatural whiteness nudged at a memory, dredging it from the depths of her consciousness.

"The cravat," she said slowly.

Pettifer looked sideways at her.

"Why do I get the sense you're about to do that thing again?"

"What thing?"

"My job."

She pulled a face at him, but continued.

"Riverton was hanged with a cravat. That's always bothered me, for the same reason you've just said. Why would the murderer make their life so difficult? I mean, they were in a theatre dressing room! There was rope around, ribbon, braid from soldier's uniforms..." She broke off for breath. "Any of that would have been an easier choice ... so why a *cravat*? Unless..."

"It meant something." Pettifer finished thoughtfully. "A symbol of some sort."

Finally, he was with her. She could feel excitement building, colouring her voice as she carried on:

"One victim strangled with a cravat." She began to tick off her fingers. "Another poisoned by makeup. A carriage accident." She opened her hands wide, looked at him expectantly. When he didn't jump in straight away, she blurted out impatiently, "There's a Georgian theme there! Surely you can see that? They're *Georgian* murders."

He didn't look suitably thunderstruck. She felt a damp fizzle of disappointment, like a sparkler put out in a bucket of water. Instead, he raised an eyebrow sardonically.

"And are you about to tell me that hook-a-duck is a quintessential Georgian game?"

"Well ... no," she admitted. "That is a bit of a hole in my theory. "But..." she continued quickly, before he could shut her down altogether. "Iris's death has always seemed different somehow, hasn't it? I know you think so too, so don't try and deny it."

"It hasn't ever quite fitted in my mind, no," he conceded, albeit grudgingly.

"Exactly! The rest were all meticulously planned, almost *over*-planned, whereas that … it seems to have been spur-of-the-moment, a crime of passion."

"A different murderer, perhaps?" Pettifer suggested, far too matter-of-factly for Felicia's liking.

"Oh God, don't say *that*." The thought was enough to send a tremor through her. "One's more than enough." She wrapped her arms around herself, a motion which only served to remind her uncomfortably of her corset. "I suppose I can take this dress off now, can't I? I mean, it's definitely over?"

Apparently, four murders and a poisoning had been too much for even the impressive tenacity of the powers that be, who'd finally caved and cancelled the rest of the day's events. Felicia couldn't say she was sorry to see the back of the Georgian Fair, although she fervently wished it were under different circumstances.

"I think we can fairly safely say that, yes." Pettifer was looking around him, clearly perplexed by the unabating crowds. "Not that it appears to be putting people off. Why are they all still here?"

"Everyone loves a bit of intrigue. They're probably hoping that if they stick around, something else exciting will happen." She folded her arms. "I should warn you though, Dexter's not happy that you axed his event. Apparently it pains him to have to," she clasped a hand to her heart and feigned a dramatic mien, *"let down his fans."*

"Hmm." Pettifer rumbled. "I think I can live with that on my conscience."

"You're a hard man." She grinned, reaching down beside her. "Now here, take your poncy coffee. Before it gets cold."

He winced.

"You remember my saying that?"

"Hard to forget such an august turn of phrase." She eyed him as he took a hefty swig. "They seem to have grown on you since, mind."

"I like the syrup," he muttered, then scowled as she began to laugh. "Now stop that; I'm ashamed enough of myself as it is. But I can't help it; I'm hooked." He held out the cup towards her. "Butterscotch. It's a good one; you should try it."

"No thanks." She grimaced. "I think I'll stick to a plain flat white."

He shrugged, taking a plangent slurp.

"You Londoners are all the same. No sense of adventure."

"I'm not sure I was ever really a proper Londoner." The confession tumbled automatically from Felicia's lips, taking her by surprise. She fiddled with the lip of her takeaway cup, feeling slightly self-conscious, yet aware that now she'd begun, she had to finish. "But I'm not really a Stamfordian anymore either."

"Aye, well, we're in the same boat there." Pettifer's reply came robustly, without a hint of embarrassment. "My vowels'll always be too short for this place, no matter how long I stay, but back home they can pick up my soft Southern edges a mile off."

Felicia rolled her eyes.

"This is the Midlands, Sergeant. Don't you know that by now?"

"Only Midlanders keep on insisting the Midlands exist. Where I'm from, this is the South. Although full disclosure? I don't mind some things about being a Southern Softie." He raised his cup, then eyed her nervously. "You won't tell anyone about this, will you? I've got a reputation to maintain."

"So long as you don't tell my father that we've actually *paid* for a coffee when there's a perfectly good kettle and jar of instant inside." She looked apprehensively over her shoulder towards the rose-smothered cottage, hoping they weren't being observed from within. But to her relief, there was no movement behind the leaded panes.

"Is that why we're sitting out here?" Pettifer seemed amused. "I did wonder."

"In part." She crossed one leg over the other, settled back. "But otherwise, we're just two misfits enjoying the view."

There was a pause, although not a very tranquil one. Pettifer was making little huffing sounds, tinkering with his coffee cup. The lid came off, then went back on again, then came off. Felicia waited as patiently as she was able while this ritual was performed. Then, after what seemed like an age, he finally did the awkward throat-clear which signified he was ready to speak.

"Felicia, I'm sorry for what I said."

She sat, absorbing his words for a moment, letting herself work out how she wanted to react rather than simply firing off the first thing which came into her head.

"Which part are you referring to, exactly?" She asked levelly. "The bit about me losing the plot, or when you called me a liability?"

He, too, seemed to take a few moments to consider before he replied. When he did, though, his voice was sincere.

"The part where I told you I wasn't treating this as a murder case." He inhaled deeply. "For what it's worth, I thought I could protect you by keeping you out of it."

"I ... see." She wasn't entirely sure how to feel about that.

"I still meant what I said, mind. I do think you're getting too close ... but that's a discussion for another day," he added swiftly, as her expression darkened. "The point is, I was trying to keep you safe..." he faltered, the first time she'd ever known him do so. "And I failed."

She looked at him, startled, but he held up a hand to indicate that he wasn't finished.

"Not just you; everyone in this town. That's my job. And yet look at what's happened. What's still happening." He slumped forward, looking utterly defeated. "There's a maniac on the loose, and to be honest, I'm a little frightened myself. Not for me, but for what might come next."

Felicia opened her mouth, her natural impulse to comfort him, but then she closed it again. She knew him well enough to sense that wouldn't be welcome. He didn't want pity, or reassurance. That would only make him castigate himself all the more.

"And now Ambrose is suffering too." Pettifer's massive hands screwed into fists. "All because I can't do my *bloody* job properly."

"Do you think they have enough to charge him?" Felicia tried to get him focussing on the practicalities. "I mean, what about the other deaths? Surely if they can't connect him to those too, then..."

"Don't underestimate Heavenly." Pettifer's voice was bleak. "Even if he can only get him for Riverton's death, that's what he'll do. One arrest is better than none, after all." He looked at her for a long moment, clearly trying to work out whether to confide in her further. Eventually, his face set in resolution. "I've been desperately trying to work out anything which might link the four victims, but nothing. All I've got is this." He foraged in his pocket, producing a clear bag containing a charred scrap of paper. "I found it in the fireplace at Iris Breadmore's rental cottage."

So he'd noticed the fireplace too, had he? And he hadn't been able to resist going back to check. The temptation to say something about that was overwhelming, but she resisted. There were times to be the bigger person. Instead, she took the bag, holding it gingerly between her fingertips, much to his evident entertainment.

"You know the fingerprints are on the inside, right?"

"Oh," she said, feeling a little shamefaced. "Yes. Of course." She peered at the fragment within. Its edges were brown and curling, but she could just about pick out some letters, although they didn't make much sense.

Then she saw it. Something that changed her entire understanding of what she was really looking at.

"I think it's a reference number," she said, her pulse quickening. "Or at least, part of one. More than that, I think I know where it's from."

Chapter Thirty-Six

The bottle lodges looked otherworldly in the late afternoon light. Their wedding cake-like tiers and curving turrets were catching the best of the gilded sun, rendering them closer to storybook illustrations than real stone and mortar buildings. Felicia stopped on the grass in front of them, daisies and buttercups flickering against her ankles, biting her lip in indecision. Wondering what exactly she was doing here.

Or actually, *not* wondering, she corrected herself. She didn't *need* to wonder. She knew exactly why she was here. The urge to come had been instinctive, overwhelming. It still was.

But she couldn't stay. She didn't know a lot right now, but she knew that much.

Suddenly, it struck her how foolish she must look, standing here. Thank God there was no sign of him, she thought, with a rush of relief, as she turned to leave. How embarrassing it would be if he came back and found her...

Her thoughts ground to a pitiful halt as a small, unobtrusive door at the side of the right-hand lodge opened.

Jack was leaning against the doorframe, watching her steadily from the half-shadows of the interior.

Felicia swore she actually *felt* her heart plummet.

"I like you better dressed like that," he remarked, by way of greeting. He didn't seem surprised to see her. He must have been observing her through the window, it occurred to her, with a fresh flush of mortification. Oh God.

"I was just passing," she blurted out, then realised he hadn't asked. This was getting worse by the minute.

"Were you?" He seemed to find her discomfort amusing, although he was doing a good job of hiding it. The knowledge emboldened as much as it piqued. She folded her arms, narrowing her eyes at him.

"Are you going to invite me in?"

He gave a wry smile.

"Do I need to? You don't usually wait to be invited."

Felicia felt her jaw set stubbornly.

"Fine. If you won't ask me in, I'll sit in your garden instead." She swept past him, through the magnificently arching gateway and around the back, to what would technically be more accurately described as a wilderness than a garden. There was evidence of some cultivation, but it had been a long time ago, and the residents of what had no doubt once been a show-worthy cottage garden had completely forgotten their manners. Perennial sweet peas tangled across a peeling wrought iron bench – once painted a rather fetching marine blue, if the fragments left were anything to go by. The borders were an unruly clump, foxgloves and lupins fighting for survival in a verdurous sea of ground elder. "Not much of a horticulturalist, are we?" She observed dryly.

"It's called rewilding." He'd followed her, and perched now

against a low, crumbling brick wall, which had been half claimed by a triffid-like rambling rose. "It's all the rage these days, I'm told. Although I wouldn't expect a stuffy auctioneer to know that."

There was no mistaking the teasing in his tone. She gave him a quick, assessing look, taking in his posture, the sense of lightness about him, as though he'd set down a huge weight. He was relaxed here, she realised. On his own territory. There was none of the usual edginess which accompanied him whenever he was in town. But then, perhaps that was understandable. After all, here he wasn't on the sharp end of constant scrutiny, never-ending judgement. She'd known it affected him more than he let on, but now, seeing the contrast so strongly … she felt a sudden swell of emotion towards him. Protective, perhaps, and something else. Something she tried not to think too hard about. She joined him on the wall, sitting as close as she dared.

"Nature's welcome to be nature here," he was saying now, gesturing around the garden. "Nothing artificial. No pretence of perfection."

She gave him a sideways glance.

"Why do I get the feeling there's a subtext there?"

"Because you spend too much time thinking about murders. It's made you paranoid." He spoke glibly, crossing one ankle over the other. She noticed he was wearing all black, as usual, despite the heat of the day. "So, to what do I owe the pleasure? I presume you're not here just to critique my approach to floriculture."

"I told you," she said lightly. "I was passing."

"Not very quickly, you weren't. You were standing on my front lawn for a good ten minutes."

She scowled.

"Have you never heard that you shouldn't contradict a lady?"

"Ah, but that would require me to be a gentleman. And I'm fairly sure I don't qualify as one of those around here."

His tone was arch enough, but an undercurrent had entered it, as it always did when the subject strayed in this direction. She decided to move on swiftly.

"Anyway, do I need a reason to visit a friend?"

"No." He looked her in the eye, trapped her gaze in his own. "But we're not friends."

And just like that, they weren't joking any more. She sucked in a silent breath, trying not to show how much he'd thrown her with the jarring change of tempo. She pretended to examine the head of a rose, wondering if she had the courage to step up and take the opening which had been left to her. The opening she hadn't even realised she'd been waiting for.

"What are we, then?"

Apparently, she did. She even managed it with an admirable casualness, she thought. No-one on the outside would imagine that her heart was pattering so hard it threatened to crack her ribs.

He didn't answer for a moment, and it took all of her resolve not to turn her head and look at him. She'd never be able to read him anyway. Nor would she prompt him into an answer before he was ready. The only thing to do with him was wait.

When he did speak, his voice was slow, as though he was carefully considering every syllable.

"That's a heavy question for a lovely summer's evening, don't you think?"

A tortoiseshell butterfly landed on the sleeve of her blouse, vivid against the white backdrop. She watched it for a moment, holding her breath until it took off again, flapping away into the haze.

"Yes," she said quietly, trying to swallow her disappointment. "I suppose it is, rather."

They lapsed into silence, although in reality it was anything but, the aforementioned midsummer's evening providing its own rich orchestra. The droning of bees intermingled with the chattering skirl of songbirds, notes and melodies overlapping and enmeshing together in an anthem of dying light. A pair of pigeons crooned lovingly at one another from high in the apple tree, from where they watched the golden hour cooling into a mauve twilight.

"There is ... something else," she admitted, at last. "You're right, I did come here to see you."

He didn't say anything. Just looked at her and waited, the question hanging in the air.

"Tony Chandler's dead," she said, her voice wavering slightly. "And you're the only person I can talk to about it."

He swore under his breath. When he spoke again, it was some seconds later.

"I thought Dexter was your go-to for all things investigative."

"Not this time. I only want you."

Their arms were touching as they sat next to one another, and she felt his muscles tense, although outwardly he didn't react.

"Why?"

"Because I'm running out of time," she admitted hopelessly. "Because the police have arrested Ambrose for Riverton's murder..."

"Really?" Jack interjected, frowning. "But he's still just a kid."

Felicia shook her head, trying to articulate the doubts churning in her mind.

"These killings ... they're clever. Calculated. With the best will in the world, I just can't see Ambrose masterminding them." She let her forehead drop into her palms briefly, pushing her hair back. She'd put out her one last lead and was waiting on the reply, but despite her assurances to Pettifer, she knew it was tenuous at best. She certainly wasn't about to pin all her hopes upon it. "If I can't work out who's really responsible, and *soon* ... Heavenly's determined to charge him. You know what he's like when his pride is at stake."

Jack was the only person in her life right now who she could admit this to, because he was the only person who would actually just listen. Who wouldn't tell her that it wasn't her job to work this thing out. That it wasn't her responsibility to clear anyone's name. Who wouldn't try to reassure her, or persuade her. That was why she'd really come here this evening. It was the simple truth, and it was on the tip of her tongue. But it just felt too raw, too vulnerable to express.

He leaned forwards, resting his elbows on his knees. She could tell he was taking all of this in.

"How did Tony die?" He asked eventually.

"A carefully stage-managed accident. Although there was almost some collateral damage. Whoever's doing this..." She took a shaky breath. "They don't seem to care who gets in the way."

He exhaled, looking deep in thought.

"All right," he said slowly. "So if Ambrose didn't do it ... who d'you think did?"

She blinked, utterly taken aback.

"I ... I have no idea," she stuttered.

He appeared singularly unimpressed by that answer.

"I don't believe that."

"I don't," she said, a touch testily. He shook his head.

"You have a brilliant brain, Felicia. Far more so than you give yourself credit for. And you know a lot more about this case than you realise. So, go on." He leaned back in his seat, watching her expectantly. "I'm listening."

"Well..." she began hesitantly. "I suppose Drummond is the most obvious suspect. I mean, he hates the Georgian Fair with a passion. And he's clearly intelligent; he could easily have planned all of this." To her surprise, the words were flowing easily, coming from a place in her mind she wasn't even aware they'd been hiding. Jack was right, she realised; she *did* know more than she'd been letting herself believe. She continued with more zeal. "He has an amazing knowledge of history, too; he'd know exactly how to execute historical-looking deaths. And then there's Edith ... I mean, she had every right to be furious that they'd allowed Iris Breadmore back this year. Perhaps she decided to take revenge on the whole lot of them? The organisers, the town, the fair itself..."

She trailed off, looking to Jack for a response. But he just sat there, with exactly the same expression, clearly waiting for more. So she obliged.

"I mean, I suppose I shouldn't discount Tara just because she's young and pregnant," she mused. "But I really believe that she loved Riverton; she'd never kill him. Now, if she found out that one of the others had ... that might be different. She's got a lot more passion beneath the surface than you'd think. And Nick ... well, he could have poisoned himself, I suppose, to cover his tracks, but..." She frowned to herself, dissatisfied with that. "No, I can't see it. He just doesn't seem brave enough to me. And would he really ruin the fair just for a story? Unless he has some secret history with it I don't know about..."

At last, Jack stirred, holding up a hand to stop her.

"Okay, I see your problem now."

She stared at him impatiently, feeling faintly put out. She'd thought she was doing rather well.

"I have a problem?"

"Yes, you do. A big one. You're assuming the murders are all to do with the fair. And I don't blame you, in a way. Because someone's clearly been working very hard to make you assume that."

"But..." She automatically began to protest, but he didn't give her a chance.

"Just get rid of all the dramatic trappings for a minute," he persisted. "And just think about what you actually *know*."

She wavered for a moment, assimilating the idea, reframing events in the new light of it.

All along, she'd had the uneasy sense that something about these murders was personal, despite the cool detachment of their devising. The way Riverton had been strung up – that would have taken the kind of strength only anger could fuel. Caroline's death had been graphic, public – vengefully appropriate for someone who'd spent their life exposing others. And Tony Chandler, condemned to being crushed to death ... that hadn't just been business-like, it had been actively callous.

Suddenly, her stomach swooped as she realised what a fool she'd been. Jack was right; she'd been sold a story. And she'd swallowed it without a second thought.

"All I truly know that every time I think I've turned a corner on this case I just come up against another wall." Felicia sat back down with a dispirited sigh. "I was so sure that

Caroline was the red-clad figure Nick saw down in the cellars. But then she died, and..." She trailed off as her gaze fell upon her own fingers, the tips of which seemed to be covered in pink dust. Immediately, she looked at the wall they were sitting on. The bricks in it were Victorian; a characteristic shade of pinkish red...

"Jack," she said slowly. "Do you remember the coat Tony was wearing last night?"

"Of course. It was red."

She felt a bolt of anticipation run through her, but tried to keep her tone casual.

"I would have described it as pink, but still."

"It was definitely red," Jack insisted. "I'm a photographer, Felicia. I notice colour."

"You're not wrong," she agreed. "But neither am I." At his quizzical look, she explained, "Men and women process colour differently." Thank heavens she paid attention to Algernon's science homework. "It's to do with the makeup of the eye. So if a shade falls somewhere between two colours—say lilac, or aqua..."

"Or brick red." Jack was looking down at the wall, clearly following her logic in reverse. "So what does it mean?"

"It means that I discounted Tony from being the mysterious person down in the cellars because I was looking for someone wearing red. Which to my eye, he wasn't, but to Nick..." Her hand flew to her mouth. "Oh God, of *course*! He recognised my dress. He knew it didn't belong to me. It all fits. He *had* to have been down there."

"You've lost me a little. But even if he was down there, it doesn't prove anything, Felicia. Lots of people were coming back and forth that night."

"No, but he was the only one being furtive about it."

"It's not a crime to be furtive," Jack said, a touch pointedly, she thought. "But in any event, he's dead himself. How d'you explain that, if he's supposedly your murderer?"

She hesitated a moment before she replied.

"Honestly? I can't." She sighed deeply. "But we need to be practical, and in immediate terms, only Riverton's death really matters." Her words were building momentum, getting faster and more animated as she dared to allow herself to believe they might actually be getting a break. "That's the one they're holding Ambrose for. This might cast enough doubt to get him released. Or at the very least, buy him some more time." She broke off breathlessly, suddenly aware that their faces were very close. For only the second time in months, she could see the golden flecks which fringed his pupils.

It hit her that she was dangerously near to kissing him. The thought was simultaneously world-tilting in its unexpectedness and yet the least surprising thing which had ever passed through her head.

Dimly, she realised that his lips were moving. But the words were delayed in reaching her ears, as though they were coming down a long tunnel.

"He didn't do it."

She blinked, wondering if she were hallucinating. Then she saw him wince.

"Tony Chandler couldn't have killed Riverton," he repeated dully. "I know for a fact."

She drew back, a cold douse of chariness washing over her.

"I think you'd better explain," she said evenly, folding her arms.

He was visibly reluctant, but one glance at her face swiftly changed his mind.

"I saw the two of them together that night." He shoved his

hands in his pockets, looking uncomfortable. "Outside the ballroom."

"What time was this?" Felicia demanded, not bothering to leave much of a pause before she did so. Jack was a man of frustratingly few words; he wouldn't volunteer any more than he felt was necessary.

"It was just after Aloysius had left. I'd gone out to get some air ... and there they were." He shrugged. "They were having a discussion. It seemed pretty heated. Riverton was asking if Tony had found it yet."

"Found what?"

"I didn't hear. But Iris was mentioned. Riverton said..." He faltered briefly. "He said he couldn't afford to be implicated."

Felicia looked up at the heavens.

"Riverton was alive and well when he left," Jack added. "Tony stayed outside on his phone, taking a call. I saw him come back into the ballroom through the outer doors, and he didn't leave again. So unless there was some serious conjuring trick going on, he's not your murderer."

Felicia breathed in, then out, trying to order her thoughts. The fact that he hadn't thought to say anything about this sooner was something she'd have to save for later rumination. Right now, she had to stay focused on what needed to be done.

"Okay, well first things first, we have to report this to Pettifer." She pulled out her phone and was scrolling through her contacts, when his hand suddenly closed over hers, stilling her.

"That's not going to happen."

Her head snapped up and she stared at him, but he just looked back at her calmly.

"You can't be serious," she said slowly, although she already knew that he was.

"I'm perfectly serious. I can't afford to get mixed up with the police, Felicia. You already know my reasons."

"Yes, I do," she said slowly. She could scarcely credit what she was hearing. "And I've always respected them. But this is *different*, Jack. This is vital information."

"Is it, though?" He raised his eyebrows. "I mean, it doesn't exactly help Ambrose, does it?" At her wide-eyed look of disbelief, he sighed. "Look, obviously if I genuinely thought it would help clear his name, I'd come forward."

"Very heroic of you." Her voice dripped with sarcasm. His eyes darkened.

"Don't judge me, Felicia. You have no idea what it's like to be in my position."

Then he began to walk away, towards the house. She glared at his retreating back.

"What exactly is *that* supposed to mean?"

She saw his shoulders tense. Then he turned. His expression was hard, uncompromising.

"It means that you've been coddled your whole life. Expensive schooling…"

"*You* went to that school!" She spluttered. He had a nerve, throwing that one at her. "It's your own fault you got expelled. No-one forced you to set fire to it."

He carried on as though she hadn't spoken. Clearly, this was something which had been on his chest for a while. Now he'd begun, he wasn't going to stop until he'd said his piece.

"…then Oxbridge, then onto your family's business, all neatly set up for you…"

She gasped. That was unfair, and he knew it. He'd seen for himself how hard she worked keeping Grant's going. But he still wasn't finished.

"...connected in all the right ways. Your best friend's the mayor, your husband's some kind of minor nobility..."

"*Ex* husband!" She practically howled at the heavens. But he ignored her nonetheless.

"You have no idea what it's like to be completely on your own in the world, to have to watch your own damned back all of the time." Jack looked about as angry as she'd ever seen him, his eyes flashing with green fire. "So don't you *dare* lecture me about morals."

They stared at each other across the ruins of the garden, and Felicia had the hollow sense of something slipping away. Something which had never even really had the chance to begin.

Then there came a high-pitched wailing sound. They both looked up, just in time to see a shower of pink and gold lighting up the sky beyond the lodge's domed turret.

Fireworks. Felicia's minded clouded in confusion. They must be coming from The Meadows; that's where the display had been set up for this evening's closing ceremony.

A ceremony which had now been cancelled. So what on earth...

"Someone's idea of a prank?" Jack suggested.

He might, of course, have been right. He often was. But Felicia wasn't about to stay around and chance it. She was already halfway through the garden gate, her feet taking her swiftly back down the hill towards the heart of town.

She would never know that his eyes stayed upon her, following her until she was completely out of sight.

Chapter Thirty-Seven

The Meadows were swarming with people by the time she arrived, the explosive display overhead having drawn the curious and the expectant to the scene. Felicia could see the roped-off area from where the fireworks were emanating, although the perpetrator was nowhere in evidence. She soon spotted the reason; they'd had the foresight to light one of the single ignition boxes which provided an entire, autonomous display. They were probably miles away by now, she realised.

Her phone was buzzing in her shorts pocket. She retrieved it distractedly, clamping it to her ear.

"Cass! Are you seeing this?"

As she spoke, a golden fountain fizzed to life in front of her, showering a waterfall of sparks onto the grass.

"Fliss?" The voice on the other end was faint. "Can you hear me?"

"Just about." Felicia stuck a finger in her free ear. It improved matters, but barely. "Where are you?"

"We need to talk." Even under these conditions, Felicia

could hear the worry in her friend's voice. "About that reference you sent me…"

Felicia felt herself straighten in sudden attention.

"You know what it is?"

"Yes, but…" There was a pause and for a moment, Felicia had wondered if the line had failed. But then Cassie spoke again, her voice so low it was barely audible. "I don't like it, Fliss. I don't like it at all."

"I'll come to you. Just tell me where you are."

"I'm over by…" A gasp, a muffled crackle, and then the line went abruptly dead. Felicia felt fear drop like a stone into the core of her being.

"*Cass!*" She yelled into the phone, even though she knew it was useless. "Cassie! Are you there?"

Nothing. Felicia could feel dread clawing at her throat, closing off her airways, and she fought for breath. She couldn't afford to lose her head. She needed to *think*.

Her mind scoured back over the call, desperately searching for anything unusual, anything which might help. It took her a few replays, but then she got it: a fizzing sound in the background, like static, followed by a dull bang.

Gunpowder. It was unmistakable. And it could only mean one thing.

Cassie was here. She was close by.

With a surge of hope-fuelled adrenaline, Felicia weaved her way through the throng, searching vainly for a glimpse of a familiar curly blonde mop of hair. Fireworks were still exploding overhead; one misfired, raining sparks over the crowd and prompting screams of fright and alarm. The air billowed with smoke, hot and acrid. It was pandemonium. Felicia felt her optimism rapidly fading. But just as she was beginning to despair, a cadaverous profile emerged out of the brume.

"Dennis!" She grasped his arm, suffused with a relief she'd never thought she'd feel at the sight of him. "Have you seen Cassie anywhere?"

But he didn't appear to have heard her. He was gazing around him, shellshocked. Suddenly, it occurred to Felicia that he wasn't a young man. For the first time since she'd known him, he looked lost, vulnerable ... even old.

"I ... I don't understand what's going on," he said helplessly. "What's happening?"

"Look, I need you to focus." A memory was stirring somewhere in her mind. Something about Dennis ... usually, Cassie moaned about her deputy so frequently that most of it went in one ear and out of the other, but this ... Felicia squeezed her eyes shut, willed herself to remember that day, that conversation.

They'd been in Cassie's office, that much she knew ... two months ago, had it been? Wait, no. There'd been peonies in a vase on the desk. So, May then. Last month.

"He remembers *everything*." Cassie had been pacing around, barefoot as usual. Stamford's mayor wasn't a fan of shoes, and she rarely wasted a second more wearing them than she had to. "Every council meeting, every ceremony, every bloody *planning* application ... he even remembers the reference numbers! How revolting is *that*?"

Felicia, who'd been quietly sitting on a pile of old envelopes on the visitor chair and wondering how soon she'd be able to get back to the auction house, had looked up at that. "Really? That's actually quite impressive."

"It's calculating, that's what it is," Cassie fumed. "He uses it against me. It's insupportable!"

And yet now, Felicia thought, that much-despised trait might just save her friend's life.

"Do you remember what this number refers to?" She urged, drawing up the photograph of the burnt paper on her phone. "I know it's a lot to ask, but if you could just try…"

"I don't need to *try*." Dennis's haughty tone had revived somewhat, along with the indignant colour in his sunken cheeks. "Of course I remember that case. Couldn't forget it. It's the Trendlehart field."

Felicia started.

"You mean…the land James Riverton owned? The site he and Tony Chandler planned to develop?"

"Why, yes." He looked at her curiously. "Say, how d'you know about that? This was all months ago now. Before you came back to town."

She didn't have time to even fabricate an answer to his question, so she simply ignored it, pressing on.

"Where is it? How do I get there?"

"It was quite the case, you know." Unfortunately, Dennis had rallied *too* thoroughly; he was back into standard pontificating mode. "The land's a natural wildflower meadow, so it wasn't really a candidate for development. But Tony Chandler was a persistent man, and with James Riverton behind him … well, they would have got it through eventually. *I* wasn't in favour, of course," he added hastily, giving her a sideways glance. "But I would have had to be seen to be supportive of the decision, whichever way it went."

"I'm sure you would," Felicia agreed, through gritted teeth. "But Dennis, where's the field? I need to know."

"And then the Trendlehart Trust found proof that the ruins of an old farmhouse on the land were in fact the site of his very first orphanage…" Dennis was looking mistily off into the middle-distance. "What a boon *that* was. And to think it might all have been lost beneath a modern housing estate..."

"Dennis!" Felicia snapped, finally at the end of her tether. Cassie didn't have time for this. "Just tell me where the bloody field is! *Now!*"

He blinked rapidly, apparently too taken aback to be affronted.

"Well, I mean, it's out past The George..." he stuttered. "Although you might be better to take the back route..."

Felicia felt her heart sink as he rambled on. Clearly, directions weren't his strong suit. Eventually, she grabbed her phone again, pulling up the maps app and shoving the screen beneath his long nose.

"Just show me."

Colin Creaton ambled past the diamond-paned windows of The George, humming away to himself. It was a habit he knew Margaret detested, so he tried to contain it at home, although it was difficult. Half the time, he didn't even know he was doing it, she complained. So when he was out and about, away from her sensitive earshot, he indulged freely. It sometimes earned him a wary glance or two, even occasionally a crossing of the road to avoid him, but it was worth it.

"Pom-pom-pom..." he warbled cheerfully. The melody was one he vaguely recalled from his boyhood, and he couldn't remember every bar of it, let alone what it was called. He wasn't even sure, after all of these years, if it was the same tune he'd originally been thinking of, or if improvisation had morphed it into something quite different. Not that it mattered anyway; it was only really him listening, and he was no musical aficionado. Just a man who liked to hum.

"Pom-dippity-pom-pom..."

The bottle in his anorak pocket clanked against his house keys, providing an uneven accompaniment to his efforts. Margaret had been insistent that she couldn't do without her tonic tonight – the *things* which were happening in their town these days! A disgrace, it was, and all down to that *ghastly* Georgian Fair, she was certain of it; after all, no-one had committed suicide in Stamford before it came to town ... why *would* they, in a place like this? She didn't feel safe walking the streets now, she *really* didn't – and thus, off to the off-licence had Colin been duly dispatched.

The thing was, he thought mildly, she hadn't *technically* stipulated which off-licence to go to. And so here he was, enjoying a gloriously unexpected treat: an evening's stroll around his beloved town. There really was nowhere like Stamford in midsummer, when the honeyed stone dazzled against cerulean skies and the river rippled lazily beneath the bridges, creating blurred portraits of the scene above like an old mottled mirror.

He followed the side of the ancient inn for a while, before crossing the narrow road which led towards his favourite place. It was a liberty, in truth; he couldn't afford to be too long. Poor Margaret; her nerves really were getting worse. It was only a week ago that he replaced her last bottle of tonic – although of course, he'd feigned amnesia of the fact. It wouldn't have been gentlemanly to point it out.

But he only wanted a quick peek, he reasoned to himself. Surely, *that* couldn't hurt.

He crossed the bridge with eager, shuffling footsteps. He'd heard in the off-licence that they'd shut down the Georgian

Fair early. Something to do with an incident ... but he hadn't stopped to listen to the details. He'd practically skipped out of there, such had been his excitement.

His cherished town meadows, back to their usual tranquil self. He'd probably be the only one on them at this time of night. He couldn't think of anything more blissful, more...

A keening sound ripped through the air, bringing his train of thought to an abrupt end. Colin paused, confused and uncertain, then flinched as a bang made his ears ring.

Why, that had *almost* sounded like a...

As if in confirmation, a firework lit up the sky above him, exploding into a dandelion clock of cobalt and magenta stars.

Something was wrong, he just knew it. Colin staggered across the bridge.

His first impression was that it was like a warzone. Smoke clogged the air, carrying with it the acrid tang of spent gunpowder. The grass agitated with people, chattering and shrieking in a mixture of anxiety and disorientation. Overhead, firework after firework split the night like a violent storm. Each boom seemed to shake the very ground itself.

As Colin stood there, slack-jawed, watching it all, someone barrelled past him, jostling his shoulder roughly and making his pocket clank in protest. The impact roused him from his reverie; he turned, ready to issue a reprimand – or, all right, perhaps a weakly disapproving look instead; after all, he *was* an Englishman – but he was too slow. All he glimpsed of his assailant was the back of a bronze head, melting away into the smoke.

Margaret was right, he thought sadly. This town really *was* going to the dogs. He zipped his anorak up to his chin, hunched his shoulders, and carried on his way, humming a mournful tune as he went.

Felicia flung out a hand behind her, muttering a distracted apology to whoever it was she'd just bumped into. Then she heard herself being called.

"Mum!"

"Algie." She was about to pull him into a fierce hug, then at the last moment noticed the gaggle of boys standing just behind him. "What are you doing here?"

"Septimus's house is just over there." Algernon pointed across the river. We saw the fireworks and came out to see. What's happening, Mum?"

"I don't know," she said honestly. As a rule, she tried never to lie to him, even if she couldn't tell him the full truth. "But I think it's better if you boys go back inside. Stay there until I come and get you."

His eyes went round.

"You don't want to go home?"

"Not yet, darling. I need..." A surge of emotion made her voice waver. "I just have to find Aunt Cassie first."

"Well that's easy," Algernon said. "She's here. I just saw her."

Felicia felt a flicker of hope. She crouched down, put her hands on his shoulders.

"*Where*, Algie?"

"Over there." He pointed towards the now-abandoned funfair, then frowned. "Oh. She's gone. She must have left with that soldier."

Something uncoiled in Felicia's chest. A disquieting feeling, as though she was being stared in the face by the truth, and yet she couldn't quite see it yet. It was still just around the corner, just out of reach.

"You know, the ones in the red coats?" Algernon pressed, clearly taking her silence as incomprehension. "They were talking. He was sort of leaning in, as if he was telling her a secret."

Red coats.

Felicia could feel her head spinning as realisation slammed into her. She willed herself to stay calm.

"Did you recognise him?"

"No, they were too far away." Algernon looked at her searchingly, clearly picking up on her apprehension. "But it's all right, Mum. I'm pretty sure they knew each other."

That got her attention.

"Why d'you say that?" She asked quietly.

"Because of how they were walking. Really close together. He even had his arm around her." Algernon raised his eyebrows. "You wouldn't do that with someone you didn't know, would you?"

No, Felicia answered silently. You wouldn't. Unless…

And then the answer was there, somehow even worse than before.

Cassie hadn't just disappeared.

She'd been kidnapped.

Chapter Thirty-Eight

Cassandra Lane waded through the sea of wildflowers, feeling as though she was in a dream. All around her was aglow, a jewel box of reds and purples and electric pinks ignited by the late, slanting sun. Above, the sky was a plush, cloudless violet. A more perfect view was hard to imagine, but she daren't stop to admire it. The cold barrel of the musket pressing into the small of her back warned her against that.

They trudged on in silence. It was slow progress; the grass was waist-high at this time of year, and leaves and stems snagged at the skirt of the costume she hadn't got around to changing out of. What a mistake that felt like now; the weight of the material made it impossible to even think about making a run for it. Not that she'd get very far in this long grass anyway. It was like treacle to get through, and her captor clearly knew this terrain far better than she did.

Her foot caught a rabbit hole, sending her lurching sideways. Her ankle jarred, and she gasped, staggering to a stop.

"Keep moving." The gun dug cruelly into her spine.

"Listen," she managed, between snatched breaths. Her voice sounded alien to her own ears, frightened and confused. "Whatever it is, we can talk about it. You *don't* have to do this."

Silence from behind her.

Then, out of the corner of her eye, she saw sunlight glinting off the gun barrel. Instinctively, her whole body tensed, prepared for the worst. But there was no shot. Instead, the gun kept arcing around, indicating over her shoulder to a cluster of ruined walls rising up out of the flora.

"Over there."

Cassie tilted her face upwards. In the heavens, the first evening star had emerged. She knew that she should be thinking frantically right now, working out how to get out of this. But in truth, all that occupied her brain was a single, almost peaceful thought.

It was a beautiful day to die.

Chapter Thirty-Nine

F elicia walked down the track, her feet making almost no sound on the packed dirt floor. The canopies of the trees met overhead, forming a tunnel of ever-shifting green through which only dappled diamonds of light penetrated. With every step she took, the comforting thrum of civilisation got fainter and more distant, the drone of traffic blending into the rustling of leaves until eventually the latter was all she could hear. The silence only made her more acutely aware of how alone she was, how far from help should she need it.

Dennis had said there'd be a gate. She came to it; small, wooden, with a discreet plaque declaring the land beyond it private property. Not that the warning was really necessary; no-one was likely to chance upon the place, despite its proximity to town. It didn't seem to lead to anywhere. Felicia had always blithely assumed she knew every inch of Stamford and its environs – after all, she'd grown up here – but she'd had no idea this track even existed until now. It was an odd feeling.

There was an old planning application still tied to the gate, curling and faded by weather. Felicia recognised the number at the top, although most of the page had been ripped off, leaving a jagged edge. It was a small sign of anger; the same anger she'd been able to sense throughout this case.

She braced herself, then pushed on the gate. Its bottom slats scraped across the dry grass. She could see the field beyond, a kaleidoscope of stained glass colours reflecting what was left of the sun. Then, just as she was about to take a step forward, she heard a rustling behind her, and froze.

"Will you *ever* learn to wait for me?"

The voice was exasperated, gruff … and she'd never been so relieved to hear it. She waited as Pettifer reached her side, rasping with exertion.

"Probably not," she said, with a shrug. She pointed at a thin channel in the grass, a snaking line indicating where someone had clearly passed recently. "They're here."

He nodded curtly.

"Then let's not waste time." But as Felicia forged on ahead, he began to put up a protest. "Wait, I didn't mean you *first*…" A sigh of defeat. "Oh, never mind."

He followed her into the dying light.

Cassie stood in the carcass of what had once been a house, looking around her at the tumbledown walls. Above her were the remains of the old floor, gnarled beams no longer with anything to support now finding a new use as a perch for songbirds. Their evening chorus provided a soothing lullaby to her churning thoughts.

The sense of paralysis which had gripped her through the meadow had broken, much to her relief. Suddenly, she felt lucid again, her survival instincts kicking in. The faces of her children flickered across her vision, steeling her resolve. Every cell of her body was primed, focused on one objective: *not* dying.

"You know, I'm not the only person who knows about the planning reference," she said shakily. "The police have it. They'll find out what it means. Killing me..." She swallowed reflexively at having to say the words aloud. "It won't make this go away."

"You really think that's what this is about?" The response was like a whip, harsh and disbelieving. "After what you did, how you betrayed me?"

Cassie whirled, astonishment making her mindless of the gun still pointed in her direction. Instead, she looked directly into the face she knew so well, searching desperately for any sign of humanity, of pity. But there was none.

"I would never do that," she said. "Please. You know me." When her captor didn't react to that, she repeated pleadingly, "You *know* me."

"Cassie!" And then suddenly Felicia was there, melting out of the golden haze. Cassie blinked, wondering if she was imaging things, her brain playing tricks on her before death. But then Pettifer appeared hot on her heels, and she realised it had to be true. She had a lot of time for the Sergeant, but she highly doubted he'd be featuring in her final highlights reel.

"Watch out," she yelled in warning. "He's got a gun."

But Felicia didn't stop. She kept coming towards them. Pettifer teetered on one huge foot, looking alarmed.

"Felicia," he commanded. "What are you doing? *Stop!*"

"No!" Cassie cried, as Gavin calmly swung the gun around to point straight at her best friend's chest.

Chapter Forty

Cassie's scream rent the air, sending birds exploding from the trees. Felicia stopped, inches from the muzzle of the gun, looked Gavin straight in the eye.

For a moment, everything was perfectly still. Behind her, she could hear Cassie whimpering, Pettifer breathing heavily.

"It's all right," she said quietly. "That isn't a gun; it's a musket."

She paused. Gavin raised his eyebrows.

"Oh, don't stop on my account. You were saying?"

"Muskets don't work like modern guns," Felicia continued, slightly hesitantly. She was keeping her gaze firmly fixed on him, waiting for him to make a sudden move, but to her surprise, he appeared to be genuinely listening. "There's no chamber, and no bullets. Instead, it's loaded through the muzzle." It took some courage to indicate the very thing which was aiming at her heart, but she did it. "You have to stand the gun on its end to fill it with the wadding, gunpowder and finally, the lead shot." She addressed Gavin directly now. "When we got here, you were holding it pointing downwards.

340

It's understandable; they're heavy things. Your arms probably needed a break. But it was also a mistake on your part. Because it tells me something very important. It tells me that this," she stepped forward, until the gun was pressing up against her sternum. "Isn't loaded."

Then she waited. It was easily the longest moment of her life. Blood was screeching in her ears, pulse ready to burst out of her body. Somewhat belatedly, it occurred to her that she might have been a trifle reckless. After all, despite what she'd said, she couldn't be one hundred percent certain she was right. And if she wasn't ... well, at least one of them was probably about to die. Beginning with her.

But then Gavin's lips curved in a rueful smile, and he let the gun drop.

"Well, I suppose I should have known I wouldn't get it past an antiques expert."

Pettifer moved forwards, hand outstretched.

"Come along, then, lad. It's over."

But Gavin stayed put, still smiling.

"Not quite. You see, I have a few facts of my own." He cocked his head enquiringly at Felicia. "If I may?"

Pettifer stirred, but Felicia put out a hand to stop him. She didn't know what game Gavin was up to, but she sensed danger. They had to play along, at least for the time being.

"Of course," she said neutrally. "It's only fair."

"Very sporting of you." He looked lovingly at the musket. "You also know, then, that this isn't only a gun? It's actually a multi-use weapon."

Felicia nodded, slowly.

"It had to be, considering how tricky and time-consuming it would have been to load each time."

"Exactly!" Gavin shouted, making Cassie flinch. Felicia

eyed him warily; he seemed to be slipping further from sanity with every passing moment. "There's also the bayonet." He pointed to the thin blade attached to the top of the muzzle. "Although some health and safety-conscious sort has blunted this one, so it's of little use to me. However," he hefted the gun up onto his shoulder. "There's always the most basic method. It's crude, I regret, but needs must."

The next few seconds were a blur. It took Felicia a second to realise what he was implying, and when she did, the butt of the musket was already slicing through the air towards Cassie's head. Her mouth fell open, a cry forming in her throat. But the next sound she heard wasn't her own voice.

"Gavin! *No!*"

Gavin spun around, face rigid with horror. The gun swerved off its arc, its end landing with a thud on the soft ground. Cassie, who'd shrunk back in anticipation of the blow, just stared at it, as though she couldn't quite believe her eyes.

"Hugo," Gavin said haltingly. "You shouldn't be here."

"Please, Gavin." Hugo ignored him, walking towards them through the ruined doorway. "*Stop.* Just stop."

"I can't." Gavin's features crumpled in misery. "I have to finish this."

"Finish *what*?" Cassie, who was by now slumped against the remains of a wall, wailed. "I don't understand what this is all about."

"I do." Felicia turned to Gavin, softening her voice. "This is about your brother, isn't it?"

Gavin looked back at her for a long moment. Then he seemed to deflate, his shoulders dropping. He nodded jerkily.

"Oliver...he was the only thing which made growing up in

that house bearable." His voice had lost its swagger; he sounded lost, broken. "People expected me to resent him; after all, lots of teenagers would have hated having a much younger sibling tagging along after them all the time. But I didn't." He gave the ghost of a faraway smile. "You had to have met him to understand. He was brilliant, bright as the sun. I..." He choked. "I loved him very much."

"This is the place, isn't it?" Felicia looked around them, at the slanting light, the swathes of butterfly-crested flowers. Suddenly, the pollen on his sleeve was making a lot of sense. She wondered if Hugo was making the connection too. "Where you used to come together?"

"His favourite place." Gavin's jaw trembled. "Exactly as it was when he was alive. He has a grave, of course, but I never go there. *This* is his real memorial."

"Except, it wasn't destined to stay this way, was it?" Pettifer finally spoke. "Your father wanted it built on. All of this would be gone."

Hugo looked stunned, his head swivelling between everyone helplessly.

"But ... I don't understand. Why would James want to do a thing like that? It's not like he needed the money."

"Because he wanted to obliterate the past, that's why," Gavin said bitterly. He was still gripping the musket, but Felicia sensed it was more out of a need for support than intent to use it now. "Because he thought that I couldn't move on from Oliver's death. That I wallowed in it. In his opinion, it was the cause of all the problems between us." His face clenched recollective pain. "I found out all of this when I confronted him about the initial planning application. He knew I'd find out; I work for the council, for heaven's sake. He was basically throwing out a line, forcing me to come to him."

He looked at Hugo then, eyes beseeching.

"You see, I'm not a real killer. If I were, I would have done it then and there. I could have, easily." His fingers tightened around the gun handle, his words forced out through clamped lips. "But I didn't. I let him talk. I'd assumed it was all just some pathetic ploy to get my attention; he'd done that sort of thing before, although never anything this extreme. But then he started talking about how he'd met someone. He wouldn't tell me who, but supposedly he fancied himself in love with her." His voice dripped with disbelief.

"Not just that," Felicia interjected softly. "He wanted to marry her, didn't he?"

"Oh, yes. He had it all mapped out in his head. We were going to be a family, apparently." He gave a shout of incredulous laughter. "Can you imagine it? Rosy cheeks and board games and evenings in front of the fire. And the only thing getting in the way of this delightful utopia was my *unhealthy* obsession with the past." He stabbed at his own chest viciously. "I was ruining his plans yet again. I was good at that, you see. I've always been the only person he couldn't control, couldn't manipulate into doing what he wanted. It drove him mad."

"So he decided that if he couldn't persuade you, he'd have to force you instead," Felicia guessed. But it wasn't a question. Gavin nodded, looking impressed.

"He never understood what this place meant to us; he thought it was just a symbol I'd chosen, a focus for my morbid resentments. He thought that if he could destroy it, then I would have to move on. That I would magically become the son he wanted."

"But the planning application failed," Pettifer pointed out bluntly.

"It did." Gavin smirked. "Who do you think tipped off the Trendlehart Trust about the site? My family have always known about its connection to the orphanage."

"So your father…"

"Didn't care a jot about history," Gavin confirmed cheerfully. "He just pretended to. You have to around here if you want to look good, get along. The whole town's obsessed with it." He sighed wistfully. "Oh, how I *wish* I could have seen his face when he got that news."

"But he didn't give up, did he?" Pettifer pressed. Gavin's expression soured.

"No, he didn't. I rather naïvely let myself believe that that was the end of it. That I'd outmanoeuvred him, won the game. But he was deadly serious, utterly possessed by the idea." He seemed oblivious to the irony, but Felicia wasn't about to bring it to his attention. Certainly not while he was still looming over Cassie. "I was first alerted when he insisted on having Iris Breadmore back this year. That was an odd move for him; it risked making him unpopular, and I knew it must be of vital importance for him to chance his golden boy image on. Then those stories started appearing in The Bugle…" His mouth twisted derisively. "Really, they weren't half as clever as they thought. It was obvious to me that they were trying to cause trouble with the Georgian Fair somehow. But that was as far as I got." He paused. "Until one day, they met here."

The inference being that they hadn't been aware of his presence. Presumably, he'd been hiding amongst these ruins. Felicia imagined that he knew them like no-one else.

"They were discussing Iris," Gavin was saying. Now he'd begun, he seemed keen to explain his side of the story. Felicia suspected it had a lot to do with Hugo's presence. If he weren't here … it didn't bear thinking about. "Whether she could be trusted. Caroline seemed to think her a liability. But my father said that she would do what she was told, so long as she got her money."

"To re-write her speech?" Cassie piped up. She looked pale but defiant.

"Yes. That's when I found out what they were really up to. They thought if they could make the whole thing such a disaster, such a source of embarrassment for the town ... if they could turn its figurehead into a villain ... well, they might be able to get the ban lifted on the land. No more Georgian Fair, no more problems. That was the idea."

"Although your father needed to keep up his act on the outside, so as to avoid suspicion," Pettifer added.

Gavin shrugged.

"Paying for a statue, pouring money into the fair ... that kind of money was nothing for my father. He would have seen it as a worthwhile investment." He looked at Hugo intently, as though the next part was specifically for him. "But you know, as I listened to them, I had an epiphany. I realised that, in a twisted way, my father was right. I was trapped by the pains of the past. If I wanted to move on, I had to free myself."

"...And revenge was the way to do it?"

"If that's the term you choose. I prefer closure."

"Your father, I understand." Felicia was trying to keep her voice neutral, but even she could hear the incredulity in it. "But the rest of them? Did they really deserve to die?"

"Did my *brother* deserve to die?" Gavin shot back, eyes glinting. "He was seven years old. *Seven!*" He composed himself with a visible effort, his words becoming stilted. "But I'm not a monster. I gave them all a chance. Not my father; he'd had more than enough of those. But I caught Caroline and Tony in conversation over the past couple of weeks, let it drop in how much this place mattered, what it really meant." His face turned hard. "It didn't make the slightest difference. Neither of them stopped what they were doing. If they had, they'd still be alive today."

"And Iris? Did you give her a trial too?"

"I tried to." He sighed. "I knew my only chance to talk to her would be the night before the fair started, at the drinks party. She wasn't local, so I couldn't do it before then. I also didn't really know her, so engaging her in conversation wouldn't be as easy. I decided to ... grease the wheels a bit. I heard her order a lime and soda at the bar; I got myself a double G&T, then swapped them while her back was turned. Then I waited for an opportunity."

"But she left early."

"Yes, that threw me somewhat. You can tell I was ad-libbing, because I made a stupid error. I took my glass of wine out with me." He shook his head, frowning. "I'm still annoyed with myself about that. But then ... I don't know what happened, but things weren't right. When I caught up with her, she was reeling. I couldn't get any sense out of her."

"She was newly teetotal, according to her doctor." Pettifer said shortly. "Her drinking had begun to catch up with her health, and she was trying to change. She hadn't touched alcohol in months."

Felicia's head whipped around, and she stared in shock at this new information. But he was steadily watching Gavin.

"I didn't know that." Gavin held up a finger. "It was an accident, I *swear*. She fell, hit her head ... taking out my glass on the way down, unfortunately."

Felicia didn't buy his protestations of innocence for a moment. She folded her arms.

"It might technically have been an accident, but I suppose

you had a plan for what you would have done with her, had she not passed your test. Something suitably Georgian, presumably?"

"Ah, so you got there at last." His face lit up. "You were being rather slow. I was starting to feel disappointed. Yes, drowned in the bath would have been fitting for her, I felt. It had to look like an accident, that one. I couldn't afford for the fair to be stopped. It was the perfect cover. Besides, I had it all so nicely planned out."

"And that's also why your father's death had to look like a suicide, I'm guessing?"

His mouth flattened distastefully.

"I would have liked to use a little more flair on that one; after all, he was the one who most deserved punishment. But sometimes one has to focus on the bigger picture."

"And Cassie?" Felicia jabbed a finger towards her friend, who was still clinging to the wall, looking stricken. "What did she do? She wasn't involved in any of this."

"What did she *do*?" His voice rose to a screech of outrage and disbelief, his composure, which had been precarious all along, suddenly shattering into shards of angry hysteria. "She agreed to let them build here, that's what she did. She *signed off* on it!"

"Gavin." Cassie's eyes were huge, lids quivering, but her voice was admirably reasonable. "You know I don't have any power over planning. I couldn't have stopped it, even if I'd known ... but I didn't. I swear. I had absolutely no idea this was your and Oliver's place..."

"No, of course you didn't!" Gavin spat. "Because you never *listen*, do you? You're so wrapped up in your own problems, so self-*obsessed*. I thought of everyone, Oliver and I could rely on you, but no." His face screwed up. "Turns out, you're just as bad as the rest."

He caught up the gun again, about to swing. Cassie cried out, ducking backwards.

Felicia acted on instinct. She surged forwards, blurting out wildly, "Wait!"

Gavin's head swivelled.

"Why should I?" He snarled. "I've already come this far. Who cares what I do now?"

"Your sister will care."

He froze, staring at her like a wary animal.

"I don't have a sister."

"Yes, you do." She took a step forwards. Just one. He didn't seem to notice. His eyes were utterly transfixed upon her lips as they moved. "Or you will. That was what your father wanted to tell you. *That* was the family he was talking about."

Shock and uncertainty crashed together on his face like two waves meeting. He was obviously trying to work out if this was just a stalling tactic.

"She's telling the truth, lad." Pettifer confirmed from behind her. Felicia thought she could hear a trace of sympathy in his voice.

"It's not just you now, Gavin," she said softly. "You have a sibling who needs you." She met his eye. "Again."

And then she held her breath.

For a heart-stopping moment, she thought it hadn't worked. But then his face collapsed in on itself, and the expression on it nearly broke her heart. It was that of a man staring into the abyss. He swayed on the spot, stumbling sideways. Hugo darted forwards, catching him before he fell.

The musket dropped from limp fingers, landing on its end before slowly tipping over, swallowed into the long grass.

Then, from the depths of Hugo's chest, there came the first gulps of muffled sobbing.

"I expect, Sergeant," Hugo spoke quietly but with remarkable self-possession, belying his ashen face. "That you'll be wanting him down at the station."

Pettifer cleared his throat.

"I think that would be appropriate, yes."

"Then let's go. Together."

And putting an arm around his fiancé's shoulders, Hugo led him away, back towards the distant cluster of spires which shimmered in the twilight.

Chapter Forty-One

"**M**um," Algernon ventured, as he slotted another fair pamphlet into the pile in his hand. "Can I talk to you about something?"

Felicia pushed a stack of chairs against the wall, trying to ignore the resulting protest from her shoulders. Maybe she wasn't as fit as she used to be, or maybe it was all that sprinting across The Meadows, but she was feeling absolutely knackered. She wasn't sure she could take any more confessions today.

"That's a trick question, surely," she said wearily. "Because really, it depends what it is ... which I won't know until you start telling me."

"Well..." He shuffled the cards, looking apprehensive. "You know that Caroline Boughton – the newspaper editor – she had all of those guinea pigs?"

Felicia immediately felt wary at the turn of conversation. Algernon clearly sensed it, because he began to speak faster.

"...And it turns out that they don't have anywhere to go..."

"Algie, you're not having a guinea pig," she cut him off firmly. "Not right now, at least."

"But—" Algernon looked at Dexter, dismay crossing his face.

Felicia mounted the stairs onto the rostrum.

"Your grandfather would blow his top. He's dangerously close to doing that most minutes of the day as it is." She paused, gavel in hand, relenting slightly at the sight of the top of her son's hung head. "Look, maybe when we move. And the house isn't also occupied by a semi-feral cat." Godfrey would probably swallow the poor thing whole, she thought, with a barely repressed shudder, skewered on one of his claws like pineapple on a cocktail stick.

"But *Mum*." Algernon was being unusually persistent, his cheeks flushing stubbornly. "You don't…"

"Enough, Algie," she employed her sternest maternal voice – the one which warned him in the strongest terms not to continue with this line of enquiry. "If you really want one, your father will have to keep it in his pristine new apartment."

Dexter blanched.

"Didn't think so." Felicia gave his chair a nudge with her foot. "And stop lounging about. You're supposed to be *helping*."

Clearing up after this afternoon's auction wasn't strictly a job which had needed doing tonight, but after the events of the past couple of hours, they were all too wired to just go home and sit around. Besides, she reminded herself dully, they were going to be yet another staff member down going forwards. She wasn't sure when Hugo would be ready to return, if ever. And they had a jewellery and watches auction scheduled for next week; the saleroom needed returning to its usual state.

These were all perfectly sensible justifications, not to

mention true. But in reality, she'd just wanted to be here. This draughty room, slightly eerie when it was empty, was her sanctuary. Her safe place. It grounded her, and heavens knew, she needed grounding right now.

With a put-upon huff, Dexter levered himself out of the chair, heading over to one of the tables of as yet uncollected lots. They worked on in companiable silence for a while, Felicia tidying the rostrum, Algernon collecting abandoned pamphlets from the seats, and Dexter tinkering non-committally with the items on the table, moving them back and forth without actually managing to do anything particular with them. Then, after a few minutes, he looked up quizzically.

"Felicia, someone appears to be trying to break into your auction house."

"Oh, that's just Pettifer." The sergeant had many fine policing skills, but entering a premises silently wasn't one of them – as the cacophony of scraping and creaking could attest. "I told him we'd be here. Apparently he has a few final questions."

"You mean, things he needs you to explain to him," Dexter replied sardonically.

"I'd say we're pretty even on that score." Pettifer and Dexter had a fairly prickly relationship, and she felt compelled to defend the policeman's honour. "He worked out plenty of things I didn't."

"Still, it was you who cracked it." Dexter wasn't about to give Pettifer his due readily. "I still can't believe you spotted that that planning reference belonged to council paperwork."

"Well, I've sat on enough of it in Cassie's office," she said wryly. "I should recognise it by now."

"How is Aunt Cass?" This from Algernon, small face earnest and concerned. "Have you talked to her?"

"Her family are with her now. The hospital say they'll be keeping her in for a night at least." She looked at Dexter. "She's pretty shaken up by it all."

"She'll rally," he said confidently.

"We can only hope." But privately, she had her doubts. She'd never seen her friend like this. Cassie was usually so strong, so unaffected. But now she seemed ... haunted. Closed-in upon herself. "I had to tell Dennis what's happened, explain that neither of them will be at work tomorrow."

"Bit of a bombshell for him." Dexter whistled.

"He actually seemed really upset." She'd felt quite sorry for the man. He'd looked floored. She wondered if the whole weekend had been too much for him. "It turns out that he was the only one who knew that Gavin was planning to propose. Believe it or not, they were taking dance classes together." At Dexter's expression, she added hastily, "not *together* together. Dennis wanted to learn to dance for the ball on Saturday." She recalled his exuberant steps and immediately banished the image. "Apparently, Hugo's always complained that Gavin can't dance, so he asked Dennis for the name of his teacher." Hence why he had Dennis's phone number hidden in his desk. Ironically, that mystery, which had got Cassie so paranoid, was the one with the most prosaic, innocent explanation. "It was supposed to be a surprise at the wedding."

The wedding which would never happen now. The thought dropped silently into the air between them. Felicia felt her heart go out to Hugo. After all, he was just as much a victim in all of this as anyone. What must it be like, to watch your future implode in front of you? To find out that the man you thought you'd spend your life with was a mass murderer? Usually, she was good at putting herself in other people's shoes, but that ... she couldn't even scratch the surface of imagining it.

"Evening everyone." Pettifer shuffled in, shoelaces flapping against the polished wooden floor. "Sorry it's taken me a while. I had some..." He coughed, looking embarrassed. "Er, trouble ... with the door."

"We heard," Dexter said dryly.

Felicia shot him a cautionary look, even as she prayed that Pettifer hadn't broken the thing. Most of the time, he didn't seem to know his own strength.

"Have you finished questioning Gavin?" She asked.

"Yes. He didn't cause any trouble. All the fight's gone out him since you told him about the baby. For the first time, I think he's genuinely realising what he's done. He even apologised to Ambrose."

"Who's been released, I should hope?"

Pettifer nodded.

"Without charge. Heavenly's spitting, as you can imagine."

"I can." Felicia tried not to take too much satisfaction from the image.

"Apparently Gavin never intended to frame Ambrose. He only took his coat because he knew that the lad was always misplacing things, and no-one would believe him if he said anything about it."

"Which they didn't." Felicia remembered Tara's dismissal of Ambrose's claims. "And I can see now that dressing as a soldier was the perfect cover for Gavin's purposes. He was already wearing white breeches; all he had to do was swap his green coat for a red militia one, and if no-one looked too closely, they'd be none the wiser. Nobody really notices the soldiers; there are so many of them, they all just blur into one."

"It was just an unfortunate coincidence that Ambrose happened to stumble across Riverton's body," Pettifer agreed.

"And that he picked up the phone and got his fingerprints on it."

"Hang on." Dexter threw up his hands. "You're going too quickly for my underdeveloped brain. So, *who* exactly sent the text from Riverton's phone?"

"Gavin did." Felicia stepped down from the rostrum. "That was clever, actually. It acted as a suicide note, but also provided him with an alibi of sorts. When we thought he was arriving on the scene in response to the message, he'd in fact been there all along. He just hid round the corner and waited."

Dexter looked reluctantly impressed.

"He had everything covered, didn't he?"

"Down to the smallest of things." Felicia turned to Pettifer. "I presume it was he who cancelled the lunch for Caroline before her performance?"

He gave a thin smile in return.

"As one of the fair's main organisers, it would have been easy for him. He was in a position to tinker with things, be in places without anyone questioning it..."

"But why would he *do* that?" Dexter looked mystified. "Why stop someone from having *lunch*, for Christ's sake?"

Clearly, he couldn't think of a worse sin.

"Because then he could suggest an alternative," Felicia explained. "That was vital for his plan to work."

Dexter scowled.

"Now I know you're having me on. Sandwiches were integral to a murder?"

"No," she said calmly. "Coffee was."

Dexter looked perplexedly at Algernon, who made a 'don't-ask-me' gesture.

"Arsenic powder has a bitter taste," Pettifer clarified. "Coffee is one of the few things which can hide it."

"And one of the few things you can guarantee a newspaper editor to consume plenty of," Felicia added wryly. "But it's a good thing she did, in a way. If she'd left more of it, Nick probably wouldn't still be alive."

The thought seemed to cast a sober pall over the room.

"So the figure in red..." Dexter ventured at last. "That was Gavin?"

"Yes, and to be honest, the whole red thing really threw me," Felicia admitted. "Especially when it became clear that Tony had been down there as well, and *he* was dressed in red. But he can't have been the person that Nick saw, for one simple reason: he recognised my ball gown. Edith said that all the designs were kept secret until the last minute, so the only place he could have seen the dress was when it was in the dressing room. That meant he had to have been down there *before* the ball started."

A fact which Jack had corroborated, she finished silently. But she saw no reason to mention that. She was still reeling from their argument, still utterly furious and disillusioned with him, and yet still, she couldn't bring herself to break his confidence.

Which either made her very admirable or very foolish, she thought. Only time would tell which.

"What was he even doing down there?" Dexter was asking.

"Looking for correspondence." Pettifer supplied. "When Riverton realised his plan to scupper the fair had gone awry, he began to panic about being connected to Iris. I'd been wracking my brains trying to work out how the four of them were communicating. Iris didn't even have a mobile phone, and the other three ... no sign of any contact between them." He paused. "Then Felicia had an idea."

"Letters," Felicia said, taking up the story. "It was a known fact that Iris only communicated by letter. I thought, what if that gave Riverton inspiration? It's impossible to track properly, and easy to dispose of."

"But we know that Iris wasn't really trusted by the other three," Pettifer reminded her.

"No. Despite his assurances, I think Riverton was worried she might have been slapdash about destroying her copies as instructed. So after she died, he sent Tony to look for them. As far as anyone was aware, the investigation was over. He couldn't have known that Pettifer had actually been back into the cottage looking for evidence and had cleared out the fireplace."

"But Riverton was a man who liked to cover all bases. So just to be on the safe side, he sent Tony down to check there was nothing concealed in her costume."

"But she hadn't even *worn* that costume," Dexter pointed out. "She didn't have any fittings."

"Clearly, they didn't know that. Almost everyone else had a final fitting the previous day. I suspect that Iris avoided hers because of her awkward past with Edith."

"She was too afraid to face me. *And she was right to be.*"

A booming voice rang across the room. Four heads turned.

And there, standing in the doorway, was Edith. Her head was thrown back proudly. The scarlet frames of her glasses glinted under the spotlights.

"I've come to turn myself in," she declared.

Chapter Forty-Two

It was, as entrances went, sublimely dramatic. Felicia was almost tempted to break into applause. But then Pettifer looked at her, and the exasperation in his face was enough to quell her exuberance.

"I suppose you know about this?"

Felicia just shrugged demurely.

"I had an inkling. But I needed to find out for sure. So I sent in ... reinforcements."

On cue, Peter stumped in.

"I'm afraid I'm not the most natural detective, duck," he said self-deprecatingly, pausing to rest on his crutches. "Edith here rumbled my questions straight away."

Edith rolled her eyes.

"You *were* being rather ham-fisted about it." The tailor's tone was as characteristically caustic as ever, but Felicia detected the faintest hint of something else within it ... something which sounded worryingly close to flirtation. "I think I'd stick with the antiques." Her hand settled briefly on Peter's arm, and Felicia felt a corresponding filial flicker of alarm. But then Edith turned to the room at large, face rapidly becoming more serious. "But I was glad to confess. Truth be told, it's been eating at me. After what happened to Iris…" She broke off, looking haunted. "I was angry with her, but I never would have wished … I didn't even want to hurt her. Not really. I just … wanted to see her squirm."

By now, Pettifer was evidently feeling less indulgent. He folded his arms, looking more monolithic than ever.

"What exactly are we talking about here? For the benefit of the plod."

Edith blinked at him owlishly.

"Itching powder."

Dexter appeared utterly overjoyed by this new development. He was leaning in, listening intently. Felicia tried vainly to ignore him.

Pettifer's eyes swivelled towards Felicia, demanding elucidation.

"I think, Sergeant," she suggested gently. "That Edith perhaps wanted to get her own back on Iris, after what she did to her marriage."

"She stole my husband from me!" Edith had regained some of her fire; her eyes were snapping behind her lenses. "And then she just *swanned* off, back to her glamorous life, all the while leaving mine in ruins. Do you have *any* idea what I've had to go through these past few years? The back-breaking hours I have to put in, and every penny going to pay off our debts. I never see any of it. The only thing keeping me upright most days is pride."

Pettifer looked sceptical.

"All of that for a shop which belonged to your husband? Why not just let it go under?"

Edith drew herself up proudly. She still only reached in line with Pettifer's chest, but somehow, she managed to look magnificent all the same.

"That is *my* shop, Sergeant. I'm the one who started it; I was always the one with the skill." Her scarlet lips twisted. "My husband never sewed a stitch in his life! Alas, a gentleman's outfitter needs a gentleman owner, even in this day and age. So he fronted it for me." She glared at Pettifer, so ferociously that Felicia was sure she saw him shrink back slightly. "But it is *still* mine, and I will *not* see it go bankrupt. I'll die first."

"So you put itching powder in Iris's costume?" Pettifer was evidently trying to regain his equilibrium, although he was still looking at her warily. "To punish her for what she did?"

"Not on the dress, itself," Edith corrected hurriedly, turning to address Felicia. "Only the chemise. That's why I whipped it away so quickly when Tara picked it up."

"And why she was scratching her hands when I saw her at the auction," Felicia added. "She thought it was a stress reaction."

Edith nodded miserably.

"I couldn't tell her what had really caused it. I was too ashamed."

"Wait…" Pettifer was frowning. "When I looked at Tony's body, his wig had fallen off. His head beneath … it was covered in welts. I assumed he was allergic to something in the material, but…"

"That's how I know Tony wasn't just in the dressing room," Felicia clarified. "He had to have been rifling through Iris's costume specifically. Otherwise, he couldn't have got the itching powder on his hands."

"I expect you'll be wanting to charge me, Sergeant." Edith said meekly, hanging her head. "I understand; I deserve it."

She held out her bird-like wrists together, undersides facing towards the ceiling.

There was a long pause. A ripple crossed Pettifer's face. His expression remained utterly impassive, but as he cast a glance at Felicia, she saw the edges of his lips twitch faintly.

"I don't think that'll be necessary, Ms. Babington," he said, in a convincingly stern voice. "After all, we have our killer now, and no-one got really hurt. But I'd consider this a warning, if I were you. To steer clear of this sort of thing in the future. Next time, we won't be so lenient." He paused, clearly trying to decide whether to take it further before adding ominously. "The law *will* be watching."

It was all too much for Dexter. He choked on air.

"Oh, yes." Edith was nodding fervently, relief glowing from her face. Her words were coming out in breathy gasps. "I will. Oh, *thank* you, Sergeant. You're a very kind man."

Pettifer gave a magnanimous wave of the hand.

"Go," he said, his voice resonating around the room. "Before I change my mind."

Edith scuttled out, only pausing to give Peter a shy nod on the way.

As soon as the doors banged shut behind her, Pettifer's demeanour abruptly changed. His head collapsed into his hands.

"I shouldn't have done that," he groaned. "It was highly unprofessional of me."

"Excellent value though," Dexter said spiritedly. "You've just gone up several points in my estimation, Sergeant."

Pettifer glowered at him.

"Curiously, that's not an accolade I strive for."

"Now then, boys," Peter piped up from his position by the door. "No bickering. There's still one more thing I'd really like to know." With a visible effort, he hauled himself further into the room. "And that's how the devil did Gavin get Tony Chandler sitting in a horse drawn carriage like something from a frilly novel?"

"He means a historical romance," Felicia enlightened everyone else out of the corner of her mouth. Peter swatted irritably in her direction.

"They know what I mean, duck. At any rate, it would have been embarrassing for the man. It must have taken some persuading."

Felicia briefly considered telling her father that most men these days wouldn't be allergic to the notion of sitting in a carriage, then decided against it. Sometimes, it was best to just leave him in his own little world, where men still had 1970s attitudes and shoes were all leather and tea came in only one mouth-rasping strength. He was happy there.

Also, she did actually *quite* want to know the answer to this herself. So she turned to Pettifer expectantly.

"I suspect he told Tony that he knew something about Riverton's death; am I right?"

Pettifer nodded.

"He convinced Tony that Red Lion Square was too public a place, that they couldn't be seen getting into a carriage together. Instead, he instructed him to take the first part of the route by himself up to the top of Barn Hill, where he would be able to join unnoticed."

"Thereby guaranteeing that Tony would be alone in the carriage when it hit the cobbles of All Saint's Place," Felicia finished. "Except, he wasn't alone, was he? There was the driver." She bit her lip. "For someone who claims he's not a cold-hearted killer, Gavin certainly wasn't shy about putting innocent people at risk."

Pettifer shrugged massive shoulders.

"I think he just thought his plan was invincible. He'd worked over every inch of it, after all."

"But he couldn't account for things going wrong. Like Hugo insisting they met in Red Lion's Square. That was a real problem. If Tony saw him there, he wouldn't set off alone in the carriage."

"No wonder he was so desperate to leave."

"But by acting the way he did, he caused a massive fight with Hugo, which in turn, nearly got the one person he truly loved killed."

"Well, you can't plan for everything," Pettifer concluded. "I think Gavin's learned that the hard way." He shook his head, almost regretfully. "I can't say I feel entirely satisfied with this one, mind." At the answering expressions of his companions, he continued hastily, "Oh no, we've got our man all right. No doubt about that. It's just ... well, it's a sad state of affairs. Him and young Hugo ... they could have had such a bright future together. If only he could have let go of the past." He sighed. "But no good wondering, I suppose. It is what it is now."

A pensive Sergeant Pettifer was an unusual thing. An eloquent one even less so. But Felicia couldn't help but feel he'd encapsulated everyone's feelings perfectly. The sorrow and ultimate futility of it all, the hollowness it seemed to leave behind.

"About Hugo..." She began, willing herself back to practical matters.

"He's just finishing up his statement at the station," Pettifer said. "He wanted to stay, of course, but..." he trailed off awkwardly, then coughed. "Anyway, Jess said she'll call when they're finished."

"Okay." Felicia looked at her father, who nodded. "We'll come and fetch him." He couldn't be left alone tonight, and he wouldn't want to go back to his parents. God only knew how they'd all manage in the cottage, but they'd work it out somehow.

"No need," Pettifer replied. "He's already spoken for."

He inclined his head towards Dexter, who looked faintly bashful.

"Well, look," he muttered. "I've got plenty of space; you haven't. And it's not hard to keep someone company..."

Felicia looked at him and felt something expanding in her chest. Something she hadn't felt for a long time. But before she could work out exactly what it was, Pettifer spoke up, his booming voice effectively cutting through any introspection.

"I'd say he'll be about another hour. I can drop him at yours on my way home if you'd like."

"I'll be there," Dexter promised.

"Grand." Pettifer crushed his hands into much-beleaguered pockets. "I'll be off, then. And you lot had better do the same. I'll be wanting you down at the station bright and early tomorrow for your statements." He cast a meaningful glance at Peter's crutches. "Including you, Mr. Grant. Now I know that you are, in fact, perfectly capable of getting yourself around town."

Peter had the decency to look vaguely abashed.

"Aye, well, I might be a *little* more mobile than I've been letting on..."

"And now the Georgian Fair's safely over, I presume a miraculous recovery will occur." Pettifer's smile was begrudgingly admiring. He began to make his way towards the doors, bellowing back over his shoulder, "Nine o'clock sharp tomorrow. Algernon, I'm relying on you to make sure they're there. You seem like the only one with any sense of timekeeping."

"I am," Algernon clearly couldn't resist admitting.

"Good lad." Pettifer raised a hand in farewell, then he was gone, heavy steps thudding out onto the wide pavement of Broad Street.

The room, cavernous though it was, seemed strangely empty without Pettifer's titanic presence. And suddenly, Felicia realised that this wasn't where she needed to be after all. She looked around fondly at her family, and picked up her keys.

"He's right," she said. "This can wait. Let's go."

Dexter put an arm around Algernon's slight shoulders. Felicia hesitated for a moment, then held out her own.

"Dad?" She asked haltingly.

For the briefest of moments, she genuinely thought he might say no. That they didn't do this sort of touchy-feely thing. But then he took it, looping his elbow around her hand.

And together, the four of them walked – well, three walked, Peter hobbled, his crutches clicking on the crooked paving slabs – through the sunbaked streets towards home.

Stamford glowed like a champagne pearl in the late evening light. The streets were quiet, heat softly emanating from the stone and releasing into the rapidly cooling air. The moon was a new crescent, like the white of a fingernail. It darted in and out of view as they meandered along the cobbled lanes and crossed the neat squares, playfully peeking out from behind a church spire before diving down beneath a chimney pot or slate roof.

"It doesn't *look* like a place where much happens, does it?" Algernon spoke at last, looking around him thoughtfully. "Was it like this when you were growing up here, Mum?"

"No, it most certainly wasn't," Felicia said dryly.

"Things have got a lot more ... *interesting*, since your mother came back to town," Peter admitted.

"Things tend to do that wherever your mother goes," Dexter added, with a sideways, unreadable glance at her.

They'd reached the ironwork bridge. Its delicate sage green and white paintwork was rendered in shades of lavender and dusty blue in the twilight. Through the heart-shaped scrolls, Felicia could just make out the surface of the River Welland, melting colourlessly into the night. A swan stood out starkly, glowing fluorescent against the dark water and mirroring the punchwork stars in the sky above.

Peter, with over forty years' daily exposure to a view most people only saw in travel articles and sunny mind's eye memories, barely looked at it. He stumped away towards the pint-sized cottage across the riverbank, muttering something about putting the kettle on sharpish.

But Felicia, Dexter and Algernon weren't so immune. Instead, they did what everyone else had to do, whether they be tourist, local, or simply passing through. They stopped, drinking in the magic.

It was Algernon who spoke first, his voice quietly despondent.

"I suppose this'll be the last ever Georgian Fair, won't it?"

Felicia paused, considering.

Tomorrow morning, Stamford would wake to the news that another of its own was a murderer. Yet again, the community would be shaken to its honeyed foundations.

And yet, Felicia already knew it would rally in the end. That was just what a place like this did.

That was what her *home* did. The thought, so warm and bright, almost took her breath away.

"I wouldn't be quite so certain of that," she told Algernon, ruffling his hair. "This is Stamford, after all. It's full of surprises."

And then, from the open doorway of the cottage, there came an almighty bellow. It ripped through the soft beauty of the evening, scattering moorhens across the reed-covered banks and causing a startled passing cyclist to nearly swerve into a parked car.

"Why the bleeding hell is my living room full of rodents?!"

As one, Algernon and Dexter looked at one another and winced.

Felicia closed her eyes.

Full of surprises, indeed.

Epilogue

Night had finally fallen on summer's longest day, and with it, the town's famous Georgian Fair. Stamford was silent, its streets empty, cobbles gleaming in the moonlight. The houses slumbered behind their wooden shutters. Stillness reigned.

Except ... not quite everywhere. Deep within one of its ancient churches, a scratching, scraping sound was emanating from beneath the flagstones.

For a long while, nothing seemed to happen.

Then the floor moved.

A tombstone began to slide sideways, a hand emerging from the gaping black recess within, fingers grasping the edge of the opening. An arm followed, then – after a few muttered expletives – a body heaved itself up and out of the floor.

The figure sat for a moment in the frigid transept, catching its breath. Then it got to work.

The slab was repositioned over the opening, slotting into place with a click. For a fleeting moment, the gilt lettering was illuminated as it passed across a band of moonlight.

Here lies Fitzwilliam Frederick Trendlehart...

The figure made their way towards the door, barely more than a shadow flitting between the pillars. It was locked, but they'd expected that. Even in Stamford, the churches needed to take some sort of security. But the intruder had ways around these things. They produced a bunch of keys. It was a curious selection, certain to arouse interest if anyone happened to lay eyes upon it. All of them, without exception, were ancient-looking, heavy. Many were ornately scrolled, although the one the figure selected now was among the plainer. It turned smoothly in the iron lock. The door was inched open. Silvered light spilled into the interior, then melted away as swiftly as it had come. The figure stepped out into the night.

For the first time in weeks, the air which greeted them had bite to it, and they shivered, turning up their collar against the unexpected chill. Clearly, the hot spell had broken, the English summer returning to more familiar ground. Doubtless, this would be the last clear sky for a while. Nature would take its price in the form of rain and cloud, balancing out what it had given.

All debts had to be paid, after all. No-one knew that better than the figure did.

A sound came from the darkened lane to their right, and they whirled, heart in their mouth. But there was nothing. The shadows remained solid.

Aloysius Drummond shook his head at himself. He was becoming paranoid, seeing things which weren't there. Perhaps, at last, he was getting too old for this.

Or perhaps it was only natural, he reminded himself. After all, things were changing. What had lain safe for centuries suddenly seemed a lot less secure.

A cold gust of breeze curled around him, making him shudder again. With numb fingers, he pocketed the keys.

Then with one last, nervous look around him, he scurried away into the starlit night.

ONE MORE CHAPTER

YOUR NUMBER ONE STOP

FOR PAGETURNING BOOKS

The author and One More Chapter would like to thank everyone who contributed to the publication of this story...

Analytics
Abigail Fryer
Maria Osa

Audio
Fionnuala Barrett
Ciara Briggs

Contracts
Georgina Hoffman
Florence Shepherd

Design
Lucy Bennett
Fiona Greenway
Holly Macdonald
Liane Payne
Dean Russell

Digital Sales
Lydia Grainge
Emily Scorer
Georgina Ugen

Editorial
Arsalan Isa
Sarah Khan
Charlotte Ledger
Jennie Rothwell
Caroline Scott-
Bowden
Kimberley Young

International Sales
Bethan Moore

Marketing & Publicity
Chloe Cummings
Emma Petfield

Operations
Melissa Okusanya
Hannah Stamp

Production
Emily Chan
Denis Manson
Francesca Tuzzeo

Rights
Lana Beckwith
Rachel McCarron
Agnes Rigou
Hany Sheikh
Mohamed
Zoe Shine
Aisling Smyth

The HarperCollins Distribution Team

The HarperCollins Finance & Royalties Team

The HarperCollins Legal Team

The HarperCollins Technology Team

Trade Marketing
Ben Hurd
Eleanor Slater

UK Sales
Laura Carpenter
Isabel Coburn
Jay Cochrane
Tom Dunstan
Sabina Lewis
Erin White
Harriet Williams
Leah Woods

And every other essential link in the chain from delivery drivers to booksellers to librarians and beyond!

YOUR NUMBER ONE STOP

ONE MORE CHAPTER

FOR PAGETURNING BOOKS

One More Chapter is an
award-winning global
division of HarperCollins.

Sign up to our newsletter to get our
latest eBook deals and stay up to date
with our weekly Book Club!
<u>Subscribe here.</u>

Meet the team at
<u>www.onemorechapter.com</u>

Follow us!

 @OneMoreChapter_
 @OneMoreChapter
 @onemorechapterhc

Do you write unputdownable fiction?
We love to hear from new voices.
Find out how to submit your novel at
<u>www.onemorechapter.com/submissions</u>